Comment from Malachi O'Doherty, bestselling writer, journalist, TV personality, Writer-in-residence at the Seamus Heaney Centre, Queen's University Belfast: *Gerry McCullough combines a fierce and tight narrative drive with humour, imagination and lust. What more do you want?*

Comment from Sam Millar, bestselling author of 'On the Brinks' and 'The Dark Place': *Gerry McCullough's story-telling ability to keep all the plates spinning is impressive. Effortlessly, she takes your conscious mind out of your own world ...smoothly and expertly, with page-turning ease.*

Comment from Charles Bane Jr., Poet, USA: *This is a brilliant story, and could only be written by someone of Joyce's blood ... The description...is stunning. Brilliant, Gerry. Utterly brilliant.*

Comment from author T. MacKenzie: *This is truly a book about Ireland itself, not just friendship, love and suspense ... it is true literary fiction, not just fiction. It has a VERY wide range of appeal. Seamless intro of major characters, the fleshing out/explanation/background just the right balance, touch. You cover so much ground in that first chapter, effortlessly. The swift, brutal injection of action so soon into the story works so well. HAD to turn the page . . . no going back. Your writing, your pace, just about flawless.*

Comment from Mark R. Trost, author of 'Post Marked': *You have a manner with words that moves the eye around each description. I can feel your characters. I can hear them speak. Your atmosphere is tangible. I think that is so difficult. I congratulate you on it...when a writer takes the care to add the emotional, societal, and physical atmosphere the reader can engage on an emotional, physical, and spiritual level. And then you have art. You provide that atmosphere. It's difficult. It's an achievement.*

Comment from Amelia O., author of 'A Certain Date in the Diary': *If you only have time to read one book properly it's this one. An award winning read.*

Comment from author John Burns: *You have an (seemingly) effortless pace which carries the reader onwards at a right rate of knots. You are also good at distinguishing between your several characters, making the storytelling clearer. And you are never at a loss for a sudden plot switch. I like the way you let Belfast emerge as a character in its own right, never making a big deal about it.*

Comment from author S.C. Thompson: *A great opening set piece, aglitter with high fashion . . . and intrigue most foul! "Belfast Girls" reveals insight nuanced characters struggling with contemporary challenges as the gritty plot unfolds.*

Comment from author C.J. Cronin: *I think this book is a great one. The story is moved along a nice clip: depictions of the characters set against an Irish cultural background, blend well with the tone of the narrations. Quiet on the surface, something uneasy is lurking underneath and compelling readers to move on.*

Comment from author James MacPherson: *Belfast Girls was all glamour and beauty at the start - mixed suddenly with Ulster Fry and Soda Bread, and the bhoys with the guns - a great story, with everything that's beautiful and ugly about the Province, running through it. The opening was not quite what I was expecting, but tense and then explosive at the end. Then back in time to pre Good Friday, and the innocence of youth, against the backdrop of sectarian hatred, showed the reader expertly, the transition*

Comment from author Graham Barrow: *There is always something instantly appealing about a story that promises several strands of story lines that weave together into a complete and compelling narrative cord. What immediately strikes me about your writing, Gerry, is the love of words and the understanding that good writing must have a rhythm to it in order to maintain interest - which yours does abundantly well. These chapters read with the effortlessness that suggests that a great deal of effort has gone into writing them.*

Chapter 1

Jan 21, 2007

The street lights of Belfast glistened on the dark pavements where, even now, with the troubles officially over, few people cared to walk alone at night. John Branagh drove slowly, carefully, through the icy streets.

In the distance, he could see the lights of the Magnifico Hotel, a bright contrasting centre of noise, warmth and colour.

He felt again the excitement of the news he'd heard today.

Hey, he'd actually made the grade at last – full-time reporter for BBC TV, right there on the local news programme, not just a trainee, any longer. Unbelievable.

The back end shifted a little as he turned a corner. He gripped the wheel tighter and slowed down even more. There was black ice on the roads tonight. Gotta be careful.

So, he needed to work hard, show them he was keen. This interview, now, in this hotel? This guy Speers? If it turned out good enough, maybe he could go back to Fat Barney and twist his arm, get him to commission it for local TV, the *Hearts and Minds* programme maybe? Or even – he let his ambition soar – go national? Or how's about one of those specials everybody seemed to be into right now?

There were other thoughts in his mind but as usual he pushed them down out of sight. Sheila Doherty would be somewhere in the hotel tonight, but he had plenty of other stuff to think about to steer his attention away from past unhappiness. No need to focus on anything right now but his career and its hopeful prospects.

Montgomery Speers, better get the name right, new Member of the Legislative Assembly, wanted to give his personal views on the peace process and how it was working out. Yeah. Wanted some publicity, more like. Anti, of course, or who'd care? But that was just how people were.

John curled his lip. He had to follow it up. It could give his career the kick start it needed.

But he didn't have to like it.

* * *

Inside the Magnifico Hotel, in the centre of newly regenerated Belfast, all was bustle and chatter, especially in the crowded space behind the catwalk. The familiar fashion show smell, a mixture of cosmetics and hair dryers, was overwhelming.

Sheila Doherty sat before her mirror, and felt a cold wave of unhappiness surge over her. How ironic it was, that title the papers gave her, *today's most super supermodel*. She closed her eyes and put her hands to her ears, trying to shut everything out for just one snatched moment of peace and silence.

Every now and then it came again. The pain. The despair. A face hovered before her mind's eye, the white, angry face of John Branagh, dark hair falling forward over his furious grey eyes. She deliberately blocked the thought, opening her eyes again. She needed to slip on the mask, get ready to continue on the surface of things where her life was perfect.

"Comb that curl over more to the side, will you, Chrissie?" she asked, "so it shows in front of my ear.Yeah, that's right – if you just spray it there – thanks, pet."

The hairdresser obediently fixed the curl in place. Sheila's long red-gold hair gleamed in the reflection of three mirrors positioned to show every angle. Everything had to be perfect – as perfect as her life was supposed to be. The occasion was too important to allow for mistakes.

Her fine-boned face with its clear translucent skin, like ivory, and crowned with the startling contrast of her hair, looked back at her from the mirror, green eyes shining between thick black lashes – black only because of the mascara.

She examined herself critically, considering her appearance as if it were an artefact which had to be without flaw to pass a test.

She stood up.

"Brilliant, pet," she said. "Now the dress."

The woman held out the dress for Sheila to step into, then carefully pulled the ivory satin shape up around the slim body and zipped it at the back. The dress flowed round her, taking and emphasising her long fluid lines, her body slight and fragile as a daydream. She walked over to the door, ready to emerge onto the catwalk. She was very

aware that this was the most important moment of one of the major fashion shows of her year.

The lights in the body of the hall were dimmed, those focussed on the catwalk went up, and music cut loudly through the sudden silence. Francis Delmara stepped forward and began to introduce his new spring line.

For Sheila, ready now for some minutes and waiting just out of sight, the tension revealed itself as a creeping feeling along her spine. She felt suddenly cold and her stomach fluttered.

It was time and, dead on cue, she stepped lightly out onto the catwalk and stood holding the pose for a long five seconds, as instructed, before swirling forward to allow possible buyers a fuller view.

She was greeted by gasps of admiration, then a burst of applause. Ignoring the reaction, she kept her head held high, her face calm and remote, as far above human passion as some elusive, intangible figure of Celtic myth, a Sidhe, a dweller in the hollow hills, distant beyond man's possessing – just as Delmara had taught her. This was her own individual style, the style which had earned her the nickname 'Ice Maiden' from the American journalist Harrington Smith.   She moved forward along the catwalk, turned this way and that, and finally swept a low curtsey to the audience before standing there, poised and motionless.

Delmara was silent at first to allow the sight of Sheila in one of his most beautiful creations its maximum impact. Then he began to draw attention to the various details of the dress.

It was time for Sheila to withdraw. Once out of sight, she began a swift, organised change to her next outfit, while Delmara's other models were in front.

No time yet for her to relax, but the show seemed set for success.

* * *

MLA, Montgomery Speers, sitting in the first row of seats, the celebrity seats, with his latest blonde girlfriend by his side, allowed himself to feel relieved.

Francis Delmara had persuaded him to put money into Delmara Fashions and particularly into financing Delmara's supermodel, Sheila Doherty, and he was present tonight in order to see for himself if his investment was safe. He thought, even so early in the show, that it was.

He was a broad shouldered man in his early forties, medium height, medium build, red-cheeked, and running slightly to fat. There was nothing particularly striking about his appearance except for the piercing dark eyes set beneath heavy, jutting eyebrows. His impressive presence stemmed from his personality, from the aura of power and aggression which surrounded him.

A businessman first and foremost, he had flirted with political involvement for several years. He had stood successfully for election to the local council, feeling the water cautiously with one toe while he made up his mind. Would he take the plunge and throw himself whole-heartedly into politics?

The new Assembly gave him his opportunity, if he wanted to take it. More than one of the constituencies offered him the chance to stand for a seat. He was a financial power in several different towns where his computer hardware companies provided much needed jobs. He was elected to the seat of his choice with no trouble. The next move was to build up his profile, grab an important post once things got going, and progress up the hierarchy.

In an hour or so, when the Fashion Show was over, he would meet this young TV reporter for some preliminary discussion of a possible interview or of an appearance on a discussion panel. He was slightly annoyed that someone so junior had been lined up to talk to him. John Branagh, that was the name, wasn't it? Never heard of him. Should have been someone better known, at least. Still, this was only the preliminary. They would roll out the big guns for him soon enough when he was more firmly established. Meanwhile his thoughts lingered on the beautiful Sheila Doherty.

If he wanted her, he could buy her, he was sure. And more and more as he watched her, he knew that, yes, he wanted her.

* * *

A fifteen minute break, while the audience drank the free wine and ate the free canapés. Behind the scenes again, Sheila checked hair and makeup. A small mascara smear needed to be removed, a touch more blusher applied. In a few minutes she was ready but something held her back.

She stared at herself in the mirror and saw a cool, beautiful woman, the epitome of poise and grace. She knew that famous, rich, important men over two continents would give all their wealth and status to possess her, or so they said. She was an icon according to the papers. That meant, surely, something unreal, something artificial, painted or made of stone.

And what was the good? There was only one man she wanted. John Branagh. And he'd pushed her away. He believed she was a whore – a tart – someone not worth touching. What did she do to deserve that?

It wasn't fair! she told herself passionately. He went by rules that were medieval. No-one nowadays thought the odd kiss mattered that much. Oh, she was wrong. She'd hurt him, she knew she had. But if he'd given her half a chance, she'd have apologised – told him how sorry she was. Instead of that, he'd called her such names – how could she still love him after that? But she knew she did.

How did she get to this place, she wondered, the dream of romantic fiction, the dream of so many girls, a place she hated now, where men thought of her more and more as a thing, an object to be desired, not a person? When did her life go so badly wrong? She thought back to her childhood, to the skinny, ginger-haired girl she once was. Okay, she hated how she looked but otherwise, surely, she was happy. Or was that only a false memory?

"Sheila - where are you?"

The hairdresser poked her head round the door and saw Sheila with every sign of relief.

"Thank goodness! Come on, love, only got a couple of minutes! Delmara says I've to check your hair. Wants it tied back for this one."

* * *

The evening was almost at its climax. The show began with evening dress, and now it was to end with evening dress – but this time with Delmara's most beautiful and exotic lines. Sheila stood up and shook out her frock, a cloud of short ice-blue chiffon, sewn with glittering silver beads and feathers. She and Chrissie between them swept up her hair, allowing a few loose curls to hang down her back and one side of her face, fixed it swiftly into place with two combs, and clipped on more silver feathers. She fastened on long white earrings with a pearly sheen and slipped her feet into the stiletto heeled silver shoes left ready and waiting. She moved over to the doorway for her cue. There was no time to think or to feel the usual butterflies. Chloe came off and she counted to three and went on.

There was an immediate burst of applause.

To the loud music of Snow Patrol, Sheila half floated, half danced along the catwalk, her arms raised ballerina fashion. When she had given sufficient time to allow the audience their fill of gasps and appreciation, she moved back and April and Chloe appeared in frocks with a similar effect of chiffon and feathers, but with differences in style and colour. It was Delmara's spring look for evening wear and she could tell at once that the audience loved it.

The three girls danced and circled each other, striking dramatic poses as the music died down sufficiently to allow Delmara to comment on the different features of the frocks.

With one part of her mind Sheila was aware of the audience, warm and relaxed now, full of good food and drink, their minds absorbed in beauty and fashion, ready to spend a lot of money. Dimly in the background she heard the sounds of voices shouting and feet running.

The door to the ballroom burst open.

People began to scream.

It was something Sheila had heard about for years now, the subject of local black humour, but had never before seen.

Three figures, black tights pulled over flattened faces as masks, uniformly terrifying in black leather jackets and jeans, surged into the room.

The three sub-machine guns cradled in their arms sent deafening bursts of gunfire upwards. Falling plaster dust and stifling clouds of gun smoke filled the air.

For one long second they stood just inside the entrance way, crouched over their weapons, looking round. One of them stepped forward and grabbed Montgomery Speers by the arm.

"Move it, mister!" he said. He dragged Speers forcefully to one side, the weapon poking him hard in the chest.

A second man gestured roughly with his gun in the general direction of Sheila.

"You!" he said harshly. "Yes, you with the red hair! Get over here!

Chapter 2

1993

There were so many things about her life that Sheila Doherty hated, especially her appearance, her skinniness and her hair, which was a very bright red. She was eight, and just beginning to notice boys. She knew how important it was that other people should think she looked good, and how impossible. How awful it was to be called 'Ginger', to be considered too tall, too thin, too ugly. She hated being called after in the streets, and in the school playground.

When church, Sunday dinner and Sunday school were over, Sheila wandered out into the back garden. Boredom attacked her.

The back garden was not very large and there was nothing much to do there. There was a square of grass, a border bright with flowers in spring and summer, but mostly brown or green on this dull October afternoon, and an empty rabbit hutch against the far wall.

Sheila could vaguely remember the rabbit, a furry, cuddly focus of love a few years ago when she was five or six, and her short but violent grief at his unexplained death from some unidentified rabbit disease.

She mooched over the grass, kicking aimlessly at the few still remaining fallen leaves, and leaned against the wizened old apple tree in the corner near the hutch. Although she was not to leave the garden or go out into the street by herself, it was good for her to be out in the fresh air, her mother said. It might give her a bit more colour.

Sheila's pale skin and red hair, from her father Frank's side of the family, were a source of constant irritation to both Sheila and her mother Kathy. Both would have preferred almost any other combination, but particularly the dark hair and blue eyes for which Kathy had been so widely admired in her youth – as she often told Sheila with some complacency.

Sheila kicked a few more leaves and wished something would happen. If only she had a sister, or even a brother. It would be fun to have someone to play with.

Suddenly a large ball thudded at her feet.

Sheila jumped and said, "Sugar!" Then she blushed, for she didn't often use what Kathy would call bad language. She picked up the ball and stood with it in her hands, looking cautiously around.

It seemed to have come over the wall which ran between her family's garden and the house next door.

She watched. Two hands were gripping hard on the top of the wall. Then a head rose slowly above the edge.

Black curly hair, blue eyes wide open in inquiry, a mouth which broke into a friendly grin as its owner saw Sheila.

"Hi. Can I come and get my ball?"

Sheila nodded silently.

The girl scrambled over the wall, leaving muddy smears on her light blue jeans as she did so. She advanced on Sheila and took the ball which Sheila held out to her.

"What's your name?"

"Sheila. What's yours?"

"Philomena Mary Maguire, but I get called Phil."

They looked at each other steadily for a moment. Then Phil again took the initiative.

"We've come to live next door, here. We moved in yesterday. Is this your house?"

"Yes."

"What's it like, here? Mammy said it would be fun to have a garden. Is it? Do you like it?"

Sheila had never thought about it. She had always had a garden. Didn't everybody?

"Let's play with your football," she said.

"Okay." Phil looked back. Another head had risen above the wall. Brown hair, not as dark as Phil's, grey eyes, a round freckled face with a friendly grin.

"This is my brother Gerry," said Phil. "Can he come over, too?"

"Yes, g-great!" stammered Sheila.

A moment later, Gerry, who was obviously a year or so older than Phil but still small for his age, had scrambled over the wall and given the football a vigorous kick, only just missing Kathy's favourite rosebush. Sheila giggled. This was going to be fun.

They played happily together for the rest of the afternoon. Phil and Gerry were inclined to take the lead and to suggest new games.

Sheila didn't mind. It was interesting. Phil was fascinated by the rabbit hutch and the apple tree. She made Sheila see the back garden with new eyes, as an exciting place of endless possibilities.

"We could make a swing from the tree if we had some rope," Gerry suggested enthusiastically. "We could use the clothes line."

"I don't think my mammy would let me –" Sheila began.

But he had already pulled down the line and was starting to tie it to the tree. So Sheila and Phil joined in and helped him. It was great.

The afternoon whizzed by, and there was Sheila's mother, woken up from her Sunday afternoon nap, calling Sheila already for her tea.

"I won't be allowed out after tea," Sheila said. "It'll be too dark. Maybe I'll see you at school tomorrow?"

"St Columba's, mine's called," said Phil. "I won't know anybody yet, so it'd be nice if you were there."

Sheila was disappointed. "I go to Alexander Primary, so I won't see you. But we could play after school?" she suggested hopefully.

"Okay," said Phil. "See you, then."

She and Gerry scrambled back over the wall and Sheila went in. St Columba's was the nearby Catholic primary school, she knew. Alexander Primary was Protestant. She thought maybe she wouldn't mention her new friends to her mother, just yet, though Kathy would have to know sometime that the new neighbours were Catholic.

From then on Sheila and Phil were inseparable.

Gerry was a good friend too, but he had his own mates to hang around with usually and, as they all got older, it was only occasionally that he would join in with Phil and Sheila's games. After all, they were only girls.

It was Phil who stood up for Sheila now when people called her 'Ginger,' or 'Carrots', and made fun of her.

"You leave her alone or I'll twist your elephant ears off!" she ordered Chrissie Murphy when she tried to pull Sheila's hair.

And, "Leave off my mate or I'll get my big brother to give you such a hidin'!" when Sandy Bell was teasing Sheila more than usual.

Occasionally Sheila would turn to Gerry to help her and the 'big brother' would soon deal with any persistent trouble makers, going so far as to punch big Geordie Patterson in the eye on one memorable occasion.

When they moved onto secondary school, although they were still separated during the school day, their friendship remained strong.

It was against all the rules, they knew, vaguely, for a Catholic and a Protestant to be best friends but, thought Sheila and Phil, who cared?

Chapter 3

The week leading up to the twelfth of July celebrations was always an exciting one. School was over for the summer. Everyone was out collecting wood and cast off furniture for the bonfire. Sheila and Phil collected together.

Phil's brother Gerry was particularly enthusiastic. He and his mates dragged an old sofa and chairs, which Mrs Fagan was throwing out, the whole length of the street to the green patch at the end where the bonfire was to be. Gerry was thirteen by now, more than a year older than Sheila and Phil, but still small for his age, so it was quite a feat.

All the children of the neighbourhood joined forces for the collecting. As the pile grew, they boasted happily to each other that their bonfire would be heaps bigger than the ones in the nearby areas. Not every street would have a bonfire. A number of streets would work together, the arrangement springing up naturally among children who normally played together.

Sheila and Phil were still best friends. They had been playing together after school for nearly four years, now. They had other friends, mostly from their own neighbourhood, and some from school, but none of them were so close. Although they could not help being aware, more so as they grew older, that the religious difference seemed important to some people, they and their friends thought very little about it. Phil and her family were Catholic, Sheila and her family were Protestant. So what?

The twelfth of July celebration was something which had little meaning to them except as an excuse for a bonfire.

On the evening of the eleventh night, Sheila, Phil, Mary Branagh from Phil's school, and Jeanie and Margaret Gillespie from a few houses away, sat along the wall beside the bonfire. Time hung heavily on their hands. The bonfire was ready. There was nothing more to be done. The older teenagers had decreed that it was not to be lit until dark. In July, dark would not be for several more hours.

"Are you going to see the parade tomorrow, Sheila?" Jeanie asked. "My daddy will be walking with his Lodge, and mammy's taking me and our Margaret down to Carlisle Circus to watch them set out."

"I expect so." Sheila was vague. She was used to getting up early and going with Kathy to see the parade, but this year apparently her daddy, Frank, was not walking. He had made various remarks to Kathy about not wanting to be part of it any more, which Sheila had only half listened to, or understood. Kathy hadn't been pleased, she knew that much.

If Daddy wasn't walking, was it worth the effort of getting up early on a holiday morning, just to see the other men? And would Mammy be planning to go, anyway? Sheila had no intention of going by herself.

She told Jeanie none of this, however. It was a family matter and no-one else's business.

"Let's go round and see the other bonfires, see if any of them are as big as ours," suggested Mary Branagh. Mary never liked sitting doing nothing.

This was hailed as a great idea.

"The only thing is perhaps we should get some of the boys to come with us, in case there are any roughs hanging about?" suggested Margaret.

"Okay, why not?" said Phil. "There's our Gerry and his mates over there, I'll ask them." She scrambled up onto the wall and waved vigorously. "Gerry! Gerry! Do you and Danny and Tommy fancy coming round with us to see the other bonfires?"

Gerry, who had recently developed quite an interest in Sheila, though he wasn't prepared to admit it yet, agreed readily.

"Good idea. C'mon then, kids."

"Do you think we should tell our mammy where we're going?" asked Jeanie doubtfully. The youngest of the group, she was less independent than the rest.

"Not when we have the boys with us, stupid," said her big sister Margaret. "We'll be okay."

Gerry and his mates sauntered over.

"You're getting bigger every time I see you, Sheila," Gerry said, grinning.

Sheila was embarrassed.

"It's these new shoes I'm wearing with the block heels," she muttered.

"It's not your height I meant, Sheila!"

"Oh!"

Sheila's face was scarlet.

"Come on," interrupted Phil briskly, "let's get on for goodness sake!"

They trooped off happily, chattering, laughing, and pushing each other off the edge of the kerb in their normal manner.

The nearest bonfire was satisfactorily small compared to their own. They hung around for a while chatting with the local kids who were mostly familiar faces, if not friends. Then they moved on.

They had gone much further afield and visited a number of bonfires by the time darkness began to fall.

"I think we should go back," said Jeanie. Her voice sounded nervous. "This is what our mammy calls 'the back streets', and I don't think she would like me and our Margaret to go here, if she knew."

"Aw, come on," scoffed Tommy Watson, who was in the form above Margaret and Sheila at school, and qualified as a 'big boy'. "Look, there's one down that street over there, I bet it's a giant. And look, it's lit! You can hear them shouting and singing round it - listen!"

Raucous singing and shouting were coming from the entrance to a narrow street leading off the main road. Curiosity led them to approach nearer. An enormous bonfire was piled against the gable end of the house furthest away. Flames erupted from it, and round it a horde of people, adults as well as children, were dancing and singing. Many of the adults were waving cans and bottles from which they slurped noisily between bursts of song and shouts.

The children were fascinated. As they came nearer, a cheer went up. Someone started up a new song.

*"It is old but it is beautiful
And its colours they are fine!
It was worn at Derry, Aughrim,
Enniskillen and the Boyne!
Oh, my father wore it as a youth,
In bygone days of yore,
And on the twelfth I love to wear
The sash my father wore!"*

"They're singing 'The Sash!'" whispered Gerry Maguire to his sister "What's "The Sash'?" asked Phil innocently.

"Hush!" said Gerry, who was beginning to feel a little uneasy.

The crowd round the bonfire came to the end of the verse and added their own unofficial chorus.

"Valdaree, fuck the Pope,
Valdara, fuck the Pope,
The sash my father wore!"

"What are they saying about the Pope?" Phil asked.

The singing and shouting continued and the language grew more uncontrolled.

Phil looked at Sheila. There were tears in her blue eyes.Then she burst out, far too loudly, "Why are they saying those things about the Pope? The Pope's a good man - why don't they like him?"

Sheila didn't know what to say.

A woman who had been among the most uncontrolled of the crowd, turned round and looked at Phil.

"Ho, what have we got here?" she mocked. "Listen here, Billy, it's a wee fenian bitch, so it is!"

The man beside her, Billy, was big, red faced, and very drunk. It took him a few moments to take in what the woman was saying.

"A wee fenian bitch, Billy! A pope lover!" she screeched again. "Get her, Billy! Teach her a lesson!"

The man called Billy lumbered forward. To the horror of her companions, he seized Phil by the slack of her T-shirt and swung her up in the air dangerously near to the bonfire.

"How's about a taste of hellfire, wee fenian?" he roared. "Give you some idea of where you're heading for?"

He laughed loudly and swung Phil through the air, nearer and nearer to the flames.

Sheila heard the terrifying sound of clothes ripping.

Gerry and Tommy and Danny simultaneously rushed forward and lunged themselves against the big man, punching and pummelling him, kicking his shins, wasting breath in calling him names Sheila had never heard before.

Sheila found herself rushing forward, too, kicking the big man's legs, biting his bare, tattooed arms fiercely. "Let go of her! Let go of her!" she screamed. Mary Branagh followed, punching the man from the other side. Sheila could hear the woman who had urged Billy on laugh contemptuously.

Suddenly it was all over.

Billy, staggering partly from whiskey and partly from the attack, let go of Phil, luckily at a point in his swing where she was well away from the fire. Phil landed in a heap on the ground. Sheila grabbed her by one hand and hauled her to her feet. Mary seized Phil's other arm.

"Come on!" Mary panted briefly.

They pelted at top speed away down the street and round the nearest corner. Gerry and the other two, giving up their attack, had the sense to follow on the girls' heels.

Jeanie and Margaret had already gone. Sheila and Phil and Mary, and the boys, found them lurking far down the next alleyway. With one accord, they hurried for home.

Phil was very silent.

"Pay no attention, Phil," said Margaret, primly. "Only people like that, roughs from the back streets, would behave that way."

But lots of other people think the same sort of thing, even if they don't say it or act on it, thought Sheila. She took Phil's hand and gave it a little squeeze.

"Let's go and get our own bonfire lit," said Gerry. He had been much angrier than his sister at the attitude of the crowd, but had no inclination to cry. He could understand, he thought, how people took up the gun against men like that - though the woman had been worse. If he had been older...

They went back to their own bonfire and lit it, and afterwards roasted potatoes in the embers, but it wasn't as much fun as it had been last year.

Sheila knew all about the boring Troubles which had been going on for years and which had never really affected her, living in one of the safe areas of Belfast, but this was the first time she had really noticed at first hand how much was wrong with her country

Chapter 4

Phil and Sheila continued to be close on through secondary school and shared secrets which they told to no-one else. Together they cautiously experimented with cigarettes and helped each other with homework.

Sheila would say to Phil over the garden wall "I've got something to show you when you're round, Phil."

The something would be a pale, pink, frosted lipstick which Sheila had bought out of her pocket money, unknown to Kathy. To her mother's mind, Sheila was still much too young for make-up, but Sheila and Phil saw the question differently. Anything that could be spared from their scanty pocket money went on lipstick, mascara, or eye shadow, and they practised putting on the various items in each other's bedrooms after school. On all social occasions now they would wear make-up if they possibly could, and this usually involved a great deal of secrecy, slipping out of their houses and back in without being seen, or else putting on lipstick after they were out of sight of home.

As they reached their middle teens, when they got together after school or at the weekends it was to grumble about the amount of homework they had to do, with GCSEs coming up, and, more and more, to talk about boys.

Phil was very popular. She could have had her pick of most of the boys of their own age who were attracted as much by her lively personality as by her pretty face. But Phil had written them all off and was only interested in older boys. Sheila still had no boyfriends. She wished she was as pretty as Phil and envied her, but still felt happy, even privileged, to have Phil for her friend.

One bright evening in late spring, Phil lay on her front on Sheila's bed with her shoes kicked off, propped on her elbows and smoking furiously, and talked non stop about her latest boyfriend, Davy Hagan.

"Why can't he turn up when he says he will?" she asked. "Last night I waited nearly an hour outside the pictures for him! I don't take that from anyone."

"What did you do?" asked Sheila. She was sitting beside the window on the chest with the quilted top which Kathy called the Ottoman, smoking with less assurance. She had only recently taken up smoking and was about ready to drop it again for good. She was on the alert to open the window and, she hoped, disperse the smoky atmosphere quickly, at any sign of her mother's approach.

"I went in by myself," said Phil sharply. "Sammy Hunter was there and, when he saw me, he came over and asked if he could sit with me, and I was so mad I said yes. Now I'll have Sammy round my neck for the next few weeks till I convince him it was just a one night stand." Sitting with someone at the pictures, as Sheila well knew, was a euphemism for a kissing session.

"I can't make out," Phil went on," if Davy's interested in me or not. Why would he ask me out and then not turn up? I suppose he thinks I'm just a kid? I think I'll stop fancying him and go for someone else. But all the boys I know are so young! Maybe there'll be some talent at Mary's birthday party on Friday night."

"Well, he *is* a lot older," Sheila said reasonably. "After all, he's sitting his A levels and he'll be starting University this October."

"So what?" said Phil. "We'll be there ourselves, at Queen's, in a couple of years!"

"I won't if I don't get this Geography revision done," sighed Sheila. "It's all right for you, Phil, you'll sail through everything."

"Sister Attracta doesn't think so," said Phil, giggling. "You should have heard what she said to me the other day. "Philomena," she proceeded, making her voice into a squeaky imitation of the nun's, "'you'll be the death of me. You need to pull your socks up or it's washing dishes in Burger King you'll end up instead of university. She seems to think life should be nothing but work, work, work."

Sheila giggled, too. "Who else is going on Friday night?" she asked.

"Oh, everybody," said Phil vaguely. "It should be a laugh."

Sheila felt excitement welling up in her.

Anything might happen.

In fact, something was going to happen that would change her life.

Chapter 5

Mary Branagh's house, which was noticeably bigger than Sheila's or Phil's, was full of people when they arrived there on the Friday night. There were double doors between the two front rooms and these were thrown open to allow extra space and movement for the guests. Mary's parents, who were an easy-going couple, gave her more freedom than either Sheila or Phil were used to at home. They hadn't gone out but they were keeping to the small back sitting room and allowing Mary to run her own party, a celebration of her sixteenth birthday. There were soft drinks provided and a finger buffet, and Mary had the use of the stereo system to play her own choice of music. It was more like a grown up party than anything Sheila or Phil had been to before. They were both excited. Sheila didn't know Mary very well. She was more Phil's friend. Mary had a reputation for wildness - her party was expected to be different from the usual run. Anything could happen.

Or so they hoped.

Phil was anxious to see if Davy Hagan would turn up. In spite of her threats to Sheila, she had no intention of forgetting him. He was in a different league from the boys of their own age who pursued her eagerly. He was older, he had the use of a car - his mother's - and he was said to run with a dangerous crowd. Phil, who had so far met none of his other friends, was not quite sure what was dangerous about them, but it all added to Davy's fascination. She had bullied Mary into inviting him on the excuse that he was in the same form as Mary's brother John, who would certainly be at the party with some of his friends.

Sheila was fizzing with excited anticipation. She had been allowed a new frock for the occasion, in a dark blue shade which flattered her hair. As she left childhood behind, she had thankfully observed that its bright ginger had darkened slightly to a more attractive colour. It still seemed to her a notable handicap but at least boys no longer shouted "Hey, Ginger, do you snap?" after her in the streets. Recently she had even noticed a tendency in them to whistle after her instead. If only she wasn't so tall. She sometimes felt that she towered over every boy she had ever known.

Mary greeted them at the door and accepted their birthday presents - perfume and a necklace - with unconcealed glee.

"Wait till you see what I've got!" she whispered dramatically. "Come over here where people can't see." She dragged Sheila and Phil into the kitchen and produced a bottle which had been hidden in a wall cupboard behind some saucepans. Sheila looked at it in some bewilderment.

"Vodka!" said Mary triumphantly. "I'm going to add it to the orange juice and we'll have screwdrivers - that's what it's called."

Sheila, who was actually rather shocked, did her best to arrange her face into an expression of pleasure. Phil managed a more blasé reaction.

"Lime would be better," she instructed Mary, "then you have what's called a gimlet - much more sophisticated."

"Let's try one now, anyway," Mary giggled. She took three tumblers of the type used for whiskey from a glass fronted cupboard and poured a generous measure of vodka into each glass, topping it up with orange juice from the fridge.

"Shouldn't you measure it or something?" asked Sheila nervously.

"Don't be daft - knock it back!" said Mary blithely. "Happy birthday to me!" She raised her glass to them, then drank deeply.

Sheila and Phil followed suit. It tasted to Sheila much like any other glass of orange juice and she finished it quite quickly. She had begun to suspect that Mary's 'vodka' was really only water.

It was halfway through the evening, and several 'screwdrivers' later, that she realised her mistake as her head began to swim. The noise of the music, the chatter, and the laughter seemed to have been turned up to full volume, and the lights and colours were brighter and more dazzling.

She was dancing with Phil's brother, Gerry Maguire. It wasn't very exciting, since she knew him so well but it was better by a mile than sitting at the side of the room as a wallflower, watching everybody else dance past her. Suddenly there was a sound of new arrivals at the front door. Mary's laugh could be heard above the loud music and the voices, and then, amid more noise and bustle, three or four older boys came in from the hall. Sheila was pleased for Phil's sake to see Davy Hagan. She had begun to be afraid that he wasn't going to show

Chapter 6

The party threw Phil and Davy Hagan together again. They spent the evening with each other and, afterwards, when Davy took Phil home, he invited her to go to the pictures with him the following weekend.

Once the exams were over, and they had the summer before them, their dates became a regular, accepted thing. Davy borrowed his mother's car, and took Phil for drives. They went to Bangor, Carrickfergus and, once, leaving earlier in the afternoon, as far afield as Portrush on the north coast.

The evenings developed their own pattern. They talked and laughed together, stopped the car and walked for an hour or so, then as dusk crept around, stroking their cheeks seductively with velvet fingers, they would take the car to some secluded spot and spend as much time as possible kissing. As the months went by, these sessions developed into more and more of a struggle. Phil was determined not to go much beyond kissing. Davy, for his part, wanted more and more to go further. Phil found her will power being gradually eroded.

She and Sheila still shared all their secrets, and they talked together about the situation.

"If I could be sure he wouldn't just drop me once he got what he wanted," Phil would sigh. "If I knew he didn't just want to boast about it to the other boys....."

"You wouldn't want everyone to say you were easy, Phil," Sheila encouraged her. "It would be horrible to know people were talking about you the way they do about Maureen Connor."

Maureen Connor had the reputation of being ready to sleep with anyone, and both Sheila and Phil knew that, although boys queued up to take her out, the remarks they made about her afterwards were mostly unpleasant. Even now, girls who slept around were 'sluts' or 'tarts' or worse.

"But I really want to, Sheila," Phil confessed. "That's the trouble. If I could be sure he was serious about me, I'd give in like a shot. But then suppose I had a baby!"

"That would be just the end," agreed Sheila with a shudder.

One hot evening in August, Phil and Davy drove up to the grounds of Belfast Castle, parked the car, and climbed to the higher reaches of the Cave Hill. It was a beautiful evening. The heather hill stretched far around them on all sides, and down below was the breathtaking view of Belfast Lough, gleaming silver and pink in the rays of the setting sun. The air was saturated with the scent of heather and pine. Phil's heart felt near to bursting point, swelling with a mixture of romantic longings and simple sexual desire.

Davy put his arms round her and drew her down onto the soft, grassy hillside. They were so completely alone that they might have been the only people left in the world.

"Oh, Phil," he said in a soft murmur, "don't hold me off any more."

Davy was aware of a strange mingling of emotions. He knew that Phil mattered to him in a way no other girl had ever mattered. He didn't want to do anything to hurt her. Alongside this feeling was a strong belief, ingrained over the years, that a boy should always try to persuade a girl to go as far as possible, that it was something which was expected of him, and that he should try to chalk up as many sexual triumphs as possible. But stronger than any of this, overwhelming in its effect, was his desire for the warm, soft body he held in his arms.

He began to kiss her and to stroke her back gently. Phil felt herself slipping away. Was it worth holding out any longer? She felt sure that she really loved Davy. Was it really so wrong to be so close to him, to be even closer?

Then she felt a familiar twinge in her stomach. She had almost forgotten - but, yes, it must be.

"I'm sorry, Davy," she told him. "But even if I wanted to, I couldn't tonight. I'd forgotten that my period was due and I'm afraid it's just started."

Davy sprang to his feet and walked away from her.

"Hell!" he said.

He fumbled in his pocket for his cigarettes, pulled out the packet, and lit one for himself without offering them to Phil. He stood with his back to her some yards away, looking down over the Lough. Then, eventually, he turned round, and with an effort said "Well, it can't be helped. We may as well go back, now."

"Have you got any tissues?"

"Me? No, what would I have tissues for?"

"I might have some in my bag. Sling it over will you?"
Phil spoke coldly. She was angry at Davy's attitude.

Fumbling in her bag, she found a handful of tissues and stuffed them down the front of her jeans, inside her pants. She felt the pain of cramps coming on but was unwilling to mention this to Davy in case he thought she was looking for sympathy. If he didn't care, then he didn't. So what?

They walked back down to where the car was parked in silence. Phil was still angry. It wasn't her fault that she had a period, was it? She said nothing, waiting for Davy to speak, to apologise, to sympathise, or even just to make some friendly remark. But they reached the car without any word from him and he dropped her home with only a brief "Bye, then. See you soon."

A week later, Sheila saw Davy Hagan having coffee with a girl she didn't know. She said nothing to Phil about it. Other friends were less careful, however. Before long, Phil knew that Davy was going out with a girl called Julie Simmons.

"Well," said Sheila, "she may not be Maureen Connor, but I've heard that she's the next best thing."

"That's one of the most spiteful things I've ever heard you say, Sheila Doherty," Phil retorted, grinning. "You don't have to pull the girl to pieces just for me. What do I care who Davy Hagan sees?"

All the same, it seemed to Sheila that Phil was a lot quieter these days. Then she started going out with boys again, on the basis of "Let's see how many I can get this term."

Sheila found it worrying.

Chapter 7

Eighteen, and going to Queen's!

Sheila was on top of the world, floating above the clouds in the sunshine. She found herself breaking out into grins as she walked along the road, and passers-by smiled back at her indulgently.

She was on her way to the Freshers' Reception, held in the Great Hall of the university, and anticipation was mingled in her mind with apprehension at being on her own. For various reasons, none of her friends had planned to be there.

Although it was October and already some of the leaves on the huge trees that lined University Road were offering a choice of yellow and orange and brown as well as the predominant green, it was a bright, sunny day, not hot but still pleasantly mild. The enormous Victorian Gothic building that was Queen's University loomed up on Sheila's left, beautiful and hugely impressive.

The hall was crowded, mostly with new students, but with some of the final year people who were there to extend a welcome. There was a buffet arranged along both sides.

First came speeches welcoming the 'freshers' from the Vice Chancellor and from the president of the Students' Union.

When the formalities were over, Sheila made her way over to where plastic cups of wine and beer were ranged alongside cocktail sausages, chicken or mushroom vol-au-vents, and miniature sausage rolls.

She wished Phil had been able to come, and by way of alternative support, helped herself to some of the white wine and took a large gulp. Gazing round, she tried to find a familiar face. At the other end of the long hall, hemmed in by the crowd, stood a tall, dark, bony faced boy of slim but muscular build, who looked very familiar. Sheila studied him for a few moments.

Yes, it was John Branagh, her friend Mary's brother. Sheila took a deep breath, gulped down most of the rest of her wine, and pushed her way over to him.

"Hi!" she said.

John looked round, and stared at her. Their eyes were very much on a level except, Sheila realised, that John was looking down on her by a couple of inches. This was pretty unusual and she liked it quite a lot. It was clear that he had no idea who she was.

"I was just thinking that I'd like to get to know you better," Sheila went on. Then she stopped and flushed as she realised the gaucheness of her approach.

John was looking at her in amusement.

"That's a good line," he remarked, grinning.

Sheila pulled herself together. "You're John Branagh, aren't you? Mary's brother? You don't remember me, do you?"

It was John's turn to look embarrassed.

"Oh - sorry, I didn't realise - you're one of Mary's friends? Can I get you another drink? What is it, white wine?" He covered his embarrassment by turning to the buffet table which ran along the side of the hall behind him and handing Sheila another of the plastic cups.

"I'm Sheila Doherty."

"Good to meet you, Sheila. So, are you coming up to Queen's this year then?"

"Yes, I'm doing English. But I thought - someone told me, John, that you were going to be a priest. Don't you go to Maynooth or somewhere to train?"

"Not necessarily. You can do a degree first." John hesitated, then said "But as it happens, I changed my mind about that. I'm not going on for the priesthood any longer. I'm going to be a journalist."

"Oh, good!" said Sheila without thinking.

John laughed, but there was a wry note in his laughter.

"Good? I don't think so. I found that I wasn't the right type. But I still wish I was."

Sheila said nothing, but looked at him. "Not a question of belief - just a matter of not being strong enough."

Suddenly John shrugged and grinned. "Why are we being so serious? Tell me about yourself. You're a good looking girl, Sheila Doherty, do you know that?"

"Am I?" said Sheila nervously.

"Have you had enough of this reception? I think I've done my duty stint now - some of us were asked to turn up and be friendly to the freshers. I should be able to consider it done if I go on being friendly to this particular little fresher, don't you think? Would you like to come for a drive? I have my mother's car this afternoon. We could go for a walk by the Lagan, out by Shaw's Bridge, and you could 'get to know me better', if that's what you really want to do."

They went out by the great front doors of the university to the narrow gravel courtyard where cars were parked.

The late afternoon sun was still bright outside.

It shone on the grass, on the beds of neatly planted-out brown and yellow wallflowers, impregnating the air with their sweet scent, and on the cars parked like sardines in a tin, the gleam of the sun which shone on their silver and coloured flanks enhancing the resemblance.

John drove his mother's Fiesta through the city streets on out to the beginnings of country, until he reached the tow-path by the river. He pulled up by Shaw's Bridge, a secluded spot, with parking space for far more than the half dozen or so cars scattered about.

They sat silently, looking out at the sun rippling on the quiet water of the River Lagan. The long grasses sprinkled with vetch and clover dripped over the bank's muddy edge and soaked their fingers in the cool green reflections.

It would have been possible to leave the car and walk along the footpath at the river's edge. Neither John nor Sheila, however, felt any inclination to do this.

Sheila thought "I suppose I shouldn't have come out here with him if I didn't mean to let him kiss me. I suppose that's why he's brought me here. All boys are like that, aren't they?"

She felt no reluctance, only a certain shyness which made her hesitant.

As the silence continued, she suddenly wondered if John was shy too. He didn't look shy - but that meant nothing. Did she need to encourage him?

Turning towards him, Sheila saw that John was looking away, out through the window, his thoughts apparently miles distant. She put out one hand and touched him on the arm.

"John," she said, "what was it you wanted to talk about?"

He leaned towards her, his eyes very bright. Sheila's hand reached on up to touch his cheek, then she found herself leaning slightly forward and suddenly his lips were pressed against hers, his tongue forcing her mouth open.

It was a long, long kiss. Sheila found herself sinking under the surface. She didn't want to stop. It seemed that John didn't want to stop either. Much later, Sheila began to realise dimly that things were out of control, that his hands were all over her, but it didn't seem to matter.

It was John who sat up and pulled away.

"Sorry," he said after a moment.

"It's all right," Sheila said.

"No, it isn't!" John said passionately. His face was pale and hurt looking, full of pain. "Why didn't you stop me sooner?"

Sheila looked at him in bewilderment. What had she done?

"I didn't expect you to be that sort of girl," John said violently. "You don't look as if you were."

Sheila said nothing. She had no idea what to say.

"Come on," John said. He was flushed and angry. "I'll drop you back at the university. I expect you can make your own way home from there? And let me give you a word of advice - be a bit more careful next time you pick up a stranger and snog with him. The next one may not have as much self control."

Sheila, in turn, was angry. She had nothing to say, so that was what she said.

John put the car into gear, and they moved off.

It was still bright and sunny. The drive led along country lanes where the hedges, laden with blackberries and rosehips, brushed the windows of the car and back up to the dual carriageway. The University was less than half a mile away, just at the edge of the town.

John pulled up in the car park outside the Great Hall. They hadn't been away for long. The last stragglers were still drifting away from the reception.

Sheila gathered her dignity around her like a comfort blanket and scrambled out of the car. It didn't seem necessary to say goodbye.

She hoped seriously that she would never see John Branagh again.

Chapter 8

In Mid-December, Sheila and Phil went to a Christmas party given by the English Professor, Dennis Logan. The whole of the English Department had been invited, for the house was large enough to contain them.

Sheila wavered for some time before making up her mind to go. It was more than likely that John Branagh would be there. But then, why shouldn't she meet him on a purely social level? Why should she miss what promised to be an interesting, and even important, event just because of embarrassment over an episode now long past?

Professor Logan lived not far from the University, just on the edge of the city. His house was old and rambling, with large rooms and widespread gardens. It had been in his family for a couple of generations but had been modernised recently in an unusual and personal style. One room was devoted to music, another to books. A wooden spiral staircase ran up the central spine of the building and the polished wooden floors of the open plan main reception area were scattered with bright oriental rugs.

When Sheila and Phil arrived, Professor Logan was welcoming all comers from a position near the centre of the reception area.

A table placed just to one side of him, plentifully laden with beer, wine and sherry enabled him to pass on those he greeted either slowly or quickly according to status, on the excuse of directing them towards some refreshment. The student element as a whole was only too eager to pass on.

Sheila was glad to be with Phil. It made the occasion very different from the Freshers' Reception where she had been on her own, obliged to start conversations herself. Yet it was not so different in one way, for the first person she saw, standing at the far end of the room, just as he had done then, and looking sardonic and aloof, was John Branagh.

Quickly, Sheila turned away.

She said to Phil "Let's go and explore."

They headed for a door to the left and found themselves in the music room. A keyboard occupied one corner, guitars, bouzoukis, mandolins and other such instruments hung on the walls, and a harp had pride of place. A slim brunette in a white, Grecian style dress with a low scooped neckline was perched on a stool plucking a classical guitar and singing softly and melodically in French to a small group of people. Sheila found that she could pick up one or two of the words.

As they joined the admiring group, Phil whispered to Sheila that this must be Lois, Professor Logan's wife, a well known poet 'in her own write', and a frequent guest on Radio Three. She had set some of her own poems to music but so far had made no big hit.

The song ended and the buzz of talk grew louder. A fair haired final year student standing nearby had been watching them. He came up and began to talk to Phil in a low voice which deliberately excluded Sheila, on Phil's other side, from the conversation. Sheila sipped her glass of wine and looked round for more interesting company.

A tall, lean man in his twenties with a dark moustache appeared at her elbow. He was carrying a spare glass.

"Care for another? White wine, very harmless." He smiled lopsidedly and Sheila smiled in return and took the offered drink.

"Like to dance?"

"Why not?" Sheila said.

They left the side room and found the area where a few other couples were dancing, to music downloaded from iTunes.

"Francis Delmara," her partner mouthed over the music, pointing to himself.

"Hello!" Sheila mouthed back. The combination of the wine and the loud music was making her slightly dizzy.

"Did anyone ever tell you how beautiful your eyelids are?" Francis breathed in her ear.

He gathered her closely to himself, smooching rather than dancing. It was all very pleasant. Sheila felt special and desirable.

"You remind me of a painting by Botticelli," Francis said, "Aphrodite arising from the waves. But you have more clothes on, alas."

Sheila giggled. It sounded funny as well as flattering.

"It's hot," said Francis. What about a breath of fresh air? And another drink?"

Detouring first by the refreshment bar, he led Sheila out through the patio windows.

Fairy lights were strung along the edge of the patio. Beyond was a darker area, grassed over, partly lawn and partly a wilder growth.

Sheila had every opportunity of discovering this as she and Francis, hand in hand, wandered in that direction. In a short time they felt dampness round their ankles from the grass and other undisciplined green things springing up at random.

"We must boldly go where no lawn-mower has gone before," Francis said lightly.

Sheila, whose head was muzzier than ever, had almost forgotten that he was there, although it was his arm which was keeping her from stumbling.

"Look, isn't the moon beautiful?" he said, his voice growing more husky. "But not as beautiful as you, my lovely girl."

He bent his head to kiss her.

Sheila found herself responding. Her knees began to buckle under the weight of his body pressing against her. She found that she was being dragged slowly to the ground. There was no desire in her to resist. Then she was lying back in the soft damp grass and Francis' hands seemed to be everywhere.

This wasn't what she had intended, Sheila thought.

Her right hand, spread floppily out like the hand of a rag doll, came in contact with something metal. Idly she twisted the projecting handle.

Suddenly Francis stopped nuzzling Sheila's neck and began to shout very loudly in her ear instead. Then he sprang to his feet and began to dodge wildly about.

Sheila sat up slowly and watched in surprise.

As well as music and romance, there was wetness in the air.

It took her another minute to realise that water was spraying all around, at no great height from the ground and in a misty arc rather than a soaking stream.

Her idle twist of the metal handle had turned on the sprinkler and it had started to water the lawn.

"Turn it off!" shouted Francis. "Turn it off!"

His shirt was soaking where the sprinkler had caught him and he was shivering in the cold December air. He had got by far the worst of it, for Sheila had been protected by his body. In the end, he had to find the handle and turn it himself, for Sheila was giggling helplessly and was not sure even yet where the handle was.

They staggered back to the house.

The romance seemed to have gone out of the atmosphere. As far as Francis was concerned, a warm, dry towel was higher on his list of priorities than Sheila's body. As soon as they entered the house again by the patio doors, he disappeared in search of a bathroom.

Sheila felt rather wet and shivery too, though still inclined to giggle.

Somewhere deep down, ready to surface when the light-headedness had cleared up, was relief that things had stopped when they did.

She found another bathroom and a towel for herself, gave her hair a rub, and wiped down her dress. Then she felt able to rejoin the throng.

Phil was still chatting with the fair-haired final year student and it seemed better not to interrupt them.

The atmosphere had hotted up.

Lois, the Professor's wife, was dancing with someone whom Sheila recognised as a celebrity from local television, Ronnie Patterson.

Someone seemed to have turned up the volume and also speeded up the video, for everyone's movements were in fast, jerky motion, like an old Charlie Chaplin film.

Sheila was hesitating, wondering whether to help herself to another drink or to be sensible, when she heard a voice in her ear.

"Hello. I think we should get to know each other better."

It was John Branagh, with a glass in each hand, and a determined expression.

Sheila laughed. Suddenly she felt very happy.

"That sounds like a good line."

"Come and sit down," said John.

He led her to a sofa to one side of the room and handed her one of the glasses when she was seated.

"Now," he said, "let's try to start on a better footing, this time. Tell me something about yourself."

Sheila, who usually found herself at a loss for conversation with boys, suddenly found that she could talk.

They sat together and laughed and talked and, later on, they danced a little.

John talked in his turn and told Sheila about his feelings and beliefs with a freedom that surprised himself.

As the evening wore on and more people were dancing, they smooched dreamily round the room, saying less and less.

Later, John drove her home, and asked her if she would like to go with him to see a film they had discussed. Sheila agreed happily.

"Goodnight," he said, and leaned over to kiss her gently. Then he got out of the car, and went round to open her door.

Sheila got out, not sure whether to be glad or sorry that there was to be no more kissing.

"Goodnight, John," she said, and went into the house.

She had never been so happy in her life.

Chapter 9

It was at a debate in the Mandela Hall, in the basement of the Students' Union, that Phil met up with Davy Hagan again. She and Sheila, trying to become more involved in university life, went along out of curiosity, mainly to see the guest speakers who were all local celebrities.

Sheila and John were going out together regularly. It was several months now since the Christmas party. Sheila felt everything was perfect. If only they saw each other more often. But John, in his final year, needed to spend most of his time working. He rationed himself and Sheila to one meeting a week, and even then was careful to bring her home far earlier than Sheila liked. So Sheila had plenty of spare time and spent most of it with Phil.

It was Phil's idea to attend the debate. The subject 'That this House believes cannabis should be legalised,' was one that interested her. Secretly she had an unacknowledged feeling that this was the sort of thing that Davy Hagan would want to support for, if the truth were told, Davy Hagan still popped up in Phil's thoughts far more frequently than she would have wanted anyone to know, even Sheila. Davy had never tried to encourage Phil to smoke blow after one early offer which she rejected sharply, but Phil knew he smoked regularly himself.

The chairman introduced the speakers. The debate warmed up. Opinions from the floor came fast and furious.

"The current laws criminalise this harmless plant!" shouted Aidan McKimmon, an unpopular loud-mouthed politician with an independent stance. "I say this house needs to stand against these laws and insist on change!"

It was halfway through the evening. Noises suddenly erupted outside. A crowd of protesters burst into the hall hurling eggs at the speakers in favour of the motion, and particularly at Aidan McKimmon.

The porters, helped by a number of the older students, furiously tried to push the protesters out of the hall, back towards University Road.

"Help! Let's keep out of this!" gasped Phil.

Sheila was in full agreement.

The girls drew back and to one side as more people, those who had been at the front of the Mandela Hall, emerged into the corridor and began to push their way forward and upstairs to the ground floor to find out what was going on. A familiar voice behind Phil's back said "Let me through, there, can't you?"

She turned round and found herself looking directly at Davy Hagan.

For a moment he failed to recognise her. Then his eyes widened and his mouth broke into the reckless grin Phil remembered so well.

"Who'd have believed it? Little Phil - after all this time."

"Not so much of the little," Phil retorted, nettled. "I'm a big girl now."

"So you are - indeed you are," said Davy, his eyes raking her thoughtfully. He seemed to come to a decision.

"Don't go away, sweetheart," he said, "I'll be right back. I'll take you for a drink or something. But right now I need to get out here and teach these guys a lesson."

He pushed his way on down the packed corridor to the entrance.

Phil watched him go. Part of her wanted to run - but even if she tried to, it would be impossible to get away just now. She wasn't sure that she wanted to get involved with Davy Hagan again but she knew that she didn't want him to get hurt in whatever was going on outside.

There were renewed noises, shouts and jeering from the front of the building, then came the sound of cars screeching to a halt, sirens, a voice over a megaphone. The police had arrived.

Relief flooded through Phil. It didn't take the police long to clear the crowd from University Road. The students who had poured out to the front steps came trooping back in. Davy thrust his way over to her.

"Let's get out of here," he said. "Come on and I'll buy you a drink in the Bot."

With a whispered word to Sheila, Phil found herself following him outside.

Did he really think that he could just take things up where they had been two years ago? Did he think that she had forgotten how he had treated her? But it seemed he did think just that.

And the awful part, Phil realised, was that she seemed to think so, too.

Chapter 10

"Sheila!" called John.

He stood outside her bedroom window, like Romeo, shouting up. But it wasn't night time. Instead, it was a beautiful early spring morning at the start of the Easter break and Sheila was still loafing in bed, getting up by slow stages. Her parents had both left for their respective jobs some time ago.

"Why doesn't anyone answer the door in your house?" John complained. "I've been banging for ages!"

"Everyone's out except me," Sheila said, "and I'm not quite up yet, sorry!"

"Well, get up now!" John exclaimed impatiently. "I've got my Mum's car for the day. I'm going to take you up the Antrim coast road. That is, if you'd like to go?" it occurred to him to add.

There was nothing Sheila would have liked better.

"Oh, brilliant!" she called down to him, hanging out of the window wrapped only in her white fluffy dressing gown, her red gold hair a tangled mass of curls around her shoulders and flopping in uninhibited strands across her forehead. "It won't take me a minute to get ready. Well, actually," she added truthfully, "it will, but I'll be as quick as I can, really! Hang on, I'll come down and let you in."

"No, don't," John said sharply. "Not until you're dressed. I'll wander about out here till you're ready."

Sheila was surprised. She wasn't proposing to bring him up to her room after all, or to dress in front of him. Still, she had become quite philosophical about John's ideas and attitudes by now, and reckoned that the best thing to do was just to take them in her stride.

"Okay," was all she said.

She ducked back into her room and began to drag clothes hastily out of her wardrobe and her cupboards, looking for something good enough. A whole day out with John! It sounded like magic. A quick shower, rubbing her hair and leaving it to dry naturally in the sun, and she was ready to scramble into a sleeveless bright green sundress and to put on a little make-up.

Suddenly it occurred to her that the short sleeveless dress wouldn't get John's approval at all. Quickly she snatched a white cotton jacket from its hanger and struggled into it as she sped downstairs.

"Ready now, John!" she called, reaching the front door and flinging it open.

John came across the lawn towards her and Sheila bounced joyfully into his arms, the bright spring sun sending sparkling reflections of itself cascading from her still damp curls. For a moment John held her tightly, his mouth fastening eagerly on hers. Then he detached himself gently from her clasp.

"Come on," he said briefly, breathlessly, taking her arm, "let's get into the car."

Slightly cast down, Sheila followed him meekly. She was quite aware by now that John was reluctant to kiss her or hold her more than a very little. He had standards which he was determined to keep. Sheila respected him for it. Goodness knows, it was so much better than the other boys she had known, before she began going out with John, whose only thought was to get into her pants, as the saying went. She had hated that sort of attitude. All the same, she sometimes asked herself, did John take things too much to the opposite extreme?

But John had his own rules to keep to. When he was younger, he had seen himself as a priest, a strong man gently helping others to keep to the rules he found worked for himself. But it had not been long before he had found that celibacy was something he regularly struggled with. He found himself, quite without meaning to, getting involved with more than one girl, finally sleeping with one.

He gave up any intention of becoming a priest but, fiercely angry with himself, he clung more firmly than ever to the basic rules he lived by. He would never again, he promised himself, have a casual sexual relationship with any girl. With Sheila, he was determined to be careful. He would resist any temptation to sleep with her as he had done with that other girl, but there were times when it was very hard.

He opened the door of his mother's bright red Fiesta and installed her carefully in the passenger seat. Sheila held her skirt tightly round her, edging in hips first. She didn't want a repeat of the remarks John had made once before, when he considered that she had shown too much of her legs in the course of climbing in.

Then John turned the key, pressed his feet on the pedals and they were off, heading out of the city towards Carrickfergus with its mediaeval castle, then on through industrial Larne and finally on to the open line of the coast where the road ran beside the sheer white cliffs on their left, and the sea was only yards away on their right, with beach after sandy beach leading away into the clear blue distance as the little Fiesta roared happily round bend after bend. Each small bay was outlined in heavy pencil strokes of white or grey rock, and ahead, stretching up the coast, the headlands stood out like giant slices of birthday cake, white and brown with a lush green topping against the brilliant blue of the sea. Sheila drew a sigh of deep content as she felt the heat of the sun caressing her shoulders.

"This is so good, John," she said. "What could be better?"

John smiled at her, a swift sideways smile, before returning his full attention to the road.

"Some things, I should think. But, yes, this is pretty good."

Sheila wasn't sure what he meant, but was happy to leave it unexplored for now.

In the early afternoon, they stopped in a small layby, scrambled out of the car, and made their way across to a wide grassy ledge perched over on the far side of the road, but at a lower level, which gave them a certain amount of privacy from passers by. Small yellow and white flowers, which had been scattered by an artist with a generous hand and an eye for colour, peered up brightly amongst the soft greens of the varied grasses. Several large white rocks, probably deposited there by glaciers in the Ice Age John told her, loomed up between them and the road as guardians of their privacy.

John had brought a picnic, some egg sandwiches which he had coaxed his mother to provide, although he didn't tell Sheila this, and a litre of fruit juice. Sheila, who had noticed the picnic in its bag on the back seat, was just a little bit disappointed. She had been visualising something a bit more romantic. Sandwiches were nice, of course, but maybe chicken drumsticks, or even smoked salmon, would have been more exciting. Too dear for John's student grant, she realised, reproaching herself for her thoughtlessness. But a bottle of white wine would have been so much more special than fruit juice and surely one of the cheaper brands wouldn't have cost so very much more these days.

They settled down on the grass in the shade of the big white rocks. Sheila lay back and closed her eyes, raising one arm to shield her face from the direct rays of the sun.

"I thought I'd better not bring any wine," she heard John's voice. "I know you like white wine, honey, but, to tell you the truth, the effect it has on you is way too dangerous to risk when we're here on our own!"

He was laughing, pretending to tease her, turning it into a joke, but Sheila stiffened.

"Not much risk when you're always so careful yourself, John," she said coldly. Sitting up, she reached for an egg sandwich. The magic of the afternoon seemed damaged. She tried to resurrect it but without much success. Presently they packed up the remains of the picnic and drove on.

Mile after mile of incredible beauty sped by. It was early evening, though the sky was still blue and bright, when John pulled up the car by a smooth sandy beach visible beyond a short track. The track led down from the edge of the road, weaving its way through the rough grasses of the sand dunes which here were sprinkled with the gentle blush of sea pinks, until it reached the soft golden sand.

"Let's go for a walk along the beach," John suggested. Sheila, who had long since put her annoyance behind her, agreed enthusiastically.

Hand in hand they scrambled wildly down the steep little path and raced over the dry sand until they reached the damp firm stretches at the edge of the sea. Slipping off her sandals, Sheila splashed noisily into the shallow waves.

"Isn't this great!"

John, laughing, bent to scoop up water in his hand and splash it over her. Then he in turn pulled off his trainers, slung them by their laces round his neck, and rolled up his jeans, joining Sheila in the shallow water.

"Wouldn't it be lovely to have a swim?" Sheila sighed. The heat of the sun still beating strongly on her body made the idea delightful.

"Well, in the first place, it's probably as cold as ice a few more feet in," John remarked reasonably, "and in the second place, we don't have bathers with us, do we?"

Sheila thought of suggesting that they could strip to their underclothes. She looked speculatively at John's face, and decided against it.

"True," was all she said instead.

There were some small smooth pebbles along the sea edge. Sheila and John picked up a handful each and began to skim them, counting the number of jumps in friendly rivalry, making their way slowly along the beach towards the further point, feet sometimes in and sometimes out of the water.

Sheila was once more ecstatically happy. There was no-one in the world like John. So he had his bad points. So what? She would never love anyone else as much as this.

The beach led to a low ridge of rocks reaching out into the sea, like an arm encircling the sand. Sheila and John hopped over it easily, eager to explore, to see what was on the other side. The cliffs were sheerer here, rising high and white to many feet above their heads.

"There's a cliff path, do you see, over there?" John indicated a narrow, twisty track, rather like the one they had come down but quite a bit steeper, going much higher up. Sure enough, from what they could see, it probably continued along the top of the cliff.

Taking Sheila's hand, he led her to the foot of the path. Here they shook the sand from their feet, redonned their footwear and looked doubtfully at the climb.

"Well - shall we go for it?" John asked.

"Okay."

John went first. Sheila scrambled after him, John turning every now and then to give her a hand where necessary to make sure that she was managing. Finally they stood on the cliff top.

The amazing view was their reward. East across the sea, the day was so clear that they could see Scotland green and sharp, the Mull of Kintyre in its greens and browns set against the calm blue of the ocean. To the North lay the nearer islands, first Islay, and behind it what seemed to be Jura. Eastwards, beyond the Mull, John, who was long sighted, pointed out Arran, Ailsa Craig, and the further shore of Scotland in the distance.

For some time they stood looking out.

"Worth coming for this alone," John said presently. He took Sheila's hand again and they began to stroll gently along the cliff top path. Immediately to their right, Sheila noticed, instead of one of the sheer rocky cliffs there was a less abrupt slope now, well grown over, covered in tall grasses just coming into seed, scattered with golden whin bushes and with gleams of wild flowers, white of daisies, bright yellow of dandelions, purple and white of clover, lighting up the picture. The vanilla scent of the golden whin blossom hung sweetly in the evening air.

They passed a weather-beaten notice warning of the danger of landslips at the edge of the path, and Sheila noticed that there seemed to have been one recently. At least, there were trails of brown earth across the path occasionally rushing on down over the edge.

She peered over cautiously and saw that beyond the safer slopes, the cliff turned abruptly into a steep cliff edge. A good idea to walk carefully, she thought. Once over the edge of the path, a slithering slide would take anyone very quickly to the cliff edge and from there it would be the easiest thing in the world to continue on into outer space, ending up on the beach below with at the very least broken bones. She held John's hand more tightly and stepped cautiously as far from the edge as possible.

Ahead of them, to the North West, they could see the sky beginning to reflect red and gold streaks from the sun, as it made up its mind to sink gradually lower and closer to the horizon.

"I wish John would kiss me," Sheila thought. She turned her face to his and smiled encouragingly and, at that, John leaned towards her.

It was a kiss, certainly, but such a gentle one. Sheila, while thoroughly enjoying it, could have wished for a little more passion. Still, she supposed she should be grateful for what she had.

John leaned away again. The kiss was over.

It was just at that moment that they both heard it.

A faint moan, so weak as to be almost beyond hearing.

John dropped Sheila's hand and rushed to the edge of the path. Sheila was just behind him.

As the sky wasn't dark yet, it was still easy enough to see down the grassy slope. Looking over they could both make out a small figure. A child. A little boy, they both thought.

He was wearing a bright red T-shirt, which was a good thing. It made it that bit easier to be sure he was there. In the fading light, brown or green would have made it harder to distinguish him against the surrounding slope and its grassy ledges.

He was clinging to the inside branches of a whin bush and seemed to be crying.

Chapter 11

"Hullo!" John called down.

The little white face below looked up at once and split into an incredulous grin.

"Hullo!" the boy called up to them in a wavering voice. "Please, can you help me?"

"Yeah, sure thing," John called back. "Just stay still, right?"

"The path slipped!" the boy called back. He was clearly eager to explain. "I was playing on the beach with Mum and Dad and our Kevin, he's just a baby, and I thought I'd explore a bit round the corner, and I came up here and walked along a bit, and the ground just flippin' gave way. I shouted and shouted, but no-one heard. Maybe they've gone looking for me the other way, like…"

"Yeah, well, never mind all that now," John said authoritatively. "Just hold on, see? We'll sort something out." He fished in the pocket of his jeans and produced his mobile. "If I can just get a signal." He walked away along the path. For a few moments he pressed buttons, then, with a sigh of relief, began to speak into the phone.

Sheila watched.

"Hi, is that emergency? We have a kid here who's fallen over the cliff. I can give you the rough location."

He did his best to identify the cliff path for the listening rescue services, hoping he was being coherent. They seemed to recognise his description.

"Can you send out - oh, a helicopter I should think it would have to be? You need to hurry, he might slip some more. Good. Right. We'll do our best here in the meantime." With a sigh of relief, he folded up the mobile and returned it to his pocket.

Sheila, who had been trying to keep the child cheerful while John rang for help, turned her face away from the cliff top and spoke in a low worried tone which she hoped only John could hear.

"John, how long do they expect to be?"

"Twenty minutes."

"But, John!" Sheila's face wore an expression of horror. "That's way too long!"

"It's the best they can do." John spoke irritably.

"John, the ground's still slipping! Some of it went by while you were on the phone! He might be swept away any minute!"

"Okay." John was thinking. "We'll have to do our best for him, then. We can't just wait." As he spoke, he was unbuckling the belt of his jeans. "Look away, Sheila," he instructed. "I'll have to see if I can make a long enough rope out of what I'm wearing. It won't be easy to tie the things together with a firm enough knot, but we'll see."

Sheila spoke indignantly. "Look away, indeed. Give me a minute and I'll add my stuff to yours." She slipped off her jacket, and began to unbutton the front of her sundress. Then, seeing the horror in John's eyes, she added firmly "This is no time for nonsense, John. That kid's life may depend on it."

John shrugged. He was forced to acknowledge, in spite of all his instincts, that what Sheila was saying was right. As quickly as he could, he tied the various articles of clothing to each other, stretching out his jeans to get the length of both legs, making sure that each knot was firm and secure, working each one, tugging and pulling until he was convinced that nothing would come asunder. Sheila tossed over her jacket, then her sundress, and watched him adding them to the rope, concentrating on not looking at her.

He leaned forward over the edge of the path, and called down.

"What's your name?"

"Barney," said a quivering little voice.

"Well, Barney, I'm going to lower a rope to you, and I want you to take hold of it carefully. Don't just grab or you might end up dislodging some more soil. When you're sure you've got a good grip, let me know and Sheila and me will pull you up, okay?"

Barney nodded. Then, realising that there was too little light by now for anyone to see the movement, he managed to call in a voice made shaky by tears "Okay!"

John leant carefully over the edge of the path, dangling the home made rope at arm's length.

It was still too short.

"I'll have to go down," he said. He was measuring the distance with his eye as he spoke. There was another warning sign just beside them. The post was firmly concreted into the ground.

"Sheila. I'm going to tie the end of the rope round this post but I need you to hold it as firmly as you can, just for backup. Brace your feet against the post and hang on, see? I'll climb down and let's just hope I can reach far enough."

Sheila took the end of the rope, which a short while ago had been her white jacket. She set her teeth grimly. Her biggest fear was that John's own movements as he made his way down to Barney might send the earth slipping again and dislodge the little boy from his precarious perch.

John moved forward cautiously, sliding over the edge face first, moving on his stomach. It seemed the method least likely to displace more ground.

Sheila watched anxiously. Most of her mind was concentrated on holding the improvised rope tight. One part of her, however, couldn't help noticing the beauty of John's slim, muscular body, naked except for his boxers and wishing wistfully that he hadn't got quite such rigid ideas.

She could see over the edge of the path. John was nearly down as far as the little boy, Barney, now. He was holding his end of the rope by one hand and with the other stretching down as far as he could reach.

"Barney." John spoke quietly, gently. Above all, he was concerned not to stampede the child into any sudden movements which might dislodge the whin bush from the edge of the hill. "Barney, I want you to keep as still as possible and see if you can quite slowly and carefully reach your hand out to me."

"Okay."

Barney gulped. Moving slowly, just as John had instructed him, he stretched out his right arm. A moment later, John had him in a firm clasp round his wrist.

Then came the worst time.

John needed to retreat as carefully as possible up the side of the hill. He wasn't convinced that he could do this, pulling the boy with him, without ending up by starting another landslide. And if he did, what would become of them? It might have been better to let Sheila come down, he thought, for then he could have pulled her and the boy to safety. But he knew Sheila would never have the strength to pull them both up.

"I want you to be very brave, now, Barney," he said, "and let go of the whin bush. Then I'll be able to pull you up to me."

For a moment he was afraid Barney would be too frightened to obey. He could see the boy's eyes large with fear, looking at him. Then, with a shuddering sigh, Barney let go of the bush and John began carefully to pull him across the short distance until he could grasp him more firmly round the shoulders, and then round the waist. For the first time, John let himself think there might really be a chance of bringing the child to safety.

"Sheila!" he called. "I'm going to tie Barney to the rope. Do you think you could manage to pull him up if I push from this end?"

Sheila wasn't at all sure that she could, but she braced her legs even more firmly against the post and said only "Go ahead."

Pulling and pushing, with earth sliding around them on both sides, they hauled Barney over the edge and onto the path. Sheila gathered the child into her arms and sank to the ground, holding him tightly. John, less concerned now about caution, came scrambling after him. As he gained the security of the cliff path, a rumble to their left signalled the start of yet another landslide, coming from much further up the high cliff on their other side.

They watched with white faces as the rocks and earth swept past them, carrying all before them and snatching the whin bush to which Barney had been clinging so recently, uprooting it and hurling it far over the cliff.

It was another ten minutes before the rescue helicopter turned up.

Chapter 12

John's first concern, to Sheila's annoyance, was to get her respectably covered up again as soon as possible.

He sat on the path, wrestling grimly with the knots he himself had tightened a few minutes before. No easy task, for the one anxiety previously had been to make them secure enough to take his weight for the descent. He kept his eyes turned stubbornly away from Sheila as he struggled to free, most importantly, her dress and jacket before working on his own T-shirt and jeans and belt.

Sheila, at first unaware of his preoccupation, spent the time hugging Barney She sat on the grass at the edge of the path with the little boy on her knee and tried to comfort him after his ordeal.

"Hell!" burst out John suddenly. "I'm never going to get this done in time. I wish we'd never phoned for that helicopter. They'll be here any minute and you still half naked!"

Sheila stared at him in amazement. "We'll still need the helicopter, John," she pointed out. "Barney's in no condition to walk back along the path and back to our car, and that would be the nearest place we could take him. It's probably more than a mile away. Even then, we'd have to drive him to the nearest hospital or police station or something."

"Yeah, you're right." John sounded ashamed of himself for a moment. But a second later his obsession had overtaken him again, and he was once more struggling fiercely with the knots. At last, to his relief, he felt something loosen. Snatching up the white jacket, now smeared with shades of brown and grey, he hurled it at Sheila.

"At least get that on."

Sheila, while annoyed at what seemed to her nonsense, obediently pulled on the jacket. John was still struggling with her green sundress when they heard the nearby whine of the rescue helicopter. In another minute it was hovering above them. With a savage snarl, John dragged his clasp knife from the pocket of his jeans and slashed at the dress. While Sheila stared at him in amazement, he managed to rip the dress free and threw it to her.

"Quick!"

"My good dress!" Sheila was angry.

"Get it on!" John ordered. His face was white and twisted.

Sheila sensibly saved up her comments for later. She buttoned the dress round her, noting the rips which had spoiled it forever, and put her jacket back.

John's mobile was ringing. Pulling himself together, he answered it.

"Yes, this is the emergency call. We managed to get the boy up to the path but he'll need to be air-lifted now."

The next ten minutes passed swiftly. John struggled back into his clothes. A paramedic descended by rope from the helicopter and checked Barney for injury. Reassured that the child was mainly suffering from cold and shock and bruises, he quickly fastened Barney into the seat at the end of the rope. They watched thankfully as the rope was pulled up and Barney was safely stowed in the helicopter.

"What about his parents?" Sheila asked.

"Oh, they know we're rescuing him," the paramedic told them cheerfully. He was a small but tough looking young man, somewhere in his thirties, with a pleasant, freckled face. "They reported him missing a good while ago, so when we got your phone call, we were able to let them know he'd been found."

They should report to the nearest police station and make a statement, he told them. The parents would want to thank them. He took their names, then disappeared in turn into midair, hopping nimbly into the seat when his colleagues, having taken Barney on board, swung the rope down again. The helicopter, with a final wave from its passengers, buzzed busily off into the distance.

John and Sheila looked at each other.

And grinned.

"Well," John said, "we did it. Got him up before the bush went over the edge."

"Yeah," Sheila agreed. She didn't know whether to laugh or cry, and in fact as the thought went through her mind, she found to her astonishment that tears were streaming in hot gushes from her eyes.

"Oh, John!" seemed to be all she could say. "Oh, John!"

They moved forward simultaneously and were suddenly clinging desperately to each other, as if they could never let go.

Presently John, detached himself gently. He led Sheila to the grassy inner edge of the path and sat her down beside him, his arm round her shoulder.

"You were great, sweetheart," he said into her hair.

"*You* were great, John."

"Okay, we were both great. Listen, Sheila - "

John paused. He looked out over the darkened sea.

"When I graduate this summer, I have a job lined up with the BBC. It won't be a lot to start with, but enough. I'd like us to get married as soon as my finals are over."

Sheila stared at him. She could only see his profile as he still looked away into the distance.

"But, John!"

He turned to look at her.

"I love you, Sheila. I want to marry you!"

"Oh, John, I love you too, it would be great, but shouldn't we wait a bit longer - ?"

"I can't bear it any longer, Sheila! Especially just now, seeing you almost naked, it's more than I can manage, to keep my hands off you. If I knew it wouldn't be much longer, maybe I could keep control of myself." He groaned, stood up suddenly and walked away from her. "It's more than I can bear, Sheila, and you don't help, you know you don't help!"

"John, I'm sorry." It was a miserable little whisper.

"Oh, I know you don't do it on purpose, but you don't understand. I want you so much but I don't want to spoil everything. I don't believe in sleeping around. Sex is for marriage, right? I've always believed that. Sheila, it's as much as I can do not to grab you right now. The only answer is to get married as soon as we can, don't you see?"

"Okay, John."

Sheila stood up, and put her hand gently on his arm.

"I do love you, John. I want us to get married. But what about *my* degree?"

"Can't you go on with it even if we get married? I don't see why not."

Sheila considered, then her face broke into a wide beam.

"Yes, why not? As long as we don't start a family straight away, why not? Yes, John, let's get married this summer!"

John seized her in his arms and swung her round. An ear-splitting wild west "Yippee!" broke from his lips, sparking off a fit of the giggles from Sheila.

"Darling, darling, we're going to be so happy!"

He bent his head to kiss her once, briefly, then, taking her hand, led her back along the cliff path in the direction of the car.

Sheila, following him happily, nevertheless felt confusion rising up inside her. Was she happier than she'd ever been in her life or was she worried - frightened?

She had no clear idea.

Chapter 13

It was the night when he was beaten up that Phil slept with Davy for the first time.

She had known for years that Davy used illegal drugs but it had come as a bit of a shock to learn, not long after they had started going out together again, that he was trading in them.

Just on a small scale, Davy assured her. Really only for friends. And, okay, it gave him a bit of an income, but so what? He was the one running the risks, surely it was only fair if he made something on it? Not much, just enough to be reasonable. The drug barons were exploiting ordinary people who just wanted a bit of pleasure, a bit of relaxation. Just because the law was against them, people had to go to criminals for what they wanted. Davy, he argued virtuously, was saving them from that.

Phil knew perfectly well that Davy was fooling himself but she had no idea how dangerously until one Spring evening.

They were walking along Malone Road on their way back from the Botanic Inn, when the car squealed to a stop beside them and two men, hooded and dressed in black, jumped out and seized Davy in a vicious grip. She had hardly had time to cry out before they bundled him into the car and with a violent U turn roared off up the road.

In spite of her horror, Phil kept her head. It was important to make a mental note of the car's number. She tried desperately to do this, meanwhile hauling her mobile phone out of its carry case and calling the emergency services.

"Police!" she shouted into the phone. "A kidnapping. Two men in a car. They grabbed my boyfriend!"

It was hard, battling with extreme shock, for Phil to make herself clear. She gave the location in response to questions, tried to give the car number accurately, gave her own name. Then she crawled round to the nearest police station, her knees weak with terror, hardly able to walk, and sat there for what seemed hours, drinking weak coffee from a machine, giving a formal statement, and shivering uncontrollably as she waited for news, and wondered desperately what the news would be.

Too often, a snatch like this was followed by the discovery of a body, or of the victim beaten, kneecapped and dumped.

She heard at last.

A police car had located Davy.

The hoods dumped him from the car, bloody and bruised, on the outskirts of town. He crawled to the edge of a main road where he was visible in the street lights, then he passed out.

"Lucky he wasn't shot," said the fat, middle-aged sergeant cheerfully, passing the information on to Phil some time after he had received it. "They're taking him to the Royal for stitches and a check over. Could have been a kneecapping, if not worse, when these boyos get hold of you."

Phil took a taxi to the hospital.

They kept her waiting there in a bare, unhappy room with other friends and relations of the night's accident victims and would tell her nothing.

Phil could not bear to leave. She had been wounded to the heart by the thought of Davy, beaten and bloody, after the attack. She sat, mute and numb, for hours, waiting for him to be released, both unable and unwilling to talk. No-one bothered her except to offer occasional cups of tea. In another room, Davy received the medical help he needed.

At last he came. He pushed open the door, saw Phil, and came straight over. Putting his arms round her, he said in an unexpectedly shaken voice "Poor Phil!" He hugged her tightly. Phil hugged him back wordlessly.

"Are we going,now?" she asked when she could speak.

"I'll just get a taxi organised," Davy said.

"I'll come with you." Phil couldn't bear to be left alone any longer.

They walked to the car park where Davy had asked the taxi to pick them up and got in. They sat close together in silence.

They drove round the outskirts of the city to avoid traffic. Davy had a room in an old three storey house in a street just off the Ormeau Road. It couldn't be called a flat. He shared kitchen and bathroom but his own room was private, with a door which could be locked.

They paid the taxi driver, went in and upstairs. There was no-one else about. Davy closed his room door behind them and sat down on the bed, burying his face in his hands. He had not spoken since they left the hospital.

Suddenly a groan broke from him and he cried out, "Why? Why?"

Phil went to him and knelt on the floor beside the bed, on the threadbare carpet, putting her arms round him.

"Hush, dear, hush. It's all right."

"It's not all right," he said vehemently. "It's all wrong. We're helpless, Phil. The big bosses won't let the ordinary, independent traders operate in peace. What harm does it do them? They have ninety per cent of the customers, why can't they leave just a little bit for other people? It'll never change."

"So, that was what it was all about?" Phil asked slowly. Mixed with her anger at the attack on Davy was equal anger with him. How could he be such a fool as to put himself at such risk? And didn't he have any feeling of right and wrong? Surely he knew he should never have started this?

"Yeah, Big Jim Murphy's boys," Davy said absently. "Said it was an object lesson. Didn't know they were familiar with concepts like that." He made a weak attempt at a grin. "Said I was working on their turf." His face grew white again. "Why should they think it's *their* turf? And why should they think they have the right to do this to me?"

"Because they're greedy, vicious people or they wouldn't be involved in this in the first place," Phil said. But she could see he wasn't listening.

She pulled his dark head down and stroked his hair, whispering endearments to him as if he were a child.

"Oh, Phil, Phil," he groaned. He lifted his head from his arms and looked at her. There was a plaster across his forehead just below the hairline to protect the stitches he had got in the Royal Victoria Hospital.

"You're so lovely, Phil. Don't let go of me."

"I'm not going anywhere, Davy. I'm right here."

She could not remember ever having seen Davy, casual, self-possessed Davy, looking like this before. He seemed lost, even frightened, clinging to her as if he would never let her go. Phil felt as if her heart would break.

"It's all right, dear," she said again. "It's all right."

It was a dismal setting. The small attic bedroom on the third storey of the old house held only a single bed, a chest of drawers, a table covered in books and papers, and a single bar electric fire. Through the sash window the roofs of Belfast could be seen, grey slated and wet, stretching into the distance. The late moonlight, slanting in, picked out the frayed patches of the ancient carpet.

But Phil noticed none of this.

Gently disengaging herself from Davy's grasp, she stood up and went over to the electric fire. Bending down, she switched it on. Then she went over to the door, checked that its Yale lock had caught and put on the snib. She turned back to the narrow single bed where Davy sat watching her and, shrugging out of her jacket, began to unbutton the blouse she wore beneath it as she moved back towards him.

She sat down beside him on the bed, put her arms round him again and drew him towards her.

For a moment her lips brushed his cheek tentatively. Her hand stroked his hair. Then her mouth fastened on his and they kissed hungrily, ferociously.

It was Davy who broke free.

"No, Phil!" he said, speaking with an effort. "I know this isn't how you want it." He buried his face in her shoulder as he spoke.

But Phil said nothing. Instead, she lifted his right hand and placed it gently against her breast. Then, lying back against the pillow, she pulled him close against her, beginning to kiss him again with greater and greater passion until Davy forgot all his resolves.

"Hide me, Phil," he said. "Hide me and keep me safe."

"Yes, Davy," Phil whispered back softly, her mouth pressed against his chest as he bore down upon her. "Yes, yes, yes."

Chapter 14

On a soft afternoon in the very early summer, with a hint of roses in the air, Sheila and John drove out to Shaw's Bridge and parked John's mother's car, intending to walk on the towpath. They had not been back there since the first time they had met.

They had been engaged privately for nearly two months now. Sheila was very happy. Her only complaint, one which she did not make out loud, was that John seldom kissed her, except for a brief goodnight, and clearly intended to keep it that way.

They left the car and strolled along the towpath by the edge of the river. They had been walking for about twenty minutes or so when John suddenly slapped his forehead with the heel of his left hand.

"What a fool! I forgot! I have to meet Dennis Logan in ten minutes and hand over the keys of the Department library - he lent them to me yesterday. I might just get there before he gives up and goes, if I sprint like the hammers back to the car and fly round there."

"Okay, no problem," Sheila agreed. "You go on - I would only slow you down in these shoes. I'll wait here. It's a lovely day for a rest on the river bank."

"Thanks, darling," John said, smiling gratefully. "I don't want to get in his bad books just before finals."

John was expected to do well in his exams and had a job lined up with the BBC ready to walk into if all went well.

"I'll be right back," he added, and was away almost before he had finished speaking.

Sheila sat down on the edge of the bank and leaned over, trailing her fingers in the water. Time passed. Presently, a shadow behind her made her turn her head.

"Aphrodite!" said Francis Delmara, approaching along the towpath and stopping beside Sheila. "Springing, not quite from the waves but something like that. How nice to see you, beautiful."

"Francis," Sheila said. She hadn't seen him since the Christmas party and her memories of what had happened then were embarrassing, though vague.

"That's right," said Francis, "I'm glad to see you remember me, beautiful. But I never learnt your name?"

"Sheila Doherty," said Sheila.

"Hullo, Sheila Doherty," said Francis softly. He sat down on the bank beside her.

"You disappeared rather quickly, that night, darling."

"I thought it was you who disappeared," Sheila responded. "And just as well, too."

"Was it?" asked Francis. He smiled. "I don't agree, beautiful. It was the major tragedy of my life."

Sheila laughed. "You seem to have survived."

"One always survives. That's what makes it a tragedy," said Francis. He leaned over and took Sheila's hand, still wet from the river. For some reason, inexplicable to herself, she allowed him to take it.

"Tut, tut. This needs dried," Francis said and, producing a large clean handkerchief, began to dry her hand carefully, one finger at a time. Sheila, to her horror, found it incredibly sexy.

Then Francis looked deep into her eyes. "I wonder if you realise how beautiful you are, Sheila Doherty?" he said.

* * *

John arrived at the English Department Library just as Professor Logan appeared round the corner.

"Ah, Mr. Branagh," said the Professor amiably. "Good, good. You have the key?"

John, as a potential TV journalist, was a favourite with Dennis Logan who lost no opportunity of extending his contacts with the media. Any and all publicity was meat and drink to him.

John handed over the key and they chatted in a friendly manner for a few minutes about the reference he had been looking up in the more specialised books in the Department library. Then the Professor nodded and went in, and John went back to the car.

As he drove back to Shaw's Bridge in a rather more leisurely manner, John allowed his thoughts to drift back to Sheila. He had been so mistaken about her when they first met. He had written her off as promiscuous and untrustworthy, living only for sex. How different she had turned out to be in the months since they had met again at the Christmas party! He thought of her as chaste, virginal, above all faithful. He was sure now that she would never hurt him by flirting, or worse, going with someone else. He felt secure and happy in their relationship. He was prepared to wait to fulfil their love until after their wedding. It was hard, almost unbearably hard, at times. John didn't care. He was ready, willing to be hard on himself when necessary. He had never considered that it might perhaps be hard for Sheila too.

He left the car in the park at Shaw's Bridge and began to stroll gently back along the river path, enjoying the spring air.

Francis sat beside Sheila on the river bank and played with her hand.

"I hoped we might meet again," he said. "But I've been out of the country for the past few months. I only know Dennis Logan through his wife - she buys some of her clothes from me."

"You sell clothes?" Sheila asked.

"Design and sell them," Francis corrected. "I'm just starting but before long you won't need to ask that question. Everyone will have heard of Delmara Fashions."

Sheila smiled.

"But let's talk about something more interesting," said Francis. He dropped his voice to a murmur. "Now that we've met again, beautiful, why not go back to where we left off? It seems the ideal opportunity."

Sheila began to say something but Francis paid no attention. Instead, he leaned over, put his other arm around her shoulders, and began to kiss her. It was like the night of the Christmas party. Sheila was as sober as a judge this time but she felt as if there was no resistance in her. Something about this man attracted her at a purely physical level. She found herself lying back against the grassy slope, all among the primroses, and everything seemed to be floating.

Including, a moment later, Francis.

A bellow of rage sounded in Sheila's ear. John's angry face flashed before her as she opened her eyes. There was a splash that seemed to soak the surrounding countryside and, as Sheila scrambled dizzily to her feet, she saw that Francis was struggling frantically in the middle of the river.

It seemed funny to Sheila at the time. At first she laughed helplessly. Then she saw John's white, bitter face.

"John! It's all right, it was nothing -"

"*Nothing!*" John could hardly speak.

Francis climbed out of the river and stood there, wet and dripping.

"Every time I touch you, pet, I end up soaking," he said to Sheila. "It must mean something."

Ignoring John, he strode off in the opposite direction.

Sheila stood looking at John.

"I don't want to speak to you," John said. "I can't trust myself - I want to kill you ."

He stood with his back turned, not looking at Sheila, his hands tightly twisted together.

"John - don't - !" Sheila stammered incoherently.

Then he began to speak, or rather to shout. When he had called Sheila all the evil names she had ever heard, and some more besides, she managed at last to interrupt him.

"John - you don't understand. It didn't mean anything."

"That makes it worse - much worse," John said. He had gained control of his voice and spoke quietly again. "You and I are streets apart, Sheila. I don't ever want to see you again."

Then he turned and walked away.

Sheila stood quietly beside the river. The sun poured down, lighting up her hair, and she could still smell the primroses in the air.

It was a long time before she could begin to walk back along the path to catch a bus home.

Chapter 15

Phil was running across the grass. She was late, which wasn't too unusual. But this time, she was late for Davy, not just for some lecture. Even at university, Phil had still not brought herself to take work, with its lectures and tutorials, too seriously. As she ran, she could smell the roses from Botanic Garden's famous rose garden coming nearer. Just past the rose garden was a secluded little rockery with a bench seat where she and Davy often met. Davy hoped to graduate this year and move on to Ph D work at the Ashby Institute where he already spent many of his working hours. The gardens made a convenient halfway house for their more casual meetings. But often Davy could only stay for a short while before going back to his work. Phil didn't want to miss him.

She stopped running as she came nearer to the meeting place and stood for a moment to get her breath back. It would never do to let Davy see her running to meet him. One still has one's standards, thought Phil, grinning. After a moment, she walked on, still hurrying, but ready to look casual as she came round the final corner of the path. There were voices coming from the direction of the rockery. It sounded like Davy, and a stranger.

"Knickers!" thought Phil to herself. "It sounds as if someone Davy knows has come along. What a pest."

She walked on past the last bush and saw Davy talking to a middle-aged man whom she had never seen before. They broke off abruptly when they saw her.

"This is Phil," said Davy quickly to his companion. "My girlfriend."

"Nice to meet you, Phil," said the man. He was medium height, thin and with sandy hair beginning to show some grey. His eyes, which Phil particularly noticed, looked hard. She felt as if he had taken in everything there was to know about her at one swift glance. For some reason, which she could not have explained, she felt an instinctive dislike of him.

"Sorry I can't stay," the man went on. "Nice to run into you again, Davy. See you around. Cheerio." He smiled at Davy, then at Phil, and moved off with a casual half wave. Phil stared after him. When he had gone out of hearing, she turned to Davy.

"Who was that?"

"Oh, just a guy I've met a few times."

Davy was embarrassed. He wasn't used to lying to Phil.

"I don't believe you," Phil said.

There was a lump in her throat. She felt as if she might burst into tears any moment.

"Well, what do you think he is, then?" Davy asked coolly.

"He's one of the boys, isn't he? He's part of the Belfast Mafia. Mixed up in drugs," Phil said fiercely.

"Shut up, can't you? If he is, all the more reason not to shout about it."

"Are you getting involved, Davy? You are, aren't you? How can you, after what they did to you!"

Davy looked at her.

"This is a different lot. O'Brien's people. Not like Murphy's boys. O'Brien's civilised."

"Maybe!"

"I got involved in this long ago. You know that, Phil, even if we don't talk about it. You knew what I was doing."

Phil shuddered.

"Yes," she said slowly. "Yes, I suppose I did know it." She thought back. "Yes, you talked about it. I thought you had met some of the people but I didn't think it had gone any further."

"And why should you think that it has, now?" demanded Davy. "Why are you jumping to conclusions just because you see me with someone you haven't seen before?"

"I don't know," confessed Phil miserably. "It's just - you seemed so familiar with him." She tried to explain. "As if it was nothing new, as if he knew all about you and you often met and talked."

Davy turned away. Fumbling in his jacket pocket, he produced a packet of cigarettes and lit one.

"Here." He tossed one back to Phil.

"Thanks."

"Okay," he said presently. "Yes, you're right. I haven't said anything to you, Phil, because it's better for you not to know. I've been working with O'Brien for a while now. Since the night Murphy had me beaten up. It was that or quit altogether. It's too dangerous out on your own. I first met Sean - the guy who was here - a bit before that, but I didn't make up my mind until after what Murphy did. After that, I didn't think there was much choice."

Phil was silent, remembering. She had thought, in common with many of the ordinary people of Northern Ireland, that the ceasefires and then the Good Friday Agreement, would put an end to the terrorism and bring in a time of peace and contentment for her country. Disillusionment had been gradual but in the end it had been clear that the vacuum left by the disbandment of the terrorist forces had been filled by crime and by a renewed, different violence. Drugs, prostitution, all the crime so infrequent in Northern Ireland before the Troubles, had come in like a tidal wave to fill the empty house.

Phil remembered, too, Davy's white, bitter face that night after the beating up. He had escaped relatively uninjured but all around him he had heard of others shot in the knees, beaten or killed. He could not forget it. For some nights afterwards even the comfort of Phil's arms could not help. She would hold him while he wept and then he would make love to her in a hard, fierce way which was new in their relationship. She had been frightened, not so much by his rough, painful approach to her, as by what lay behind it. He had been scarred in a way which she was afraid might never heal. But a few days later, when they met again, he had lost all his harshness and was gentle with her, with a tenderness in his love-making which moved her deeply.

It must have been, she now thought, during those few days that he had made his decision to join O'Brien and in that decision had found the safety which she had been unable to give him.

"Davy," she said at last, "I understand that you feel that you must do something important with your life. That you want to make money, be successful. But not this. You are hurting too many innocent people. I wish you would pull out before it's too late."

But he only smiled at her, and repeated her words. "Too late."

Then he took her hand, and held it tightly saying, almost casually, "It's too late already, Phil."

Chapter 16

Mary Branagh, John's sister, had come up to Queen's too.

Sheila had never known Mary all that well but she liked what she had seen of her.

One day, drinking coffee in the union with Sheila and Phil at the start of their second year, Mary invited them to a party.

"Not for anything special," she explained. "Just a get-together, for a laugh. Charlie Flanagan took me to the first one and then I keep getting invited on."

Phil frowned.

"Davy told me Charlie Flanagan's well into drugs," she said.

"So what?" said Mary lightly.

"Well – maybe not a good idea?" said Phil slowly. She had always been the leader of the pack. She didn't specially want to seem dumb but it really wasn't right for Mary to try to drag Sheila, who was so innocent, into that sort of stuff. Sheila had no idea how to look after herself.

"No way!" said Mary happily. "A *very* good idea, I think!"

"Well, I won't be there," said Phil firmly.

"How about you, Sheila?" asked Mary, turning persuasively to her other friend.

Sheila thought about it. There was no way she wanted to get into drugs, but ....

Mary was John's sister. She really, really wanted to keep up the relationship. Maybe there was a chance that if she saw a lot of Mary, she would bump into John one of these days.

She turned to Mary and smiled enthusiastically.

"I'd love to come!" she said.

Every Saturday night after that, Mary and Sheila went to parties.

Once into the circle, there was never any problem getting invited on the next occasion, and there seemed to be something on every weekend. Sheila, at first invited on Mary's say so, found to her surprise that there was a crowd of fifty or sixty regular party goers whom she had never met before. They were mostly a few years older, maybe that was why. Most of them were students. On any one evening, at least twenty of them would gather, usually in someone's flat, for parties which seemed to Sheila to be in a whole new world from her school days' socialising

On the first evening, sitting on the floor beside Mary in a large, scantily furnished room with a low table, a number of cushions on the floor, and a few large armchairs where people sprawled with legs thrown carelessly over the chair arms, she said as much.

"This is good, Mary. I feel good about this."

Mary grinned. The dim lighting sparkled on her sleek blonde hair and on her white teeth. The Beatles' Sergeant Pepper album was playing in the background. Retro music

"You smoke, don't you?" Mary asked

"Oh, yes," replied Sheila confidently. Hadn't she and Phil been stealing fags from their mothers' handbags since they were twelve, before their pocket money stretched to buying their own?

"Here."

Mary handed her an already lit cigarette. It looked home-made.Sheila had seen home rolled cigarettes before. Some of the boys she knew had resorted to that when they were hard up. This one looked a lot bigger, but so what? She took the offered cigarette and had a puff. Her eyes opened wide. She took the cigarette out of her mouth and turned to stare at Mary

"It's – "

"Blow. What did you think it was?" Mary asked lightly. She seemed quite unmoved.

Sheila looked at the joint again.

Yes, it was much longer and thicker than the hand rolled cigarettes she had seen previously. Otherwise it looked much the same. She sniffed it cautiously. The smell of cannabis was unfamiliar to her but it was clearly different from tobacco. She put the end back into her mouth and inhaled slowly

"Pass it on," said Mary.

Sheila obeyed. Then she leant back against the wall and felt good. She was relaxed, happy. There didn't seem much reason to worry. When the joint came back to her, she inhaled deeply again and felt even better.

There was a vase of roses in shades of red and pink on the low table against the far wall. She lay back with her eyes fixed on the roses, contemplating them dreamily.They seemed to shine at her.The red petals seemed redder, and the pink, pinker, than anything she had ever seen before.

Chapter 17

On New Year's Eve, Mary, Sheila and a crowd of the regular party-goers went down by car to Whitehead, a quiet little seaside town with an elderly population. They parked near the sea front and walked down to the promenade in a noisy group.

The moon shone peacefully over the sea, reflecting the ripples in a broad path. Mary stretched out her arms theatrically towards it and declaimed in a sing-song voice,

"Oh, the moon shines bright on Mrs. Porter
And her daughter,
They washed their feet in soda-water...

before breaking into giggles halfway through

She and Sheila linked arms and ran wildly down the pebbly beach to the sea. Kicking off their shoes and turning up their jeans to their knees, they ran into the rippling, shallow icy-cold waves and splashed about

"Let's walk round the cliff path to Black Head," someone suggested

Laughing and chattering, the group gathered itself together and made its way slowly along the concrete path at the edge of the shore beneath the looming cliffs which led in the direction of Islandmagee. Mary and Sheila carried their shoes in one hand waiting for their tights to dry out. After a while the rough surface became too uncomfortable and Sheila stopped to slip hers on again, leaning for the purpose on the arm of Charlie Flanagan who was a regular at the parties and, Sheila thought, the main source of supply. Charlie now attempted to get his arm round Sheila when she had finished putting on her shoes but she pushed him roughly off and ran on ahead.

Shrugging, Charlie turned his attention instead to a more accommodating girl.

Sheila caught up with Mary, who had wandered on by herself, and the two skipped happily along, giggling and singing to themselves. After a while, the party came to an open space where some trees grew, and Mary, who had been there before, pointed it out to Sheila.

"That's the Magic Forest."

The words seemed to be taken as a general signal to stop. Bumping into each other and looking round vaguely, the group came to a standstill. The trees formed an attractive background although they were in no sense a forest.

"Let's go and sit down," suggested a boy called Tim.

Leaving the path, they wandered carelessly over the ground with its thick covering of pine needles. Presently they came to a halt in a more open place and began to settle down, in ones and twos, in some sort of rough circle under the branches. A joint was lit up and passed from hand to hand.

The moon slanted down through the trees, lighting up the young faces, intent or dreamy. Sheila leaned back against the trunk of a tree and inhaled deeply. At some level, she was aware that this might not be the best thing to be doing. John, she knew, would be not only shocked, but angry, ragingly angry, she supposed, if he knew what she was getting into.

So what? If John cared about what she was doing, he would have got in touch ages ago. Heaven knows, she thought bitterly, I've tried hard enough to contact him. He won't even let me say I'm sorry.

All around her, she became aware, with a heightening of her senses, of the brightness of the moonlight, the sharp smell of the pine trees, the soft, prickly feeling of each individual pine needle beneath her. Her ears picked up the gentle lapping of the waves and the rustling of the wind among the branches, and she could hear her own breathing magnified a hundred times as she focused her attention on it. The pine needles shone as if lit up by electricity, bright green mixing with gleaming bronze.

She became aware, after what seemed to have been years, that people had begun to jump up and run and dance among the trees. There was a great deal of shouting and laughing. She sat still, feeling relaxed and at peace, with no inclination to join in.

Then all of a sudden, a desire came over her to dance and leap and shout. She sprang to her feet, moving with a wild vigour and pleasure, and began to dart about among the trees, chasing the others, running away, coming back again.

Without really knowing when she had first become aware of him, she realised that Charlie Flanagan was following her closely. From time to time, he reached out, trying to catch hold of her but always she managed to elude him. It became a game. As soon as Charlie came within reaching distance, she would spin happily round and escape him again.

It was fun. Sheila found herself laughing a lot. Then suddenly it was no longer fun. Unexpectedly, Charlie managed to catch her and, before she could avoid him, he pulled her down and was lying on top of her, with his arms round her.

The feel of his coarse, tickly hair on her cheek roused Sheila from her dream. She didn't even like Charlie Flanagan. She found him disgusting. Thumping his back with her fists, she tried to push him to one side. But it was too hard.

The effect of her last smoke began to kick in. She felt her head begin to whirl. Suddenly it seemed a pity to stop Charlie. With one part of her she no longer cared; with another part she quite wanted him to go on. She felt, as if at a great distance, his hand tugging at the zip of her jeans and his struggle to pull her clothes down over her hips.

Something in Sheila pushed and struggled its way to the surface, screaming through the mist in her mind "No! No!"

What way out was there?

Sheila found that Charlie had managed to undo the buttons of her blouse. Reaching under his arms to pull the material closed, her hand encountered something metal attached to her bra strap.

Of course!

Just before coming out, too late to stop and sew it properly, she had discovered that her bra strap had come apart and had effected hasty repairs with a large safety pin.

Putting out all the strength she had left, she clicked the pin open and dragged it from her bra. She picked a spot high on Charlie's inner right leg where he had pulled his jeans eagerly down and left himself unprotected by their thick cloth. She thrust the sharp point of the pin viciously home. Charlie, suddenly aware through his drugged consciousness of an agonizing pain in a precious and vulnerable region, leapt clumsily to his feet screaming.

Sheila scrambled away, crawling on hands and knees at first until she was able to stand. She ran over to Mary who was still sprawled beneath a nearby tree.

"Let's go," she said abruptly. "This lout is giving me a pain."

But nothing to the one I just gave him, she giggled internally.

"No rush," said Mary dreamily. She continued to gaze at the moon, a peaceful smile lighting up her face, moonlight gleaming on her blonde hair.

"Yes, there is," said Sheila.

She felt angry but, although she pushed at Mary, there was no noticeable reaction. Mary continued to half sit, half lie where she was, shrugging off Sheila's hand as if she was hardly aware of it.

It was no use.

Sheila sat down again beside Mary, leaning against the same tree. The effects of the cannabis seemed to have worn off and she hesitated to smoke again, although another joint was circulating. When it reached her, she passed it on untouched to the nearest person.

No-one seemed to notice or care.

She had no desire to have any further relations with Charlie or, for that matter, with any of the other boys present. Not, to be honest, that Charlie seemed to want to have anything more to do with her! But if she smoked more blow, who knew, she wondered, how she would react if he, or any of them, grabbed her again.

There seemed little danger of that. Charlie lay on his stomach, groaning loudly, oblivious to everything and everyone but his injury. All around her, Sheila was aware of the rest of their company, some lying down, others still moving about and exclaiming in loud voices in reaction to their heightened perception of the sky, the trees, the sea. It would be a long time before they wanted to leave.

Sheila had permission to stay overnight with Mary for New Year's Eve, so she was not worried about her parents expecting her back. The party, which had begun in Mary's house, had moved on to a nearby flat in time for midnight. She had hoped to meet John at Mary's house, but apparently he was out, working on a BBC New Year's Eve programme. Sheila told herself she didn't care.Then had come the suggestion of the trip to Whitehead.

"A trip in both senses," Mary had giggled.

No-one seemed to expect to go home that night. Sheila shivered and pulled her jacket more tightly round her. At least it wasn't raining. She supposed the others were insulated from the cold by the effects of the cannabis. She herself had felt warm and happy until Charlie's attempt to get too friendly.

Perhaps she should have another puff. It was going to be a long, cold, miserable night otherwise. But looking at Charlie lying on one side, with his arms stretched out, snoring now, she shuddered instinctively.

Anything was better than risking a repeat of that. Surely, even if she was higher than the birds, she wouldn't let him near her, but she knew that it was only too possible.

That settled it. For the rest of the night, Sheila sat huddled against the pine tree, trying to get some warmth from Mary's back which was next to hers, wishing glumly that she had stayed in instead for the family New Year party as she had always done before. At least she would have been warm, if very bored.

Thank goodness she had stopped him in time and was still a virgin. Supposing she had got pregnant? That would have been too awful for words.

Dawn came at last, a pale sunlight breaking over the mostly sleeping company. Hours later, they packed themselves up, and wandered back to their cars

Chapter 18

"I told you so," said Phil.

Sheila had to admit she was right.

And as for getting in touch with John Branagh again through his sister Mary, well, that had been a complete failure, hadn't it? She could only hope John would never realise what she been doing these last months. Never again, she told herself.

She stopped going to parties with Mary. It wasn't worth it. She hadn't met up with John and she realised now that if she had met him in the sort of company Mary kept, he would have hated her even more. Time to forget John, to forget Mary's friends, to be her own person.

She knew she had been neglecting her work, doing badly in her essays, falling behind with everything. Time to get a grip. She began to work harder, aiming to do well in her end of term exams to eventually get herself a qualification and a good job. To try to learn who she was herself, and to live her own life.

And to forget about John Branagh.

Sheila saw less and less of Mary as winter retreated and exams drew near. The attractions of the weekend parties had long since faded. The idea of being thrown out of University was one which she was not prepared to live with. She spent more and more time working and regularly excused herself to Mary when she suggested a Saturday night break.

Mary, on the other hand, was showing less interest in work as the year went on. She missed classes regularly and often seemed to sit through those she attended in a dream. Sheila guessed that often Mary was tripping at these times or recovering from the after effects. She thought it likely that Mary had moved on from cannabis to the harder drugs. She seemed to have changed from the bright, lively girl Sheila had liked. Instead, she was quiet, withdrawn, dreamy.

Then came a stage when she became completely unpredictable. Suddenly, for no apparent reason, she would explode into anger, and shout at Sheila in a way which both upset Sheila and turned her off. Mary became, from one of Sheila's closest friends, a person she would rather avoid.

One day at the start of February they met in town to do some shopping together. Mary had had a birthday. She wanted to buy herself something nice to wear with some of her birthday money. It seemed a pleasant, normal sort of plan. Sheila looked forward to it.

They wandered round the shops for a few hours, trying on skirts, tops and dresses, giggling and happy. Then Mary began to get jumpy. She snapped at Sheila, apologised, then a few minutes later snapped again. They were in the changing room at Principle's at the time.

"For goodness sake take that off! You know I wanted to try it myself!" Mary shouted. She began feverishly to pull at a pretty, lilac coloured top which Sheila was trying on, almost ripping it in the process. Sheila was afraid that the top would be damaged and that they would be forced to pay for it. Hastily she gave Mary all possible assistance to get it off, but she felt very angry with Mary.

"People are looking at you, Mary," she said coldly. "Calm down or I'm going - now."

"Sorry." Mary rubbed her forehead, and pushed her hair back from her face in her habitual gesture. "Sorry, Sheila. Let's go and get a cup of coffee, shall we?"

"All right."

They pushed their way out of the shop and walked round to the Knightsbridge, a popular coffee bar in Donegal Square at the side of the City Hall, down at basement level. They plunged down the steps, found an empty table and ordered their coffee.

When it came in a tall pot with wide white porcelain cups and a plate of scones, Mary sat slumped over the table nursing her cup in both hands.

"Sorry," she said again.

She sat back, fished in her shoulder bag and produced a small pill container.

"Coffee sweeteners," she said with a grin which invited complicity. "Have one?"

"No, thanks," said Sheila sharply. "Mary, don't you think you should wait till you get somewhere more private before taking that?"

"Why?" asked Mary, in a deliberately provocative manner. "What's so private about sweetening your coffee?"

Sheila shrugged.

Mary swallowed one of the tablets, washing it down with coffee. For a few minutes she continued to sit slumped over the table, then she straightened up and began to talk and laugh loudly. Sheila, rigid with embarrassment, hoped no-one was watching who could interpret this behaviour correctly. She drank her coffee as quickly as possible and stood up.

"Bye, Mary," she said. "Time I was heading home."

"Don't go, Sheila!" Mary said, suddenly changing from laughter to a clinging dependency. "I haven't finished shopping yet. Don't leave me! Stay for a while longer."

Sheila was firm.

"No. I'm going now."

"When will we get together again? How about next weekend?"

"No, I don't think so, Mary. See you around."

That was the last Sheila saw of Mary for the some time. She looked back as she left the coffee bar. Mary was still sitting where she had left her, slumped over her coffee cup again. Her eyes were half shut, her mouth hung open. With one finger she was pushing her cup by the handle round and round its saucer. Her bright, fair hair hung limply over her forehead and she was giggling quietly to herself.

Chapter 19

Nearly two months passed and Sheila heard nothing more of Mary until an evening in late March.

The message came through a friend who had been a frequenter of the weekend parties, Timmy White. He rang Sheila one evening while she was reading various critics on Milton in preparation for an important essay.

Sheila's first reaction was annoyance at being disturbed.

"Timmy White?" she repeated down the phone.

Then memory clicked into place.

Of course. A tall, pleasant looking boy with light coloured hair and a pale, freckled face.

"Okay. Yes, Timmy, this is Sheila Doherty. Long time, no see."

"Yeah." Timmy paused. "It's - well, Sheila, I thought you would be the person to ring. It's Mary, you see. You're her best mate, right?"

"Not really, Timmy." Sheila was brisk. "I haven't seen Mary for ages. Not since the beginning of February."

"Oh. Oh, I see. I didn't know that. But maybe you could come anyway? I don't know who else to call, except her parents, and I'd rather not involve them, right?"

"I see." Sheila thought for a minute. "What's the problem, Timmy?"

"I'm not sure. Mary passed out, here in my flat a couple of hours ago and I don't know what to do with her. She'll have to be brought round and taken home. I thought a girl would know better what to do - and - well - could you come?"

"Okay," Sheila said. "Give me the address and I'll see if I can borrow my mother's car. I'll need it to take her home."

Timmy's flat wasn't far away. Ten minutes later, Sheila, in the car which she had quite recently learned to drive and which Kathy had allowed her to borrow with many warnings about taking care, pulled up at the kerb beside the tall house in the university area.

An anxious face at one of the upstairs windows disappeared and, a moment later, Timmy was opening the door.

"Up here," he said.

Sheila followed him along the hall and up the narrow flight of stairs to the second floor.

Timmy's flat was like most student digs but with a large front room. On the shabby old sofa Mary was stretched out full length, breathing heavily. Sheila went over to her.

Mary's face was very red and her breathing sounded strange. All of a sudden Sheila felt frightened.

"What was she on?" she asked, trying to keep her voice steady.

"Different things," Timmy answered vaguely. "She had her own stuff, I didn't ask. There was some shit, we all had that, but that was ages ago. Everybody else finished tripping and went home a couple of hours ago but Mary had had some tabs as well, I'm not sure what, maybe E, and she just seemed to conk out round about the time everyone was going. If I'd realised, I'd have made some of them stay and help, but it was only when I came back from letting the last people out that I found her lying there like that. I thought she'd just sleep it off, but then I got worried. I'm glad you're here," he finished with obvious relief.

Sheila, she thought to herself, wasn't glad. But in a way that wasn't true - she was glad someone responsible was there even if she would have preferred it to be someone else. Perhaps she could do something. Timmy was clearly helpless.

She bent over Mary, felt her pulse, listened to her breathing, then she shook her a little but with no result.

"Right. This has gone far enough. I know you don't want Mary's parents to find out, Timmy, but you should have had the sense to realise that Mary needs help. Go and call a doctor - quick!"

Timmy gaped at her then, obeying the autocratic note in Sheila's voice, he went obediently to the phone which was outside his door on the communal landing.

It was a coin box and Timmy had no more change.

Sheila felt like screaming as his worried face re-appeared round the doorway asking for money.

Hurriedly she searched her pockets for small coins, and at last the call was made.

Then there was nothing to be done but wait.

The doctor, not best pleased at being called out in the evening, was inclined to be irritable at first, but as soon as he saw Mary this changed. He said very little, examined her briefly, and then went to ring for an ambulance.

Sheila went in the ambulance with Mary to the hospital. It seemed somehow important not to leave her with strangers. Timmy stayed behind. He had promised the doctor to ring her parents and let them know the name of the hospital.

At the Royal Victoria Hospital, where Mary was taken, people wanted Sheila to answer questions, to tell them what drugs Mary had taken.

"I don't really know," she kept repeating to different nurses or doctors. "I wasn't there. I don't really know. She used to be my friend but I haven't seen her for ages. I only got there a few minutes before we rang the doctor. I told Timmy to ring as soon as I saw her. I don't know what she had taken - Timmy mentioned heroin."

The nurse or doctor would nod gravely and hurry away, to be replaced a few minutes later by another one who would ask the same questions.

In between this, Sheila sat forlorn in the waiting room on a hard chair beside a table covered in out-of-date magazines and Readers Digests.

She didn't feel like reading anything.

Presently, she was joined by a couple who she remembered vaguely as Mary's parents. John's parents, too. The woman was smartly dressed with tinted blonde hair which had probably once been as fair as Mary's own.

They both looked bewildered, unable to take in what was happening.

Each time a fresh person came to ask Sheila the same questions, she tried, when she had done her best to give answers, to get an answer in turn to the only question which she could think of, the only one which mattered.

"Will she be all right?" she kept asking. "Will she be all right?"

And one after the other, the people whom she asked would shake their heads and reply as if it was some sort of stock answer "We'll just have to see. It's too soon to say. We'll just have to see."

It was after midnight when a doctor in a white coat and with a stethoscope round his neck, which gave him the artificial air of someone in a TV programme, came in and called Mary's father out to speak to him privately.

Sheila waited with the woman who was Mary's mother.

After a while, the father came back in. His face showed nothing but he went to his wife and put his arms round her.

"It's all over," Sheila heard him say. "She's come round. She's going to be all right."

They went out together, the man's arm still round his wife.

Sheila sat on.

Presently a nurse, passing the waiting area, noticed her and came in.

"Didn't someone tell you?" she asked. She was a kind-looking, plump, middle-aged woman.

"Tell me what?" Sheila asked. She knew the answer. For some reason she needed to hear it in words.

"It's okay, pet," said the nurse. "It's good news. Your friend came round half an hour ago. She'll be okay."

Sheila looked at the nurse and was unable to speak.

"Okay, pet," the nurse repeated. "You'd better go home now. There's nothing here to wait for. You can't speak to her tonight. If you need a taxi, there's a phone just round that corner down the corridor."

Kathy's car was still sitting outside Timmy's flat. It was within walking distance although they had come in the ambulance. Sheila went out and walked across town until she came to it then drove home. She felt a curious numbness.

How could Mary so nearly have been dead?

The world seemed to be wrapped in cotton wool. Everything seemed very far away.

She wasn't going to faint or anything stupid like that.

She just didn't seem to be in very close touch with reality.

After a while, she drove slowly and very carefully home. She parked the car, went into the house, and went straight up to her room. In the last few hours, the whole world had changed, and yet there were the books about Milton just as she had left them when Kathy called her to the phone.

Sheila sat down on the bed and found that she was crying as if her heart was breaking.

Chapter 20

That same March, Phil put into action a plan which had been in her head for some time and moved in with Davy.

She told her parents that she would be living in a shared house with some friends and they inquired no further. She was never sure if they really believed in the friends, supposedly female, or if they simply turned a blind eye for the sake of peace.

Davy, who had graduated last year with the sort of good degree which opened the door to him for research as he had hoped, had left the small, badly furnished room in the house off Ormeau Road and taken a more up-market flat, self-contained, in Thomas Street. It was still not one of the more expensive residential areas, for even as a post graduate student Davy's income would not run to much, but it was private and good enough for the time being. It was also within reasonable distance of the University.

Phil had spent her time trying not to know what Davy was doing. She had made up her mind to accept him as he was, without preconditions.

But as the situation worsened and the loose cannons among the ex-paramilitaries more and more turned into gangsters, and shootings of rival drug dealers became a commonplace, it became harder and harder to pretend that this had nothing to do with herself and Davy.

There was one particularly horrifying day when the news seemed to consist of nothing but drug trafficking and stories of illegal immigrants forced into prostitution.

Phil sat curled into a miserable ball in the largest and softest of the armchairs in the flat, listening to the news on the radio and wishing Davy would come back.

She was half listening and half dreaming, wondering when it would all end, when she caught a familiar name.

"Crackle crackle....." said the radio, "Tomas Peter O'Dade, aged twenty three, of Malone Avenue, Belfast, was shot and killed today by masked gunmen believed to be involved in the trafficking of heroin. O'Dade, who was dead on arrival at hospital, is believed to have been a drug dealer himself on a smaller scale and to have been involved in a number of incidents concerning drugs where ...... crackle crackle crackle..."

Phil leaned forward and turned off the radio.

She felt numb.

Tomas O'Dade.

He had been one of Davy's closest friends since before Phil and Davy had met.

It must be the same Tomas O'Dade. The age and the address put it beyond all doubt.

Phil could not cry. She was beyond that easy relief.

It was so horrible that someone she had known, someone Davy knew so well, was lying dead and himself responsible, if the report was true, for so much misery in other lives.

Only a few years ago, he had still been at school - they had all been at school - with no vague premonition of what so short a time would bring.

It was impossible.

So Phil reflected with the surface of her mind.

Underneath something worse stirred and refused to be entirely pushed down.

It could just as easily have been Davy.

Chapter 21

Spring came round again, lighting up the candles on the chestnut trees, smothering the cherry and apple trees with soft pink and white blossom, scenting the air with the smell of newly cut grass. In pursuance of her good resolutions, Sheila sat with her feet up in the Reading Room at the Students' Union quietly eating a Chocolate Flake and getting to grips with Samson Agonistes.

There was a noise of clattering feet at the far end of the room and Gerry Maguire appeared.

Sheila looked up.

She had a class test tomorrow and the last thing she wanted was to be interrupted.

But it seemed clear from his smiles and gestures that Gerry had been looking for her, had seen her, and was now heading in her direction.

Gerry, now a final year law student, had changed noticeably in the last couple of years. He had grown and matured, and would have impressed someone meeting him for the first time as a responsible, adult person fully in control of his life.

Sheila, however, was quite aware that beneath this surface stability there still lurked the old, reckless boy, the rule-breaker, she had known since childhood, and his first words confirmed the suspicion generated by something in his expression that Gerry was up to something again.

"Sheila, honey, am I glad to see you!" he greeted her, in something which, while clearly intended as a take-off of an American accent, suffered in dramatic impact from the need to whisper.

A tall, blond boy with gold rimmed glasses looked up from the next carrel and frowned angrily.

"Shush!" he said.

"Shush!" said Sheila in turn, putting her finger on Gerry's mouth.

"Ooh -sexy!" he said, grinning. "All right, I'll shush, but you'll have to come on out of this morgue, I need to speak to you."

Sheila shut her book resignedly and followed Gerry out.

The Union bar, which sold beer and low alcohol wine, was nearby. Gerry seized Sheila's hand, and propelled her inside.

"Sheila," he began, as soon as they were sitting at a table in a convenient alcove with lager for Gerry and Coke for Sheila in front of them, "I've had a brilliant idea. Now, stop me if you don't like it - "

"Stop," said Sheila.

" - don't mess - Sheila, have you ever thought of entering a Beauty Contest?"

Sheila looked at him.

"No," she said.

"Seriously. The heats for Miss Northern Ireland are about to be run. The cash prizes are amazing - well, compared to grants! You would walk it, Sheila, no question. Wait - " he held up his hand as Sheila tried to speak, "- what I thought was, if I do all the organising for you, sort of like an agent, then you might think of paying me a 10% fee out of your winnings. I've had my eye on a second hand car for ages but I couldn't think how to get the money together - but this would be a cinch. If I did all the agent's side of things for you, I could feel I'd really earned the fee and we'd both be happy!"

"Gerry, if you were depending on a fee from my winnings you'd be waiting a long time for your car," Sheila said, shaking her head to clear it.

"No, really, Sheila, you've always underestimated yourself. There's no question, you'd be up there in the top three at the very worst. Give yourself a chance, girl!"

Sheila, about to laugh, caught the gleam in Gerry's eye and suddenly paused.

Was it such a crazy idea?

The money would be very nice to have. And if Gerry did all the organising, it wouldn't interfere with her work.

Could she possibly have any chance of winning?

Accustomed all her life to thinking of herself as unattractive, Sheila had just begun over the past few years to realise that some people thought otherwise.

Who was right?

If she entered this Beauty contest and got, say, through the first heat at any rate, it would prove to herself once and for all that she could be considered pretty.

But - a Beauty Contest? People like them, Kathy would have said, just didn't have anything to do with such vulgar things. It was against all the rules.

Sheila suddenly found herself consumed by a fierce longing to show everyone that she could do it, to prove that she was attractive not just to a few weird people but to the official judges in these matters. It was a bit like taking an exam - once you had passed it, everyone had to accept that you were good at that particular thing. If she didn't enter, she would never know for sure.

Well, Gerry," she said. "Tell me more. What would I have to do?"

Chapter 22

The preliminaries for the Miss Northern Ireland Beauty Contest were to be held in a hotel outside the city in nearby Lisburn. Contestants were to present themselves there at 10.30 in the morning which seemed like a strange time to Sheila.

"It's because this is just the selection round," explained Gerry, waving the letter he had received in response to his application in Sheila's name. "They just use this as a weeding out stage. They've already decided you may be a possible on the strength of your photo, and now they need to see you in person. After you pass this round, there'll be a series of heats and then the final."

"How am I to get out to Lisburn for this preliminary by 10.30 am?" asked Sheila. "I could take a train or a bus, I suppose, but supposing it rains and I get soaked on the way? It won't be a very good start."

"No problem," Gerry said, "I'll borrow my Da's car. Now, what are you going to wear?"

They ran through Sheila's wardrobe, discarding one item after another. This was too dull, that was too old fashioned.

In the end, they went out together and bought brown, shiny, satin very short shorts with a low bib and teamed them with a green top with tiny buttons down the front which Sheila had always liked, and which Gerry pronounced acceptable provided several buttons were left open to give a more plunging neckline.

Phil had a pair of green stiletto heeled shoes which were still at home and Gerry made Sheila borrow them to complete the outfit.

Sheila put the lot on and said "I look like a tart."

"Rubbish!" said Gerry enthusiastically. "You look great! Magic!"

Sheila smiled weakly.

Inwardly she wondered what John would think if he could see her. He had always been particular about what she wore, forbidding her on one occasion to go out with him in a mini skirt which she had planned to wear to the pictures, and frequently buttoning up her blouses at the neck when, to Sheila's eye, they were already quite respectable.

A shiver of defiance ran through her.

"Who cares!" she thought, not for the first time. "John doesn't care about me - why should I worry what he would think with all his silly rules?"

It seemed a long time since the days when she had been so happy, when she had been seeing John regularly.

It was over a year since that catastrophic row on the river bank.

At first she had hoped desperately to make it up. She had written to him saying how sorry she was. On one humiliating occasion, over six months ago now, just before Christmas, she had phoned the house and asked to speak to him and, after a pause, Mary had come back on the line and told her that John was out.

Sheila knew that Mary was lying.

Although she knew that it was from motives of kindness, and although Mary tried to keep up a friendly, chatty conversation and pretend that nothing was wrong, Sheila could not manage her own end of it.

She rang off abruptly. She found that she was shaking violently, mostly with anger.

John had written her off because she didn't fit in with his own image of what she should be.

He had never cared for the real Sheila, only for his own idealisation of her.

Okay, then.

She would put John's ideas behind her.

From now on she would be herself.

And if John didn't like it, tough for John!

She accepted that it was over.

John had finished his degree course now and had taken up the post he had been promised with the BBC as a trainee journalist.

He had gone out of Sheila's life, and the more she could accept that the better. She really thought about him very seldom these days, she told herself.

The beauty contest, when it came along, was one more way of showing John Branagh how little she cared now for his opinion.

* * *

The preliminaries went off very successfully. Sheila and Gerry turned up at the hotel at the right time and, after Sheila had walked up and down for the panel of judges and had answered a few simple questions, they were told that she was through to the first heat and would be given details of the time and place within the next few weeks.

There were a number of heats but each contestant would take part in only one and the eight finalists would be the heat winners.

It seemed straightforward enough.

The information about the heat arrived in due course.

Only one costume was required although for the finals those who qualified would need to appear in a bathing costume and in evening dress as well.

Sheila and Gerry decided to stay with the shorts and top outfit which had been successful so far.

Gerry drove them to another out of town location, this time in the evening.

Sheila had so far refrained from mentioning to her family or friends what they were doing.

"I don't know what my Dad will say when he knows," she said to Gerry, swearing him to secrecy for the time being. "Time enough to let him come to terms with it if I get to the finals."

"If! Strike out that 'if'!" Gerry ordered.

But he agreed that there was no point in meeting trouble halfway.

If - sorry, when! - Sheila won the title, the publicity attached would make it impossible to keep her parents in the dark, but meanwhile, why not?

Chapter 23

It was a time when Phil needed to avoid hearing things and picking up information.

By nature bright and observant, she began to train herself not to notice when casual remarks of Davy's revealed that he had been somewhere, or met someone, connected with drugs. She began to take herself out of earshot when he picked up the phone, and to ignore letters or notes left lying about, in case her eye should accidentally pick up a betraying phrase.

If she was very careful, she could convince herself that the only things Davy was involved in were very minor, on the outskirts of events.

She had been living with Davy now in his new flat in Thomas Street for two months.

She had taken over some of the more practical aspects like shopping or calling each month to pay the rent with cash handed over casually by Davy, who was only too glad to be relieved of these responsibilities.

She was working hard for her finals, which would be at the end of next year, and hoped to do well. Davy's Ph.D. work continued, giving him, it seemed, a very free rein, for he sometimes took himself off for days at a time without apparent trouble from his supervisor.

One night, when summer was almost upon them, Phil lay wakeful beside Davy in the attic bedroom.

The moon gleamed through the drawn curtains.

Outside, she could see the outline of a huge chestnut tree. It was thick with leaves now, and its delicate spring shape was nearly hidden, its branches smothered.

As Phil watched, a strong gust of wind detached one of the new leaves and, against all Nature's rules, it fluttered, still green, and yet over and done with, to the ground.

A sudden piercing sadness struck her to the heart. It seemed as if her days of youth and innocence were already gone, falling with the leaf while they were still new and green.

What had happened to her, to Davy?

At the street door, several floors below, someone was knocking.

Phil nudged Davy with one foot and he stretched sleepily beside her.

"Whaa.... whaa....?"

"Someone knocking. Who would it be in the middle of the night?"

Davy was fully awake now. He sat up and began to pull on jeans and a sweatshirt.

"Go back to sleep, Phil. It's probably nothing - a mistake. I'll go down and check."

He was gone.

Phil lay down again and stared out of the window at the tree. She felt exhausted with emotion, with trying not to know what was going on.

She felt also a small sting of anger beneath it all.

Presently she heard soft footsteps on the stairs and the creak of the living room door opening and then quietly closing again.

There was a murmur of voices.

She could not make out any of the words even if she had wanted to, but the continuous murmur, just on the verge of hearing, repeated itself in her head for what seemed like a long time.

She had seldom felt less like sleep.

At last Davy came back, creeping quietly into the room and into bed.

"What was it?" asked Phil sharply.

"Oh. I thought you were asleep."

"No, I'm not."

"Just an old mate, looking for a bed for the night," Davy said. "You've met him. Sean Joyce. I've put him on the sofa in the living room - so don't go wandering in there in the morning before you're dressed."

He was trying to turn it into a joke. For some reason, this made Phil even more angry.

"He'll probably be away before you're up, anyway," Davy said.

"Okay."

Phil turned over and said nothing.

Davy went back to sleep.

In the morning, there were few signs of the stranger's brief presence.

A smell of cigarette smoke and a few stubs in an ashtray on the coffee table.

The folded up sleeping bag, which Davy had lent him, placed neatly on the floor at one end of the sofa.

A glass rinsed out and placed upside down on the draining board, when Phil went into the kitchen.

There was really very little, when you thought about it.

So why did it make her feel as if she, or the flat, had been violated?

Chapter 24

At the heats, there was another panel of judges and again Sheila walked up and down, smiled, and answered some questions about her ambitions.

It was hard to avoid noticing that one of the judges never looked above her legs and the eyes of a second judge, although they moved further upwards, still did not seem to reach the facial region.

The third, the token woman, on the contrary, looked only at Sheila's face. When she caught Sheila's eye at one point, Sheila was surprised to see that the judge looked extremely embarrassed as if she wished she had never agreed to take on her present role.

Then the results were announced and, half to her surprise, and yet half with a sense of inevitability, Sheila heard that she was through to the finals.

Frank Doherty was horrified when Sheila broke the news to him.

She had carefully enlisted her mother's support first.

Kathy Doherty, still unused to the idea that her skinny daughter with the ginger hair had become attractive almost, as it seemed to Kathy, overnight, could not help feeling pleased that Sheila had won her heat.

"Who would have thought it!" she said tactlessly, and Sheila, even with victory under her belt, could not help a momentary return to the childhood misery of knowing that she was considered plain, if not downright ugly.

Frank shouted at first.

"No daughter of mine is going to display herself in public like that! I won't have it, do you hear?"

Sheila, who had long since begun to take her father's rages calmly, waited until he had finished.

"It's a very respectable contest, Daddy. The finals will be on television. Wouldn't you like to see me on the screen?"

Frank paused. Television? There was something very impressive about that idea. Perhaps a contest which was televised should be considered in a different category from the vulgar, back street affairs he had in mind?

It took Sheila and Kathy much longer than that, of course, to bring him round, but in the end he agreed that Sheila could go ahead.

"Especially," Kathy shrewdly remarked to her daughter, "since, when it comes right down to it, he would have no way of stopping you, short of throwing you out of the house. And I'll say this for Frankie, the thought of such an action would never so much as cross his mind."

* * *

On the night of the Finals of the Miss Northern Ireland Beauty Contest, Sheila found that she was keyed up beyond expectation.

Everything was on a higher scale than the earlier rounds had prepared her for.

The hotel, the Marine View at Portrush, was much more luxurious and expensive than the hotels used previously.

The panel of judges was composed of celebrities of at least local fame.

There were even the heralded TV cameras. Plans to record the contest were being carried out, and the place was buzzing with the extra excitement. The show would be recorded tonight, and broadcast sometime next week, Sheila had been told.

Moreover, the Chairman of the panel of judges was to be Ronnie Patterson, a household name for his chat show which drew the largest audience of any show broadcast locally. One of the other judges was the factory owner, Montgomery Speers. Sheila knew his name, although she had never met him.

Sheila found herself trembling with excitement and experiencing that fluttering, sick feeling known as 'butterflies in the stomach'.

She fought hard for control and achieved a calm, remote expression which in no way reflected her internal state of mind.

The finalists assembled according to instructions an hour before the contest was due to start, in a room which had been set aside for changing and for the entrances and exits.

Gerry, who was not supposed to penetrate behind the scenes, gave Sheila a hug and a quick kiss on the cheek, and left her to go in, making his own way to the front of the audience.

It was too long a wait.

The girls were all relieved when a knock on the door heralded a waiter with a red rose for each contestant and an invitation from

Ronnie Patterson to join him for a few moments in a nearby reception room for a 'good luck drink', as the message put it.

Everyone was glad to accept.

The room was packed with journalists, TV people, and musicians, besides waiters with trays of champagne glasses, containing something fizzy.

Ronnie Patterson hurried forward to greet his 'guests of honour' with a big smile.

Patterson was a man who was good at his job and sensible and reliable when dealing with men, but he had a reputation for being quite the opposite when it came to women.

Sheila found him repulsive.

He edged up closer than she wanted and slid his arm round her waist.

"Hey, beautiful - you're something else, baby. Now, you wouldn't try to bribe the judge, would you?"

He squeezed Sheila's waist, smiling to show it was all a joke.

He was big and beginning to run to fat, and the wrinkles round his eyes could have been caused by laughing too much but Sheila didn't think so.

His light blue eyes looked cold in spite of all the smiling.

"No," she said, "I wouldn't."

"You wouldn't have to try, darling," Ronnie Patterson murmured, coming even closer to breathe in her ear. Sheila flinched away. "It just seems to come to you naturally."

Sheila was beginning to feel that she couldn't put up with any more of this and would have to snub him more bluntly, when one of the officials tapped Patterson on the shoulder.

Keeping a firm hold on Sheila's waist, he turned his attention for a moment to the newcomer.

Sheila looked round for help and became aware that someone on the far side of the room was watching her.

She looked over and caught John Branagh's eye.

Why had it not occurred to her that he might be here? He was a TV journalist now, and the room was packed with his colleagues.

Sheila pulled herself sharply away from Ronnie Patterson and started to cross to John.

He was still staring at her with a fierce, angry gaze.

"John!" she called but there was so much noise that she was not sure if he could hear her.

Whether he could or not, he could see her coming towards him. With an abrupt gesture, he set down the glass he was holding on the nearest surface and swung round on his heel.

A second later, he was pushing his way through the crowded reception room, bumping into people as he went.

Sheila, her way blocked by a noisy group, tried vainly to reach him.

By the time she had navigated the people in her way, it was too late. He had gone.

The reception was over and the contestants were herded back to their dressing room, and a girl with a clipboard told them to keep calm and listen carefully for their names to be called.

Then out into the bright lights, moving up and down the catwalk in the first stage, in swimwear, trying not to blink, and above all not to look round again for John.

The contestants paraded first together, then singly. There were ten minutes between rounds to allow them time to change into evening dress.

Sheila had practised beforehand - step into the dress, pull it up and slip the swimming costume down, without disturbing hair and make-up.

Then the essential quick check in the mirror to ensure that all was well.

And then out again to glide up and down the walk to nostalgic Thirties style music - 'I get no kick from champagne'.

And finally the moment most of the girls had said they dreaded - standing, trying to look cool and special, while the judges asked their questions.

Yes, Sheila told them, she would love to travel, she loved children and old people, she owed so much to her parents' support.

She would have felt like giggling if it had not been for the dull ache which she had pushed down somewhere, until she had time it take it out and look at it again.

The ache which had come from seeing John and seeing him turn away from her.

Back in the dressing room, she stared blankly at herself in the mirror. What was she doing here, putting a final full stop to any hope of persuading John Branagh that she was not an immoral woman?

The girl who had been next to Sheila came off the stage and burst into tears.

"I've made a mess of it," she wept. "I wanted the money for my kid, he needs more than I can make to keep him, and now I'll have to work more overtime instead, if I can get it."

Sheila looked at her in amazement.

She looked about eighteen, if that, as if she should still be a child herself with loving parents, not trying to support her own son.

"Don't worry," Sheila said awkwardly. "I think you have a very good chance. Don't give up yet."

Then it all became too much and Sheila had to get away from the whole thing - the tears, the bright lights, the heightened emotions.

She slipped quietly out of the door at the back of the room and locked herself into one of the lavatory cubicles.

Time stood as still as a frozen pink elephant.

Aeons later, there was the sound of running feet and someone banging on the door.

"Sheila! Sheila Doherty! If you're in there, come out quick!"

Sheila opened the door cautiously and was seized by a dozen pairs of hands.

"Come on, come on, your name's being called!"

She found herself propelled down the passage to the stage door.

Then the other girls drew back.

Sheila caught her breath and straightened up.

A voice from the front was repeating, "Are you there, Sheila? Once again - first place, and the winner of the title Miss Northern Ireland - Miss Sheila Doherty from Belfast!"

The lights, the music and the tension combined to make it seem like one of the most important moments in Sheila's life.

Chapter 25

As she walked out in front of the applauding crowd, she could see Gerry grinning at her from the front row and noticed with vague pleasure that the crying girl with the little boy had gained third place and at least some sort of money prize.

Then Ronnie Patterson was kissing her on both cheeks and putting the crown on her head, and last year's winner was draping her with a sash and cloak.

The music played louder, the hands thundered applause, and Sheila felt as if something, probably herself, was about to go bang.

Ronnie Patterson whispered in her ear "Now, don't disappear afterwards, sweetheart. All sorts of exciting things happen now."

Sheila vaguely thought of photographs and a further reception.

There were photographs, certainly, and Gerry supported her through the next hour of hype and flurry.

Everyone in the world seemed to want to speak to Sheila and take her picture and plan future engagements for her.

Quite suddenly, it seemed, everyone disappeared and, with a head more than a little muzzy with the repeated glasses of champagne thrust upon her, Sheila found herself alone in a room with Ronnie Patterson.

She was vaguely aware that Patterson had managed this very adroitly, whisking her off on the excuse of important business to discuss, the date for a TV interview to settle.

He had managed to exclude Gerry as well as the crowds of press and well wishers.

Sheila, not very clear what was happening, knew only that the ache inside was rapidly making its way to the surface again.

She had looked in vain for John among the reporters milling around.

Ronnie Patterson poured her yet another glass of champagne and advanced upon her, holding the glass out.

"Alone at last!" he said in his jokey manner.

"Are we?" said Sheila, looking round. "So we are."

She felt for the moment unsure what to say.

Where was everybody else? Why was Patterson locking the door?

Warning bells began to ring in her head.

Ronnie Patterson set down the champagne glass which Sheila showed no signs of taking, and put his arms round her.

A moment later, Sheila found herself being pulled down on what was certainly a bed, while Patterson pressed his unpleasantly thick lips on her mouth.

For a minute she was helpless, unable to speak or struggle to any effect.

Then, coming very rapidly to her senses, she dragged her lips away and lowered her head so that her mouth was out of range of further kissing.

"Let go of me at once!" she ordered furiously.

Patterson laughed. "I like a girl with spirit," he said.

Even at that moment, Sheila could not help an inward grin at the cliché.

Then, as he showed no sign of releasing her, she began to panic.

What was she doing alone in this bedroom with a man she didn't even like? She must have been crazy to let him bring her here.

Okay, she'd dealt with this sort of thing before, she could deal with it again.

When several more pushes had no effect, Sheila remembered her stiletto heels and kicked Ronnie Patterson sharply on the legs, meanwhile beginning to scream in good earnest.

She didn't want to hurt him badly but, on the other hand, he seemed to have no reservations about hurting her.

She was on the floor, struggling wildly, with the famous Ronnie Patterson on top of her tearing at her expensive hired dress, when she heard a furious hammering at the door of the room.

"Help!" Sheila shrieked. "Help me, someone!"

"Sheila!" a voice outside shouted. "Sheila, is that you in there?"

"Yes!" Sheila shouted back. "Help me!"

The door flew open.

Gerry was standing on the threshold, looking red and belligerent.

Behind him hovered an anxious looking figure with a bunch of keys whom Sheila recognised as the hotel manager.

Ronnie Patterson looked round and blinked. He got slowly to his feet, saying nothing.

Sheila scrambled up.

She stood swaying for a moment, then rushed into Gerry's arms. They seemed very solid and comforting.

Gerry, his arms round her in turn, patted her soothingly on her back.

"Sheila," he said, anger and worry making his voice rough, "are you all right? I should never have got you involved in this business. It was a big mistake. I didn't realise the sort of thing I was letting you in for."

He glared at Ronnie Patterson who stood brushing himself down, and smiling.

He seemed, incredibly, to have recovered his public image already and to be ready to laugh the whole episode off as a bit of a joke.

A pay-off to the hotel manager, no doubt, in order to avoid bad publicity, and he would carry on as if nothing had happened.

Except, Sheila thought, for the steadily growing rumours which would catch up with him one day.

"But, Gerry," Sheila said, "I won!"

"I know you did, pet - you were great. I knew all along that you would. But it wasn't worth all this."

"Yes, of course it was," Sheila said. "It's one of the best things that ever happened to me. I'm glad I did it, Gerry. I'll always be grateful to you for suggesting it, and for encouraging me."

She leant over to kiss him, and then stepped back from his still supporting arms.

"Mind you, I was never so glad to see anyone as to see you just now!"

"All part of a manager's job," said Gerry flippantly.

He looked at her doubtfully, still uncertain about her true reactions to the evening.

"Come on," said Sheila. "Let's get away home out of here."

She smiled at him, slipped her arm into his, and propelled him out of the room amid the muttered apologies of the hotel manager.

She thought, as she held onto his arm, still feeling very much in need of protection, that Gerry was a really nice person.

What a pity she hadn't fallen in love with him instead of with her other friend's brother.

Gerry had always been so kind to her.

But she knew that he would never be more to her than a close friend, someone who she thought was almost as much her brother as Phil's.

She looked up at his worried face and smiled at him.

What she had told Gerry was true.

She said, partly to encourage him, but mainly because if she didn't go on talking she would probably burst with the excitement of it all, "I feel like a million dollars!"

"And you look like it, too!" Gerry said happily.

"Gerry, I really think I'm going to burst, it's all just so great!" Sheila told him.

And, she thought, although she didn't say so, to hell with John Branagh!

Chapter 26

To Mary, slowly recovering from her overdose, living was a strange experience at first. She went back to Queen's as soon as she could. She had decided to stop taking drugs. It was easier than she had expected. A revulsion rose up in her which made her feel physically sick at the bare idea.

But to stick to her decision, she needed to cut herself off from her party friends.

This was also easier than she had expected. They seemed to be avoiding her, perhaps unwilling to be identified with her by the authorities. She was on her own.

The first weeks reminded her of her early days at Primary School when the sea of strange faces threatened to overwhelm her. She could hardly remember it, now. Ever since then, she had had the comfortable feeling of knowing at least someone wherever she went. Phil had been her friend through Primary School and all through the Dominican Convent days. Suddenly she had no friends.

Mary, daring and adventurous, found that loneliness was a bad enemy. She seemed to herself to be a different person. It was as if her role in the play had come to an end and she was left standing in the centre of the stage, surrounded by people who knew their next lines, while she did not know what to do next; or in the middle of the playing field, completely ignorant of the rules of the game she was supposed to be playing. For so long, rules, for Mary, had been just a thing to be ignored.

It took some time for the feeling to pass away.

She had missed the end of the spring term and had come back into the last term of her second year.

At first, she relied greatly on planned meetings with Phil or Sheila for coffee in the Students' Union between lectures.

Gradually, she began to make new friends.

There were class tests due at the end of the term. Mary, panicking one day in a Physics lecture because she seemed to have lost an important chunk of notes which would be essential for revision, was searching frantically through her file when a neighbouring student tapped her on the shoulder.

Looking round, Mary met a friendly smile.

"If you need to borrow any notes, I can lend you whatever you need."

"Orla Greaves," added the owner of the smile.

"Oh - thanks, that would be great." Mary smiled back. "I can't think what I've done with them."

Orla looked at her gravely. "How about going down for a cup of coffee after the lecture and then we can decide what you need and sort something out?"

They had almost completed the transaction when it occurred to Mary that Orla seemed strangely unaware that she would need the notes herself for the forthcoming test.

"I'll copy them and bring them back to you on Monday," she promised eagerly.

"That's fine," said Orla off-handedly. "I'm sure you will."

Mary laughed. "Well, I will - but you don't seem very worried. Suppose I don't bother and you don't have any notes yourself to revise from?"

"Oh, I think I can trust you," Orla answered. She looked at Mary seriously. "You seemed upset about having lost your own notes. I don't mind taking the risk."

Mary looked at this strange girl.

She had already noticed her in previous lectures, for Orla's appearance was striking. She had a pale, smooth skin, with mid-brown hair cut to shoulder length which fell straight around her face. She wore clothes which to Mary's eye seemed to have come from the second hand clothes shops, shapeless dresses hanging to an unfashionable length. She was not exactly pretty but no-one could have called her plain. This was partly because of her wide, generous mouth, but mostly because of her eyes. A light, bright grey, set beneath thick black eyebrows which seemed to mark out her face as one which mattered, they burned with a fire which Mary could not put a name to.

She thought of it as the face of a martyr - a twentieth century Joan of Arc.

Over the term, Mary began to see more and more of Orla.

She found Orla an interesting person, quite different from anyone Mary had known before.

She had very little sense of humour. When Mary made a joke, Orla would look at her blankly, and then laugh, but only as if she knew that it would be an unnecessary unkindness not to do so.

Her voice was strong, deep and yet musical. She spoke seldom but, when she did, it was to the point.

Mary talked to her about politics. Although Orla agreed with Mary about the state of the country, she could never be persuaded to go with Mary to any political meetings.

"People need to change from the inside," she said to Mary one day. "All the political agitation in the world won't alter things if the tribal divisions continue. We need to stop hating each other and learn to forgive. Only God can teach people how to do that and He'll only do it if we allow Him to."

Mary had never heard anyone say things like that before - or if she had, it had been people who she despised as woolly thinkers or smug hypocrites.

But Orla couldn't be put into that sort of category and dismissed.

One day, when Mary was teasing Orla again to come to the New Ireland Society, Orla suddenly gave one of her rare smiles - a wide, charming smile which showed her even white teeth and gave her an unexpected beauty.

"All right," she said. "Fair's fair. I'll go to your Society meeting, Mary, if you come with me to a meeting I go to every week. We meet in the Church of Ireland Centre but it's not a denominational thing. Anybody who wants to can come - Catholics like you and me, and Protestants of all the different types you can name. I'd like you to come and see for yourself."

Mary hesitated.

It didn't sound like her type of thing at all.

But as Orla had said, fair was fair.

If she wanted Orla to come to her political meeting - and she really did, for some reason - then she ought to go to what, in her own mind, she labelled as "Orla's religious meeting."

It need only be once, after all.

And it might be quite interesting, at that.

Chapter 27

On a bright morning at the end of term, Phil wandered restlessly round the flat, barefooted and still wearing an old shirt of Davy's which she had shrugged on when she got out of bed. Davy had gone early to the Ashby Institute where he had an experiment to work on for his Professor.

Some vestigial instincts of housewifeliness prompted her to begin a little tidying. Davy, as usual, had left everything he used lying behind him. She picked up some items of clothing, folding some and dropping others into the basket for washing. Then she walked around for a while with a folded tee shirt in her hands, thinking about nothing and forgetting to put the tee shirt away. In the end, she pulled open a drawer at random, in the chest of drawers in the bedroom, and placed the tee shirt on top of its contents.

As she was doing this, Phil noticed that there was something hard and bumpy one layer down. She lifted the top layer of tee shirts and found herself looking at a gun.

It was a handgun. Not, Phil guessed, a particularly powerful weapon, in fact quite small. Phil stared at it for a few minutes, still holding the tee shirts she had lifted. She connected it, without any real evidence, with the man who had stayed over in the flat not long ago. But the stranger could not have put it in this drawer. He might have given it to Davy to look after and Davy had slipped it in there. Perhaps he had forgotten it.

What was she to do now?

Phil didn't know.

The gun might have been used in one of the punishment shootings or murders which regularly filled the news bulletins now. She had no way of telling. If it had not already been used in this way, there might be plans to so use it at some time in the future. It should be handed over to the police.

If Phil took it and gave it to the police, perhaps by some anonymous means if she could think of any, would they be able to trace Davy's connection with it?

It seemed to Phil that this was the crucial point.

She put the tee shirts into the drawer and shut it carefully. Then she went and made herself a cup of coffee, and sat down with her hands cupped round it while she thought.

If there was any chance at all of the police tracing this gun to Davy, she could not give them that chance. On that question, she was not in doubt.

If this gun was likely to be used to kill someone, then she needed to do something to prevent that. But what?

If she told Davy that she had found it, what would his reaction be? Phil realised that she had no clear idea of that.

Would it be possible to persuade him to hand it over, anonymously?

Phil didn't think so.

Suppose she took it away and got rid of it herself? She could, for instance, throw it in the river.

The trouble with that solution was that Davy would know at once that she had taken it. There was no-one else. So she might just as well speak to him about it.

Back to square one.

Phil felt lost.

In the end, she stopped thinking. Dressing carefully and trying to distract her mind with thoughts of work, she went out to her lecture.

It was lonely, in many ways, not having Sheila next door now. Phil had made many other friends, but Sheila was special. If she went home, and Sheila was there, Phil would be able to talk to her about the gun, perhaps. But at the thought of the gun, her mind squirmed away again, and she tried once more to blank it off. There was Mary, too. There had been a time when she could have talked to Mary about anything, but she had grown very far apart from Mary in the last two years. It was hard to remember when they had last talked together in any depth.

Phil felt very alone.

In the afternoon, avoiding her friends, she walked around Botanic Gardens looking at the new buds and smelling the sweet, powerful scent of the roses which were blooming freely. For a while she sat under a tree and watched some children and a dog racing about with a football.

None of this seemed to help particularly.

Finally, she went back to the flat.

There was no sign of Davy but Phil had her own key, and she let herself in. It was in her mind that she might collect up her possessions and think about going home for at least a few days. But she would go into the kitchen first and make herself a cup of coffee while she came to a decision.

As she entered the kitchen, she stiffened. There was a smell of cigarette smoke in the air but not from the type of cigarettes she and Davy smoked. This was a ranker, stronger smell. By the sink, an empty tea cup had been left, upside down, rinsed out, on the draining board. Phil knew it had not been there when she left that morning. It would not be Davy's - he had his own mug which he always used, and which was hanging in its usual place by the wall cupboards.

Phil discovered that her mind was now made up.

Was she seriously planning to break it off with Davy?

Even putting that thought into words gave Phil a sick feeling. No, that wasn't what she intended. It was just that she needed to detach herself for a little from this place which had become curiously frightening.

She wandered round the bedroom, gathering up the odds and ends of her belongings. The books would be the most bulky item, that and her notes. Perhaps she would not take those, just yet. It would be such a final step. Her clothes would go into one bag. She had kept very little in the flat.

She stood for a moment looking at the chest of drawers. Finally, with a mental shrug for her stupidity, she pulled open the drawer, unable to resist the compulsion to check again that she had really seen a gun.

There was nothing there but the shirts and underclothes.

Although she knew that there had been no imagination, nothing but cold fact, in her previous sight of the weapon, Phil felt illogically as if a weight had been lifted from her shoulders. The gun had not vanished from the face of the earth, she realised. It was still around somewhere and might be used to destroy lives. But short of betraying Davy's connection with it to the police - an impossible action - there was nothing left that Phil could do. She had no further decision to make now that the gun was no longer there to be handed in or disposed of.

She gathered up her belongings and hurried out of the flat as if the devil himself were after her.

Chapter 28

The letter dropped through the Dohertys' letterbox just after Sheila had left for the first lecture of the day some weeks into the new term. It was June in her second year with exams looming. All the hard work that she had been promising herself she would do 'nearer the time' was beginning to take on a dreadful urgency.

It was a short day. After her second and last lecture, Sheila came straight home. It wasn't worth hanging about for coffee. Instead, she would go to her room, sit at the new desk she had bought herself with some of her prize money, and really plan out a detailed scheme of work for her exam revision.

The letter was lying on the hall table where her mother always scrupulously left her post unopened. Sheila picked it up and carried it to her room with an armful of books. Looking at it curiously as she went upstairs, she realised that the handwriting was unfamiliar.

'Dear Sheila,' she read, "I saw you winning the Beauty Contest and a thought came to me. As you know, I am getting more established as a fashion designer. I've recently been promised more backing and I want to branch out a bit further. What I need most at the moment is a really striking model who is already in the public eye. I have a couple of girls who are trained, but from a public relations point of view they are nothing special. How about it? The job's yours if you want it. Any training you need, I can easily give you myself. If you are interested, we can discuss terms but I will happily pay the top of the market to get the model I want. Let me know quickly at the Belfast office address above. Love, Francis Delmara."

Sheila read it again. It still said the same thing.

"Mum! Mum!" she called, then remembered that Kathy wasn't at home. There was no-one in the house to tell.

She rushed next door but, of course, Phil, as she knew, had moved in with Davy and Gerry was out, too.

Sheila felt a mixture of excitement and frustration. Nothing like this had ever happened to her before and there was no-one to talk to about it.

By the time Kathy arrived home from her afternoon's shopping, Sheila had made up her mind.

"I'm going to accept, Mammy," she said. "I'll regret it all my life if I don't."

Kathy Doherty was at a loss. The feminine part of her was almost as thrilled as Sheila at the prospect. The sensible, forward thinking part, on the other hand, was horrified. What security was there in a job like that? And what about Sheila's degree? She had been doing so well and Kathy had been looking forward to having a daughter who had graduated, and who was in a nice, secure, respectable job for life - teaching, most likely, she had always thought.

"A woman needs to be able to look after herself in this life, Sheila," she told her daughter. "If you have your qualifications, you can always be sure of getting a good job, whatever happens. If you get married, you won't need it, but who knows?" Kathy belonged to a generation whose married women worked only in the home. "Mind you, you may well marry, you've turned out good-looking after all, but who knows even then? If you're in a position to support yourself, you'll never need to be dependant on anybody."

"What an attitude, Mum! Whether I marry or not, I'm not going to spend my life in the kitchen. But I don't need this degree to get a job. Look what this letter says. I could make more in a month's modelling than in a year's teaching."

"Ah, but, Sheila, will it last? That's the thing. In a few years' time, maybe you'll be out on the dole and with no degree behind you."

"Don't fuss, mammy. I'll save while I'm earning good money and who knows what it may lead to? I've got to take the chance, don't you see?"

"Maybe you could go back and finish the degree in a few years' time," speculated Kathy. "Though who's going to pay for it, I don't know. The Government will hardly give you another grant if you walk out now. And what's your daddy going to say?"

And at this thought, mother and daughter paused and looked at each other. The thought which had been at the back of both their minds suddenly thrust itself forward into prominence.

"He'll kill you, Sheila," said Kathy at last. "He'll not stand for it. That Beauty contest business was bad enough, but this - he'll never let you throw up your degree and leave Queen's!"

Sheila was thoughtful. She knew that Frank would be hurt and disappointed by her decision. She didn't want to quarrel with him. But she had already made up her mind and there was nothing Frank could do or say to change it.

When he came in from work, she was waiting and ran to fetch his slippers and the Belfast Telegraph for him to read by the fire while Kathy put the finishing touches to his tea.

"Hey, hey, what's all this?" Frank joked. "Getting spoiled, am I? You must be after something, Miss Sheila."

Sheila smiled sweetly, sat on the arm of his chair to put her arm round his shoulder, and kissed the top of his head.

"Can't fool you, daddy, can I? Yes, I want you to be specially nice and wise and sensible, like you always are, and listen to me. Now, don't say anything until I've finished."

Frank looked suspicious.

"If this is about borrowing my car again - " he began.

"No, no, nothing like that, Daddy. The fact is, I've been offered a job - a really good job. But taking it means leaving Queen's now, not finishing my degree. I want to finish, naturally, but this is an opportunity that may not come again. Mum thinks I should stay on but I think you'll be more sensible about it. I don't want to spend the rest of my life teaching and regretting that I missed this opportunity." She fastened big, serious eyes on him. Frank melted.

"Sheila, I hear what you're saying, love and there's a lot of sense in it. But your mammy has a point, too. A degree's something well worth having. If you don't finish it now, maybe in a year or two you might regret it badly. Anyway, what is this job? A lot depends on how good it really is."

"It's working with a fashion designer, Daddy. Modelling clothes."

"What!" Frank's roar brought Kathy rushing from the kitchen in dismay.

"Now, Frankie, don't be shouting at the child. She's got a right to live her own life, not just to do what we want."

To Sheila's amusement, Kathy seemed to have about turned in her opinion.

"I'm not doing anything," said Frank indignantly. "But surely you don't want our Sheila to give up all her good prospects for a miserable job like this?"

"It's not a miserable job, Daddy," said Sheila urgently. "Look, here's the letter, see for yourself. He's offering top rates. That means as much in one month as I could make in a year teaching! Models are really well paid nowadays if it's one of the top designers. I could save enough in the first year to go back to Queen's if it ever came to that, but why should it? Once I get a start, who knows how far I could go?"

Frank took the letter. He was bewildered. Sheila was his only child. He had always wanted to see her well established. And this modelling - was it any more respectable than showing your legs in public? But both his women seemed to see it differently. The money Sheila talked of was a surprise to him. It was certainly an opportunity anyone would hate to miss. All his life Frank Doherty had taken risks with his own career, moving on when something good was offered at the risk of losing security. He looked at Sheila's eager, anxious face, and knew that he couldn't stop her from taking the same risk. She was his daughter, after all.

"I can't say I'm happy about it, love. But, there - I suppose you'll do it anyway, eh?"

"I don't want to fight with you, Daddy," Sheila said.

Frank grinned. "But you will, if you have to, won't you love? Obstinate as a mule, always have been."

"And where does she get that from, Frankie Doherty?" remarked his wife.

"All right, Sheila. I tell you what. You think about it for a few days. Don't jump into anything. And if you're still set on it, I won't say no."

"Oh, Daddy!" Sheila flung her arms round him in delight.

"But, now, make sure you get a contract signed before you do anything drastic. There'll be no need to let them know anything about it at the University for a month or so, anyway, till you know how it's going."

"That's very sensible, Frankie," approved Kathy. "Listen to your daddy, Sheila, and don't be burning your boats till you see if it's going to work out."

"Now, mind, I want you to think about it first. Maybe when you wake up tomorrow morning you'll see it all differently. Or maybe in another day or two."

"But he says to let him know straight away, Daddy," Sheila argued anxiously.

"It'll do no harm at all to keep him waiting a few days," Frankie said shrewdly. "From the tone of his letter, he's very keen to have you. Don't make yourself cheap. It never does any harm to look as if you're not overly keen. You don't want to look ready to jump at a moment's notice."

With this Sheila had to be content. She went to bed that night with her head in a whirl and, when sleep came at last, dreamt of fame and fortune, of famous men falling in love with her, and of clothes, clothes, clothes.

Chapter 29

In the morning, Sheila hadn't changed her mind. It was a bit like her decision to enter the Beauty contest - she couldn't help being a little frightened, but mostly she was excited and eager to go ahead.

The opportunity to talk to Phil about it came after their first English lecture that morning. Phil was almost as excited as Sheila.

"You could end up a film star - that often happens to really famous models," she told Sheila. "Go for it, kid. You'd be mad not to."

They were drinking coffee in the Union, elbows on the table and heads close together in the familiar gossipy, giggly way. Sheila felt a sudden pang at the realisation that there might be only a few occasions when they would ever to do this again. But the feeling was momentary.

"Here's the letter," she said, fishing it out from her shoulder bag. Phil read it with interest.

"This is the guy you met at the Prof's Christmas party last year?" she asked. "Well, you watch out for him, then. You know he's after you."

"I can look after myself, don't worry," said Sheila light heartedly.

"Oh, yeah? What about your man after the Beauty contest? Gerry turned up just in the nick of time, didn't he?"

"Okay, but I'd have more sense now," Sheila protested. "I didn't think what I was letting myself in for. I'd know better another time."

"Well, let's hope so." Phil didn't sound convinced. "So have you rung this Francis Delmara yet?"

"No, Daddy made me promise to think about it for a couple of days first. I'll ring him tomorrow."

She rang Delmara's number the next afternoon when once again she had the house to herself.

"Francis - It's me, Sheila. I got your letter."

"Ah - Sheila." The drawling voice sent a familiar shiver down her spine. "So. I hope you've got good news for me?"

"That depends." Sheila spoke cautiously. "Would there be a contract? And what exactly would the agreement be?"

Francis laughed. "For you, beautiful, anything. Yes, a contract by all means. I would want to sign you up for at least a year at an agreed rate - towards the top of the scale, as I said in my letter. Then we'll see."

"I'd like to read the contract before I agree to anything," Sheila said firmly. "And I need to know a bit more about what would be involved."

"You would be agreeing to model exclusively for Delmara Fashions for the specified period," said Francis. He sounded amazingly businesslike all of a sudden. "This would include dress shows in various locations including Dublin and New York if I can set it up. It would also include photographic sessions for magazines, etc. You would be prohibited from modelling for any other fashion house or undertaking any outside work without the written permission of Delmara Fashions - i.e., me. But if it was going to be good publicity for us, I would give permission, naturally. Travel to the various locations, and accommodation where appropriate, would be paid for by the company."

Sheila, who had been silently reacting to the mention of Dublin and New York, recovered herself sufficiently to sound businesslike in return.

"And this would be in writing?"

"Sure thing, honeychile," drawled Francis, with a return to his familiar manner. "Suppose you call at my office tomorrow afternoon? I can have something ready for you to sign by then. Vetted by my solicitor, so you needn't worry about it."

Warning bells rang in Sheila's head. Solicitor?

"I think I would like my own legal advisor to read the contract before I sign," she ventured. "I'll bring him with me, if he's free tomorrow. If not, I'll let you know when would suit him."

"Fine by me," said Francis. "See you then, beautiful."

He rang off.

Sheila sat with the receiver in her hand for a breathless moment, then hurriedly pressed the hand rest and dialled Gerry's number.

"Gerry? You know the way you've almost qualified now, and have this trainee post lined up with these solicitors? Well, do you know anything about contract law? You do? Oh, brilliant! Listen, I want you to do something for me....."

Gerry owned a suit, purchased in anticipation of his expected graduation this summer. On Sheila's instructions, he was wearing it and had combed his hair with great care when they met by arrangement at the City Hall the next afternoon.

"You look great, Gerry," Sheila told him enthusiastically. "Okay, now the main thing is to look as serious as possible. It will make you seem older, mid-twenties or so, an experienced solicitor. I just hope you know as much about contract law as you think."

"No problem, Sheila. I passed that module last year and I had a read through my notes last night after you phoned. I know as much now as I will after I've qualified as a solicitor, so what's the difference?"

"A few years of experience, maybe," Sheila said. "But never mind, Francis Delmara won't know any better. I want to impress him as businesslike, Gerry - but I also want to make sure that I don't sign anything stupid."

"I can see to that for you, Sheila. I know enough law to make sure it's all in order. Quietly confident, that's the story." Gerry grinned, at once making himself look about sixteen instead of twenty-something.

"Don't grin!" Sheila ordered him bossily. "Get into practice looking serious, for goodness sake."

"Sorry," said Gerry unrepentantly. "Just one other thing, Sheila. I'm doing this as a friend, not as an agent, so no percentages this time. I just wouldn't have time these days to take on the work that would be involved. So once the contract's signed, you're on your own, baby - okay?"

"Fair enough, Gerry," Sheila nodded. "Thanks for today, anyway. Okay, then, let's head."

They strolled round to Delmara's office, above a shop in Upper Arthur Street. There was a name plate saying 'Delmara Fashions' on the door beside the shop front which opened into a porch where an arrow pointed to a flight of stairs. They went up slowly, trying to look adult and dignified.

At the top of the stairs was a passage, and off it a newly painted door said again 'Delmara Fashions'. They knocked and went in, and were in a small ante-room furnished with a modern looking desk, telephone and computer, but with little else except the thick, expensive-looking carpet and one modern print on the left hand wall.

A secretary, very fashionably dressed as befitted the company she worked for, was sitting at the computer keyboard, typing, and she looked up and smiled as they came in.

"Yes? Can I help you?"

"Sheila Doherty to see Francis Delmara," said Sheila in a firm, pleasant voice. It was at times like these that she found her height an advantage.

"Mr Delmara is expecting you, Miss Doherty," said the girl. "I'll just let him know that you are here."

She pressed a button on the telephone and spoke into it. "Mr Delmara will see you now," she said, and stood up to open the door which was behind her to the right. Sheila and Gerry walked meekly in.

It was all much more formal and awe inspiring than Sheila had expected.

And yet, after all, when Francis, rising from behind a similar desk in his own office, came forward to greet her, it was just Francis.

"Sheila, my lovely," he murmured. "How delightful. And this must be your legal advisor."

"This is Mr. Maguire. Gerry Maguire," Sheila said.

Francis shook hands with Gerry solemnly. "How do you do, Mr. Maguire? Do sit down, both of you. Coffee?"

"That would be lovely," said Sheila, trying not to giggle.

It was really strange to see Gerry and Francis pretending to be adults - for that was how she thought of it. Sheila was pretending to be grown-up, and so were they, but was it any more of a reality for Francis than for Gerry and herself? And did they all know the rules?

Then she remembered that someone had actually backed Francis with real money, enough to run this place, pay a secretary and design clothes for a real dress show.

Perhaps everyone was only playing at being grown-up all the time. Perhaps everyone felt inside as if it was all a game. A game without any clear rules, Sheila thought, a game whose rules seemed made only to be broken.

"I wanted Mr Maguire to look at the contract before I made any decision," Sheila said.

"Very wise," Francis purred. "I have it here. A standard form, as signed by my other models, and vetted by my own solicitor. You can take a copy away with you, if you like, and come back to me when you feel happy about it."

"That may not be necessary, if the contract is as standard as you say," Gerry said.

He was balancing the cup of coffee produced by the secretary, holding the saucer in one hand and taking careful sips from the cup.

Sheila thought he looked worried about breaking it or spilling it. At least it prevented him from grinning and giving away his age.

Francis lifted the form from his desk and passed it over. There were several closely written pages and Gerry settled down to read them with care. Francis Delmara smiled at Sheila.

"You're looking especially bewitching today, beautiful. I love the hat. But you shouldn't cover up your hair."

He reached over and twitched off the black velvet cap Sheila was wearing, releasing her red-gold curls so that they tumbled about her shoulders.

"Ah, yes," Francis sighed to himself. "Yes, definitely."

It occurred to Sheila, memories of her previous meetings with Francis springing up, that she would have to keep tight control of herself if she and Delmara were going to spend much time together. It would never do if certain episodes were repeated, especially if they were to maintain a good working relationship.

"When do you expect to have your next show?" she asked, to relieve the tension in the atmosphere.

"There'll be several in the late summer - my autumn and winter lines. I'll give you some training between now and then. And in late winter, there'll be my spring lines.I'm planning to go to Dublin for that one."

Gerry coughed importantly.

"There are one or two points, Mr. Delmara. Firstly, the photographic sessions mentioned. It appears that the terms of the contract, as stated at present, allow Miss Doherty no veto on the type of work involved. If she should be unhappy with the work suggested, she would have no option other than to break the contract or to co-operate. We would like an option inserted giving Miss Doherty the right to veto any work she deems morally unacceptable."

"That will be no problem, my dear Mr. Maguire." Francis Delmara seemed unmoved. "There is no intention of involving Miss Doherty in anything of a sleazy nature. Delmara Fashions has no desire to acquire that type of reputation."

"Good. Then, as to the terms, I suggest that after the first six months, the rates should be raised by ten percent. That seems reasonable, since Miss Doherty will by then have absorbed any necessary training and will be a much greater asset to you."

"H'm. Yes." Francis paused in thought for a moment, tapping his slim fingers on the desk. Then he leaned forward, smiled sweetly and said in a tone which brooked no argument "Seven percent."

"Agreed," said Gerry quickly. "Then, if you will have the necessary changes made to this document, I shall advise my client to accept your offer. Miss Doherty, you will wish to read the document yourself." He coughed importantly again and passed Sheila the contract.

"If you aren't in a great hurry, my secretary can make the changes to the contract on her word processor in a very short time," said Delmara. "Meanwhile, perhaps another cup of coffee. Or may I suggest a glass of wine to drink to our future? Our joint future?"

Sheila sat back and sipped her white wine while the contract was adjusted and listened with half an ear to Delmara's chat, occasionally making a comment.

She looked relaxed and in control, but inwardly her mind was buzzing.

She had agreed and was about to sign something that would change her life. By the end of the year she would be in Dublin, taking part in a major fashion show, at the start of a career which might lead anywhere.

But strangely enough, these were not the thoughts which were uppermost in her mind. Instead, she was thinking of the gleam in Francis Delmara's eye as he raised his glass to their 'joint future'.

What exactly did he have in mind?

Sheila was aware that she would have to be very careful.

Delmara was a dangerous man, dangerously attractive. He was determined to get what he wanted. If, as she had every reason to believe, Sheila herself was part of what he wanted, she would have her work cut out making sure that he did not get it.

Especially as she knew that, in some moods, she was more than half on his side.

She sipped her wine, gazing round at the carpet, the picture on the wall, anything, principally from a determination not to look Delmara in the eye too often or too seriously.

As she did so, there rose up in her mind again, unbidden, the face of John Branagh, never long absent.

What would John think of her new career?

He was bound to hear of it sooner or later through Mary if in no other way.

Sheila felt instinctively that he would hate it.

If, that was, he cared at all, by now.

What did it matter? After that scene by the river, she and John were irrevocably finished. She would never trust herself to a man who could behave like that, even if his opinion of her changed enough to make him want her again.

And after his reaction to seeing her at the Beauty Contest, nothing seemed less likely.

She could not be more finally separated from him by becoming a model than she already was.

The memory of John's hatred for her fell like a cloud over the bright summer afternoon.

Sheila bit her lip hard, swallowed the rest of her wine in one defiant gulp, and yet again tried determinedly to put John Branagh completely out of her mind.

Chapter 30

Third year, and the new term, had already arrived by the time Mary went with Orla Greaves to the meeting she had spoken of.

It was evening and darkness was beginning to fall.

The lights gleamed on the wet pavement as Mary and Orla walked down Elmwood Avenue at the side of the Students' Union to the Church of Ireland Centre.

Mary felt rather nervous.

"What do I have to do?" she asked Orla.

Orla smiled her rare smile. Her dark grey eyes, burning under the heavy eyebrows, regarded Mary seriously.

"Don't worry," she said. She smiled her warm smile again and Mary felt oddly comforted.

"You don't have to do anything," Orla said, "unless you want to. There are no rules here."

They went into the Church of the Resurrection. About twenty people were sitting around chatting.

They had pulled some chairs into a rough circle and it looked unexpectedly informal to Mary's eyes.

"Hello there, come and sit down," said a young dark-haired man in a clerical collar.

"Hi, everybody, this is Mary," said Orla, sitting down on an empty chair and pulling another one over beside her. "Come and sit down, Mary."

"Hi, Mary!" said a number of voices.

Orla went round the circle, giving a string of names for Mary's benefit, not one of which stayed with her for more than a moment.

She was aware of bright, friendly faces and a general attitude of welcome.

"Perhaps we should make a start," said the man in the clerical collar.

Someone struck a chord on a guitar and everyone began to sing.

Mary noticed in surprise that everyone sang with their eyes closed. Some were holding up their hands as if ready to receive something. She tentatively closed her own eyes.

Mary didn't know the song but the words were very simple and repetitive and, when they came to the end, the group just began again, and kept on singing. After a while, Mary found that she was familiar enough with the words to join in.

"He is Lord
He is Lord
He is risen from the dead.
And He is Lord......."

As she sang, she felt a great peace beginning to invade her.

Chapter 31

For Phil, the months passed slowly. She had moved back home, saying nothing to Davy about her reasons, giving a vague excuse about needing to work. She sat exams at the end of the summer term, did fairly well, and waited for the results. She saw much less of Davy. Work had made a good excuse. The flat had become a place with bad associations. She no longer wanted to spend time there.

The summer passed, the new term began.

Davy did not seem to notice. It was incredible to Phil that he could be so blind. Didn't he realise she was going through an emotional turmoil?

But Davy was becoming more and more deeply involved with O'Brien and his drug ring. He did not speak of this to Phil after a few early attempts at justification which met with outright rejection. Phil saw things differently from him. It was no use to talk to her but the end of open communication between them put a strain on their relationship which he had not foreseen.

Gone were the days when they argued cheerfully about everything under the sun and always ended in the harmonious agreement that it was 'time things were changed'. Davy and Phil drifted silently further apart until neither fully understood any more, what the other thought or felt.

One day when the autumn was already almost over, and Phil realised with a shock that almost a week had passed since she last saw Davy, she decided the time had come to make some decisions. She was not willing to continue with this situation. Either they must make a clean break or they must try to get back unto the old footing. She would go and see Davy and make him talk to her, and then - well, they would see what happened.

Phil rang Davy's number but got no answer. The best thing was to go over to the flat where she could be sure of catching Davy sooner or later.

It was early evening when she reached Thomas Street. Davy might possibly be home by now and making himself something to eat. She still had her key and, when there was no answer to her ring, Phil let herself in through the unlocked front door which was the common entrance for all occupants of the house and went upstairs to unlock the door which closed off Davy's share of the building.

She went in familiarly and sat down on the shabby old sofa in the living room. Throwing her bag on the floor beside her, she leaned back with a sigh, preparing to wait.

She was in too tense an emotional state to pick up one of the many books scattered around and pass the time by reading, although normally that would have been her automatic solace in such a situation. Instead, she rested her head against the back of the sofa, closed her eyes, and tried to relax.

There were noises coming from the kitchen. It took Phil a few minutes to realise this, but suddenly it sank in. The vague rustlings, not at first identified as someone moving about, abruptly culminated in a rattling noise too loud to be mistaken for anything but the sound of another person's presence.

Phil's first thought was that Davy was there after all and hadn't heard her ring. She jumped to her feet and headed for the kitchen, calling out "Hey, half-wit! Why didn't you answer the bell?"

Halfway along the passage way she froze, her mouth dropping open, and speech dying on her lips.

The kitchen door opened quickly and a man stood there looking at her - the man she had seen before with Davy in Botanic Gardens. Sean, that was his name. A man who had some connection with O'Brien, the drug dealer.

"Oh - sorry - I thought it was Davy," she said, when she had recovered the power of speech.

The man said nothing.

"I'm Phil, Davy's girl-friend, you remember?" Phil babbled nervously. "I suppose you don't know if he'll be back soon? I meant to wait, but if he isn't going to be here until late, I might just go on......."

"How did you get in?" the stranger asked abruptly. He was a man of medium height, thin, with sandy hair beginning to turn grey, but with a pale face with heavy jowls and thick eyebrows which gave a scowling intensity to his words.

"I have a key," Phil said.

"I didn't know anyone else had a key to this place," the man said.

Phil said nothing. For a moment they stood staring at each other. Then came noises on the stairs, footsteps approaching, and a bang on the door. Davy's voice could be heard calling cheerfully,

"Sean! Sean! It's me, Davy! Let me in!"

Phil thought "He lent his key to this Sean, otherwise he could get in without knocking." She moved back down the passageway to the door and opened it, and Davy came in. He was carrying a paper parcel which smelt like fish and chips. His expression of shock on seeing Phil holding the door open would have been ludicrous if Phil had felt like laughing.

Davy recovered himself quickly. "Phil - good. I didn't know you were coming. You've met Sean before, haven't you? He's staying over with me for a day or two. Listen, let's you and me go out for a snack and a quick pint. Sean can stay here and make do on the carry-out, okay?"

"Okay," said the man called Sean. His face, like the face of a good poker player, gave away none of his feelings.

Phil allowed Davy to shepherd her out of the flat. Outside, she turned to face him.

"Davy. It's time we had a chance to talk. There are things we have to say. Both of us. This episode today just underlines the need."

"Okay, Phil," said Davy. He seemed irritated but not, Phil thought, at her. More at the way things had happened. "Let's go down to the Bot."

They sat in the Botanic Inn with glasses of lager in front of them and tried to communicate. Phil felt hopeless.

"I don't want to get in your way," she said.

"You couldn't," Davy said positively. "How could you? You and I belong together, kiddo."

"Do we?" said Phil. "We seem quite far apart in a lot of ways now, Davy. I know your ideas have changed. We haven't talked much about it. Perhaps you could try to tell me where you're at these days? All I know is you're into something that takes up most of your time and energy and, unless I'm prepared to be in it too, we're bound to be apart too much. Not just because we never have time to see each other but - you know – because we're growing apart in our thoughts and feelings too."

"Yes. I know." Davy was silent for a moment, staring into his glass.

"There are things I want to talk to you about, Phil," he said, presently, "but not here. And we can't go back to the flat with Sean there. Let's go for a walk down by the embankment. It seems a long time since we've done that. Maybe I can explain to you where I'm coming from, and maybe you can think about it."

The trees along the Embankment had lost their leaves and stretched slim beautiful arms towards the pale moon, still bright against the half light of the early evening sky of late October. They reminded Phil of the many times she and Davy had walked under the same trees with the moonlight reflected sometimes on the slight new leaves of spring, sometimes on the thick leaves of summer, and the shimmer of water nearby; when they had first come together and everything had seemed new and beautiful.

They walked hand in hand in a strange return to innocence and Davy tried to explain.

"You see, Phil, I've always believed people have a right to recreational drugs if they want them. What right has the law to ban them? They claim drugs do so much harm. But what about drink? Doesn't it do just as much if it's misused? The whole idea is to treat us like children, Phil, with a set of rules laid down for us by the so-called adults that we have to obey. But we have the right to be treated as adults ourselves, adults who can make their own decisions and use either drugs or drink in their own way, okay?" he said passionately. "The other thing isn't working – it's like Prohibition in America. When you put the use of drugs outside the law, everybody wants to use them even more. The only way then is to break the rules."

Phil tried not to jump in quickly with an argument. This was too important.

"I see what you're saying, Davy," she answered after a moment. "I do, really. But doesn't supplying these drugs cause endless misery? Isn't it a vicious circle? Won't it only make things worse?"

"Yes, perhaps, if people are stupid," Davy explained eagerly. "But that's the thing, Phil. If we would only make drugs legal, it would be so different. We daren't do less. If we let it drag on, it will escalate and get worse, as you say. Nobody wants that."

"But, Davy - the people who are suffering are innocent victims. Often they are the very people you say you want to help. Justice isn't an abstract thing, it means actual people having better lives. But it's actual people who are worse and worse off because of drugs. It isn't some sort of game."

"You don't understand, Phil," he broke in, stopping and turning to face her as the pent-up emotion he had tried to control took over.

"There are always casualties in any fight! I want to win freedom for you and me, Phil. Why shouldn't we make some money out of this crazy situation, enough money to get away, out of this rat race? How many ways are there to do that - to get enough to escape?"

"Davy," said Phil gently, "it's me you're talking to, not an audience. Don't preach at me. The victims in this case are your own innocent countrymen. Even your friends. What about Mary Branagh? She was nearly dead! Doing something which claims to make life better for people and ends up killing them doesn't even make sense to me! And we don't need to escape, to run away. All we need to do is to sort out our lives here!"

They stood, glaring at each other, battle lines drawn up. Then Phil broke.

"Oh, Davy! Let's not fight. I promise to go home and think about it. But won't you promise me to think about what I've said?"

Davy looked down at the path and then at the water beside them. The moon had brightened as they talked and now shone down at them from a clear, dark, autumn sky.

"I will think about it, kiddo," he said slowly. "But in a way, it's a bit late. Even if I wanted to, I wouldn't find it easy to draw back now. I know things, I've been told things. I'm not sure they'd let anyone walk away knowing the things I know. That's one reason I've kept you at arm's length for the past few months, Phil. There are levels of knowledge I don't want you mixed up in. The risk is too great. Even today, seeing Sean at the flat - I wish that hadn't happened. I'll tell him when I get back that you don't know anything and that, even if you guessed, you could be trusted. But don't go there again without me, dear. Promise."

Phil promised in a shaky voice.

"It's being used as a halfway house to store stuff, you see," said Davy very quietly. "And I didn't tell you that. But you're not such a moron that you hadn't guessed. So now, forget all about it."

Phil nodded silently.

Davy put his arm round her, drew her close and kissed her.

It was a very gentle kiss and it went on for a long time. To Phil, it meant more than all the talking. For the first time in weeks, she felt close to Davy again. It seemed possible that they might be able to maintain the delicate balance of their lives, in spite of everything.

Chapter 32

Mary and Orla walked beside the river and talked about life.

It was late autumn, almost winter, in their third year. The air was fresh and cool and the sun still held the remains of the day's unusual warmth as it sparkled off the ripples in the quiet water.

"What will you do when you finish your degree?" Mary asked.

Orla had no doubt or hesitation. Her curious dark grey eyes shone beneath the thick, heavy brows.

"I'm going to Africa to help the developing countries out there. Perhaps the Sudan - or perhaps not. It will depend which door God opens up at the right time."

"And how will you help them?" asked Mary curiously.

"I hope by then I'll be qualified to teach some of what I've learned myself. That's why I chose to do Science. Science is the gateway to so many opportunities for the developing countries today. Education is one of the chief needs. When people are educated, they can help themselves."

Orla's eyes glowed with enthusiasm, her thin bony face lit up by an inner fire.

"It sounds good," Mary agreed.

"People are starving, Mary. Just for lack of the elementary knowledge to allow them to manage their country well, to produce a livelihood. It sickens me to realise the luxury we live in here, compared to two thirds of the world. We need to help in whatever way we can."

"Is that why you dress the way you do?" Mary teased. "All out of the second hand shops, so you can send all your spare money to Africa?"

"Yes, since you ask," Orla replied calmly. "What do clothes matter, compared to saving the life, or the eyesight, of a child?"

Mary felt humbled, though she was clear that Orla had not intended any rebuke.

They walked on in silence for a moment.

"Wouldn't it be better to teach some basic farming methods, then?" Mary suggested. "Or to do medicine and go out as a doctor?"

"Those are important things, too," Orla agreed. "But not for me, that's all. My own calling has been clear to me for some years now, Mary, and it's what I said, to teach science and free the African people through education. To give them an equal status, if you want to put it like that, with Western man."

"It sounds exciting," Mary said, half enviously.

"Oh, it will be hard work," Orla said matter-of-factly. "But I need to make my life count, you see. Mother Teresa, Albert Schweitzer, Doctor Bernardo - those are the people I admire. If I can do even a small part of the sort of things they've done, I can be at peace."

"It's all to do with believing in God, isn't it?" Mary asked tentatively.

"I suppose, if you believe in Him, everything is about that," Orla said.

"I don't really know if I do believe or not."

Orla said nothing and Mary went on thinking aloud.

"I know I used to believe when I was small. About nine or ten. Then I seemed to lose it somehow. I don't think I ever thought about it even. I just drifted out of believing for no real reason."

"It seems a big decision to reach at so young an age," Orla remarked teasingly. "Haven't you ever thought it out again since you grew up?"

"I suppose I haven't. I don't know much about it. What are the reasons for believing? Why do you believe, Orla?"

Orla paused for a moment and looked at Mary.

"I haven't always believed. About five years ago, if you had asked me, I would have said much what you've just said, Mary."

"And what made you change?"

Orla thought again.

"I suppose, when I started to think about it, I couldn't make any sense out of life in any other way."

Mary was silent.

"Have you read anything about it?" Orla asked presently. "'Mere Christianity', by C.S.Lewis, for instance? I could lend you that, if you like."

"Oho," said Mary, "indoctrination, now?"

"No indoctrination," Orla said, unperturbed. "The offer stands. But if you want the book, you'll have to ask me for it now after that crack."

"Well," said Mary, "is it very boring? And all about keeping to the rules? That's never been my sort of thing, you know."

Orla laughed suddenly. "Rules don't come into it, Mary. It's about learning to be your real self, about knowing the Person who made you the way you are. And I don't think you'd find it boring."

"Okay, then," said Mary quickly before she could change her mind, "I suppose it's only fair to give it a go. Could you lend me it next time we meet?"

Orla nodded gravely. "Let's turn back now," she said. "We might have time for a cup of coffee before the lecture."

Chapter 33

Sheila floated down Grafton Street with her head in a whirl. She found it hard to keep from breaking into a run or starting to skip.

All around her were the noises of Dublin.

The strange accents, the voices which seemed louder, echoed in her ears.

A flower seller sat at the entrance to a side street surrounded by enormous bunches of flowers stuck into buckets of water.

In a shop doorway, a group of young men played popular music with an open guitar case on the ground beside them for contributions from the passers-by.

The glittering shop windows were full of exciting things: perfume, clothes, books.

She wasn't going anywhere in particular - that was one of the best things about it. They had arrived in Dublin a few hours earlier and booked into the Shelbourne Hotel in O'Connell Street. Then, after lunch, Delmara had said,

"I won't need you this afternoon, Sheila. Have a rest, or go and sight-see - whatever you like. Be here at six, okay? I have plans for tonight."

So here she was, on her own in Dublin, free as a bird and feeling as if she was fifteen again.

Why was Dublin so much more exciting than Belfast? Perhaps only because it was strange and new.

She darted into the nearest shop, which happened to be Brown and Thomas', and began to examine the clothes on display.

There were French perfumes on one counter and Sheila sprayed herself lavishly with the free tester of Chanel No.5.

Then she picked out three dresses which caught her fancy and wandered over to the changing rooms to try them on.

Time went past quickly.

Sheila bought herself a cup of coffee in Bewley's, going upstairs so that she could sit in the window and look out at the crowds in Grafton Street.

She felt sophisticated and adult, a woman of the world, as she leaned back in the rickety wooden backed chair and stirred her coffee.

A glance at her watch told her that it was time to go back to the Shelbourne.

In fact, she might have to run if she didn't take care. Delmara had plans for tonight - it was important that Sheila didn't cause him any hassle by being late.

In the four months since she had signed her contract, Sheila had already learnt that Francis Delmara was a man to be taken seriously. As her boss, he sometimes seemed a completely different person from the man who had pursued her so light heartedly from their first meeting.

She hurried back over O'Connell Bridge and was relieved to find that she reached the hotel with ten minutes to spare.

Delmara was in the reception lounge, sitting elegantly at ease in one of the enormous, comfortable chairs, and chatting with two men, when Sheila, strolling casually and with her breath under control, appeared.

"Ah, Sheila, beautiful," he greeted her. "Perfect timing, as always." He rose to his feet and came over to her.

"Let's go into the bar," he said, "and have a drink while I explain my plans for this evening." He waved casually by way of farewell to the two men and steered Sheila into the cocktail bar.

Presently they were seated in a secluded corner with Brandy Alexanders before them.

"Now," began Delmara, "I want fashionable Dublin to be talking about you before the show opens, precious. So tonight I plan to introduce you to some quite important people. First of all, we'll attend a preview of Sebastian O'Rourke's new exhibition of paintings in the Charlton Gallery. Then we'll move onto a party some friends of mine are throwing where all the right people will be making an appearance. The important thing is that you should look good. I'll manage it so that you can make a grand entrance and set people talking. I know exactly what I want you to wear - but be warned, darling, guard it with your life! If a single spot, smear or rip appears on that gown, I'll have you out sweeping the streets tomorrow. Only joking, love," he added quickly, as Sheila's eyes grew large in amazement, "I'm letting you wear one of my new models for the sake of the advance publicity. I want your picture in every newspaper tomorrow on the front, and the name of Delmara Fashions beside it."

Sheila smiled. "It sounds a good idea, Francis, but suppose no-one wants to take my photograph?"

"I'm not worried about that, beautiful. When they see you, they'll be knocked for six, no question. Now you see why I wanted you back in good time. Drink up and we'll go and start work. It'll take a couple of hours at least to get you ready."

Sheila sipped her Brandy Alexander cautiously. "Maybe I should eat something," she ventured. "I don't want to pass out on you."

"A good point. Let's get something now." He clicked his fingers at the barman and ordered open sandwiches for both of them.

"Just tell me when you're ready, Sheila," he said, leaning back in a typically relaxed poise. But Sheila could see the tension vibrating through him beneath the surface.

Afterwards, she could look back and appreciate how skilfully Delmara had stage managed the evening.

First there was the dress.

A dream of a dress.

Long, slender, clinging, in a soft silky material, in pure silver, with a back and cleavage which plunged to the limit and then some.

Chrissie, who worked at the dress shows, was on hand to do Sheila's hair in the simplest of styles so that her mass of red gold curls hung down her back almost to the low backed dress, and with a thin silver ribbon which sparkled with diamonds threaded through the curly wisps which fell over her forehead.

With it, long silver ear-rings and silver stiletto heeled shoes which added enough inches to her height to bring her more than level with Delmara.

When Chrissie had finished with her, Sheila stood up and Delmara carefully twitched the gown into place.

Sheila stared at herself in the long glass and saw a stranger.

A tall, red haired woman, fragile and fine-boned, with white delicate skin and a finely cut nose, looked back at her with enormous green eyes fringed with dark lashes.

Sheila had become used to the fact that she had grown up 'quite good-looking, really', as Kathy had put it. Enough people had told her so by now, for the truth to have sunk in and been accepted.

But underneath, she still thought of herself often as the pale, skinny child with the ugly coloured hair who had longed for dark hair and blue eyes.

In the few moments while she looked at herself in the long glass, that image vanished for ever.

This was a woman, not a child, and a woman of great and individual beauty.

She was also, to Sheila's amazement, poised, confident, and a little withdrawn.

How could an exterior be so misleading? Where was there any sign of the butterflies churning and fluttering in her stomach?

"Yes," said Delmara softly, looking over her shoulder at her reflection. "Yes, indeed."

He stood for a moment, his gaze fixed on her, then pulled himself together.

"Now, Sheila, we'll go in another few minutes. One last word. Don't look in mirrors or try to tidy your hair once you're on display. Don't smile or try to talk too much. Let other people make the effort. You don't need to be witty or clever. You just need to let people look at you and fall down like ninepins. Right?"

More rules, thought Sheila.

But she didn't really mind these ones.

"Ready to go?" Francis asked.

Sheila nodded. Excitement welling up in her made it impossible to speak.

"I've booked a taxi," Francis Delmara said. "It makes things easier. Let's go."

Chapter 34

Outside in the crisp, frosty air, the darkness was hung with glittering lights.

As the taxi carried them effortlessly through the centre of Dublin to the Charlton Gallery in Lower Abbey Street, Delmara talked.

"You don't really need to know this, but Sebastian O'Rourke is probably the best painter to come out of Ireland this century. You may not like his work. It's very strong, with hard lines and angles, and strong colours. Mostly people but none of your traditional Irish character stuff. There will be a lot of well known people there tonight, the Minister of Arts and possibly the President and, of course, the cream of society - the rich and the thick. The Charlton has the ideal layout for making a grand entrance. I'll go first and get people's attention. Then I want you to play it absolutely professionally, as if you were on the catwalk. Don't smile. I want that remote look."

Sheila nodded.

"The doors lead to the top of a staircase and the gallery is at the foot of the stairs. Think of Walt Disney's Cinderella and you'll get the picture. So everyone looks at the stairs when someone comes down if it's timed properly. You can leave that side of it to me. Just pretend you're Cinderella at the ball, or Audrey Hepburn in My Fair Lady. Okay?"

"Okay, Professor Higgins," said Sheila.

She smiled.

The butterflies seemed to have packed up and moved out, temporarily at least.

This was going to be good. Prickles of excitement ran up her spine.

The taxi pulled up before one of the old Georgian houses which make up so much of the centre of Dublin. Delmara came round to open the door for Sheila and she stepped out, carefully holding up the trailing hem of her dress. How dreadful if she caught the heel of a stiletto in the fragile stuff! But all went well.

Inside Sheila was dazzled for a moment by the lights and the ear assaulting noise. They were, as Delmara had described it, at the top of a flight of stairs leading directly into a long basement gallery where people were packed like sardines.

"Pause a moment, then follow me down when I call you," Delmara instructed.

He went forward, stood a few steps down the stairs, and then called loudly, his voice pitched to cut through the noise and bring a momentary hush, as people turned to see what was happening.

"Sebastian O'Rourke, you old scoundrel! Come here, I want you to meet the most beautiful woman in Ireland!"

Sebastian, a tall, burly, sun-tanned figure with a balding head and very blue eyes, turned from the crowd of guests who had been buzzing round him and approached the foot of the stairs.

Francis Delmara ran lightly down the remaining steps, hand outstretched.

On the lowest step, he paused dramatically, seized Sebastian O'Rourke's hands in both of his, and exclaimed, still in that very loud, attention grabbing voice,

"Here she is, Sebastian! Look your fill! The fabulous Sheila Doherty, Delmara's latest and most stunning acquisition!"

Then he dragged O'Rourke to one side and turned to look up, giving Sheila a clear passage.

Sheila came slowly down the stairs.

As Delmara had prophesied, all eyes were on her.

Now that the moment had come, she felt no remnant of nervousness, only a fierce exhilaration.

Inside she felt laughter bubbling up, and sternly pushed it down. She would not spoil this moment by bursting out giggling.

Yet a part of her thought in wonder,

"Why are they all looking? It's only me, Sheila, the gawky, ginger haired kid. It's all a gigantic game."

As she reached the lower steps, she became aware of Sebastian O'Rourke's blue eyes fixed on her with a piercing gaze which seemed to penetrate through to the back of her head and out the other side.

"Sheila, this is my friend Sebastian," said Delmara easily.

O'Rourke took her hand and, with a graceful movement unexpected in so large a man, bent to kiss it.

Sheila smiled at him fleetingly, in spite of Delmara's instructions, but the look in his eyes had already quelled in her all desire to laugh. She regarded him solemnly, her eyes large and wondering.

O'Rourke, too, seemed momentarily at a loss for words. Then he recovered.

"Beautiful, indeed, Delmara," he said. "It's not often that word is used so accurately. It's a great pleasure to meet you, Miss Doherty - or may I call you Sheila? Come and I'll show you my paintings."

Retaining his hold on Sheila's hand, he began to lead her round the gallery, watched covertly or openly by almost everyone in the room.

Already Sheila had been aware of the flash of cameras several times and she hoped that she had not been caught from an unflattering angle.

But there was nothing to be done about it, so remembering Delmara's repeated orders, she forgot about her appearance and refrained from so much as patting a curl back into place now that she was on public view.

Sebastian stopped at each of the paintings to explain it and praise it. Sheila had never heard anyone before blatantly praise his own work like this. Yet O'Rourke did not strike her as conceited, only fiercely honest and realistic.

"I'd like to paint you, Sheila," he said abruptly. "Have you sat for any other painter?"

"No," Sheila said. "Would you make me look like that - all angles?"

She indicated the picture in front of them.

"No," said O'Rourke slowly. "No. With you it would be a more delicate approach. Flowing lines. I'd have to think about it. But there's something there I need to capture."

He stared intently at her.

Presently Delmara came over to them and handed Sheila a glass of wine.

"Someone wants to meet you, beautiful," he said to her. "Come on, Sebastian, your turn's over. Give her back, she's mine."

O'Rourke laughed.

"For a while, Delmara. But take warning. You have a serious rival now. Probably many," he added, looking round at the eyes fastened on Sheila, openly or otherwise, from all sides. "Who do you want her to meet?"

"The President," said Francis Delmara in an off-hand tone. "And after that, we must move on."

Sheila met the President.

Then they met the Minister of Arts.

Then a well known playwright and poet.

Then a number of journalists.

The cameras flashed again.

Then at last they moved on.

The rest of the evening seemed to Sheila, high on adrenalin as well as wine, to consist of a series of flashes.

They went to a party where Delmara stage-managed another 'entrance' for Sheila.

The large crowded rooms, full of lights and people, were beginning to make her head whirl.

Catching sight of herself in a mirror at a point much later in the night, and at once looking away in obedience to Delmara's constantly repeated rule never to be caught studying her own reflection in public, she found it hard to believe that the cool, poised, woman reflected in the glass was herself.

The hosts of the party were a young married couple, Tod and Sally Kilpatrick, friends of Delmara. They were the daughter and son-in-law of the well off owner of a chain of supermarkets, Hugh Frazer Knight.

Sheila reflected that neither of these well dressed, elegant people gave the slightest impression of being connected even remotely with tins of baked beans but was careful not to say so even to Francis.

The husband, a school friend of Delmara, although apparently recently married showed a disturbing tendency to hang around Sheila, pressing her to drink.

She was relieved when Francis collected her smoothly and led her off to meet a string of other fashionable people, some with vaguely familiar faces and others whose claim to importance seemed to consist of their wealth rather than their talents.

Halfway through the evening, Francis introduced Sheila to Pat Fitzwilliam, the racing driver.

She had seen Fitzwilliam occasionally on television, winning Formula One races and being interviewed afterwards, or appearing on chat shows.

He seemed a pleasant, naive young man, with a lock of fair hair falling over his forehead and a friendly grin.

Sheila found him good company and smiled at his jokes. With this encouragement, he managed to manoeuvre her into one corner and gazed earnestly at her while he talked of his last race and his future prospects.

"Warm in here, isn't it?" he suggested presently. "How about a bit of fresh air?"

"I don't think so," said Sheila firmly. "Tell me some more about New York. I may be going there soon myself."

Pat resumed, but the desire to make further progress with Sheila was strong and soon he had thought of another method.

"This is a very historic house," he began. "Sally's father bought it for them from the O'Hara family, and it still has some of the original pictures and trappings. Have you seen the portrait of the Lady O'Hara whose husband was Lieutenant Governor in the nineteenth century? I ask because it's amazing how like her you are.Only you are so much more beautiful, of course."

Sheila laughed.

"You must come and see it," Pat said enthusiastically. "It's just down this corridor."

He seized her hand and led her through the nearest door.

The portrait was further away than Pat had implied.

Rounding a corner of the passage, Sheila found that they had come to a less well lit part of the house.

While she had no doubt of her ability to keep Pat under control, there was no sense in asking for trouble.

"I think we'll leave the portrait viewing for some other time," she began. "Let's just go back, now..."

Instead, Pat seized her in his arms and began to kiss her passionately.

Since Sheila had been alert for some such attempt, he succeeded only in kissing one of her ears as she turned her head to one side.

In another dress, she would have felt like using her knee at this point, but the precious Delmara gown must not run the risk of being ripped.

Instead, she kicked sideways with the heel of her stiletto shoes and at once distracted Pat Fitzwilliam's attention to his own shin.

Hopping on one foot and groaning while he clutched his leg, Pat mumbled incoherently "Ow - sorry - oh - you shouldn't be so lovely - ow – "

Sheila glared down at his bent figure and swept majestically away down the corridor, luckily in the right direction.

137

Chapter 35

Much later, as she listened to the would be witty remarks of two men trying to out vie each other for her attention, she was once more collected by Francis and taken to meet, this time, an older woman.

This was Roisin Boyd Cassidy, the very elderly widow of Stephen Boyd Cassidy, one of the heroes of the Republic who had taken part in the 1916 Rising.

Roisin Boyd Cassidy, friend of Yeats and the subject of one of his lesser known poems, looked incredibly old to Sheila.

Her face was lined but her hair was blue rinsed and carefully set, and her gown was elegant and expensive.

She had been talking to two young men as Delmara approached, but dismissed them with a wave of her wrinkled, claw-like hand as she turned to greet her friend.

Sheila caught a brief glimpse of the younger of the two men. For a moment she thought she recognised him. Could it be Charlie Flanagan? Charlie, who had caused her such grief back in her party going, drug taking days? No, surely not.

She very much hoped not.

And what would someone like Charlie be doing at an up market gathering like this?

She must have been mistaken.

The young man disappeared from sight, leaving her still uncertain.

The other man, rather older on closer inspection, was slight and sandy haired, with something indescribably tough about him. Sheila was glad to see him also melting politely away at their approach.

Mrs. Boyd Cassidy smiled benignly at Sheila and took her hand.

"So young, so beautiful," she murmured. "You make me hear Time's winged chariots, my dear."

Sheila smiled politely, at a loss for a reply, but it didn't matter. The old lady was happy to supply the conversation.

"You remind me of such happy times," she continued. "Delmara tells me that you are to model for him. Ah, if only I had had a model like you in the days when I was still designing! Coco Chanel would have had to acknowledge my supremacy then, for my style would have suited you exactly, my dear. But Coco, with her little suits, was always much more ordinary, although she would never admit how much I out classed her. I was always imaginative, extravagant, in my ideas. To tell you a secret, my dear, naughty Delmara has copied some elements of my style, I really believe. Not any one design, of course, he wouldn't dare do that, but the whole atmosphere, the ambience, of my gowns - but don't tell him I said so! He would only deny it. And, after all, since I no longer care to design clothes myself, why should not he, rather than someone else, keep the House of Roisin influence alive?"

Presently Francis, seeing signs of fatigue in the old lady, returned to take Sheila away.

"That lady is still one of the most influential people in Ireland. If I can get her support and custom, everyone else will follow like sheep. I think she liked you, which means she will probably come to the Show."

"Why is she so important?" Sheila asked later as they sat in a taxi on their way home.

She had asked very few questions all evening but this one came out before she could stop it.

How could someone so old still matter?

"Her husband was an important politician until his death twenty years ago," Francis told her. "She herself was a famous dress designer, as you no doubt gathered, which makes her opinion in matters of fashion still valued, but also she has great clout because of her own links to the government. Then there are the rumours. She's incredibly rich. People wonder where she got her money. How she still gets it. As to that I couldn't say. But it all adds to her celebrity status, people being what they are. All we need to know is that her influence can help to make the reputation of Delmara Fashions - and to make yours too, beautiful." He smiled as if something had amused him.

"Did you notice the man she was talking to when I took you over? Sandy haired fella. That was Sean Joyce. One of the most notorious people in Dublin. Used to be an IRA activist. From the North, of course, as most of them were, but he had to shift down here early on. They say he's moved into drugs in a big way these days. Who knows? But it's knowing people like him, keeping in touch with them, that gives Roisin her slightly dodgy reputation."

Sheila found it hard to believe. Was Delmara really serious?

But, tired out and half asleep, she asked no more questions that evening.

Chapter 36

Delmara Fashions held its dress show early in January, several weeks after Francis and Sheila and the rest of the team had arrived in Dublin.

Delmara had hired a large function room at the Shelbourne and invited everyone he could think of.

His advance introduction of Sheila to the fashionable world had paid off. Everyone was eager to see the beautiful new model who had attracted so much attention.

Those who had already met her wanted to see her again.

Those who had missed her wanted to catch up on the latest sensation.

The clothes were very much a secondary consideration. Delmara gambled on the fact that most of his prospective clientèle would fall for the dresses as soon as they saw them, particularly when they saw them worn by Sheila.

He was right. The evening was a triumph. Suddenly, everyone wanted to look like Sheila Doherty. Everyone wanted to dress like Sheila Doherty.

Delmara Fashions were booming.

Francis Delmara was pleased with his strategy and its success.

He was especially pleased when Roisin Boyd Cassidy came to the opening night and bought two of his evening gowns.

Afterwards, he made a point of speaking to her at some length to show his appreciation.

"Your little girl, the model," Mrs Boyd Cassidy said abruptly, after a few minutes of fashion talk. She was rubbing the palm of one incredibly wrinkled hand with the fingers of the other in an agitated manner. "Who is she?"

Francis was thrown. "Her name is Doherty. Sheila Doherty," he ventured.

"Yes - you told me her name. She looks so like - " She broke off and sighed. "Never mind. She reminded me of someone. Bring her to see me when you can get away from here, if it's not too late."

Francis bowed his acquiescence to the order, for such it was.

He had expected a gathering in the Boyd Cassidy town house, but instead the old lady was alone. When they were shown in, she looked up and smiled.

"Come and sit here, my dear," she said to Sheila. "You, Delmara, you can go and look at my early collections, the photo albums in the library. Reilly will show you."

Reilly, the tall, grim-faced maid who had been in Roisin Boyd Cassidy's service for most of her life-time, held the door for Delmara, and perforce he followed her out and along the passage to the library where the records of the famous designer's early triumphs were laid out in album after album of fading photographs.

Mrs Boyd Cassidy turned confidentially to Sheila. "I wanted to speak to you alone, my dear, because I am so struck by your resemblance to a dear friend of mine. I am sure you must be related to her in some way. Do you mind telling me a little about your family?"

Sheila tried not to look surprised. "My family? We're very ordinary people," she said. "What can I tell you?"

"I wondered - " said the old lady. She paused. "But I am behaving badly. I haven't offered you refreshment. What would you like? Tea, coffee, a liqueur? I have an excellent liqueur brandy which, alas, my doctors have now forbidden me to drink. You would be doing me a favour by having some - removing temptation from my way." She laughed vivaciously, showing some rather decayed looking teeth. Sheila did her best not to feel repulsed.

"The liqueur sounds lovely, thank you," she managed.

Mrs Boyd Cassidy touched the bell on the low table beside her armchair and presently Reilly reappeared.

"The liqueur brandy, Reilly. A glass for Miss Doherty. And bring the decanter."

Reilly went out, looking cross. But then, she had looked like that when showing Sheila and Francis in, so perhaps it was her normal expression.

In a few moments she returned with the brandy and two glasses on a tray which she placed on the table beside her mistress.

She poured a glass, offered it to Sheila, and then went out.

As soon as she had gone, Mrs. Boyd Cassidy, with a roguish glance at Sheila, whispered, "And now I'm going to be very naughty. Reilly would scold me if she knew, but we won't tell her."

She lifted the decanter in her thin, spindly hands with the utmost concentration and poured herself a glass while Sheila watched, fascinated, expecting any moment to see the decanter drop and spill.

At last the manoeuvre was complete and the glass was raised to Sheila.

"To you, my dear. And now, tell me..."

"Anything I can," said Sheila. "But, really, I know very little about my family. I take after my father's side, I'm told, in looks. He was a County Clare man, and his grandmother's family name was O'Hara, but I never knew either her or my great grandfather Doherty. They both died when my father was still a child or so he's told me several times."

"I knew it!" Roisin Boyd Cassidy burst out triumphantly. "You're an O'Hara to your fingertips, my dear. Let me show you something."

She fished down into a large, black leather handbag which was placed on the floor beside her chair.

"Here."

Sheila put out her hand to take the small object the old lady was holding out to her.

It was a tiny, miniature portrait of a young girl, not much more than sixteen.

Her red gold hair cascaded in a mass of curls around her shoulders and her green eyes gleamed under black lashes against her white skin.

Sheila felt an odd sensation, as if she was looking, impossibly, at her own reflection.

Chapter 37

Sheila stared at the portrait for some moments, then looked up to see the triumphant expression in her hostess's eyes.

"You see?" she said. "It's you, isn't it?"

"Not me," Sheila objected. "She looks like me, yes, I can see that -"

"Because she was your great grandmother," the old lady said. "My dearest friend, almost eighty years ago. Brenda O'Hara."

Her face softened and she looked at Sheila and smiled.

Sheila said "You know, there are lots of O'Haras about. I don't think it's really all that likely that this is the same family - "

She was interrupted again.

"You know it must be! How could anyone look at that portrait, and at you, and doubt it?"

The old lady was determined to believe that she was right.

Sheila gave a mental shrug and decided not to argue.

It wasn't important.

Why destroy Mrs Boyd Cassidy's illusions? If it gave her pleasure to think that she had met the great grand-daughter of her friend, then there seemed little reason to take that pleasure away.

Who knew, she might even be right? It was certainly possible.

Call it, Sheila estimated, a ten thousand to one chance.

"Let me tell you something about her," Roisin Boyd Cassidy said. "She was the daughter of one of the wealthiest men in Dublin back in the early days of this century - Fitzroy O'Hara, whose grandfather was Lord Lieutenant under Queen Victoria. She was brought up a member of the Ascendancy, but it wasn't in Brenda to accept blindly all the rules her family taught her. She was eight when I first met her, several years older than me, and already thinking for herself. She and I were thrilled by the 1916 Rising, though we were still children at that time, and in the early twenties we worked together behind the scenes to help get this country established.

"Brenda, though still in her early teens, was in a position to gather useful information from her family connections. She passed it on to me. I knew the key people on our side and I was able to give them Brenda's information on a regular basis. Between us, you could say, we changed the course of history."

She was a traitor, Sheila thought. I hope she wasn't any relation of mine.

But she said nothing aloud.

The old lady continued, in a dreamy voice. She was living again the days of her youth, full of romance and excitement, untouched by the bitter reality of maturity.

"It was through me that Brenda met Patrick Stevens, one of the leaders of the Rising. They fell in love at once. Brenda was a very beautiful girl - so like you, my dear - and Patrick was a dashing, good-looking fellow with a reputation for a wild sort of courage, although nearly twenty years older than Brenda or me when we met him in the early Twenties. We were all mad about him, but it was Brenda he fell for.

"Of course, her family knew nothing about this. There was a well-off young Englishman whom they wanted her to marry - she'd been introduced to him on one of the family's socialising trips to London - but Brenda would have nothing to do with him, although she couldn't tell her parents the real reason.

"Then things came to a head. After the nation won its freedom in 1921, the Free State was set up. "There was no place for people like Fitzroy O'Hara under the new regime. He was offered a Government post in London and he told his family that they would be moving there in a matter of a few weeks.

"Brenda was in despair.

"She came to me, crying, one night, and said "What am I to do, Roisin?"

""Don't go," I told her. "You and Patrick want to be together. You belong together. Go to him, then. Run away from your family and hide out with your lover until you can get married and be free of them."

"It was then that she told me that there was more to it than her reluctance to leave Patrick and go to England.

" 'I'm pregnant, Roisin," she said, looking at me with those huge green eyes, "I'm carrying Patrick's baby.'

" 'All the more reason to go to him,' I told her.

"She accepted that. It was what she wanted to be told.

"Her family were very angry.

"And worried, too, no doubt.

"She left them a note, saying she was going to her lover, but not naming him, in case he got into any trouble from her powerful connections.

"I didn't know where she was any more than they did, for months, and I worried about her, I'm sure, at least as much as they did.

"Then the civil war broke out. We were no longer Irishmen fighting against the English oppressors, but Irish against Irish.

"Patrick was in the thick of it, I knew, but I never heard where he was based.

"Then I got a letter from Brenda, with no address. I can remember every word. I still have it. I've read it so many times, I don't need to read it again.

"'My Dearest Roisin,
I am writing to you because you have always been my closest friend. My baby is due soon, and I am in good health, but I worry constantly about my dear Patrick. The fighting continues all round us, even in this quiet place where we are hiding out. I am frightened for him, he has so many enemies who want him dead. What will I, and the child, do if he is killed?
Perhaps I will be able to come and see you after my baby is born.
Till then, all my love.
Brenda.

"She never came. For a long time, I heard no more.

"Then, one day, a friend told me that information had come to him in a roundabout way about Patrick Stevens.

" 'You remember him?' he asked. 'He used to be a good lad but he chose the wrong side when the fighting broke out.'

"Remember him? Of course I remembered him. But I kept Brenda's secret and hid my concern.

" 'What about him?' I asked.

" 'Bad news, I'm afraid,' my friend told me. 'He was shot a few weeks ago. He was hiding out in the back of beyond, but you know how it is. They tracked him down, and shot him dead.'

"My heart ached for poor Brenda.

"I had no means of finding her, but I hoped and hoped that she would come to me. She never did, though.

"Then, when I had almost given up hope, I got another letter.

"She gave no address this time either, and said only that her baby was well and growing, and that she was about to leave the country and put it all behind her.

"About two years later, I got a letter saying that she was going to marry a good man who loved her.

"So I lost my dearest friend and, until this day, I never knew what had become of her."

"It sounds as if she went to America - or somewhere like that," Sheila ventured.

In spite of herself she was moved by the old woman's story, although she felt that the advice Roisin had given the young Brenda had been the worst possible.

But then she had been young and romantic herself at the time, not much more than a child. Who could blame her?

"I thought as much myself," Roisin admitted. "But I know better, now. She went to the North. The man she married must have been called Doherty, and your father, or I suppose it would have been your grandfather, would have been the son she bore to Patrick Stevens - brought up with her husband's name."

Sheila smiled kindly at the old lady.

Such a sad story, and so many years ago.

If it pleased her to believe that she had reached some sort of happy ending, it would be cruel to cast too much doubt on it.

Sheila, however, was clear in her own mind, that her grandfather was not the offspring of Patrick Stevens and Brenda O'Hara.

For one thing, she thought she remembered Frank saying that his grandmother's name was Sheila. That was why Sheila had been given that name.

And Frank Doherty was a very ordinary man. There was no aristocratic streak in his parentage, she felt clear. He was the source of her colouring certainly.

But Sheila was well aware that her fine bone structure came from her mother. Kathy had often remarked on it, complacently, in the more recent past.

Sheila was not really so like her father. She was the product of the mixture of both parents.

So her likeness to Brenda O'Hara was just one of those things.

Sheila smiled kindly at Mrs Boyd Cassidy and thought how awkward it all was.

It was hard to know what to say.

Francis Delmara pushed open the door and came into the room.

Sheila felt a surge of relief.

She could escape now and would not need to invent comments on a bygone tragedy which was nothing to do with her.

"Roisin, darling, your albums are truly wonderful, but I must tear myself away. This lovely girl needs her beauty sleep. Sheila, beautiful, time to go."

"Tomorrow I'm having a small party," Mrs Boyd Cassidy said graciously. "You must both come. There are some people I want to introduce to Miss Doherty."

Sheila would have liked to refuse, but Francis was already accepting. Afterwards he told her "Roisin Boyd Cassidy can be very useful to us, Sheila. She's taken a real liking to you, so let's make the most of it."

Sheila would not have minded if she had not had a very definite worry at the back of her mind about the people Roisin Boyd Cassidy wanted her to meet.

She felt almost frightened.

Was something about to happen which would not be at all what she wanted?

But there seemed to be no way of avoiding it now.

Chapter 38

Mary had gone with Orla several times to the meeting in the Church of Ireland centre at Queen's.

Something about the atmosphere of the place gave her a feeling of peace and release.

Over the last few months there had been some excitement. Mary, on the fringe of things, gathered that there had been some visitors over from America who were concerned about the situation in Belfast.

It seemed strange, Orla said, that other countries had begun to send missionaries to Ireland - for centuries it had been the other way round.

The leaders of the meeting were full of fresh enthusiasm now.

"The rest of the world looks at us," one of them said, when he and Orla and Mary were sitting chatting over a cup of coffee one evening in late January. "They've seen Christians fighting each other for years in the name of God. What do you think He feels about that? Now they see us unable to make terms for peace and let go of the past. We need to show the world that some Christians at least can love each other, whatever label they grew up with."

His eyes were bright with enthusiasm.

"What about your own plans, girls? You'll be graduating at the end of this year."

Orla flashed a look at Mary, her fierce grey eyes bright under their thick brows. "I'll be all ready for Africa when I get through finals."

Orla still meant to go to Africa to teach.

It was what she had meant to do for so long.

Mary, who was not looking forward to seeing Orla disappearing from her life, said nothing.

"So it's still going to be Africa, Orla?" asked Tony. "Don't you feel that you might have a calling to stay here? Surely the need at the moment is just as great?"

Orla smiled one of her rare smiles.

"I can't argue with that, Tony. All I know is Africa is where I've been told to go. There's no change there."

How can she be so sure? wondered Mary. It's all very well to say she knows she's been called. What does that mean? Has she heard a literal voice?

No, not from anything she's ever said.

It was hard to believe that Orla was talking about something real.

Yet Orla herself had impressed Mary, right from their first meeting, as someone who knew where she was going and what the reasons were.

On the following Monday, Orla and Mary went to the meeting together.

As always, they sat round in a circle and sang, quietly at first, and then more powerfully.

Mary felt again the strange peace which she always experienced at these meetings. She had sometimes asked herself why she continued to come. It was not in order to keep Orla's friendship. She knew that was something she would always have, no matter what the future held.

These people mostly believed things which Mary, in spite of the teaching of church and school, was not sure she herself could truthfully say she believed. They were good people. She liked nearly all of them. But she felt a wide gulf between herself and them.

God, now. Did she really believe in God? She hadn't thought about that for years, not until recently. She could remember when she was about six saying prayers at night and expecting God to answer. When had the last time been? Was it when she had confidently asked for a new tricycle for her seventh birthday and been given a doll instead?

Perhaps she had prayed while she waited at the hospital to hear that she was well enough to go home?

No, she thought on the whole that she had not. Her mind had been too numb.

The strange peace lapped over her again. Eyes closed, she allowed herself to sink into whatever it was.

There was a pause in the singing, and a girl's voice read from the first chapter of Genesis:

"And the Spirit of God moved upon the face of the waters ....
........and God said 'Let there be light,' and there was light."

Mary became aware of a great brightness shining all around her, and through her closed eyelids. She lifted her face and felt the light bathe her.

Inside her head, she heard someone speaking.

"Mary."

Mary sat quietly, her whole being flooded with peace and light.

"Mary," said the interior voice again. "What is it you want?"

Mary said nothing aloud, but inside her head her response was a great cry. "This is it! This peace, this feeling. This is what I want."

She gave the voice no name as yet.

"Mary," the voice spoke again. "I can and will give you these and other gifts. But do you want only my gifts or do you want the giver of the gifts as well?"

Mary's heart was bursting.

"Do you want me, Mary? I can only come to you as Lord."

Mary bowed her head into her arms. No-one else was aware of it, even Orla on her right hand, as they sang on with closed eyes.

"Yes, Lord," she said, in the quiet of her own heart. "You are what I want."

A sense of release flooded through her as she spoke.

Suddenly she realised that she wanted to jump up and dance as she had done when she and Sheila and the others had gone to the Magic Forest.

But there was no hidden fear mixed in with this present delight.

She found that she was singing loudly, along with the other people in the room, a song which had become familiar to her over the past months. Suddenly it was filled with new meaning.

"He's my Lord
He's my Lord
He is risen from the dead,
And He's my Lord ...."

Mary sang as if her heart would burst. She opened her eyes and looked round at the familiar faces.

She felt a swelling of love for them all, and especially for Orla.

"Let's all hold hands and sing that last song again," said Tony suddenly.

They held hands and sang.

Mary took Orla's hand in hers and looked round to smile at her.

"What is it, Mary?" whispered Orla, immediately aware that something had happened.

"I'll tell you afterwards," Mary whispered back. "But it's something good - something very good."

Did everyone here feel what she had just experienced? No wonder they were so sure of what they believed.

Mary felt as if she had come home after long wandering.

At the same time, she felt eager and ready to begin on an unknown journey which would take her to undreamt of places, on a road which ran clear before her feet from that very moment.

She felt that she had wasted her life until then, looking for things in the wrong places and finding nothing. She felt a wild regret for the way she had lived, together with an assurance that it was past history - forgotten.

She could be at peace, and cease to regret, and go forward confidently.

Where she was to go, she had as yet no idea.

But presumably that was Someone else's business, and no doubt He would tell her everything necessary in His own good time.

She was ravenously hungry and, when coffee and sandwiches came round presently, she found herself wolfing the food down.

When she went home, she went straight to bed and, for the first time for many months, she slept deeply for nearly ten hours.

Chapter 39

Sheila found that being a celebrity was fun.

During the first weeks after her introduction to fashionable Dublin, she found herself showered with invitations. She was interviewed by the Irish Times and found her photograph staring at her when she opened the paper.

Pat Fitzwilliam was particularly pressing with his invitations.

Delmara, who had taken it upon himself to censor Sheila's social life, and who had weeded out and rejected many of the requests for her company, was happy to encourage her to be seen with Pat.

"It will all help to build up your public image, beautiful," he told Sheila. "Image is everything. Fitzwilliam is popular and well-known himself - the papers will be all the more eager to mention you if you are with him. It gives them double value."

So Sheila lunched with Pat Fitzwilliam, danced with him, and was taken driving by him whenever she had a spare moment.

Spare moments were scarce, however. Sebastian O'Rourke was also a contender for Sheila's company. He had decided to paint her and wanted to begin straight away with rough sketch work.

Here again, Delmara was encouraging.

"To be painted by Sebastian O'Rourke is the acme, darling," he told Sheila. "But don't agree to it unless he wants you to wear Delmara clothes."

Sheila was happy to comply. She gave O'Rourke to understand that he could paint her under Delmara's condition, and he groaned.

"Gowns! Dresses! I'm not interested in what you wear, girl, I want to paint your face, your body!"

Sheila managed not to giggle, and regarded him gravely and inquiringly.

"The clothes don't matter, as long as they don't conceal your shape," O'Rourke said. "But I warn you, Sheila Doherty, if I paint you, I'll make love to you."

"Oh, yeah?" was Sheila's inward response. "That's what you think!"

But she did not say it aloud, and contented herself with raising one sardonic eyebrow.

O'Rourke was exciting and Pat Fitzwilliam was sweet, but Sheila felt no inclination to let either of them make love to her.

She was, she believed, through with all that sort of thing, since John Branagh had dropped out of her life.

She was a career woman and had no further interest in love. So she thought.

One bright spring day, she drove out with Pat in the early afternoon in his private sports car, a Lamborghini.

They headed south, as far as the Wicklow hills.

Bare spaces, empty of people for miles around, stretched out on every side. The sun picked out the purple of heather and the green of the fresh new leaves beginning to appear on the hedges that lined the narrow roads where they drove at a leisurely pace. Sheila delighted in the scattered primroses and violets along the nearby banks.

Presently they parked the car in a high grassy area and strolled peacefully about, enjoying the clear air and the spreading views of green fields and misty mountains.

Pat raised the subject again of Sheila's resemblance to the famous Lady O'Hara.

"I don't know who first noticed it, Sheila," he began, "but I've lost count of the number of people who've mentioned to me that you're the spitting image of that portrait in Loughry House."

"The one you offered to take me to see, Pat?" asked Sheila sweetly.

Pat blushed. "Yes, that's right. You never did get to see it, did you?"

"Tell you what," Sheila said thoughtfully. "I'm quite anxious to see it by now. Suppose you point it out to me next Tuesday. That is, if you're going to this lunch party of Sally's?"

"That's a date," agreed Pat happily. "Mind you, she's not as good-looking as you by a mile, Sheila. Her nose is too short to my way of thinking. But there's definitely a look of you about her."

Sheila grinned. It was nice to be told that you were better looking than a famous beauty. She still hadn't quite got used to the idea.

Sally Kilpatrick's lunch party was held in due course in the town house which had previously belonged to the O'Hara family and which had been bought for Sally and her husband Tod as a wedding present by her wealthy parents, Hugh and Rosemary Frazer Knight.

Sheila was seated part way down one side of the long table with its shining white linen damask cloth and gleaming silver cutlery.

Lifting her sparkling glass of Waterford crystal in one hand, she gazed at its gleaming rim and sighed with pleasure as a delicate china plate of melon and strawberries in a red wine coulis was placed before her.

Her neighbour, a stout red-faced man whom she had met several times before, but whose name she had so far failed to remember, misinterpreted the sound.

"Bored?" he asked in a low voice. "These large affairs are all like that. Why don't you and I slip away as soon as possible afterwards and go somewhere more interesting?"

Sheila shook her head at him with a gently mocking smile. "At three o'clock I'm due at the Burton studios for a photographic session for "Now" magazine, no excuses accepted. I'm a working woman. My life runs to a strict time-table."

"Some other time, then." The words were spoken with obvious regret. "I'd like to show you my yacht. It's moored down at Dun Laoghaire - a short run in the car. Any time that suits you, suits me too."

"I'll have to check. Delmara sets up assignments without letting me know half the time." Sheila smiled vaguely and turned to her other neighbour. A yacht sounded good, but not if it meant fending off her red-faced acquaintance for several hours.

Pat, sitting on her other side, was only too glad to seize her attention, given the chance.

"I made Sally put me beside you," he told Sheila as soon as she had turned her face to him. "I had to use all sorts of threats and bribes, but it was worth it. But you must talk to me, when I've gone to so much trouble, instead of turning your back and wasting time on Jack Kavanagh there."

"Fine by me," Sheila said, smiling at him.

She had become quite fond of Pat by now, and was happy to fall in with Delmara's plans and spend time with him. Occasionally she hoped, vaguely, that he wouldn't think she was encouraging him seriously. She didn't want him to end up hurt.

"Remember to show me this portrait when the meal's over," she said, and concentrated for a few minutes on the exotic chicken dish which had replaced the melon.

Further down the table, Sally Kilpatrick was conducting a two-handed conversation. On one side of her was Finley Boyle, a Member of the Irish Parliament, a TD, to whom she was talking seriously about the current political situation. On her other side was Tricia Scanlon, the only daughter of a shipping millionaire and a member of the international jet set to which most of the guests belonged. With her, Sally was chatting frivolously about a recent scandal among their acquaintances, dexterously conjuring with both conversational balls at the same time.

Sheila, half listening to Pat Fitzwilliam, could hear snatches of this conversation at the same time.

".......said she had never even seen the prince, but the photographs showed..........."

"..........so we need to talk to the Assembly about more cross border co-operation..."

"..........and if the papers once get hold of that, good-bye to her chances of a Spring wedding, or any wedding at all......."

".........need to show solidarity with the Nationalist people in the north........."

The T.D. was interrupted by a well known columnist, Terry O'Hanlon, from the Irish Times, who was sitting opposite.

"Hey, Sally," he called out, "do you know why Ian Paisley gets on so well now with Martin McGuiness?"

"No," said Sally obligingly.

"Marty promised him he'd have a word with his old comrades about Peter Robinson!"

Everyone within hearing laughed. Sally, laughing with the rest, suddenly broke off and spoke down the table to Sheila.

"Sorry - I didn't think. That wasn't funny to you, I suppose!"

Sheila smiled. "Don't worry, people in the north make jokes like that all the time. As a matter of fact, I first heard Mr O'Hanlon's joke last year, in Belfast."

O'Hanlon groaned cheerfully. "That's me shot down in flames. I'll have to be more up to date in future. It's the journalist's nightmare, to be behind the times."

"Whereas you, O'Hanlon, are normally at the front of the Times - the Irish Times!" called out someone else.

When the meal was over and people had pushed back their chairs and begun to wander about, Pat touched Sheila's arm and led her unobtrusively out of a nearby door and along a corridor.

"Just around this corner, I think," Pat said. "It gets a place of honour because she's so famous. Tod and Sally bought it with the house, naturally."

The portrait hung at one end of a long drawing room elegantly furnished in the latest styles, though not in keeping with the Georgian period of the house.

Bare parquet floors shone, and the low tables, bureaus and chairs in which the room abounded were cut on straight, uncluttered lines.

Wood predominated, giving a clean, natural look, in rejection of the frills and fuss of an earlier generation. The comfortable chairs were mainly in soft leather, in warm reds and browns.

On the furthest wall, carefully placed to catch the available daylight while avoiding the dangers of direct sunshine, and with artificial lighting set up for the evenings, hung the famous portrait by Millais.

Barbara O'Hara, wife of the Lord Lieutenant of Ireland in the mid eighteen hundreds when England still held sway over the whole island and Home Rule was still a burning issue, gazed out at them with wide green eyes.

A famous beauty in her day, Barbara O'Donnell had come from the wilds of Connemara and married into the Anglo-Irish ascendancy because, so the story went, Fitzroy O'Hara had fallen madly in love with her at first sight of her face.

The Irish peasant girl had quickly learnt to be a great lady and had moved freely through the society of both the London and the Dublin of her day.

She had been presented at court and Queen Victoria had written in her Diary, concerning the red-haired Barbara, "O'Hara has tamed the wild vixen, but let him look to his cubs!"

Or perhaps it was Disraeli who had fed Her Majesty this epigram.

Whatever its source, it contained an element of truth.

There had been a wild streak in the O'Haras ever since.

Brenda O'Hara, friend of rebels who had eloped with her lover Patrick Stevens, was only one example of that continuing streak.

Sheila stood before the portrait and studied it gravely.

She could see clearly the resemblance between the famous beauty and her granddaughter Brenda, whose miniature portrait she had been shown by Roisin Boyd Cassidy.

The red hair, white skin, and green eyes under dark eyelashes were there in both O'Haras. She could see, also, why others compared these two people to herself and remarked on her likeness to them.

But now, looking at the portrait in cold daylight, Sheila was more inclined to notice the differences.

Those dark eyelashes, for instance.

It was unusual for anyone with Sheila's colouring to have dark lashes - and, in fact, Sheila's own natural lashes were a much lighter shade.

She knew that by darkening them she had added something to her beauty.

How much, she could not have said, but her own opinion was, a great deal.

It was when she had begun to do this at the age of fourteen that people had first begun to call her pretty.

These O'Haras seemed to have the darker shade by nature.

(In fact, this was not true. Like most red-haired women, Barbara and Brenda had regularly darkened their lashes).

Then again, as Pat Fitzwilliam had remarked, there was a difference in the noses.

Sheila's nose was slender and delicately cut, only a fraction on the right side from being over long.

Barbara O'Hara's nose was much shorter and did not have the same delicate line.

Sheila was well aware that her fine features came from her mother, Kathy. She concluded, inwardly, that people had not really looked much beyond the general appearance and the colouring in remarking on the much discussed resemblance.

Sheila knew that Pat, in telling her that many others had compared her to Lady O'Hara's portrait as well as himself, was speaking no more than the truth.

Even the journalist who had interviewed her for the Irish Times had mentioned it and had made a passing reference to it in his completed article.

Sheila would have preferred to hear no more of the matter, but Delmara, she knew, saw it differently. His nose for publicity accepted this as an interesting extra strand in Sheila's public image.

"When we go to New York next month," he told her, "I think we might play up this resemblance, my pet. A touch of mystery and romance - especially for the Americans, who love anything to do with Ireland's romantic past. You needn't confirm it, Sheila but, when it's mentioned, don't deny it either."

Sheila would have preferred to bury the whole idea but it was, after all, Delmara's business and Delmara's clothes and designs which she was there to promote.

She sighed inwardly but was willing to go along with most things he suggested.

It did not seem worth while to make a big issue out of this one. The story would undoubtedly die a natural death before long.

Meanwhile, if Francis Delmara saw it as a useful way of increasing public interest in Delmara Fashions, she would not stand in his way.

She gave the portrait a final inspection and then turned to Pat Fitzwilliam.

"Thank you, Pat," she said. "It was interesting to see it. Now take me back to Sally and Tod. I must say goodbye to them and get moving. I have to be at the Burton Studios in about half an hour to get ready for this photographic session, remember."

Chapter 40

John Branagh finished an article for the BBC Web site on the new plans to increase tourism and pushed his keyboard back with a sigh.

He felt bored and restless. He had a good life, on paper. He was young, free, doing work which he enjoyed doing and being paid at a rate well above the Province's average.

There was the possibility in the pipeline of a move to London, carrying with it promotion.

So what was wrong with him?

Even to himself, John refused to admit that the disappearance of Sheila Doherty from his life could have anything to do with his unhappiness.

He glanced round the noisy, busy office where he worked and caught the eye of a girl sitting not far away who had been watching him with a hopeful expression.

She was about twenty, slim, small and fair-haired, and her wide open brown eyes always reminded him of a dog he and Mary had owned as children.

"Hi, Rosie," he said, smiling pleasantly because it seemed cruel not to acknowledge her.

"Hi, John," Rosie Brennan responded eagerly. "Finished? So am I. Feel like a drink?"

"Good idea," said John easily. "Brian, Tim, Katie - anyone else? Rosie's trying to turn us all into alcoholics."

"The only way to survive in this office," called big Tim Cameron, from his desk across the room. "Let's get stuck in."

John did his best not to see Rosie's disappointed expression as four or five of the journalists trooped out together to the nearest bar. He was well aware that Rosie had hoped to get him on his own, had been trying to attract his attention for months.

The favourite pub was Murphy's and they piled into the crowded, noisy warmth, laughing and chatting together.

"Talk about a Zoo!" said big Tim, settling himself comfortably at the corner table they had taken over. "More like a snake pit than anything else, isn't it? Which reminds me, what did St Patrick say when he was driving the snakes out of Ireland?"

"What?" John asked lazily.

"Are yis all right in the back, there?"

Everyone laughed, Rosie after a pause for thought.

Looking round, John realised that he knew most of the people there as they were TV journalists, people whose job it was to get the news even if it meant being up late.

Brian Gallagher, a friendly balding man with a noticeable paunch, began to talk about his experiences that day interviewing some of the family of the victims of a bank robbery the previous night.

"Ex para-militaries, it looked like," he said. "They've moved into this stuff now we've got the ceasefire. Just out for the money, a bit extra to what they make from the drug trade, I guess. The Belfast Mafia, they call them."

"That's happening more and more these days," said Katie Acheson, a haggard but still attractive blonde in her late thirties who was one of the staff reporters with a regular spot on the News. "Crazy. We get rid of the terrorists and what do we get in return?" She sipped her gin and tonic with a cynical shrug.

"I had to interview the parents of the guy who got shot, and his girlfriend," said Brian. "A bad experience, I can tell you. I'll let you do it, next time, Rosie."

Rosie shuddered. "No way, Brian. I'm sticking with the Women's News."

"Very wise," said big Tim. "D'you think they would let me join you?" He winked at Rosie in a mock lecherous way.

Rosie, determined to stop the talk of horrors, began to chat about her own area.

"I was listening to some interesting stuff about the new fashions just now. This Sheila Doherty looks like being a big name," she said. "You must have read about the splash she made in Dublin with Delmara Fashions. Good to see someone from here starting to make it big. They'll be off to New York soon, I'm told. Gnash, gnash - wish I was her."

John Branagh winced and said nothing.

Brian showed signs of interest.

"Some smasher, isn't she?" he commented. "I saw a write-up about her last month in Now magazine. She was wearing one of these new mini skirts that are even shorter than the originals. Cor - legs a mile long. I think I have a copy of it somewhere about. I'll show you when I get back to the office."

"Right on," agreed Tim. "I told you the Women's News was the stuff to work on."

John felt his face becoming frozen in the effort to show nothing.

Sheila showing off her legs in a popular magazine.

The idea stabbed him painfully.

What was it to him? he asked himself savagely. She was always the same. Nothing but a tart. He was well rid of her.

Turning to Rosie in desperation, he began to ask her about herself in a determined effort to change the subject. Brian, Katie and Tim became involved in a discussion of their bosses, working conditions, and the chance of a pay rise. As John knew, once started on those subjects they could go on for hours. He continued to talk to Rosie and, when the others got up to go, found to his dismay that he seemed to have committed himself to giving her a lift home.

Later, when he stopped the car outside Rosie's house and she gazed up at him with those pathetic brown eyes, it seemed very natural to John to kiss her good-night.

It was a gentle kiss and John gave it with every intention of leaving things at that.

But Rosie clung to him, making it difficult for him to draw away without hurting her.

The mixture of hurt and anger which boiled not far beneath the surface of John's emotions demanded some sort of outlet.

He continued to kiss Rosie.

It was a long time before he managed, with the exercise of great will power, to call a halt.

He drove home cursing himself for his stupidity.

He, who had been determined to be different, to maintain his own moral standards in the face of a degenerating world, had allowed himself to become the victim of his own desires.

He had no love for Rosie. He had simply been making use of her.

He knew that he could not afford a repeat of tonight's experience. Next time round, or at the most, a few times later, he would find himself drawn into the kind of casual sexual encounter he most hated.

Stupid, stupid!

The problem was, with Rosie working in the same office, it would be almost impossible to avoid her.

He didn't want to hurt her, either.

For once in his life, the decisive John Branagh found himself confused, uncertain what to do. He wished for the hundredth time that Sheila had been different, that she had not been the sort of person she had turned out to be.

After a while it occurred to him to wonder if there was so very much difference between Sheila, and himself as he had been tonight.

Chapter 41

One day, at the end of the summer term, at a time when the sun had begun to pour out his generous warmth again and to raise up spirits from their winter depths, Mary ran into Phil in Botanic Gardens. They had not met for nearly a year. Their paths had veered apart and, for lack of deliberate planning, occasions to meet had become rarer and rarer.

Mary, full of energy and bounce herself, was surprised to see how unhappy Phil looked. She reproached herself for having failed to keep in touch for so long with a girl who had once been so close to her.

Phil was mooching slowly along one of the paths and Mary, who had been hurrying on her way to the library, pulled up at the sight of her. Phil's head was bent, her eyes fixed on the ground and an air of melancholy seemed to emanate from her bowed shoulders.

"Phil!" exclaimed Mary. "Goodness, it's nice to see you."

Phil looked at her for a moment as if she was a stranger. Then, pulling herself together with an obvious effort, she broke into a smile.

"Mary Branagh, for heaven's sake! I thought you must have emigrated."

"Not just yet - maybe never," Mary laughed. But, Phil, don't disappear now I've got you. We should keep in better contact. If you haven't got to be anywhere particular for the next half hour or so, let's go for a coffee and catch up on the gossip, okay?"

"Fine," agreed Phil, looking pleased. "Good to see you, Mary."

They headed by tacit agreement for the Union.

"So, Phil, how's it going?" asked Mary, setting her coffee down on the table opposite Phil and flopping down on one of the plastic chairs. "You passed your exams okay?"

"Yeah. I'll probably go on and do an MA now." Phil's lack of interest in this subject was obvious. "And you?"

"So far, so good," Mary said. "I'm planning to do a teacher training Cert. after the summer." She hesitated. "Look. I know we haven't been in touch but we're still friends, aren't we? So don't mind me asking - is anything wrong?"

Phil looked amused. "Does it show so badly? Well, since you ask, yes, things are wrong. But there's not a lot anyone can do."

"You're not - " Mary hesitated and Phil laughed outright.

"Same old Mary - straight to the point. No, I'm not pregnant, if that was what you were going to ask."

Mary blushed and then caught Phil's eye and laughed. "Well, it was always the ultimate calamity, wasn't it? Though I suppose if we were married it would be a different matter."

"Yes," agreed Phil indifferently.

"So - what is it, then?"

"Oh, Mary!" Phil sighed in exasperation. "What was it, ever?"

Mary knew the answer to that. "Davy Hagan."

"Right."

"But - I thought things were really good for you and Davy now?"

"Oh - in some ways." Phil was aware of an intense longing to pour it all out, to hear Mary's sensible, down to earth reaction, to share some of the weight with her friend. But she realised without even having to think about it how impossible that would be.

"It's nothing you could help with, Mary," she said instead. "I wish it was. Oh, I'm making a drama out of nothing. We just have a few relationship problems. Doesn't everyone? We don't see eye to eye on some things which seem important to me. Davy lives by different rules - or by breaking the same ones I try to keep. Oh, don't let's talk about it. Let's talk about something else. How are things with you?"

Mary stirred her coffee thoughtfully.

"These areas where you don't see eye to eye. They would be stuff to do with drugs, right?"

Phil nodded silently.

"You and Davy used always to agree to differ about him being a user. And I don't think you've changed your views. So it must be Davy who's changed, yes?"

Phil's head jerked up and she stared at Mary with something of the horror she felt showing in her eyes.

"Don't, Mary. Leave it. It's not something I can talk about."

Mary nodded. "I think I understand. It's all right, Phil. We'll leave it. But any time it helps to talk, ring me. You know me. Silent as the tomb when it matters. We've shared a lot of secrets in the past which never came out. This one won't either."

"Oh, knickers, Mary, you haven't changed!" Phil grinned in sudden appreciation. "It's good to see you again, you old pest!"

Mary smiled at Phil's reversion to the swear words of their schooldays.

"Subject closed," she said lightly. "Now I'm going to talk about myself, so just shut up and drink your coffee and listen."

She began to tell Phil about the things that had been happening to her, haltingly at first and then with increasing confidence as she went on. She had shared so many things with Phil when they were children. It seemed very natural to share these things, too.

When she had finished, Phil, who had been letting her coffee grow cold while she continued to stir it absently, looked up.

"Oh, Mary," she said, "you seem so happy. So peaceful. I wish I could be like that."

"Well," said Mary, "I don't have a monopoly on it, Phil. It's there for anyone who wants it."

"I don't know," Phil said. "I don't know."

Mary, whose natural instinct would have been to push on with her own opinions, and insist that Phil should adopt them as her own, suddenly found an unaccustomed wisdom. For a moment she said nothing. Then she said,

"Well, like I said, any time you want to talk, you know where to find me. But tell me, have you heard anything from Sheila Doherty lately? I haven't seen her for ages. I hear she's hitting the high spots in Dublin, these days?"

Phil suddenly looked animated again. "Yeah, isn't it great? Did you see the photos in Now magazine? If anyone deserves it, Sheila does. She's a great girl."

"Yes," Mary agreed. "And how about Gerry, and your family, and so on? Tell me all the news."

They continued to chat for another half hour, reminiscing about school, the nuns and the pupils, the times when they had been in trouble together, events which had been painful at the time but which now, in the haze of nostalgia, seemed both funny and full of the warmth of past security.

When at last Phil noticed the time and realised that she would have to rush to avoid being late for Davy, she was surprised to find that she was feeling more cheerful than she had done for a long time.

"Let's keep in touch, Mary," she said impulsively as they separated outside the Union. "I think one of the main things wrong with me is not having a good mate like you to talk to when I feel down."

"You've got a point, there," Mary said. "I'm glad we met. I'll be in touch."

She smiled as she waved a casual goodbye.

But when Phil was out of sight, her smile disappeared.

This was not the cheerful Phil she had once known.

Mary wished with all her heart that she could free Phil from the sadness which seemed now to have her in its grip.

Chapter 42

Sheila went for a sitting with Sebastian O'Rourke one afternoon about a week after Sally and Tod's lunch party.

He was waiting impatiently for her and flung open the door as soon as she approached, pouncing on her and dragging her in, rather, Sheila thought, like some wild animal seizing his prey and dragging it into his den.

"Francis will be here in a moment," Sheila said coolly. "He wanted to discuss with you what you want me to wear. He's thinking in terms of some special creation for the occasion."

O'Rourke growled. "Something light and floating. That's all it needs to be."

His studio was on the top floor of an old house out towards Rathmines and the rather dilapidated exterior gave the visitor no clue as to what to expect inside.

In fact, Sheila discovered, O'Rourke had completely rehabbed the place and she found herself impressed.

The keynotes were light, space and air. There was no clutter.

At the top of the stairs, four doors opened off the small landing, giving a glimpse of bedroom, kitchen, bathroom and studio.

The studio itself was a large room, two or three rooms thrown into one, Sheila guessed. There were windows on three sides as well as roof lighting.

Brushes, paints and other tools of the artist's trade were arrayed with meticulous neatness in a made to order cabinet on the fourth side, by the door.

Canvasses were stacked carefully on a set of shelves in one corner and the painter's easel was set nearly in the middle of the room.

To one end was a red velvet chaise longue, obviously for a sitter.

The only other seating arrangements were two simple wooden chairs with straight backs against one wall and a few enormous cushions in bright colours flung down on the polished wooden floor.

Apart from the radiators, which diffused a gentle, regulated heat, that was all.

"Go over and sit on the couch," ordered Sebastian O'Rourke, almost before Sheila had come through the studio door. "I want to get a general impression first - remind myself of what it was about you that I wanted to paint."

Sheila went over to the red couch and sat, and O'Rourke immediately roared out "No! Get away from that red!"

He rushed to the cabinet, flung open one of the lower doors, and pulled out a couple of spreads, one black, one a pale cream.

These he arranged in turn over the couch, placing Sheila against each, standing back and frowning.

By the time he had decided on the black cover, a ring below signalled the arrival of Francis Delmara.

O'Rourke plunged down the stairs to greet him, let him in, and at once began to argue fiercely about the need for his presence.

"Interference!" he said loudly. "That's what it is. Why should you have any say in what I decide to paint?"

"Because," said Francis Delmara calmly, "the only reason I am permitting Sheila to sit for you is that it will be more publicity for my designs. So I shall - not decide - but discuss with you what she will wear. Sheila, my dear O'Rourke, is under contract to me and has signed an agreement not to undertake any outside work without my consent."

"Work? This isn't work. It's art!" burst out O'Rourke. "As for what she should wear, suppose I decide that I want her to wear nothing at all? Where would Delmara Fashions come into the picture then?"

"My dear Sebastian," Delmara was beginning in the languid tones in such complete contrast to O'Rourke's roar, "any paid activity is work, although it may be art at the same time - "

Sheila stood up and moved forward.

Her voice when she spoke was soft but it managed to cut off Sebastian O'Rourke's renewed bellowing almost before it had begun.

"Don't I have any say in this? Delmara is quite right, Mr O'Rourke. I am under contract to him and I'm always grateful for any advice he gives me about public appearances. If Francis was unhappy about it, I wouldn't have agreed to sit for you, contract or not. As for wearing nothing - think again, my friend."

O'Rourke suddenly smiled his charming smile. "Please don't call me Mr O'Rourke, Miss Doherty. I thought we were on better terms than that. Okay, let's all discuss it. It's my picture, but let's have a general discussion about what I'm going to paint! No, sorry, sorry, I didn't mean that. Well, Francis - what have you got to suggest?"

"That's more like it," Francis Delmara approved. "Now, Seb, this is what I had in mind."

He began to pull cuttings of material from the small folder he had brought with him and the two men became absorbed in discussion of shades and textures.

Sheila wandered over to the window and gazed out.

She saw a busy city road leading in to the heart of Dublin, chock-a-block with traffic and pedestrians. On the opposite side, the road was lined with the tall, three or four storey houses so typical of Dublin, with their small city gardens and, in many cases, a railed flight of steps leading down from pavement level to basement.

A slim, dark-haired young man, lean but quite tall, appeared abruptly in one of the doorways opposite.

He turned to fling a casual goodbye over his shoulder.

Then he hurried down the low flight of steps towards the street.

Sheila, gazing at him absent-mindedly, felt her heart suddenly stop.

John.

A moment later, she had realised her mistake. The young man was a total stranger, with only a superficial resemblance to John Branagh.

Sheila bit her lip.

She had not realised that the thought of John was so near the surface of her mind.

All that was over!

Sheila felt fiercely angry with herself.

"Well, what's the decision?" she asked, turning back to the two men in the room behind her.

"This is the one," Delmara said, holding up a swathe of almost diaphanous chiffon in the palest shade of white. "I shall design a very simple robe - almost Pre-Raphaelite - as light and clinging as air - and O'Rourke will paint you lying on the couch which will be draped in black velvet, with your hair trailing to the floor. It's decided."

"It will be a stylised subject," O'Rourke broke in. "An irony, you understand. A parody. But beautiful - beautiful. Half tribute, half mockery of a bygone romanticism which we can no longer capture. And yet, in your beauty we'll see it apparently captured again, Sheila - that's your appeal."

Sheila smiled. O'Rourke's enthusiasm demanded a response of sympathy and understanding.

It was pleasant, too, to be identified as a symbol of romantic yearnings, a symbol which in itself, being out of reach, underlined the impossibility of its attainment and mocked what it presented.

She felt proud that she would contribute to a work which she knew instinctively would be important in its impact on its century and perhaps on future generations also.

Something in her suddenly shivered and she felt her face harden.

O'Rourke's insight frightened her.

Romantic yearnings - what did they mean? What did they lead to?

She had believed that she had put all such desires behind her and accepted that love was only a game.

But had she?

Why, then, had she imagined that she had seen John Branagh?

Did he still mean something in her life?

And if not, what was left?

The smile faded from Sheila's lips and again she shivered.

Chapter 43

Sheila had not forgotten Mrs Boyd Cassidy, and she, in turn, had not forgotten Sheila.

Their paths had crossed at a number of social events but Delmara Fashions had been moving around, over to London and to Paris, and it was not until the autumn, when they returned briefly to Dublin, and Delmara had begun to talk more definitely about his proposed show in New York, that the old lady made a further opportunity to talk to Sheila.

The occasion was Roisin Boyd Cassidy's ninety-fifth birthday party and she had pulled out all the stops.

The rich and famous from three continents gathered to do her honour.

Roisin Boyd Cassidy's contribution to the founding of the present day Republic of Ireland had won admiration for her from one set of people, while her successful career as a couturière of world-wide renown had spread that admiration through a very different set.

The big city centre house was crammed with people and ablaze with lights when the taxi carrying Sheila and Francis pulled up before it.

Sheila had grown used by now to the glittering night-life arranged for her by Delmara, but she still felt the familiar thrill of excitement as she stepped out of the taxi.

In the months that had passed, first in Dublin and then moving around, winter had turned to spring, and now summer had gone in its turn.

The light, clear nights when evening parties began in daylight were already beginning to pass and darkness was creeping on.

Inside the house, flowers were everywhere and their perfume mingled with the more exotic fragrances of the guests.

Sheila paused in the doorway almost overwhelmed by the noise which hit her like a blow from the crowded rooms.

She was wearing dark blue silk. For a moment, as she dressed, her mind had gone back to the dark blue dress she had worn at Mary Branagh's sixteenth birthday party and the excitement she had felt then.

It seemed a million years away.

That had been the first really grown-up party she had ever been to, and it had been the first time she had been told that she was pretty - by Gerry Maguire.

It had also, she recalled with no difficulty at all, been the first time she had met Mary's brother, John.

Tonight's dark blue dress was a very different affair from the simple schoolgirl style of the one she had worn then.

From its plunging neckline to the thigh high slit on the left side, it was not the dress for a school girl.

Sheila, fastening it round her slim body, shook off her mood with an effort and went down to meet Francis.

Now, as she stood in the doorway, she saw that people had turned to look at her in the way that had become familiar.

For a moment there was a brief pause in the conversation.

Alerted by the sudden silence, Mrs Boyd Cassidy, surrounded by an admiring group, looked up and saw her.

She came forward at once.

"Sheila, my dear. How glad I am to see you."

She looked immensely elegant and impossibly old in a gown of deep green satin, personally designed in her own individual style for this special night.

"My dear, there are some people I want you to meet tonight who have been looking forward very much to knowing you. But let's leave that until later. Francis, take this little lady to the buffet and see that she gets something delicious to eat and drink."

Sheila had an internal grin at being called a 'little lady' by the petite couturière but accepted it as it was meant, as a term of affection.

She and Francis Delmara went off obediently to the buffet where Sheila's attention was immediately claimed by Terry O'Hanlon, the columnist she had first met at Tod and Sally Kilpatrick's lunch party.

Terry wanted to talk to Sheila not only because she was beautiful but also because his journalist's nose told him that here was material for an interesting section for his column.

Rumour had it that there was some mystery about her background.

What a scope for the O'Hanlon column to be able to announce the solution to the mystery conclusively, once and for all, on the authority of the lady's own personal revelation.

So he put himself out to be at his most charming and witty, and Sheila laughed and enjoyed his company, and was very careful to tell him nothing whatsoever that he did not know already.

"Tell me," said Sheila presently.

She was curious, and saw no reason why she should not use O'Hanlon's expertise to fill out her own understanding of the present situation.

"That man over by the far wall, talking to Mrs Boyd Cassidy - you see him?"

O'Hanlon looked across the room at the tall grey haired man with the intelligent face who was leaning over with a smile to listen to his hostess.

"Yes," he said, "you mean Seamus O'Donnell?"

"Is that his name? I'd forgotten. But what I wanted to ask you was this. Someone pointed him out to me as a hero of the IRA. If he was known as an IRA activist, why was he never arrested? Up North, he wouldn't be arrested now, since the ceasefire, okay, but before that, they'd have been onto him like hounds on a fox."

"You don't understand," said O'Hanlon, laughing.

"No, I don't," Sheila said frankly. "So explain to me, please."

"O'Donnell wasn't necessarily an activist in the present troubles," O'Hanlon began. "He fought, back in the Twenties, in the Irish Civil War, when the nation was divided between the supporters of Michael Collins, who signed the treaty with England and accepted the division of this island into north and south, and De Valera and his followers on the other side who called Collins a traitor and fought to the bitter end to resist the agreement. Peace was made eventually, but it was one of the worst and most bloody wars in Irish history. It was in that conflict that O'Donnell took part. You can see he's not a young man. He must be in his late eighties, I suppose."

"So you're saying he was a hero of an IRA which had really nothing to do with the terrorists of these recent troubles?" Sheila asked.

"Okay," O'Hanlon conceded, "that's about right. But even if he had been fully involved, he could safely go up North for his holidays now since the ceasefire, as you say. The paramilitaries have bowed out. The authorities are more concerned with the gangster element that's sprung up to fill the vacuum. Some of them are ex-paramilitaries, okay. And they're into drug dealing in a big way and trafficking in illegal immigrants, prostitution, you name it. It's always been bad in

Dublin, but now Belfast's getting caught up in the rackets too. Now, if you'd asked me about some of the other people here tonight....." He broke off and grinned tantalisingly at Sheila.

"Do you mean..........?"

"Oh, yes, any number of drug dealers here. I don't say that everyone in the room knows that. In fact, I suppose very few people do. I happen to be the exception because I have a certain amount of inside knowledge. It's my job to know things. But some of the younger men here - Roisin keeps in touch, you see. She knew them all in the old days, the ones that were paramilitaries, was involved herself, and from what I hear, she still knows most of what's going on. They call her the Celtic Tigress. The economy being the Celtic Tiger, see?"

Sheila was uncertain if she should believe him. Journalists always exaggerated. They wanted everything to be a good story.

Surely that pleasant, rather pathetic, old woman couldn't be involved in drug dealing or any other criminal stuff, either here or up north?

But she knew that at least part of O'Hanlon's information was true. Mrs Boyd Cassidy herself had talked of her activities in the days when the Republic was first set up. She knew people like O'Donnell. Why should she not know their successors? And the loose cannons who had turned criminal?

Why even should she not know something of their plans?

For a moment Sheila thought "No, she's only an old lady. No-one would be silly enough to let her know about that sort of thing."

She looked over.

Just at that moment, Roisin Boyd Cassidy looked up and Sheila caught her eye.

Such an eye.

Sharp, alert, the eye of a clever, scheming woman half her age.

Sheila found that she had given an involuntary gasp and looked hurriedly away.

No, it was not impossible. Roisin Boyd Cassidy was no ordinary old woman. Bright, intelligent, much admired for her activist part in the early days of the setting up of the Irish Free State. Sheila had not gathered if she had been pro-treaty or anti-treaty.

But if she had been a supporter of the IRA in those times, she might well have kept abreast of the later campaigns. And if her principles had turned into something very different - if she had let herself get involved in gangsterism - then her advice and quick planning brain might still be valued by the Mafia element who were trying to run the country.

Sheila felt torn in two.

She owed something to Delmara.

He had introduced her to this woman and encouraged her to be friendly, to build up a good relationship.

This was what she had done.

How could she now sweep out of the house in moral outrage, as she felt like doing, on the word of a journalist whom she hardly knew, and who might or might not be trustworthy in his information?

And yet -

Sheila felt a shuddering reluctance to stay and enjoy the hospitality of someone who had encouraged, perhaps even planned, so much death and misery among the innocent.

The voice of Pat Fitzwilliam in her ear had never been more welcome.

"What do you mean by monopolising this lovely girl for so long, O'Hanlon, you villain? Come and dance with me, Sheila?"

Pat was amazed and uplifted by the warmth of the smile which Sheila turned on him.

Silently, she followed him to the edge of the dance floor and melted into his arms. She was badly in need of someone whose innocence she could be sure of, someone she could trust without further question.

It was much later, and Sheila had recovered her poise, by the time Mrs Boyd Cassidy came to seek her out among the many guests.

"There you are, my dear. Come with me. I want you to meet some friends of mine."

Sheila followed her reluctantly, her face a polite mask.

The decision, she found, had been made.

She could not insult Mrs Boyd Cassidy in her own house by leaving or by refusing to be introduced to her friends, simply on the word of Terry O'Hanlon.

She allowed herself to be led over to a party of men and women who had been prominently in her hostess's immediate circle for most of the evening and was relieved when the first introduction was to a well-known Senator and his wife.

"And I needn't introduce you to Stephen Connelly," Mrs Boyd Cassidy went on."You must have seen his face on television almost as often as you see your own face in the mirror, if you ever watch the box at all."

Sheila, who was unfamiliar with the programmes on RTE, the southern television station, was grateful for the clue.

She recognised Stephen Connelly's name more easily than his face which was much less familiar to her than her hostess assumed.

Tall, dark and smiling, he took Sheila's hand in both of his in a rather American manner, and said, with all the charm which had put him in his present position as host of RTE's most popular chat show,

"And you need no introduction, either, Miss Doherty - or may I say Sheila? I hear about you on all sides. I hope to be able to persuade you to come and talk to me some Friday night."

Since Friday was the night of the Connelly Show, as even Sheila knew, this was, she supposed, an invitation to appear on television with him.

Sheila smiled her cool smile and said "That's very sweet of you, Stephen. Francis Delmara would be the man to talk to about that. He handles all my public life. I'm just a puppet in his hands!"

Stephen Connelly laughed politely. "A very beautiful puppet, if I may say so. Yes, I've already mentioned the possibility to Francis. We must fix a date."

"Come, Sheila," Roisin Boyd Cassidy broke in at this point. "I want you to meet Sean Joyce, over here."

She led Sheila across to a group of rather younger looking men, standing nearby.

The man Mrs. Boyd Cassidy wanted to introduce to her had sandy hair and was of a thin build. He looked, Sheila thought, tough, ready for anything, and somehow faintly out of place in this gathering of the rich and pampered, although his evening clothes were correct enough to pass muster.

To her horror, Sheila realised that Sean Joyce was talking to someone Sheila badly wanted to avoid. Charlie Flanagan. Charlie, who had tried to rape her that New Year's Eve, when she and Mary had gone with the party crowd to the Magic Forest. Charlie, who had always been into drugs in a big way. Had he moved on, now, to a professional connection with these gangsters?

She remembered that she had thought she caught a glimpse of him talking to Mrs. Boyd Cassidy the first time they had met but had hoped she was mistaken.

Now, however, he politely moved off with the other young men as he saw Mrs Boyd Cassidy approaching Sean, obviously wanting to speak to him privately.

By the time the two parties converged, he had disappeared across the room. Sheila didn't think he had seen her or, at least, recognised her. He had probably never known her full name in those days. And tonight, she knew, she looked very different from the scruffy student she had been then.

She remembered that she had seen Sean Joyce before, also talking to Mrs Boyd Cassidy just before Delmara had first introduced her to the famous designer. She remembered that Delmara had pointed him out to her as an ex-IRA activist who, rumour said, had now turned to drug dealing. Sheila had only half believed Delmara at the time.

Phil would have recognised him, too. He was the man she had met in Botanic Gardens, talking to Davy, and later in the flat.

Sean Joyce, when introduced, at first spoke to her formally and politely.

"You come from the Six Counties, Miss Doherty?"

"Please call me Sheila. Yes, I grew up in Belfast."

"I was born in Belfast myself, but it's a while now since I've lived there. But I go up and down there a lot."

There seemed to be some particular meaning to this statement which was spoken with a peculiar emphasis, while his strange, light glittering eyes bored into Sheila looking for a reaction.

"That must be pleasant," she said after a pause.

"Pleasant?" He gave a bark of laughter. "Not the best description. Not really very pleasant for the customs guys. And the PSNI mightn't think it was too pleasant if they saw me." He was speaking mainly to Mrs. Boyd Cassidy now, laughing as if at a private joke, as if Sheila couldn't hear him or would be too dumb to understand. She realised, suddenly, that beneath the social façade, he was very drunk - too drunk to guard his tongue.

Even so, he hadn't let slip anything you could pin down, she thought.

"I've told Sean about your great grandparents," Roisin Boyd Cassidy interposed hastily, in a quiet voice, at this point. "He knows where your loyalties lie. Otherwise he wouldn't speak so freely - would you, Sean?" The last words were spoken with an edge. Sean was being given a not too subtle hint to be more discreet, it seemed. "Things have changed now, haven't they? Sean has had to find other things to do, now the cause has been betrayed again."

Sheila was stricken dumb for a moment.

By the time she had recovered sufficiently to know what to say, her hostess was sweeping her on for more introductions.

Had she just been talking to an ex-IRA activist who had assumed that she was on his side, or had she not? And had there been a hint that his present activities were something criminal or had she got it all wrong?

It was hard to believe, but what other interpretation was there of the words of both Sean Joyce and Mrs Boyd Cassidy?

She shook hands, and smiled, and spoke politely as the introductions continued.

Then her hostess said "Sheila, dear, I want to get out of the crowd for a short while. Come and sit with me in my own little room, and we can talk privately for ten minutes."

She drew Sheila with her, tucking Sheila's arm into her own crooked elbow, and made her way to the far doors.

Chapter 44

Through these doors were a hall, a flight of stairs, and then the room where Roisin Boyd Cassidy had shown Sheila the miniature of her friend Brenda O'Hara whose lover had died so young.

Sheila followed, torn between worry and curiosity.

"That's better," Roisin Boyd Cassidy said, closing the door behind them. "Come and sit here beside me, dear."

She slid down into the big arm chair where she had sat to talk to Sheila before, and motioned Sheila to the little stool by her feet.

Sheila obediently sat, wondering what was coming.

"I want to show you some of my memorabilia of the days when Brenda and I were so close," the old lady began. "I have no-one else I can talk to about her. When you get older, dear, but you wouldn't realise this yet, when you get older, you find that you remember more and more about the days when you were young, and you want to talk about them. But, unfortunately, no-one is really very interested. That's why it's such a pleasure for old friends to get together. They can talk about the things they all remember, things they were all involved in, and everyone is interested, instead of sitting trying not to look bored."

She laughed, a very sweet, young sounding laugh, and Sheila felt again the sympathy she had felt before.

"But I have very few old friends who remember, my dear, and no-one who really knew Brenda as I did. So that's why I really need someone who will be interested in hearing about her - and I think you are that person."

Sheila, who had intended to deny firmly once and for all that there was any connection between herself and Brenda O'Hara, other than a coincidental likeness, found to her dismay that her heart was refusing to let her deal the old lady such a blow. If it comforted her to think that Sheila was the great grand-daughter of her dead friend, what harm could it do?

"Perhaps you would like to pass me the box on the little table over against that wall, dear?" Roisin continued. "It has some things that you might like to see. A ring of Brenda's, a brooch she gave me. Theatre programmes and dance programmes. Things like that."

Sheila got up obediently to fetch the box.

"No, not that one!" called Mrs. Boyd Cassidy, her voice suddenly sharp. "That's something quite different. The box with the red velvet cover."

Sheila, who had begun to lift up a locked wooden box from the back of the low oak table against the far wall, released it as if she had been stung.

After a brief pause, she decided to ignore the sharpness in her hostess's voice.

Instead, she lifted the red velvet box from its place beside the other. Her momentary sympathy for the old lady had been eroded a little, but enough remained.

"Look, I really think you're making a mistake -" she began.

Just at that moment, there was a knock on the door and a voice called, "Roisin! The ambassador has arrived after all. The car is just pulling up outside. You'd better come down quickly if you want to be there to welcome him. He'll be mortally offended if you're not. You know what he's like."

Roisin Boyd Cassidy hesitated for a moment, then she stood up.

"I'd better go down," she said to Sheila, "but stay here, for me, my dear. I'll be back in a few minutes. If you'd like to look at the things in the box while you're waiting, the key is in my desk over there."

She waved vaguely in the direction of a large formidably solid and business-like desk at the other end of the room, then hurried out, shutting the door behind her.

Sheila, who would quite have liked to go with her and meet the ambassador of wherever it was, was half annoyed and half amused by this autocratic disposal of herself and her time.

She had no desire to waste the party by hanging around in this room by herself.

However, she supposed that, in decency, she would have to allow the old lady five or ten minutes to return before going back downstairs.

It might be interesting, something to pass the time at any rate, to look at the contents of the red velvet box.

Sheila went over to the desk indicated by Mrs Boyd Cassidy and found a bunch of keys in the top drawer.

Taking them over to the low oak table where the two boxes were placed, together with a number of miscellaneous objects, she began looking for the right key.

Several minutes later, when key after key yielded no results, she began to feel frustrated. Finally, her patience ran out.

She thought, "This is ridiculous. I'll wait until she comes back or go if she takes much longer. This is probably the wrong bunch of keys."

Then, more from motives of boredom and idle curiosity than anything else, she thought "I wonder if any of these keys fits this other box? And I wonder what can be in it which is so secret and important?"

At the back of her mind a faint suspicion was stirring, the beginnings of an idea that perhaps the wooden box held secrets which should be revealed.

Lifting the bunch of keys which she had dropped unto the table in disgust, she began to try them again but this time on the wooden box.

To her surprise and slight apprehension, she found the right key almost immediately.

There was a satisfying click and the lid was open.

Sheila hesitated.

This was none of her business.

She was poking into her hostess's private affairs without excuse.

Probably she should stop it right now.

But, on the other hand, suppose the things Terry O'Hanlon had been saying were true? Suppose Mrs Boyd Cassidy knew about at least some of the drug dealers' plans?

The presence of Sean Joyce tonight seemed to suggest that O'Hanlon was right, if Sheila had interpreted that conversation correctly.

If there was even a remote possibility that the box contained valuable information, then didn't she have a duty to open it?

If she was going to do it, then the sooner the better, before her hostess came back and found her.

Sheila hesitated no longer. With a hand which shook slightly, she raised the lid.

The box was full of papers. She lifted some out, trying to be careful not to disarrange anything too obviously. To her dismay, they were in some sort of code. She shuffled through them but could see nothing which made any sense to her.

Then, almost at the bottom of the box, she noticed a half sheet of paper with a few scribbled lines on it which she could understand.

"*Roisin*" the note said

Sean's found us a new safe house. We're using it to store stuff in transmission. The boys can go there any time, but tell them not to over use it or someone will catch on. The address, in case you've forgotten, is 3a Thomas Street.

The plans are underway for dealing with Knight's supermarkets Jan. 21.

I'll be in touch when things are finalised.

Burn this when you've memorised it.

O'Brien.

Sheila stared at it. It seemed to be something which supported her suspicions. Was the Sean mentioned the man she had just met downstairs? The notorious drug dealer?

The address of a 'safe house'.

That must be connected with criminal activity surely.

Sheila hadn't really believed until now that that sweet old lady, with her sad memories of the past, could actually be involved in crime, in drug dealing and worse, but here was something which she thought must put it beyond all doubt.

What should she do?

But was this letter really evidence of much?

She had no idea where Thomas Street might be, whether in Belfast or some other town in the north, or even on the southern side of the Border.

As information, it seemed rather useless.

Was it her duty to report it to the Gardai?

Would it be any use to them?

Suddenly panic gripped her.

If this box really held secret criminal information, she mustn't be found poking in it.

Hurriedly she replaced the papers, shut down the lid, turned the key.

Then, moving quickly but as quietly as possible, she went back to the desk and shut the keys safely into the top drawer.

When Roisin Boyd Cassidy returned a few minutes later, Sheila was drooping sleepily on the footstool by the big armchair, looking patient, bored and innocent.

Chapter 45

Delmara Fashions went to New York in November.

Sheila had been looking forward to this since Francis had first mentioned the possibility. She had never been to America before.

The excitement crowded out all other thoughts.

The letter from Sean to Mrs Boyd Cassidy dropped silently from the surface of her mind to the unseen depths.

If she remembered it at all, it was to argue that such vague information could only be useless.

Books and films had prepared her for an arrival in New York by sea, with the famous skyline of Manhattan appearing in the distance, followed by a close-up view of the Statue of Liberty.

Flying in to Kennedy International Airport was, she discovered, a very different matter.

For one thing, they arrived in the middle of the night, and although for the first half hour adrenalin, pumped by excitement, kept Sheila alert, she found that in the end the late hours, the bustle, and the well-known jet-lag all caught up with her, and it was almost necessary to lean on desks and chairs for support.

One airport is very much like any other. It was only when safely relaxing in a taxi which hooted and crawled its way through traffic which still seemed heavy even at this time of night – three o'clock by now, Sheila noted, glancing at her watch – only then that the feeling of being in New York really hit Sheila and suddenly lifted her spirits.

The flashing neon lights, the tall buildings which made the sky seem so far away and hard to see, the noise – all combined to produce an atmosphere which spoke of life, excitement, important things happening. Sheila found herself sitting up and gazing out eagerly, hoping to identify famous landmarks.

"There's the Empire State building," said Francis helpfully. He was watching her in some amusement, enjoying the naivety of her response. "The very tall one. You can see it over the other buildings. Look."

Sheila looked, and identified what had once been the tallest building in New York – or was it in the world? - before the building of the Twin Towers. And now they were gone again, did that make it the tallest once more? She gazed around and Francis continued to point out landmarks at intervals.

"There's Bloomfields. I hope they're going to be a big client of Delmara Fashions...... That's Broadway...... We're about to pass Central Park..... And this is the Hilton," he concluded. "Where in future years they will be putting up a plaque to say, 'Sheila Doherty slept here on her first visit to New York, November 2006.'"

Sheila laughed.

The taxi - or she supposed she should call it a cab, over here – stopped. Yes, they were at the Hilton. A very tall, impressive looking building, with a luxurious lobby, thickly carpeted and gleaming with glass and polished metal.

"We have a press conference scheduled for eleven tomorrow morning," Francis told Sheila as they shot upwards in the elevator. "Get a good sleep now. I want you looking your best. Just make sure you wake up in time - remember your body clock will be working hard to confuse you. Actually, you're more likely to wake up too early. New York is five hours behind Ireland. Have you changed your watch? Well, do it now, before you forget."

"I slept on the plane," Sheila reminded him. "In a way, I feel partly as if I'd had my night's sleep already and partly as if I'd missed a night. But I'm so tired now, I'll certainly sleep."

"Ask for an alarm call," Francis advised her. "We can't afford to miss this press conference. Publicity is crucial, beautiful."

As always when discussing business, Francis sounded concise and efficient, very different from his usual persona. As a rule this made Sheila laugh inside, but tonight she was too tired for more than a weak private grin.

The room, with its en suite bathroom, was to Sheila's eyes the height of luxury. Furnished in a peaches and cream colour scheme, with thick carpet, rugs, colour television and a mini fridge stocked with a range of little bottles, it made Sheila feel rich and pampered. She sank down on the enormous soft bed, then bounced up again. A bath, to get rid of the hot, sticky effect of her long journey would be both useful and pleasurable.

The bathroom, with cream coloured fittings and cream towels and bathrobe provided, was a match in luxury for the rest. There was even a telephone extension on a little table within arm's reach of the bath and the loo.

Pouring in enough liquid bath foam to provide a host of bubbles, Sheila lay back and luxuriated. In fact, she had almost drifted off to sleep when the telephone's gentle buzz by her ear brought her back to herself.

It was Francis.

"I almost forgot to mention, beautiful. Look out for Harrington Smith tomorrow. From the New York News. He's a real hell hound when it comes to digging out the dirt. Let me do the talking and keep your beautiful mouth shut, right?"

"There isn't any dirt for him to dig," Sheila said indignantly.

"You'd be surprised! These boys will invent it if they can't find it," Francis said. "But don't worry, they'll have enough of a story without that just at first. Beautiful Irish model, etc. Just so long as nothing you say sets them off on another tack. So the best way is to say as little as possible, got it?"

"Okay, Francis." Sheila was not pleased but the habit of agreement with Delmara was strong. And if he was right, it would be bad to start some speculation in this Harrington Smith's mind and have him make up a story about some non-existent scandal.

"Chrissie will call in about ten to make sure you're looking right," Francis said, although that had already been arranged. "And you'll wear the green micro skirt, okay?"

"Yes, you told me."

"Goodnight, beautiful, sweet dreams."

Chapter 46

Francis must be more nervous than she had realised, Sheila thought, steeping out of the shower next morning and drying herself in a leisurely fashion. It wasn't like him to repeat instructions.

Harrington Smith, who Sheila had imagined as big and burly, turned out to be a slight, innocent looking young man with large brown eyes and long fluttering lashes. He had fair, curly hair which he wore fashionably short and an eager, friendly manner of questioning.

Sheila felt that if Delmara had not warned her, she would have answered all his questions trustingly and possibly given him material to twist.

As it was, she said very little and allowed Delmara to give most of the answers.

The press conference took place in one of the hotel function rooms hired by Delmara for the purpose.

Sheila derived some quiet amusement from the duel of wits which took place between Francis Delmara and the journalists.

Delmara was determined to keep the focus of interest as much as possible on Delmara Fashions, while playing up Sheila's beauty and popularity as a means of attracting more publicity for his creations, while the journalists' aim was to provide a lively story about Sheila's personal life.

Many of the questions dealt with the now famous picture of Sheila by Sebastian O'Rourke, others with her relationship with Pat Fitzwilliam.

"Is it true that O'Rourke wanted to paint you in the nude?"asked Harrington Smith.

"No," said Sheila briefly, wondering how he could possibly know that the subject had even been raised.

"Tell us about Pat Fitzwilliam. Is it true that you and he spent a weekend together in a single room cottage in the Wicklow Hills?"

"No," said Sheila again. "Pat is a good friend of mine - nothing else."

Francis coughed warningly and began to talk about Delmara Fashions.

"You see, gentlemen, that Sheila Doherty is wearing one of our most attractive micro skirts - the newest of the new in looks. After the mini, the micro."

"What next - the belt?" sang out someone from the back of the crowd amid laughter.

A number of cameras clicked and Sheila automatically took up a suitable pose. She had had some experience by now of posing for the press, but these Americans were louder and pushier than their Irish or English equivalent.

"Show us your legs, Sheila!" seemed to be the universal cry.

Sheila was beginning to feel angry.

She raised her chin and stared straight at the photographers without any attempt at a smile, her green eyes flashing.

For some reason, this seemed to have an effect. A note of respect crept back into the comments.

But Sheila felt relieved when it was all over.

"Francis, I don't want any more of that sort of thing," she said firmly when the press had gone. "I don't see that it will help your public image either if the present attitude to your models is to assume that I'm a tart!"

"Americans are like that, beautiful," Delmara said, shrugging. "I think you got much more respectful treatment than most people, up to and including the Royal Family."

Sheila frowned, not convinced. "Wearing the micro skirt was a mistake," she said. "If I hadn't been showing my legs, they would have had less excuse."

Delmara laughed. "But such lovely legs, darling! It would be a crime not to show them."

Sheila laughed too, but reluctantly. She was not looking forward to reading what the press had to say about her.

But when it came, it was a pleasant surprise.

Beautiful Sheila, the latest Irish Explosion!

and

Top of the morning to the top of models!

were typical of the headlines in most papers, above large pictures of Sheila which mainly featured her long, slim legs.

Only the New York News took a different line. Under Harrington Smith's by-line was a photo which focussed on Sheila's face, side by side with a reproduction of O'Rourke's picture of her, and the headline read,

Ice Maiden knocks them cold!

The story presented Sheila as beautiful but out of reach, an object of desire who was herself distant and untouchable.

It was the way Sebastian O'Rourke had painted her and Harrington Smith must have based his approach on this. The text spoke of the broken hearts littering Sheila's path, featuring O'Rourke and Pat Fitzwilliam in particular, while hinting at many more.

Sheila was not sure whether to be pleased or angry but Delmara was delighted.

"Image, Sheila. Publicity is all image. The public will see you as distant, unapproachable, desirable. So they will think of Delmara fashions in the same way and they'll flock to buy them. Just wait and see.

Chapter 47

The first show, on the following night, proved the truth of his words. The hired function room at the Hilton was crowded, and by the rich and fashionable people whom Delmara needed as his clients.

The show was a resounding success.

Delmara was particularly pleased that he had been approached by several of the most upmarket stores who wanted him to supply them with his exclusive range. One store in particular, Dixie's, wanted him to let them carry not only his originals but also a more middle market range of similar styles.

"I'll need to give it some thought," he told Sheila. "The attraction for the rich who are my normal clients is in the individuality of my designs. They don't want to see an off-the-peg copy for sale. But a new range with the same style but not exactly the same designs - I think it might work. I'll think about it."

He had also, to his satisfaction, sold quite a number of frocks and outfits on the first night, mostly to the sort of clients he wanted.

These people would wear his clothes to fashionable venues where the Top Four Hundred, and the newer arrivals whose celebrity status gave them the entrée, met and partied.

Delmara Fashions would become even better known as a result.

"It's all a matter of getting your name known," Delmara said to Sheila as they drove in his hired car through Central Park. "Once people have heard of you, the battle's nearly won. All you have to do then is come up to their expectations. That's the easy part!"

It was a crisp winter day with a hint of snow in the air, and already the shops were full of Christmas. In spite of the snow, there was enough warmth in the air for Francis to have put the hood down and the fresh breeze blew pleasantly round their faces, sending Sheila's red gold curls, caught back in a silk scarf, fluttering in all directions.

Central Park looked like fairyland. On all sides the trees were decorated with snow. It made Sheila feel excited and expectant and perhaps that was why she smiled at Delmara so warmly.

Whatever the reason, it was a mistake.

Delmara pulled the car up abruptly under a fir tree and ran one hand with its long delicate fingers through the black hair which was falling forward over his face.

"We'll stay here for another month," Delmara said. "That will give me a chance to get really established with the people who matter. Then we'll go home, and you can take the rest of December and early January off. You've been working for me for over a year now, time for a little break, don't you think?"

"I'll be able to spend Christmas with my family," Sheila said with satisfaction. "Good. Thanks, Francis."

"Then, in January," Delmara went on, "I want to make a big impact on the local scene. With Dublin, Paris and New York on our track record, the local customers will come running. There's nothing impresses the Irish like a success somewhere else."

Sheila smiled. She knew this was true.

"I've had shows before in Belfast," Delmara went on, "but on a fairly small scale. Two years ago, when I was starting out. Now we're moving into the big time. I want to take somewhere really flashy in the centre of the city and give it maximum publicity. I'll aim to have all the media folks there and as many of the wealthy and well known as possible. They'll come out of curiosity. I'll get the Telegraph to do a main feature a week before the show, emphasising the success in Dublin and New York, with lots of photos of you and the clothes. That, and the offer of free food and drink will bring most of them. The rest - well, I have a few contacts. I'll work them for all they're worth."

"Where are you thinking of booking?" asked Sheila. "There aren't too many possibilities."

"No," agreed Delmara. "There's the King's Hall, of course. But I don't think it has exactly the right ambiance. No, on the whole, I think there's probably only one really suitable place. I just hope we can get it. The Magnifico. And sometime near the end of January, I think. Perhaps the 21st."

He sounded vague, as if his mind was wandering to other things. Sheila looked at him in surprise. Why was he getting so side-tracked? He was really quite a sweet person, she thought. She'd always liked him. She smiled encouragingly, meaning only to show friendliness.

"Sheila," he said suddenly, turning to look at her. "Hell, you're beautiful."

He leant over to her, put his arms round her and began to kiss her.

As always when Francis kissed her, Sheila experienced a floating sensation, and only wanted it to go on.

But this time something dragged her back sharply to reality almost at once.

She pulled back.

"Francis," she said.

"Hmm?"

"Francis, listen! We can't do this. How can we have a business relationship that works, if we're - well, lovers? It wouldn't work, Francis. You know that!"

Francis still looked miles away.

Then suddenly he laughed.

He snapped back to his Delmara persona.

"Sheila, you are so right! You shouldn't be so beautiful, darling. Good for business, of course - but a man can't always have a cool business head!"

Sheila smiled gratefully but not quite so invitingly as before.

"It's worked for us up to now. Let's just forget the last ten minutes, shall we?" she suggested.

"Easier said than done," smiled Delmara ruefully. "But certainly wise. Okay, it didn't happen. If you had wanted it, I think we could have worked something out. But clearly you don't. All for the best, I daresay."

He gazed out through the windscreen for a few moments. Then he looked back, laughed, sat up, and said "At least this time I didn't end up soaking wet." He opened the car door, stepped out and lit a cigarette, looking up at the braches of the tree above them.

With a soft sigh, the branch trembled and, with an inappropriate grace, bent slightly in the warm breeze and slid its considerable load of snow gently down onto Delmara's upturned face.

Chapter 48

The shot rang out, cutting through the still, frosty December air.

O'Brien lowered his revolver and walked over to inspect the target.

Right in the gold.

His hard, impassive face showed no particular pleasure. He removed the half smoked cigar from his mouth and examined its tip before tapping the ash carefully into the ashtray set at waist height on a beautifully engraved brass stand by his side.

Behind O'Brien stood his white, charmingly proportioned Georgian house, incongruously civilised, set in perfect perspective and situated far enough away from the city to allow him the maximum of privacy. Before him, the immaculate grounds, expensively planned by the leading garden designers of the day and kept in order by more gardeners than were employed at Hillsborough Castle, were stretched out on every side. Tall beech trees, now seeming to grow taller and more stark with the fluttering release of the last of the brown and golden leaves of autumn, lined the cultivated lawns and gardens. Beyond the trees stretched the wilder but still beautiful grounds, where bluebells and violets blossomed in spring, fungi and chestnuts appeared in profusion in autumn, a mass of broadleaved trees grew like a forest throughout the year; and in the distance could be seen the watery, silvery gleam of the lake.

"So, you see, Danny boy", O'Brien said softly, "if it turns out to be necessary, it wouldn't be too hard for me to put a bullet through you, would it, Danny boy? Right in the gold, just wherever I picked on. Just like that."

He prodded his companion lightly in the groin.

Danny, a smaller, younger man, skinny but strong looking, emitted an unintentional yelp. He stuttered "Yes, Mr O'Brien! I mean, right you are, Mr O'Brien. No way it's going to come to that, Mr O'Brien."

"So you're in, Danny? Good boy." O'Brien smiled and for a moment looked even more frightening in Danny's eyes than when his face was impassive.

"There'll be five of us altogether, but two of them'll only be doing the driving. You'll get a bigger cut, you and Charlie. Plenty for all of us, mind you. We're talking big money here, Danny boy, *big* money."

He strode back to the line and sent another shower of bullets into the target. Danny, who hadn't removed himself hastily enough, yelped again as he felt one bullet whistle by only a few inches from his cheek. He dodged aside and tripped against the brass ash stand, almost knocking it over.

O'Brien laughed.

A smoothly dressed man in late middle age appeared from the house and crossed the beautifully tailored lawn, carrying a tray of drinks. Reaching O'Brien's side, he bowed his head slightly and offered O'Brien a glass already containing a tawny coloured drink which Danny knew would be O'Brien's favourite undiluted single malt whisky, murmuring "Sir," as he did so.

O'Brien took the drink, immediately swallowing half of it, and the servant, setting the tray of drinks gently down on a white painted iron table nearby, disappeared into the house as unobtrusively as he had come.

Danny ventured to ask "But, Mr O'Brien, don't the drugs bring us in more than enough to do well on? I've never done anything like this before, Mr O'Brien, tell you the truth, I'm not much good with guns, never really used them -"

O'Brien looked at him, saying nothing.

"And what about Mrs Magic?" Danny burbled on. "Her down in Dublin, I mean? The Celtic Tigress? Won't she be mad if you start pulling something different, something that she's not in on, like?"

He caught the expression in O'Brien's eye and decided abruptly to stop talking.

O'Brien looked at him some more. Then he decided to smile.

"The revenues from the drugs are good, Danny," he said softly. "But what's wrong with a bit extra? And you'll be fine. Just as long as you do what you're told, see? And don't worry about the Celtic Tigress not being in on it. When was she ever not in on something?"

Danny nodded miserably. As far as he could see, he didn't have a choice. No way was he going to say no to O'Brien. O'Brien, even if he didn't have him shot, would shop him to the police for his involvement with the drug pushing without a second's hesitation if he didn't fall into line.

He nodded again even more miserably.

O'Brien watched him narrowly, then shrugged.

"Okay. Now, have you got it clear? I've picked on 21st January as D Day. I happen to know they'll both be going to a fashion show, so they'll be right out in public with no bodyguards round them. They'll be expecting nothing. That'll be our chance, if we take it properly, see?"

"Fashion show?" Danny asked in surprise.

"Yes. Top of the range, I'm told. Some new super model who's getting all the headlines. Sheila Doherty. She'll be grabbing all the attention. No-one'll be expecting us to turn up. Until it's too late." He smiled his unnerving smile again.

"That'll be our moment, Danny boy. 21st January. The Magnifico Hotel. And then a life of luxury for us all, Danny boy. Provided I don't have to shoot you first!"

Danny, his eyes popping out of his head, dimly realised that this was a joke, one that O'Brien probably thought very funny.

But, looking ahead with terror to 21st January, Danny felt quite unable to laugh

Chapter 49

It was all very well, Phil thought, for Davy to tell her to keep away from the flat, but where else were they to go to be private?

For a few weeks, they tried to meet elsewhere but it didn't work. Gradually they drifted back to the old habits and Phil began to stay overnight again on a regular basis.

As she lay in Davy's arms in the narrow bed, she felt a confused something which was not quite happiness and which lay like a thick insulating layer over the deeper feelings of guilt and anxiety which she could not wholly push away. Responsibility gnawed at her.

From time to time, she could not help picking up indications of some of Davy's activities. Snatches of telephone conversations accidentally overheard, letters occasionally left about so that she had read a sentence or two before stopping quickly, the clear signs of the presence of strangers in the flat at times when she was elsewhere. As autumn turned to winter and the months passed, these and other things scattered over the surface of her life, like fallen leaves floating singly on the quiet river waters, kept reminding Phil that beneath that smooth surface all was not well. She and Davy had entered a more tranquil, settled stage of their relationship and from that came happiness. But Phil could not continually succeed in shutting out her knowledge and with it her responsibility to act in some way to change the course of events.

Early in December, Davy disappeared, intending to be away for several weeks. He told Phil only that he had to go away for a short time. She could only guess where he had gone and her imagination presented her with pictures of tough criminal drug runners, of the police of other countries on Davy's trail, of Davy being dragged from some plane with contraband drugs discovered in his suitcase and thrown into some foreign jail to be gnawed by rats and shut up for life, or taken out just to be shot.

It was during this absence of Davy's that Phil made a discovery which forced her for the first time to face up to the dilemma of her unwanted knowledge.

She was working in the Library one evening, researching for her MA, looking up books, making notes, checking references. It had been a long day. The trek home by two cross town buses was unappealing. Davy was not at the flat but, nevertheless, Phil decided on the spur of the moment to go there rather than home to her parents' house. It was near, it was warm and she could buy some food, make herself a snack meal and continue to work there after the Library had closed.

She called in for some chicken fried rice at the nearby Chinese takeaway, then headed for Thomas Street.

She had retained her key in spite of Davy's original intention of keeping her away and when she reached the ground floor entrance to the flat she fished in her pocket and produced it.

As was often the case, the street door, used by all the tenants, was open. Phil went quietly up the carpeted flight of stairs, hoping not to disturb the other people in the house. She had never met any of them and did not particularly wish to. They kept themselves to themselves and this suited both Phil and Davy well.

On the landing outside the door to Davy's flat, she paused, key in hand.

It was strange to be going in, knowing that Davy would not be there, either now or later. Phil had entered the flat by herself many times but always in the expectation that Davy would arrive shortly. She shrugged her shoulders, unlocked the door, and went in.

The flat was empty but Phil, wrinkling her nose, smelt cigarette smoke. Surely fresh cigarette smoke, not dating from the last time she and Davy had been there, over a week ago.

It was nothing new to realise that someone else had been there in her absence, but somehow it was more creepy knowing that Davy was away. Phil, half inclined to give up all idea of staying and to go home, put the container with her chicken fried rice down on the worktop in the kitchen and looked round.

Then her native courage took over again and she laughed at herself. What was there to be afraid of? There was no-one here now.

She made herself a cup of coffee and curled up on the living room sofa to eat her Chinese while she continued reading Bleak House. Chasing the last remnants of rice with her fork, she paused to glance at her watch and realised in surprise that it was after midnight.

Tidying away carefully after herself, she gathered up book and bag and went into the bedroom. Twenty minutes later, she was asleep in the narrow bed she had so often shared with Davy. As she snuggled down and switched off the bedside light, her last waking thought was that it was somehow comforting to sleep here where Davy slept.

Much later, she jerked awake with a start and a pounding heart. Someone was moving about in the front room of the flat.

Phil lay very still, the bed-clothes clutched round her, listening.

Yes, she had not imagined it. There was someone there. In fact, at least two people, for she could hear voices.

Phil found that the instinctive courage which had made her laugh at her earlier alarms seemed to have evaporated. She had to speak severely to herself to quell the panic which threatened to take over.

Whoever was there, they could not intend harm to her. She was Davy's girlfriend, they were presumably Davy's friends. There was nothing to worry about.

But in spite of these bold arguments, Phil continued to worry.

What was the best thing to do?

In the end, common sense, if that was what it was, took control. She didn't want to stay and meet these people whoever they were. So why not leave quietly before they realised she was there?

Phil dressed hurriedly and silently. It was easy enough. She had slept in shirt and pants. All she had to do was pull on her jeans, shoes and sweater, and wriggle into her jacket.

She stuffed her book into her bag, opened the bedroom door cautiously and stepped out.

A light came along the passage from the front room. She would have to pass the door to reach the flat entrance. It was partly closed but Phil discovered a reluctance in herself to move towards it. If she was heard trying to get away, would the two people - two men, she supposed - think she was a spy or an informer?

It would be better to be discovered sleeping innocently than to be caught like that.

For a moment she considered creeping back to the bedroom. Then she rejected the idea. If she could get away, she intended to do so.

The voices which had woken her were much clearer now. The passageway where she was standing had doors leading to the front room, the bedroom and the bathroom. At the opposite end to the living room, behind Phil, it led to the kitchen. As she stood debating her next move, she realised that she could hear clearly what the two intruders were saying. She also realised with an illogical shock of surprise that one of the voices was female.

"Danny," said the female voice, "Give us a fag, will you?" A pause, then, "Thanks. Listen, are you sure you've got all the details clear?"

"Oh, I'm stupid, now, am I?" responded the unseen Danny.

"Don't be so touchy. I just think it would do no harm to run over it again. You know we can't afford to put any orders in writing."

"Well, Maire, you go ahead then and tell me all over again." Danny didn't seem to have lost his grouch, but Maire, ignoring his attitude, went straight ahead.

"Maybe I'd better, then. I won't be there at the time to help you, you know. I'm not a part of this gig. The date is January 21. The place is the Magnifico. The time is nine forty-five. Okay so far?"

"Okay so far, mastermind."

"Willie and Con are the drivers. No need to go into that. You'll be going in with the boss and Charlie. When you've made the snatch, you get out quick and then away like the hammers and up the Falls in the cars. Do as the Boss tells you and I don't see where you can go wrong. But if everything gets mucked up and you have to split up and make a run for it, don't be coming back here, now. You'll need to get as far away as possible. You know two or three places where you'll be okay, right?"

"Right," Danny grunted.

"Got it?"

"Of course I've got it!" Danny's irritation at the unnecessary repetition of his orders became even more evident.

Maire, however, continued imperturbably. "Well, I hope you have. The boss is trusting you with a big job. If you do okay there'll maybe be something even better next time."

"Next time? I thought this was a one-off?"

Danny sounded alarmed. Phil heard Maire laugh.

"Poor little Danny, scared are you? Come here and maybe I'll give you something to cheer you up."

There was the noise of Danny moving across the room, then what seemed to be the sounds of the preliminaries to lovemaking, kisses and scuffles.

Phil was clear almost at once what she had heard. She stood rooted to the spot and found that although panic was lurking somewhere at the back of her mind, ready to pounce if given half a chance, her surface self was suddenly icy calm.

It was no longer a question of being found innocently asleep or risking being caught as she attempted to slip out of the front door. These were serious criminals planning the details of a city centre kidnapping, it seemed. If they knew she was there, they were unlikely to be pleasant and trusting.

The kitchen, she remembered, her brain working busily, had a fire escape outside the door which Davy used for carting rubbish down to the bin in the backyard. It seemed to Phil to be her best bet.

Silently, thanking heaven that the flat was fully carpeted, she moved along the passage and pushed open the kitchen door. Earlier in the evening she had left it ajar, something else to be thankful for.

Using the utmost caution, Phil slipped into the kitchen and drew the door quietly shut behind her. She held the handle until she was sure the snib had fitted into place, then released it slowly and carefully. There was no question of turning on the light. Phil groped her way across the room, finding her way by the gleam of moonlight filtering through the two windows. The door to the fire escape had a lock and Phil had never acquired its key, but she saw now with relief that it was, as she had half remembered and half hoped, a Yale lock, so that she would be able to open it from the inside. She eased it open with equal care and a moment later was standing at the top of the fire escape, breathing the cold night air with immense thankfulness and with a pounding heart.

The episode was not over yet. She had still to get safely down without making enough noise to disturb the two intruders and then make her way out of the yard. Beyond that, she need not think for the moment.

At last it was done. The back yard door, like the kitchen door which led to the fire escape, was protected by a Yale lock and, in its case, by the addition of a sturdy bolt. Both good protection against attempts to enter but neither presenting any problem, except the dangers of noise, to someone whose only desire was to get out and away.

Phil turned the lock carefully, and eased open the bolt.

She pulled the door shut behind her, took to her heels and put several streets between herself and the flat.

Only then did she pause to take breath, and to consider for the first time the new problem which now presented itself to her. Where was she going to spend the rest of the night?

It was mid December, and cold. Her own home was a long walk away. Belfast streets, at this time of night, were not the best place to walk alone. More, what on earth would her parents say if she arrived at this time of night? The last problem was the least important. She had her own key, Kevin and Annie would be long since in bed and fast asleep, she would be able to slip in unheard. In the morning, there would be nothing to reveal at what time she had arrived home.

The long walk was not a major problem either. Phil was young and fit, and quite capable of walking a good deal further if necessary. Besides, the exercise would keep her warm.

The real problem was that Phil didn't want to walk through Belfast alone at night. It took her only a few minutes, however, to make the decision.

There was no help for it. She was going to have to walk home because she had no-where else to spend the night. It wasn't something she would have done by choice but, as things were, it was clear that she didn't actually have a choice.

Wasting no further time, Phil began to move, keeping up a steady pace.

Much to her relief, her journey was undisturbed apart from one incident when she had already been walking for half-an-hour when a large grey cat suddenly jumped up from almost under her feet as she rounded a corner, making her bite her tongue in shock.

She reached home in the small hours, beating the milkman, and gained her room without waking anyone.

Sliding thankfully between the bed covers, sure that she was safe again, she was able to think for the first time since her own danger had swamped every other consideration,

"What am I to do now? How can I let this go on? But how can I tell without involving Davy?"

It was the gun business all over again, but so much more serious.

Her thoughts churned round and she lay, tense and sleepless, until the light of morning began finally to creep in through the window.

Chapter 50

Each night, Phil lay awake fretting herself into a fever, unable to eat or to rest by day.

In the end, after many days of this, she succumbed in her weakened state to a virus. She was confined to bed with a serious attack of flu.

Christmas came and went and still Phil lay in bed, tossing and turning. Her parents and her doctor grew more worried as she showed no signs of recovery. Day by day she grew paler and thinner.

Annie Maguire sat on the edge of her daughter's bed and held her hand.

"Phil, dear, you must try to eat something. Please, dear. You can't go on like this."

Phil turned her large, listless eyes towards her mother. For the first time for days she became aware of the presence of someone who was not just a figment of her own mind. Her mother looked desperately worried.

A sudden feeling of compunction seized Phil.

"Oh, mammy, I'm sorry. I didn't mean to worry you."

Easy tears came to her eyes.

Annie leaned over and brushed her daughter's tears away.

"Well, you have done," she said gently, doing her best to look more cheerful. It was the first sign of recovery Phil had shown. "Daddy and I love you very much. We need you to get better."

"I will try," Phil promised weakly.

"I'm going to bring you some good home made soup," Annie said. "If you could manage even a bit, it would help you."

Phil obediently took some of the soup, Annie spooning it to her as if she were an infant.

Then she slept.

The hot flush of the fever seemed to have receded.

To her mother's eye, Phil looked a little better and she was thankful.

It was several more days before Phil was ready to leave her bed for a few hours in the afternoon. January was already a week old before she was able to think clearly again.

"What date is it, mammy?" she asked Annie on her second day out of bed.

"January the twelfth," Annie told her.

Suddenly everything came back to Phil with a sickening rush.

She said nothing but a clear intention to act in some way took possession of her.

There was so little time left. Just over a week.

She must get her strength back and then make some sort of plan

It was the next day that Kathy Doherty came in to see Annie in the evening while Phil sat with her mother watching television.

Kathy and Annie had reached a stage of friendship by now which included occasional calls when there was something important in the way of news to share.

"It's a pity you've been sick the whole time Sheila's been here, Phil,' said Kathy when she was comfortably seated with a cup of tea and Annie had turned off the television. "She was saying she'd have liked to have a chat with you. Now she's back to work again, getting ready for this new show. Mr. Delmara likes her to be on the spot when there's something big coming up. She has this wee flat now near his showroom where he can call her in any time for fittings. Makes her work evenings as well as days, she tells me. But there, the money's good, so it's well worth it."

"What's the new show, Mrs. Maguire?" asked Phil languidly.

"It's supposed to be the Delmara Spring Fashions," replied Kathy eagerly. "Bit early in the year for that, I would have thought but it seems that's how they do it." Proud of her daughter's success, Kathy was only too ready to talk about it and indeed had come in for no other reason."It's to be held in the Magnifico Hotel and there's all sorts of famous people expected to turn up, Sheila tells me. On the twenty-first of January."

Phil's heart leapt into her mouth. There was a dull ache in the pit of her stomach.

"And Sheila is going to be there?" she managed to ask presently.

"Oh, she'll be the star of the show!" Kathy laughed. "I'd love to see her but it wouldn't really do. I'd never fit in with all the glamour."

"Nonsense, Mrs. Doherty," protested Annie Maguire, flourishing the teapot hospitably. "I'm sure if Sheila thought you'd like to be there she'd get you a ticket. More tea, Mrs. Doherty?"

"Well, maybe just a drop."

The rest of the conversation flowed over Phil's head. She sat numbly, feeling slightly sick.

There was no longer any question. She must pass on a warning, for Sheila's sake, if for no-one else.

On the following day, she told Annie that she thought a bit of fresh air would do her good. She would just walk down to the shops and back.

Annie agreed.

Phil made her way instead to the nearest telephone box.

There was a confidential number for giving anonymous information. She tried it first.

But things were not to be so easy.

There was no answer to be had on the confidential line. Time after time Phil pressed redial, only to get an engaged signal.

Her legs were beginning to give way. She knew she couldn't stand in the box for much longer.

In desperation she tried the local police station.

"Hello," she began, "I want to report a threatened kidnapping at the Magnifico - "

"Name, please," said a brisk voice at the other end.

"I don't want to give my name - "

"Name, please. We need your name for the record, madam. It can be kept private, probably.'

"This kidnapping - it will be on January 21."

"I need your name, madam, if I'm to take this seriously. There are too many hoax warnings, you know. Why don't you just give me your name and we'll go on from there? And what about a password to show you're genuine?"

Phil replaced the receiver with a trembling hand. Surely they would act on the information she had given them.

But she knew that the constant stream of hoax warnings, a habit built up during the Troubles, were against her. They would likely put this down as another one.

It was hopeless.

And indeed, at the local station the desk sergeant was replacing the receiver with a shrug. Another hoax, he thought. He would pass on the gist of the warning to his superiors and they could do what they wanted with it. The Magnifico. And had she mentioned a date? He thought perhaps she had but he hadn't caught it properly. There was always a lot of security at the Magnifico, anyway.

Phil made her way home with some difficulty and went straight back to bed.

Annie, worried that she was trying to do too much too soon, kept her to the house for the next few days.

By the time Phil was allowed to venture out again, it was the twenty first.

She walked along the road aimlessly. Where should she go? The Magnifico?

She shuddered away from the thought.

Instead, she took a taxi to Davy's flat.

Still weak and shaky from her long bout of 'flu, she was very tired by the time she reached Thomas Street.

She was cold, too.

She expected to have the flat to herself. A card, kept for her by her mother until she was well enough to read it, had arrived at Christmas. It said only,

'Held up for longer than expected. Don't expect me before the end of next month. Love, D.'

She remembered the warning words of the woman Maire to Danny. They were to get as far away as they could as soon as they could. They were not to go back to the flat. So no-one would be there.

She climbed the stairs wearily and let herself in.

It seemed a lifetime since she had been here, just before Christmas, and had overheard the conversation between the gangsters.

Maire and Danny.

She remembered crouching, frozen with fear, in the passage outside the kitchen, listening to their voices.

Like an old video, the sequence re-ran itself in her head. She saw herself as if in a dream and wondered if the whole thing had been a nightmare or a hallucination. Had there been any kidnapping at all?

It seemed even longer ago, an eternity, since she had seen Davy.

He had disappeared back in early December.

Still she did not know where he was or when he would come back.

Or if he would come back.

Confidential business, he had said. Can't tell you anything. Better not knowing.

Yes, perhaps, but Phil thought she would have felt happier if she at least knew where he was. If she knew when she would see him again.

Sorting out some problem with the drug pipeline, she guessed. Further afield than down south, or surely he would have finished by now.

Wandering into the kitchen, she looked around. Was it worth making herself a cup of tea?

There would be no milk.

Phil had never learnt to enjoy either black tea or black coffee.

It wasn't worth the effort.

Phil began to shiver. She realized that the flat was cold.

She had not noticed at first.

She switched on the electric fire and for some time crouched before it, trying to get some heat into her body.

Presently she wandered into the bedroom and lay down.

It was too big an effort to undress.

She pulled off her shoes and her jeans, lay down in shirt and underclothes, dragged the covers around her and dropped into a deep sleep.

Chapter 51

Inside the Magnifico, Ronnie Patterson, the local TV chat show personality known to Sheila and heartily disliked for his assault on her after the Miss Northern Ireland finals, murmured confidentially in one corner with Liz Heron from the Belfast Telegraph.

Gavin Phillips, a young barrister whose face had recently become well known, sipped his G and T in a leisurely fashion while groaning at the jokes of self-styled comedian and club entertainer Paddy Moore.

Well-heeled businessmen and their wives chattered animatedly, excited as much by the presence of so many well known faces as by the occasion, or by the clothes they were about to see.

In one corner, Pat Fitzwilliam, the racing driver, gazed into his brandy and soda, a lock of fair hair tumbling over his forehead as usual, and waited for the action to begin.

He was present, as he was on every occasion when Sheila Doherty was on view, solely because his first sight of her, just a year ago in his native Dublin, had affected him in a way which a less cynical generation would have described as falling in love at first sight.

To Pat, Sheila was a magnet. When she was to be seen, he found that more and more he needed to be there.

Not that he was happy about this.

Only last season, he had made the transition to Formula One racing. His life was opening up before him, full of excitement and glittering prospects. A woman's face and body had no business to come between him and the happiness of achievement and the fulfilment of a lifetime's ambitions.

He scowled at the pretty young journalist who was attempting to start up a conversation with him and was deaf to the attempts of his friend and fellow driver, Artie Mulligan, a colleague from his earlier days in Formula Ford racing.

Artie wanted to claim his attention for a scandalous discussion of their leading rival's driving skills and life-style.

"Sure, you're no fun these days, Pat," complained Artie, as Pat responded to one of his best jokes with no more than a grunt. "What's the matter with you at all?"

But Pat returned no answer.

Gavin Phillips, the young barrister, waited with almost equal eagerness to see Sheila Doherty appear for the same personal reasons as Pat. He had never met Sheila but he had seen her picture more than once and he had watched her, in fascination, on television. He wanted to know if what he had felt for her would survive her real life appearance or if he had been fooling himself when he thought that he had fallen in love.

But he managed to conceal his restlessness rather better.

Skilled through the training of his courtroom experience in presenting a public image, Gavin kept his cool without apparent difficulty.

Looking round the room, it occurred to him to wonder how many of the men waiting for Sheila to step out unto the catwalk would be untouched by some element of desire at the sight of her.

Not many, he thought.

Mrs Rosemary Frazer Knight, wife of the Jackson Knight who owned a province-wide chain of supermarkets, and mother of Sally Kilpatrick, preened herself as she caught sight of her head in one of the many mirrors which reflected the light and glitter of the room and multiplied its dimensions. She, like the famous model, was a redhead.

"I suppose there is a resemblance," she thought. "It certainly is the colour of the moment."

The resemblance existed only in Mrs Frazer Knight's mind and in the flattery of her hangers on. Her rather coarse features, and body heavy with maturity, put her in a different league from Sheila in everything but the similar colouring.

Nevertheless, Mrs Frazer Knight had bought, or forced her husband to buy, many of the clothes worn by Sheila Doherty at fashion shows, with adjustments for size, and wore them in the conviction that she now looked as Sheila had looked.

Nor was Mrs Frazer Knight alone among the well-off women present in entertaining the belief that by buying the dresses Sheila showed, they could look like her.

For, after all, it was the existence of that belief which earned Sheila the large sums of money which Delmara paid her.

Behind the scenes, Francis Delmara, an established fashion designer for several years now and trembling on the verge of a breakthrough into the very top rank, trembled literally as he anxiously supervised the last details.

This was the moment when he would have to allow his creations to appear and to sink or swim as they were, without further help.

"Sheila, beautiful, lift your skirt a little higher on the left - that's right, angel. Take it slowly, now. I want everyone to see the overall shape for at least five seconds when you first step out, before you move. Chloe, your hair! Get Chrissie to spray that strand flat into place, it's disastrous - I can't have you looking like a tramp tonight! April, not those shoes with that outfit - the green ones, sweetheart - change them at once! When will you learn to listen?"

Francis, usually so self-possessed, waved his hands about and despaired.

Sheila had never seen him so lacking in self-control.

At last, however, he could afford to wait no longer.

The show was already late in starting.

That was not yet a problem. Too prompt a start would have seemed over-eager.

But already the audience was showing signs of restlessness. To keep them waiting any longer would produce an atmosphere of impatience which would not be conducive to success.

At exactly the right time, working by the instinct which had brought him to the top, Delmara raised his hand in signal.

The lights in the body of the hall were dimmed, those focussed on the catwalk went up, and music cut loudly through the noisy chatter.

Then there was a sudden silence.

Francis Delmara stepped forward and began to introduce his new spring line.

Sitting in the front row of celebrity seats, MLA Montgomery Speers became aware that the first half of the show was over. Delmara was speaking, hoping they had enjoyed what they had seen, promising more delights after the interval, inviting them to enjoy the food and drink provided at the buffet.

Speers turned to the young, blonde girl, Karen, seated beside him.

"Take me over with you and start a conversation with Ronnie Patterson," he said.

It was an order rather than a request.

"Make it very laid back, mind. I don't want him to think I'm after anything."

Karen worked in television as a freelance researcher, and was a familiar acquaintance of the chat show host. Speers, although he had met him, was not on those sort of terms with Patterson.

Montgomery Speers had it in mind to make an appearance on Patterson's show. This in addition to his intended interview for a local news programme.

A profile raising exercise.

He would talk about his companies and allow politics to creep in only very casually towards the end of the interview.

A few minutes later, he was saying to Ronnie Patterson "Like a lot of people, I catch your show most Saturdays - quite an innovation for the province. Must give you a great feeling of power."

"Power?" Patterson laughed wryly. "Few of us have any power in this country at present. The power lies with the money men, as always. The new criminal gangs, the guys who are taking over from the paramilitaries, now the peace process is finally getting somewhere, the drug dealers and bank robbers."

It was a jarring note.

Speers turned the conversation with a shrug.

"It can't last much longer. The police know what they're doing. They're starting to see results. The country's looking up. New jobs coming in. My new factory at Craigavon, for instance - a couple of hundred new jobs there alone, to add to all the others..."

He broke off modestly to allow Patterson a chance to compliment him on what he was doing for unemployment. But instead Patterson said "I hope you're not one of these people who want to see this province becoming a milk cow, Speers, as opposed to a Celtic tiger. Squeeze out all the money and see 'The rich get richer and the poor get - children.'"

It was said with a laugh but Montgomery Speers realised that he must have made a false move.

He might have known that Patterson would be a woolly minded pink liberal - all these media people were.

He set to work to recover lost ground.

"Oh, I don't profess to have any easy solutions to repairing the damage of years - who does? I try to address the more practical issues. People need jobs and houses. I try to do my bit in that line."

Patterson looked approving and Speers saw that he was beginning to make progress.

Behind the scenes, Delmara was dealing with a firm hand with some small problems.

"Chloe, you go and put on the jade earrings for your next change – they're on that shelf. In this business, you pay attention to detail or you're out! April, you almost slipped on your last exit - do you want our clients to think you're tipsy? Make sure it doesn't happen again. And look, the seam has started to unravel in the blue playsuit for your next change! Quick, someone - Phyllis - get it fixed - you only have a minute!"

Sheila, who had almost burst into tears at this stage in her first Delmara show, remained calm.

Francis, in private life so cool and poised, was always sharper, more critical during an opening night.

It went over her head and left her untouched.

Swiftly but carefully she got into the leisure wear she was about to show and checked hair and make-up.

"I want that jumpsuit!" Rosemary Frazer Knight whispered to her husband, and he murmured back,

"Yes, darling, yes. Beautiful - beautiful."

She glared suspiciously at him.

Did he mean the suit or the girl?

But after a moment, she relaxed, and decided to believe the best. Anyway, he had agreed to buy her the jumpsuit and she would look beautiful in it, too.

Artie Mulligan nudged Pat Fitzwilliam as Sheila came out again in swimwear.

"Fancy a bit of that, eh?"

The glare he got in response silenced him.

Pat seemed to have got it bad. Not like him.

Artie grimaced to himself and decided to watch his mouth in future. No sense in falling out with a good mate over something like that, and Pat was a good mate even if he seemed to have gone haywire over a girl. A pretty special girl, Artie had to admit, but all the same - ! No woman was that important, thought the youthful Artie, unable to see into his own future.

The evening was nearly at its climax.

The show had begun with evening dress and now it was to end with evening dress - but this time, with Delmara's most beautiful and exotic lines.

Sheila changed swiftly into a cloud of short ice-blue chiffon, sewn with glittering silver beads and feathers. She went out onto the catwalk.

The door to the ballroom burst open.

People began to scream.

It was something Sheila had heard about for years now, the subject of local black humour but had never before seen.

Three figures, black tights pulled over flattened faces as masks, uniformly terrifying in black leather jackets and jeans, surged into the room.

The three sub-machine guns cradled in their arms sent deafening bursts of gunfire upwards. Falling plaster dust and stifling clouds of gun smoke filled the air.

For one long second they stood just inside the entrance way, crouched over their weapons, looking round. One of them stepped forward and grabbed Montgomery Speers by the arm.

"Move it, mister!" he said. He dragged Speers forcefully to one side, the weapon poking him hard in the chest.

A second man gestured roughly with his gun in the general direction of Sheila.

"You!" he said harshly. "Yes, you with the red hair! Get over here!

Chapter 52

For one second there was a deathly frozen hush. Then someone screamed and immediately the noise broke out - people shouting, pushing, weeping.

It was the tallest of the gunmen who took control. Seizing the microphone which Delmara had been using, he spoke firmly into it, giving his orders harshly.

"Lie down right where you are, see? Get on with it! See these guns? They'll be giving the orders if you don't listen now, right?"

He wanted everyone together, where they could be controlled, and he wanted them lying down to make it hard for them to attempt anything.

Some of the more self-controlled of the audience responded at once.

The lead given, others followed suit. The atmosphere was strained and tense. It seemed unreal.

Sheila, standing frozen in her ice-blue chiffon and feathers, jumped as she became aware of a hand seizing her by the shoulder.

"You! Come this way." The second gunman, the one who had gestured to her with his gun just before the screaming broke out, pushed her roughly forward.

She seemed unable to feel anything.

Numbly her body followed her mind's instructions and moved in the direction which the voice in her ear and the hand on her arm made unavoidable.

She found herself standing near the entrance doors still clutched in a tight unyielding grip.

Beside her, she realised, was a red-haired woman who was a stranger to her, and someone else who she thought she recognised as the millionaire sponsor Delmara had been so pleased to get, Montgomery Speers.

A harsh voice spoke in Sheila's ear.

"What the fuck? Why're there two of them?"

"Dunno," said another voice. "What does it matter? Grab them and let's get the hell outa here!"

Pat Fitzwilliam and Gareth Phillips, spurred into action by identical motives, sprang forward.

Neither of them could bear to see Sheila dragged away, helpless, by men with guns and not try in some way to prevent it. Hopeless it might be but if they made no attempt neither man felt that he could ever live with himself again.

Sheila felt her arm released as Pat landed with a thud on the gunman who had her in his grasp.

At the same moment, Gareth Phillips, coming from the other side, butted the third gunman in the face. With a howl of pain, he lowered his gun and bent over double as Gareth kicked the gun aside and then extended his kick to catch the man hard in the crotch.

Meanwhile Pat and his chosen victim were rolling about on the floor at Sheila's feet, exchanging punches.

Two of the intruders were out of action.

But the tall man had kept his nerve.

Sheila heard a rattle of machine gun fire mostly in warning over the heads of the audience who lay spread out over the floor where he had directed them to lie.

Then a moan of pain from Pat Fitzwilliam.

Pat's grasp slackened on the man beneath him and, as it did, his victim managed to wriggle free. A moment later, a sideways swipe with his gun took Pat on the side of the head, and he collapsed, his face white, drained of colour.

A round of bullets from the first man's gun thudded into Gavin Phillips.

Sheila, tears pouring down her face, heard herself screaming.

"No! No!"

"Shut up, you!" snapped the first man. "Danny, do something with this bitch!"

Sheila felt something smooth and slimy thrust over her head and all at once she was enveloped in darkness.

A moment later she was being bundled out into the cold, dark January night.

Chapter 53

John Branagh reached the Magnifico Hotel and drew up in the car park as near to the exit as possible.

He strolled slowly over to the building.

He hesitated briefly, wondering which was the best way to go, then made for the nearest door.

As he went through it, he heard screams, bustle, then saw the door of the ballroom opening. Three men were coming through, the first one turned half way round, his sub-machine gun at the ready, his eyes behind their stocking mask keen and sharp, looking in all directions. Behind him, backing out slowly, came two more men, also armed, pulling three people between them.

John couldn't see who the victims were. Black bin bags, perforated all round for air, had been fastened over their heads and round their upper bodies and arms.

John knew he couldn't achieve anything worth doing against three sub-machine guns.

He backed carefully away, hidden behind the door he had just come through, holding it against him by the handle to prevent it swinging open and revealing his presence.

Where were the security men who should be on duty at the entrances? Why hadn't they stopped this happening?

Then, as he backed further out of sight, his foot stumbled against something.

Looking down, he saw that it was a man, blood running freely from the back of his head.

For one moment, frozen, John thought that he was dead. Then, common sense returning, he realized that dead people don't bleed.

The man had been knocked out. No doubt his partner was somewhere nearby, also out of action.

What was going on?

The gunmen weren't coming in John's direction. They were making quickly for another door to one side which they seemed to have left ready, jammed open with some sort of wedge. John couldn't see much.

"Come on, move it!" one of the men snarled, pushing the people in the bin bags roughly forward.

One of them, a woman from her voice, cried out in pain and then John heard what to him was the most terrifying sound in the world, just at that moment - Sheila's voice, muffled by the bin bag but still unmistakable.

"Leave her alone, can't you? It's not going to speed things up if we all end up tripping over ourselves!"

So the worst had happened. Sheila was one of these three hostages.

John forced himself to stay calm.

He allowed the party, three armed men and three victims, to get through the door.

Then moving swiftly but as silently as he could, he went after them.

Outside in the car park two cars were waiting.

As the gunmen approached, the doors were swung open by the waiting drivers.

The prisoners were bustled into the back seats, two to the first car and the remaining one to the second. The men dived quickly in after them.

The engines started.

The cars rolled swiftly forward.

John looked round desperately for help.

There was no time to lose.

He fished frantically in his pocket for his mobile, then changed his mind. No time for that yet. Instead, he tugged out his key ring and ran silently and unobtrusively to his own car, thanking heaven that it was parked so near the exit. Dodging behind other vehicles, ducking low, he reached it.

The gunmen and their cars were still roaring towards the exit. There was only the one way out John remembered thankfully.

His car was a new Mini. The engine, he hoped, would be capable of enough speed.

He found that although his mind seemed to have gone strangely blank, his hands remembered their automatic skill.

It was a matter of moments to open the car door, to swing himself into the driver's seat, to turn the key and to find himself moving out of the car park after Sheila and her captors.

He mustn't get too close. He wanted to track them down, not to panic them into doing something foolish, like shooting their prisoners and dumping them.

John shuddered and forced himself not to think of the possibilities.

He followed the tail light of the second car, trying to keep far enough back not to appear in its mirror.

They were out on the Westlink by now, he could stay several cars back and in the inside lane, where he hoped he wasn't too obvious.

Driving with one hand, John took his mobile phone out of his pocket.

It wasn't easy to use it one handed, but he managed.

"Police?"

He had got the number okay.

"This is John Branagh. I'm following the cars used to abduct three people from the Magnifico Hotel ten minutes ago." He craned forward to make out the number plate of the rear car, the only one he could see, and read the figures out carefully.

" Moving down the Westlink in the direction of Lisburn. I'll ring again when I've a better idea where they're heading."

He rang off quickly.

Mobiles in cars. Against the law. He was breaking rules. Okay, this was an emergency, but he didn't want to be seen and be pulled over by some too zealous cop.

Anyway, he needed all his wits to concentrate on following the car in front without being noticed.

Abruptly the car he was watching pulled into a slip lane without indicating.

John, taken by surprise, almost lost them but, by dint of some inspired manoeuvring, and by earning himself a string of curses from the car behind him, he managed to get into lane in time to follow his targets as they exited on the outskirts of the city, following the motorway at first, and soon began to wind their way down country roads and byways.

It was much harder now to keep out of sight.

John realized that unless they reached their destination soon, he would inevitably be spotted.

He hung further and further back, the fear of being seen tugging against the fear of losing them - of losing sight of Sheila, of losing any hope of somehow or other rescuing her.

He managed a further brief message to the police on his mobile, indicating the direction but couldn't risk talking for long.

Crawling cautiously round a bend, he saw, to his immense relief, that the two cars he was following had turned off into an even narrower winding lane. It led, as far as he could tell, to the lights of what seemed to be a farmhouse in the near distance.

It was probably time to leave the car and make the nearer approach on foot. Yes, the cars had stopped.

John pulled up. Moving quietly, he slipped out of the car door, closed it gently behind him and headed towards the lighted windows.

Chapter 54

Sheila, flung helpless and gasping for breath into a small unidentifiable space, took some minutes to orientate herself.

She was hauled roughly upright and propped against what felt like the back of a chair. Someone, she couldn't tell who, was pushed against her, and a third person squeezing in alongside slammed a door forcibly shut.

It was only when the car engine began and she could feel the forward motion of the machine that she realized she was in a car.

The person next to her - she could tell from the perfume that it was a woman – was moaning and crying in a distressing way, so that Sheila was almost glad when a harsh voice said "Shut up, you, if you know what's good for you!" and the unhappy noises were immediately cut off. Then anger came boiling up in her instead.

It was no good trying to do anything yet.

Sheila acknowledged this to herself.

Later, if only they would take off these awful bin bags, she might have a chance, she hoped, of changing things.

How, she had no idea.

For what seemed an eternity she listened to the car engine as they raced along, then the car must have left the smooth city roads for they were bumping and jerking over uneven surfaces. Country lanes, Sheila guessed.

Then, she didn't know whether to be glad or frightened, it seemed that they had arrived at wherever they were going.

The car stopped, she heard the door opening and a moment later she was being bundled hurriedly out into the open air - she could feel the freshness of the night breeze around her legs, and the ground cold and slippery beneath her feet, and then they were pushing her in through another door.

A final push sent her reeling against something hard - a wooden chair, she guessed - and as it toppled over backwards, hard legs sticking out in all directions, Sheila fell with it. Her head banged painfully against the floor and Sheila lost consciousness.

She had no way of knowing how long it was before she came to.

Opening her eyes, she saw with relief that she was no longer trapped and blinded inside the hateful bin bag. At some point while she was still dead to the world, someone had taken it off, in the process untying the ropes round her upper body and arms.

Blinking at the unaccustomed light, she gazed round. She was in a dimly lit room with an old-fashioned flagged floor, the sort found in farmhouse kitchens or in very modern luxury homes. The ceiling was lower than would be usual in a modern house, and there were dark, soot stained rafters. Between the rafters could be seen spaces of dirty white ceiling. The furniture, which was sparse, was made of thick, dark wood and, apart from the table and chairs where Sheila had fallen, there was nothing much except for an elderly dresser with some cracked plates and cups exhibited on its shelves. Sheila thought it might be good to memorize as much about the room as possible in case she needed to identify it, supposing at some time in the future she was released.

When she was released, she corrected herself. Or managed to escape. She wasn't going to accept any other possibility even for a moment. She continued, though still fairly dazed, to look all round.

Lying on the floor not far away was her fellow prisoner, the red-haired woman she had noticed earlier. She looked miserable, frightened and disheveled, her hair a mess, her mascara running in black streaks down her cheeks where the tears had carried it.

Sheila, feeling sudden pity for the poor woman, tried to smile encouragingly.

"Hi!" she said. "This is another fine mess they've gotten us into, right?"

The woman, instead of smiling back, showed every sign of being about to burst into tears again.

"Don't let them get you down!" Sheila urged her. "Listen, we'll get out of here somehow or other. I can't think why they've taken us but they must have some reason, and people will be trying to sort it out, okay? It can't go on for all that long."

The woman sniffed but at least she nodded and made a weak attempt at a smile.

"My name's Sheila," Sheila said. She looked enquiringly at her companion.

"Oh, I know who you are!" said the woman unexpectedly. "Sheila Doherty. I've bought some of your clothes. You model the most gorgeous things!" She sighed, enviously even in the middle of her misery.

Sheila grinned, half pleased, half surprised.

"Right! Then we'll definitely have to get out, so's you can wear them! And you?"

"Sorry?"

"I mean, I've told you my name, but you haven't told me yours yet?"

"Oh, sorry. I'm Rosemary Frazer Knight. My husband," she added listlessly, as though it hardly mattered, "is Hugh Frazer Knight. He owns the supermarkets."

"What, 'Night after Knight's'?" Sheila exclaimed, quoting the famous slogan. "You must be Sally's mother, then? Wow! Your husband's a multi millionaire, isn't he?"

Rosemary Frazer Knight nodded. "Yes. For what it's worth now."

They were suddenly interrupted.

The door flew open, banging against the wall, and the third prisoner was pushed roughly in, followed by two of the men, the leader and the small one who had grabbed Sheila. She vaguely remembered that he had been addressed as Danny. They still wore their masks, she was glad to see. That made it more likely that they intended to release their captives at some point. No point in continuing to hide their identity if they were going to kill the prisoners anyway.

"Get in there!" said the leader gruffly.

A final push sent the man flying across the room, off balance, until he ended up on the floor beside the two women.

The leader seemed to be unbelievably angry.

"I'd had enough of your lies and crap!" he screamed at the man who was trying to sit up, shaking his head to regain some sort of clarity in his brain.

"Trying to tell me you aren't Frazer Knight! Bullshit!"

"But I'm not!" muttered the man weakly. "I - " Inspiration suddenly struck him. "Look, I'll show you my driving license! That'll prove it, right? Here, it's in my inside jacket pocket." He fumbled frantically in his pocket, panic increasing as his hands found nothing but emptiness.

"I know it's here!" he almost wept. "I always keep it here!"

The leader glared at him for a moment searchingly. Then he turned to shout at his henchman. "Danny! Go and fetch that stuff we took outa this fella's pockets! Move it!"

Danny scampered off. Sheila could almost see his tail twitching with eagerness to obey.

"If you're lying - " said the big man threateningly.

"No! No, I'm telling you the truth! My name's Speers. Montgomery Speers. You'll see, my license'll prove it!"

Sheila couldn't help feeling some pity for Montgomery Speers as he sat crouching, a quivering mass of fear, on the floor next to her. At the same time she wondered how anyone could show such cowardice, no matter what the danger.

"He's right, you know," she said helpfully. "I recognize him now I hear his name. I've seen him before. It's definitely Montgomery Speers. Why should you think he was Frazer Knight?"

The leader stared at her.

He turned his head as Danny came bounding back into the room, his hands clutching the contents of Speers' pockets, and snatched the license which Danny eagerly held out.

"Montgomery Cecil Speers," he read out in a voice whose coldness was even more terrifying than his previous anger. Furiously he turned upon the wretched Danny. "This is your fault, you useless piece of junk! Why couldn't you get the right man?"

"It wasn't me!" whined Danny. "It was Charlie! He got the man, my job was getting the woman, Mr. O'Brien!"

"Keep your mouth shut! Didn't I warn you not to broadcast my name, you imbecile!" the leader cut in. "And you couldn't even get the right woman, you had to grab two of them! If I find out that neither of them's the right one, you'll know all about it, you twerp!"

He walked over nearer to Sheila and Rosemary and thrust his face forward so close that Sheila could smell the tobacco and whiskey on his breath.

"Which of you bitches is Mrs. Frazer Knight?"

Rosemary Frazer Knight gave a pitiful little sigh, and fainted, collapsing onto Sheila's lap. Sheila patted her head and glared at the man whose brutality had frightened the woman so much.

She couldn't do much but perhaps she could confuse the issue.

"I'm Mrs. Frazer Knight. Why do you want to know?" Sheila demanded.

"Because your loving husband will pay me a lot of money to get you back, won't he, darling? Even if I don't have him as well, you'll do, sweetheart, you'll do!"

"That's not Rosemary Frazer Knight," Montgomery Speers interrupted, driven by fear and a self-centered concern for his own safety. His only thought was to keep on his enemy's right side. "That's Sheila Doherty, the model! Don't you recognize her?"

"What!" The leader's scream of rage echoed from the raftered ceiling. "So who's this lady, then?"

He bent over and seized Mrs. Frazer Knight by one arm, waving his gun threateningly in her face. "Tell me who you are!"

Mrs. Frazer Knight came slowly back to consciousness. Almost automatically she answered the question. "Rosemary Frazer Knight."

O'Brien stood up. The mask hid what Sheila was sure must have been a grin of triumph but they could hear it in his voice and see it in his newly confident stance.

"Okay," he said softly. "One out of three ain't bad."

"Yes it is," Sheila longed to say. "It's not even a pass mark!" But common sense kept her quiet.

"Now, my dear," said the leader. "I wonder how much your doting husband will pay for you? Not as much as if it was for this little darling, I daresay, but still, plenty! Plenty."

Sheila hated him for the unnecessary cruelty of his jibe.

"What I want from you, Mrs. Frazer Knight," said O'Brien, his tone soft but full of menace, "is your full co-operation. I'm sure you'll see the need for it. Your husband needs to be convinced that if he doesn't pay up, you'll suffer. And suffer again. Until the money comes. It won't give me any pleasure to hurt you, my dear." He laughed unpleasantly. Sheila, listening to that laugh, knew that she didn't believe him. This man would enjoy hurting for its own sake. "We'll have to think of some way to persuade him to act quickly, won't we? And then we can get going!"

Chapter 55

John prowled quietly around the house, looking for a way in.

He knew he should probably leave it to the police and he had dutifully phoned them the moment he could, when he was sure the cars had definitely reached their destination. Keeping far enough away from the farmhouse to make sure no-one there could possibly hear him, he had given them details as exact as he could make them of the farmhouse's location.

It wasn't that he didn't trust them to get here in record time and do everything possible to free the hostages without risk. Well, he seriously hoped that was what would happen.

But nevertheless he felt an overwhelming pressure to act himself, to get inside the building, to rescue Sheila before any more awfulness happened to her.

For several years now he had been telling himself that Sheila Doherty meant nothing to him.

All at once, at the second when he had heard her voice coming scornful and unafraid from the hideous black plastic bag, he had suddenly known what a stupid lie that had been.

He loved Sheila, whatever she was.

The idea of something dreadful happening to her - he couldn't even name the possibilities to himself - was unbearable.

The farmhouse was a square, two storey building, typical of the older buildings of the region, stone overlaid with plaster, painted white and roofed in slate. There were windows on either side of the narrow front door and a further row above.

John moved cautiously, treading as warily as a lion stalking an antelope, round the sides of the building towards the back. Here he found himself in a yard, surrounded on the other three sides by a series of outbuildings. A stone outside stairway ran from ground level to a door on the next floor. John examined it from his position at the corner of the house, wondering if it would make a good entrance point.

As he watched, the door was pushed open and a dim figure emerged quietly. It was one of the three men, for he was still wearing his mask, black tights pulled down over his head and face, flattening and disguising his features beyond recognition. In his hands John, peering closely, could see a sub-machine gun. As he watched, the man set the gun down and dug one hand into the pocket of his dark jeans, presently producing a packet of cigarettes. Then he thrust his other hand into his other pocket and a moment later brought it out holding a lighter.

He took a cigarette from the packet in his hand, clicked on his lighter, then gave an exclamation of disgust as it dawned on him that his mask was in the way. With an impatient movement of the hand which held the cigarette, he thrust up the tights, put the end of the cigarette in his mouth and held the lighter to it. Immediately, far from being an unrecognizable stranger, he was someone whose face was lit up and revealed in the flame of the lighter. A very familiar face to John, in spite of the swollen nose from a recent head butt. John exclaimed aloud and ran forward.

"Charlie! Charlie Flanagan!"

Charlie choked, almost swallowing his cigarette, and made a grab for the gun which was just inside the open door.

But before he could reach it, he recognized John and the double shock, the voice from the darkness and now the sudden appearance of his former friend, threw him completely and he forgot the need to keep control of the situation.

John reached the top of the stone staircase, and leapt.

He had always been able to beat Charlie in their school day fights.

He had no trouble now, adrenalin pumping through him at the thought of Sheila's danger, in bearing him down, seizing his arms, clenching his knees round Charlie's bony torso. His left hand over Charlie's mouth, he used his right hand to hold Charlie's wrists together.

"Quiet!" he whispered grimly. "If you don't want me to break your arm!"

Charlie whimpered softly. Remembering previous encounters with John, who now seemed twice as big and strong as Charlie's memory of him, he had already given up the struggle.

John, unconcerned about any possible pain Charlie might suffer, rolled him and bumped him over to the half open door.

There, he used Charlie's head as a prop to hold the door open.

Then, moving with a speed which ruled out any attempt by Charlie to struggle free, he dropped his grip on Charlie's wrists and seized the gun. A second later he had it pointed at Charlie's temple and was hissing in his ear.

"I'm going to take my hand away from your mouth now, Charlie boy. And if I hear even one little sound from you, believe me, I'll shut you up with a bullet. Okay? Nod if you understand."

Charlie's frantic nodding would have done credit to a fluffy dog in the back window of a boy racer. It was a wonder his head didn't fall off.

But John was too concentrated on his own immediate actions to laugh.

Taking his hand away from Charlie's mouth, he sprang to his feet, the gun still pointed menacingly at his trembling captive.

"Now, Charlie boy," whispered John, "you're going to tell me just what the hell's going on here? And very, very quietly, remember."

Charlie shuddered.

"It wasn't my idea, Johnny!" he stuttered. "I just got involved because O'Brien knows me from pushing the blow and gear for him, I never meant to get into anything like this but O'Brien needed two fellas to help him, and he said if I didn't come in on it he'd shop me to the filth, see what I mean?"

"O'Brien?" John repeated thoughtfully. "I've heard that name. One of the big drug dealers, right? Everybody knows it, but the police haven't managed to get anything on him yet?"

"That's right, Johnny!" said Charlie eagerly. "He made me and Danny come in with him with the guns, and he had two other guys who did the driving, I don't know their names, but they'll be round the front of the farm, O'Brien said they were to watch the front and I was to watch the back - "

"Great job you all did, too, Charlie. How come I didn't see any sign of these guys out front, then?"

"I think they both nipped in for a leak and a fag before they settled down on guard, Johnny, but I reckon they'd be back out there now, looking out for the filth turning up. Not that the filth'll have any clue where we are, I should think - "

"Ah, well, now, that's where you're wrong, Charlie boy. But get on with it! What's O'Brien's big plan?"

"He meant to pick up that supermarket millionaire and his wife, see? Frazer Knight. And he's going to make him transfer a big whack of money to O'Brien's account in Geneva, see? He said he was sick of the small time, means to retire on this loot, but me and Danny's getting a right good cut, he promised us - "

John looked thoughtfully at Charlie Flanagan. How someone could get involved in something so heartless, he was at a loss to understand. And how had they managed to take Sheila as well? Crooks were notoriously thick but how could they have been stupid enough to take the wrong woman? But it wouldn't be the first time something like that had happened, he realized. All through the troubles, there had been incident after incident of the wrong person being shot by mistake. John felt his anger boiling up.

"You disgust me, Charlie," he said softly. "Okay, on your feet. Now you're going to take me - still very, very quietly, right? – to this O'Brien guy. And just remember, if he hears any little sound to warn him we're coming, you get it first!"

"But, Johnny, he'll kill me!" Charlie whispered in terror. "You can't do this to me, Johnny!"

"Oh, can't I?" John said grimly. "I think, Charlie, that you'll find that I can. On your feet! I won't say it again."

Charlie, tears and other liquid running messily down his cheeks and from his nose, scrambled awkwardly to his feet, clinging for support to the door frame.

John nudged him, not gently, with the gun.

Then they both heard it.

A piercing, terrified scream, coming from further inside the farmhouse building.

And another.

Chapter 56

In the room at the front of the farmhouse where the big man was talking to his prisoners, Sheila's anger was also boiling up.

She looked round her desperately, searching with her eyes for some kind of weapon. She knew she couldn't successfully attempt any form of attack on their captor bare-handed.

In one corner of the room she noticed a pile of the various objects, the contents of Montgomery Speers' pockets which Danny had recently fetched and had dumped there.

She could see a mobile phone.

It must belong to Speers. Sheila, seized in the middle of the fashion show, had no handbag or any other property, only the dress she had been showing at the crucial moment.

She wondered briefly if it would be possible to get hold of the phone and get a message out, supposing they were left alone in the room even for a few moments.

Then she realized how unlikely that would be.

She might have had that opportunity while O'Brien and Danny were elsewhere questioning Speers, in the belief that he was Hugh Frazer Knight, if only the phone had been there at the time. But would the men go out again, forgetting it was there?

She looked quickly away again in case she was noticed.

But O'Brien had seen her sideways glance and understood that she was looking for some means of escape.

"Just stay where you are, sweetheart," he said evilly. "Danny here has one of those itchy trigger fingers they talk about. I'd hate to see him get too edgy and spoil your beauty, darling."

He strolled casually over to the pile of belongings.

On top was the mobile phone Sheila had noticed.

With a sickening feeling, she watched him slip it into his pocket.

Then he turned back to Rosemary Frazer Knight. Sheila suddenly noticed the tiny pale blue evening bag in a shade which matched Rosemary Frazer Knight's dress and light jacket which the woman was clutching in one hand.

Unbelievably, she had held on to it throughout all the events of the last hour.

Sheila had heard that some women will do that but it was the first time she had seen it for herself.

O'Brien leaned forward and snatched the bag roughly from her fingers.

"Yours, I believe, ma'am?" he said mockingly, brandishing the handbag at Rosemary, who sat, stunned and frightened, unable to move or answer. His threats, and in particular the realization that he would have no hesitation in hurting her, if it suited him, had left her completely demoralized.

"Yours?" he repeated angrily.

Dumbly she nodded her head.

O'Brien wrenched open the fragile evening bag, ripping one edge as he did so. The few contents scattered on to the floor. A tiny silver cased mirror, an eyeliner and a container of blusher, a slim purse and something else in a shinning blue holder which fell to the tiles with a tinkling noise.

Rosemary's mobile phone.

Sheila caught her breath as it dawned on her what O'Brien must intend.

But had he in his clumsy rage broken the phone?

O'Brien wondered that too.

With a growl of fury, he leapt forward and seized the phone, extracting it at once from its delicate holder.

Apparently it was unharmed, for he breathed a sigh of relief.

Then he turned to Rosemary with an ironical bow.

"Your phone, Mrs. Frazer Knight."

He held it out and Rosemary took it in a hand which shook.

"Now, I expect you can guess what I want you to do?"

She shook her head, genuinely unable to think from the shock and horror which filled her emotions, leaving no room for anything else.

O'Brien shook his head impatiently.

"I want you to phone your husband, Rosemary," he said.

Then, as she stared at him, trying to understand, "I want you to be very careful what you say, my dear. Any hint which would help him to find you here, and Danny would shoot at once. Better to cut our losses, you see, and get away quickly before the police arrive on the doorstep. But of course we couldn't afford to leave any witnesses, could we? So it would be goodbye to all of you, I'm afraid. Now, you do understand that, don't you, Rosemary?"

Rosemary nodded faintly.

"Good." O'Brien sighed. "I really hope you do. I don't want all my work wasted, naturally. So when I give you the phone, I just want you to say 'It's true, Hugh. This is Rosemary. Please do as he says or he'll hurt me.' Have you got that?"

"Yes." Mrs. Frazer Knight managed to say.

"Okay. Now, I expect you have the old man's number saved on this dinky little phone, yes?" Then, as she stared at him blankly, "Your husband's number, I mean. You have it stored?"

"Under Hugh," she told him.

"So I'll ring him myself and have a little chat, and then I'll pass the phone to you and you'll say just what I told you, understand? Danny will have his gun pointed right at your face. Wouldn't want it spoiled, would you? And as for you others," he swung round ferociously on Sheila and on Montgomery Speers, "I don't want a movement or a sound out of either of you, right? Otherwise, it'll be bang bang, and KO for you!"

It was so very clear that he meant it. This was no bluff.

Sheila bit grimly down on her tongue, concentrating on neither crying nor screaming.

O'Brien turned on the phone.

It took him only a moment to find the number he wanted.

They listened in a strained silence as it rang.

"Rosemary?" asked a voice, a masculine voice which nevertheless shook with some emotion. Perhaps fear.

"No," said O'Brien. "I'm afraid this isn't Rosemary. But you can speak to her presently, if you do as I tell you. Don't attempt to bring the police in on this. I'm going to tell you now that if you want you wife back, mostly unharmed, you'd better do exactly as I say. When Rosemary's finished speaking to you, I'm going to give you a bank account reference, and you are to transfer £5 million pounds to that account at once, without telling anyone, get it? Otherwise your lovely wife suffers - badly."

He handed the phone to Rosemary. "Here, sweetheart," he said softly.

As Rosemary Frazer Knight took her mobile in a trembling hand, Sheila watched O'Brien take out a cigarette and light it. Was he going to take off his mask and smoke?

She hoped desperately that he wouldn't do that. Once he had shown them his face, he wouldn't let them go alive, she knew.

But O'Brien had other plans. He raised the tights from his lips, just enough to take a quick puff, enough to keep the cigarette alight, to turn its end red hot and glowing.

Then, as Rosemary Frazer Knight stammered hastily into the phone the words she had been ordered to speak, "It's true, Hugh, it's Rosemary. Please do what he says or he'll hurt me," O'Brien stepped nearer, reached out the hand with the cigarette and pressed it firmly and callously against her wrist.

Rosemary screamed, and screamed again.

O'Brien set the cigarette down and took the phone from her. "Convincing, right, Hugh? And there's lots more where that came from. Now, get ready to make a note of that number...."

Chapter 57

John heard the screams.

He thrust the machine gun savagely into Charlie's face, knocking against a tooth.

"If that was Sheila, I'll kill you all," he promised violently. "Move, you animal!"

Charlie, blood adding itself to the other mess coming from eyes, nose and mouth, stumbled forward as John propelled him towards the noise.

It was dark in the narrow farmhouse corridor. O'Brien had made sure that no light had been turned on except in the room where the hostages were imprisoned.

But this single light was enough to show John which way to go, even without Charlie's co-operation.

The screaming had stopped and was now being followed by faint moans.

"Hurry up, damn you!" John said.

He thrust Charlie against the door.

"You're a human shield, Charlie boy, how do you like that?"

Over Charlie's shoulder, as the door burst open, he saw Sheila struggling wildly, kicking and punching a big man wearing a black mask made of tights.

At first frozen with horror at O'Brien's brutal action, Sheila had recovered her senses.

Activated like an electronic toy by sheer boiling anger, she hurled herself at O'Brien, almost making him overbalance with the shock, interrupting his message to Hugh Frazer Knight, knocking the mobile phone out of his hand.

It was only for a moment that she had the upper hand. Within seconds O'Brien had recovered his balance, both physical and mental.

"Grab the bitch, Danny!" he roared, himself seizing Sheila by her abundant hair and pushing her to her knees. "Take her off me! I need to finish this message!"

Then John fired the gun.

Impelled by his rage he would willingly have poured bullet after bullet into O'Brien's body but the risk of hitting Sheila was too great.

Instead he fired in the air but the impact was just as great.

Every head in the room turned to him, gaping with horror and shock.

Danny, about to move forward to obey his master's commands, turned into a statue on the spot.

O'Brien himself, at a loss to know what was happening, released Sheila slowly and waited to see what John's next move would be.

He had not long to wait.

Still pushing Charlie in front of him, John advanced into the room.

"The first of you three thugs to move wins the prize and gets the next round of bullets," he remarked conversationally. "It would make it easier for me to deal with you, if there were fewer of you, so don't tempt me, right?"

"John," Sheila cried thankfully.

"Don't get between me and these animals, Sheila," John said. "Have either of them got guns?"

"I don't think so, John," replied Sheila meekly. "The big one put his gun down over there when he started phoning and I think the other one dropped his ages ago when he went to fetch some stuff from the other room."

"Okay, gather them both up and put them outside the door here. Be careful coming past me, now! And then you can have a hunt around and see it you can find some rope, okay?"

Sheila, feeling rather like a schoolgirl obeying her teacher's rules, but only too happy to obey, scuttled off to find and retrieve the ropes that had been used to tie up herself and her fellow hostages. They were lying carelessly flung down on the floor of the room next door. She hurried back with them.

"Good," was all John said. "Now, you." He was speaking to Montgomery Spears."See what you can do about tying up these people. You can help him, Sheila. And, you," he turned his attention to where Rosemary Frazer Knight was sitting crouched in an unhappy heap on the floor nursing her damaged wrist, "see if your phone's still working and, if it is, let your husband know you're okay."

Although his voice was calm, John was finding it almost impossible to keep his anger in check. In spite of himself, he was aware that he was shaking.

When Rosemary made no effort to lift the phone, Sheila finished tying a tight knot in the rope she had twisted round O'Brien's arms and moved forward to take the mobile herself.

"Hugh Frazer Knight?" she said, her voice cool and sweet. "Your wife is okay. We've all just been rescued, so don't worry." She paused and looked at John for directions. "What about sending for the police -?"

"It's okay," John cut in, his voice slowing down with effort as the adrenalin began to drain out of him. "I've already phoned the police and told them where you all are. They should be arriving any time now."

The relief, to Sheila, was enormous. She was becoming less and less sure of how long John could go on controlling these people with one gun.

She felt her head growing light. She wondered how much longer she could stand up.

John, who was just as unsure about himself, felt his legs growing steadily weaker. He couldn't stand here much longer holding this heavy gun and keeping alert. And supposing the guards from the front of the building heard something or came to check that everything was okay?

It was with great thankfulness that he heard at last the noise of sirens and approaching cars and, minutes later, the thud of heavy feet on the staircase.

The rescue party had arrived.

As the first policeman burst through the door, Sheila's head finally gave up and she collapsed in a heap at his feet.

Chapter 58

Sheila returned to consciousness to find herself in a hospital bed. It took a few moments for her to orientate herself.

She struggled to sit up and a nurse came hurrying over.

"Just take it easy, pet," she said. "Don't try to get up yet."

Sheila looked round her.

She was in a private room with an open door through which the nurse had been able to keep an eye on her movements. It was painted in shades of yellow and grey, with pretty matching curtains and duvet cover. There was a small cabinet beside the bed with a yellow shaded lamp and a switch on a long lead.

Sheila looked at the nurse, a youngish woman with small neat features and light brown hair.

"Why am I here?" Sheila asked. "There's nothing wrong with me."

"Mr. Delmara insisted," the little nurse said. "He's paying for the private room, you see, and he insisted that you should be kept over night and have a thorough check-up."

"This is all wrong," said Sheila vigorously. "The beds must all be needed for people who are actually ill. All I did was faint. Where is Mr. Delmara? Let me talk to him."

"He's having a cup of coffee in the canteen. He wanted me to let him know when you recovered enough to talk."

"Then could you let him know now, please?" Sheila urged. "I really don't want to stay here tonight. It's so unnecessary."

"I'll see if someone can get hold of him," the little nurse promised. She left the room with a swish of starched skirts.

Sheila lay back and closed her eyes. To her surprise, her head had started swimming again.

Francis came into the room with his usual controlled elegance.

"Well, beautiful, so you're with us again?"

"Francis, why on earth am I here? I'm perfectly all right."

"Sheila, beautiful, I just need to be sure. You were found in a collapsed heap by the policemen who rescued you all, and carried out on a stretcher. You've been through a traumatic experience. I want to be sure there's nothing seriously wrong."

"Thank you for your concern, Francis," said Sheila dryly, "but I wasn't hurt. I just made a fool of myself by fainting. And now I want to go home if you wouldn't mind cancelling your arrangements for me. Kind of you, but unnecessary."

"Well, good," said Francis, unperturbed. "But I really think you should stay for the rest of the night, now you're here. It's after half three in the morning, you realize."

Sheila hadn't noticed it was so late.

"Tomorrow, if the doctor gives you a clean bill of health, go by all means. But I have to protect the assets of Delmara Fashions, my dear."

Sheila suddenly felt herself shaking violently.

Perhaps she was less fit to move than she had assumed. With the shuddering came further memory. Some of the events of the last few hours returned to her in vivid detail.

Involuntarily she closed her eyes and began to shake again.

Francis, watching her carefully, smiled wryly.

"So – will you stay?"

"Francis, tell me about it," Sheila burst out suddenly. "People have been hurt, haven't they? Pat? That woman, Mrs. Knight? That other man, Gavin something? Please tell me!"

Francis looked at her gravely.

"Pat is quite badly injured. He has a broken leg and some broken ribs. He also hurt his head which may be the most serious part of it. But he'll recover and, if the head injury isn't bad, he'll be back to normal eventually. But, yes, that young solicitor Gavin Phillips is dead. And two of the security men are in Intensive Care but out of danger, they say. No-one else, as far as I know. Rosemary Frazer Knight is fine. Suffering from shock, a minor burn and some bruising, that's all. Her husband took her home as soon as she had been treated. The gang have all been arrested. O'Brien and his men, I'm told. I don't really know much more than that."

Sheila was silent for a moment, assimilating what he had told her. Her thoughts raced from Mrs. Knight to Gavin Phillips whom she had never met, to Pat, and back again. And where was John? Suddenly, as the name O'Brien struck a cord, she remembered the letter in Roisin Boyd Cassidy's box.

"....dealing with Knight's supermarkets ...sometime in Jan ...

"Oh, no!" Sheila whispered. "Oh, no!"

To Delmara, it seemed as if she was reacting to what he had told her.

"Go to sleep, now, if you can," he said gently. "Don't ask any more questions tonight. You'll hear all the details tomorrow."

"Tomorrow. Tomorrow I will have to talk to the police," Sheila said. She looked whiter than ever. Delmara wondered for a moment if she was about to faint again. "There's something I'll have to tell them. Can you let someone know that, Francis, please? But not tonight. Not tonight."

She shuddered again.

"I'll ask the nurse if you can have a sedative," Francis said. He was looking worried. "You can see for yourself that this has affected you badly. You need a good sleep and a chance to recover in peace."

But long after Delmara had gone, Sheila lay awake, tossing and turning in spite of the sleeping pill.

The scenes of that evening were imprinted on her mind and came back constantly, one after the other, highlighted and stark.

But over and above everything else was the memory of Mrs. Boyd Cassidy, so old, so frail, so kind, believing she could trust Sheila because of her memories of the past, yet tied up in such horrific criminal activity.

No-one was above the law. No-one could be excused for taking part in such actions.

But Mrs. Boyd Cassidy….

If Sheila told the authorities what she knew …

But would it even be evidence?

Was it something they could take to court? Sheila didn't know.

The more she thought of it, the flimsier it seemed.

She felt trapped.

She needed badly, for her own peace of mind, to do everything she could to prevent a repetition of last night. If anything she knew could help, then she must tell someone.

She saw again Pat Fitzwilliam lying on the ground, white faced and unconscious.

Then she thought again of the old lady, so kind and trusting. It was impossible that she could be involved in such acts as this.

But what else was she to believe?

At last, at dawn, pure physical exhaustion took its toll and Sheila drifted off into an uneasy sleep.

The rattle of the nurse's trolley coming round with early morning tea finally woke her.

A heavy weight descended on her heart before her eyes were open.

It was while sipping her morning tea, propped up against pillows, that Sheila made her decision.

This information that she had couldn't be held back - the letter in Mrs. Boyd Cassidy's box.

She had read the letter and made a mental note of the contents, but then, why, she could not now understand, had she done nothing about it?

She hadn't taken it seriously enough.

She had gone almost at once to New York and when she had come home it had been nearly Christmas, and the knowledge that she held had passed almost entirely from her mind.

Now, realizing this, she felt angry at her own self-centeredness.

She must give the police the potentially valuable information which she held. She saw now that she was very much to blame for not having done this long ago.

The decision lifted a weight from Sheila's conscience.

She lay back and dredged her memory to ensure that it was accurate.

"Nurse," she asked as the breakfast trolley reached her room and the nurse came in to pull the table across her bed, "can I talk to someone from the police? Is there anyone still about?"

"Oh, there's always policemen about in this hospital!" answered the little nurse. "I'll see what I can do for you, love. If I can get hold of one, I'll send him along. Porridge or cornflakes?"

"Porridge, please," said Sheila who had a healthy appetite this morning. "Thank you, nurse."

Presently she heard a clomping of feet and a big, heavily-built policeman looked round the door and came in.

"Miss Sheila Doherty?" he inquired.

Sheila nodded, hastily finishing her mouthful of porridge.

"I'm Constable William Kirk. I'm told you're ready to speak to the police, to make a statement about last night?"

"Yes."

"Well, then, fire ahead," said the policeman, settling himself on the straight-backed chair by Sheila's bed and taking out a notebook and pen.

"But I'm afraid it doesn't really amount to much."

"We'll be able to tell that when we know what it is," said Constable Kirk unsmilingly. "Go ahead, Miss Doherty. First tell us about last night."

Sheila spoke in a nervous rush. She went through the events both at the Magnifico and at the farmhouse, with the constable occasionally asking questions. Then she went on quickly, before she could change her mind,

"About six months ago, I was down in Dublin and I was introduced to a lady called Mrs. Boyd Cassidy. I was told she had criminal - drug - connections. I've no way of knowing if that was true. No evidence to produce against her. In any case, she's living down there out of your jurisdiction. But one evening when I was in her house I saw a letter, in a locked box in her private room, written to her by someone called O'Brien, saying that they intended to deal with Knight's supermarkets on January 21. That's all, really. I don't know if it's any help. I would have told someone sooner but I wasn't sure what it meant and I thought you wouldn't find it much use. But after last night, I suppose it's clear enough now and I wanted to tell you anything that might help at all."

As she finished speaking, another shudder ran over her and she lay back against the pillows with closed eyes.

"Thank you, Miss Doherty," said the policeman briskly. "This may turn out to be very useful information or it may not. But you were quite right to tell us. You can't remember any other details about this letter?"

"No, I'm sorry, it was very short. I think it said they would be in touch about a meeting for planning soon. That was it. Oh, yes, there was an address, 3a Thomas Street, they could use as a new safe house."

Constable Kirk closed his notebook and stood up.

"Someone else may want to speak to you about this, Miss Doherty. But in any case, thanks again. I'll head on, then. The sooner this can be acted on, the better."

He made a good-bye gesture with his hand and went briskly through the door.

Sheila felt glad he had gone.

She was relieved to have passed on her responsibility. As she lay back against the pillows and drifted off to sleep again, ironically her last thought was a thankful relief that she had probably said nothing which could really be acted on which could hurt Roisin Boyd Cassidy. Such a vague letter could, after all, mean anything.

As she sank deeper into sleep, Constable Kirk's information began its journey up the line until at about two o'clock that afternoon it reached someone of sufficient seniority to act upon it and to contact his opposite number in the Gardai.

A decision was taken at a very high level that Roisin Boyd Cassidy must be questioned.

But when the very important policemen arrived at Mrs. Boyd Cassidy's house later that day by appointment, they were greeted by a sobbing Reilly.

"Oh, sir," Roisin Boyd Cassidy's confidential maid of three decades wailed out. "Oh, sir. She's gone. I don't know if she took anything or what. She told me she wasn't prepared to have to speak to you. She went up for her afternoon nap two hours ago and when I went in to see if she was ready to get up, I thought at first she was sleeping peacefully, but when I touched her hand it was so cold! She's gone!"

Roisin Boyd Cassidy had taken her own way out rather than allow the consequences of her activities to catch up with her.

She had died painlessly, the doctor reported, from an overdose of tranquilisers.

She had broken the rules for the last time.

Chapter 59

Phil slept late that morning.

She was woken by a thunderous knocking on the door of the flat.

Jumping out of bed, still half dazed with sleep, she dragged on her jeans and stumbled out into the passage barefoot to open it.

"Who's there?" she called in a loud voice. "What's wrong?"

"Open up!" came a response from outside the flat. "This is the police!"

Phil fumbled at the catch of the door and managed to release it.

At once the door was pushed wide, nearly knocking her to the ground, and several large men in uniform rushed past her. Breathless, Phil pulled herself together and tried to speak.

"What's going on? Who are you?" she managed at last.

The men had spread out and were searching the flat, throwing open doors, pulling the clothes off the bed. Phil could hear them in the kitchen pulling open cupboards and drawers, and in the living room where they seemed to be pushing the furniture about and wreaking havoc.

"PSNI," said one of the men briefly to Phil. He was tall and thin with a sandy moustache.

Half crouched by the wide open door, clinging to it for support, Phil stared at him, her eyes big with both terror and anger.

Anger triumphed sufficiently to make her snap out "Where's your search warrant? What right have you to charge in here?"

But the PSNI man gave her an unpleasant smile and answered "Haven't you heard of the Special Powers Act, love? We don't need any search warrant. We have reason to believe this place is being used for criminal activities....."

He was interrupted by a triumphant shout from the front room.

Phil peered past him as he strode through the doorway. The top half of the sofa had been dragged off the springs. One of the men was stooping over it, taking something from its hiding place there.

As he stood up, Phil could see that it was a gun and a square box.

The lid was torn open.

Inside were neatly parcelled bags which Phil could see were full of a white powder.

"Good," said the man who had spoken to her. "That's all we need. Hutchinson and Donnelly, you two stay here and finish the search - be thorough, mind. Fred, you come with me. We'll take this girl down to the station and see what she has to tell us."

Phil's face was white.

She remembered Davy's warning to her. The flat was being used as a halfway house for storing drugs in transit.

Why had she been such a fool as to ignore his words, to come here and put herself at risk?

"I know nothing about it," she stammered. "You're making a mistake."

The first man, the tall thin policeman with the moustache, took hold of her by one arm.

"You can tell us all about that down at the station. Get your coat."

Phil's coat was hanging in the hallway where she had dumped it last night. Dumbly she lifted it from the hook. The policeman released her arm long enough for her to put the coat on, then took a firm hold on her again.

"Have you a bag?" he asked.

Phil shook her head. She was at a loss what to say. She felt as if the sky had fallen on her with a crash.

The second policeman, a smaller, more burly man, took her other arm.

Between them they marched her down the flights of stairs to the front entrance, and out into a police car.

Phil's thoughts whirled.

What was she to do? What to say?

They had found a gun and a large consignment of what was probably, she thought, heroin. The fact that she was in the flat tied her to the discoveries.

How was she to explain away her presence there without involving Davy?

Phil felt tired and sick.

It was the same old problem, all over again.

But surely Davy would be involved anyway. The flat was in his name. The police could find that out straight away from the agent.

Phil stared out through the window of the car, unable to bring herself to speak as they raced through the traffic and down to the nearest police station in Donegal Pass.

Once there, she was taken into a small room and a police woman was left with her. They sat on either side of a plastic-topped table on wooden hard-backed chairs.

The police woman was middle-aged and reminded Phil a little of Sheila's mother, Kathy Doherty. She was comfortably plump and of a large build.

She seemed disposed to be friendly, at least to start with.

"Cup of tea, love?" she asked Phil, looking at the girl's tired face with some sympathy.

Phil realised for the first time that it was many hours since she had eaten anything.

"Yes. Yes, please." she said faintly. She longed to lean her head on her arms but was afraid of going to sleep before she knew what was happening.

The police woman put her head out of the door and called to someone, and presently the offered cup of tea arrived. Phil sipped it gratefully. She found that she was shivering.

"I'd like to make a phone call." she said presently.

"All in good time," the police woman said. She looked at Phil speculatively. "You haven't been charged with anything, have you? Just brought in for questioning, I was told. So what's the hurry?"

"I don't know," Phil said.

"Drink up your tea and I'll get someone to ask the sergeant what's happening about you," the police woman said. She went out of the room for a few minutes.

When she came back, the friendly expression had vanished.

"If I'd known what you were here for, you wouldn't have got that cup of tea," she snapped at Phil. "People like you are scum. My daughter got hooked on drugs when she was just a kid, it ruined her life. I tell you, you people deserve anything you get. Sit there and be quiet, and no more whining about phone calls. The sergeant will talk to you when he's good and ready."

Phil stared at her in surprise. Catching the look of cold hatred in the woman's eye, she looked hastily away. There was no human kindness left there. She had been identified as the enemy and would be treated accordingly.

For what seemed like a long time, Phil sat silently with the now hostile policewoman, waiting. What she would say when the time came, she did not know.

She would have liked to speak to her parents, or even to her brother Gerry, now a qualified lawyer working in a Belfast solicitors' office as a trainee solicitor. There seemed, however, no chance of that. She would have to rely on herself.

When the sergeant came to question her, she still had made no decision.

He came in briskly, the tall thin man with the sandy moustache who had brought Phil to the station.

"My name is Sergeant John Glover," he said. "I am going to question you about the presence of a handgun and a quantity of heroin in your flat, 3a Thomas Street, discovered there at 10.43 a.m. today. You are not being charged with anything at this point in time, merely being asked a few questions. Do you understand?"

Phil nodded.

"First of all, your name, please?"

"Philomena Mary Maguire."

"Address?"

"3a Thomas Street," Phil heard herself saying.

"So the flat is yours?"

"Rented," Phil said.

The sergeant looked pleased.

"Have you any explanation of the presence of a handgun and illegal drugs on premises which you admit are rented by you?"

"No," said Phil desperately. "I don't know how it got there. I didn't put it there. It isn't mine."

"It may not be yours - but does it belong to someone you know?"

Phil hesitated, fatally – then said "No, it doesn't!"

"I suggest that it does. That you know the owner and that you were hiding the drugs and the gun for that owner as an accessory to criminal activity, i.e. drug dealing and smuggling."

Phil stared at him. "No," she said. "No!"

"The gun has been traced by Forensic," said Sergeant Glover. "There is evidence that it was used in a hold-up at a petrol station last November and in a shooting incident last July. How do you explain its presence in the flat you rent?"

"Someone else must have hidden it there," Phil said.

"No-one could have hidden it there without your knowledge," interrupted the sergeant. He raised his voice to a shout. "You knew all about it. You helped these drug dealers by hiding their weapons and probably by hiding consignments of drugs! Perhaps you took part in some of the shooting incidents yourself. Perhaps it really is your own gun!"

Phil felt bludgeoned by the loud, angry voice, by the moustached face, contorted with fury which was thrust into hers. She pulled away, leaning as far back as she could in the chair.

"Well? It is your own gun, isn't it?" shouted Sergeant Glover.

"No! No! I don't know anything about the gun or the drugs! I don't know how they got there!"

Phil felt like weeping. Only her innate stubbornness prevented her from breaking down. More and more she longed for the support of her family.

"Does anyone else share this flat of yours?" asked the Sergeant.

"No," said Phil quickly. Without conscious decision, she knew that by no word of hers was she going to involve Davy. "I took it over at the start of September."

Would they check with the estate agent? If so, she would say that it had been an unofficial arrangement, that the previous tenant hadn't bothered to change it into Phil's name. Perhaps she could get away with that.

"So whatever is there is your responsibility?'

"I wasn't there over Christmas," Phil said. "I went home. So anyone could have got in and left the stuff."

"A rather unlikely thing to do, surely? Why should anyone hide a gun and drugs worth a fortune in the flat of a complete stranger? You'll have to come up with a better story than that, Maguire, if you expect us to believe you."

Phil had to admit the truth of his words.

As much as anything else, she found that she was upset by the sergeant addressing her as "Maguire." It seemed to show that to him she was already a criminal in the dock.

"I don't have any other explanation," she repeated. "I don't know how the stuff got there, or when. It could have been there for years."

"You forget," Sergeant Glover pounced, "this gun was used in an incident in November. A time when you were already renting this flat. It was put into your sofa sometime after that. You must have known it was there."

"I didn't know."

Phil buried her face in her hands. She had nothing else to offer by way of excuse or explanation.

"We have reason to believe," said Sergeant Glover weightily, "that this flat has been used for drug dealing and smuggling. We have other information, apart from finding this gun. We need names, Maguire. Give us some names.'

"You won't believe me. I don't know. I tell you, I don't know."

Sergeant Glover looked at her for a moment, disbelief patent on every feature.

Then, with a shrug, he began to ask the same questions over again.

As the hours passed and there seemed to be no sign of the interrogation ever ending, Phil went through the point of complete exhaustion, out the other side, and back again. She slumped in the chair, white-faced, drifting in and out of sleep, constantly woken on the point of dozing by the loudness of Glover's voice. The sergeant was replaced at regular intervals by other men in uniform, but there was no respite for Phil, and at last she reached a pit of tiredness which defied all her interrogators' attempts to keep her awake and coherent.

"Okay," said Sergeant Glover at last. "Take her away and lock her up for the night. We'll go on in the morning."

She woke hours later to realise that the interrogation had been resumed.

In the short breaks when no-one was asking her questions, Phil reflected miserably that although she knew nothing about the gun or the heroin, she had withheld knowledge which might have saved lives. The guilt at times threatened to overwhelm her. The only thing which kept her from breaking down and telling Glover everything was the iron hard determination to keep Davy out of it if this could possibly be done.

Looking back later on the nightmare, Phil could never remember if she had been in the cell for two days or three when Glover finally read her her rights and charged her.

Phil at once rang Gerry at his office.

She felt unable to deal with her parents' reactions if she rang them from the police station.

Gerry would be able to give them some support when he broke the news. And with his legal training, he would be able to advise her. Or at least get a solicitor for her who could tell her what she should do.

But Gerry, horrified and dismayed at Phil's position, found that his efforts to have her released were of no avail. The charge had been made. Phil would be brought to court in a matter of weeks. Charges against drug dealers were always pushed ahead quickly.

The most he could do for Phil was to see that she had the best legal representation he knew of.

He was thankful that in spite of the lengthy interrogation, she had admitted nothing. At least they would not be coming to court with a confession to deny.

But he had to admit to himself, although not to Phil or to his parents, that from every other point of view, the position was bad, even hopeless.

Chapter 60

Sheila left hospital soon after her interview with Constable Kirk. As she had told Francis repeatedly, there was nothing really wrong with her. Before she left, she inquired about Pat Fitzwilliam and was allowed to call in to see him for a few minutes.

Pat had a broken leg and several cracked ribs, but the most severe of his injuries was the blow on the head which had knocked him unconscious for a dangerously long time and left him weak and shaken.

He was lying in bed with the leg strapped up in plaster and a rakish looking bandage round his head. When he saw Sheila, he brightened up at once and grinned at her.

"Hello, Pat," she said, coming over to the bed and looking down at him gravely. "How are you?"

"All the better for seeing you, me darling," Pat responded in stage Irish. "You're lookin' good, Sheila – as always!"

Sheila had arrived at the hospital the previous night in the tattered remains of Delmara's ice blue and feathered creation. Her mother had brought her in some fresh clothes to wear, but since they dated from a year and a half ago when she had first moved out, they were not what she herself would have chosen to be seen in. As she pulled on the neat navy skirt and white blouse which her mother had selected from the clothes she had left behind, Sheila hoped quite seriously that there were no photographers lurking. Pat's cheerful compliment reassured her a little.

"Tell me about it," Sheila requested, sitting down on the edge of the bed carefully to avoid Pat's injured leg.

"I can only say that I courageously attacked the gunmen and really thought I was getting somewhere when the world ended – or that's what it seemed like. I'm told I was knocked unconscious by the butt end of one of their guns. The doctors were a bit worried about that for a while, but I've been X-rayed and they tell me there's no lasting damage to my first class intellect! The leg and the ribs will heal up before too long, so there's no big deal. I asked them if I'd be able to play the saxophone afterwards but the nurse said only if I'd been able to before, so that was a let-down."

Sheila groaned politely. "Very witty. But what about your driving, Pat? You'll be out of it for a while, yes?"

"Not too long, I think," Pat answered her seriously. "Six weeks at most if the leg heals up as it should. And then I'll keep that promise, and take you round the track at Kirkistown."

"I can't wait," said Sheila lightly. "I'm going home now, Pat. See you before long. All the best." She rose and bent forward to kiss him on the forehead, and went, leaving a scent of spring in the air behind her and a young man unsure whether he felt wonderful or miserable on her account.

Sheila rang her mother, promised to come round later and managed to choke Kathy off from an immediate visit to the hospital. Then she made her way to her new riverside apartment near Delmara's main workshop. She had been living here when home in Belfast between fashion shows.

It was a small apartment, best suited for one, but fitted up very comfortably, even luxuriously. One wall of the front room consisted of windows, with patio doors in the middle, looking out over the River Lagan. This gave access to a small balcony where Sheila kept some pot plants. The carpet was a thick, soft beige and the comfortable sofa and chairs were in a flowery pattern of beige and blue. The walls were painted in pale, subtle shades against which a few modern pictures in bright colours stood out dramatically. Francis Delmara, a frequent visitor to the flat, often reflected that Sheila's highly coloured beauty flamed like the sun against the pale background. There was a tiny fitted kitchen in more pale colours and a softly carpeted bathroom with bidet, shower, and corner bath, as well as the more usual fittings. Sheila's bedroom alone struck a discordant note. Piled high with clothes of all colours and descriptions, with books and furry toys from her pre-model existence, and with a dressing table where every square inch was covered in bottles and boxes of make-up and other accessories, its pale colour scheme was scarcely visible beneath the accumulation of Sheila's life. She kept her clutter to the bedroom and the rest of the flat was consistently immaculate and sparkling.

On this late January morning there was a chill in the air in spite of the weak winter sunshine which came and went fitfully. Sheila remembered that she had not been home overnight to turn on the central heating and flicked a switch as she closed the front door before sinking down into her favourite chair placed, as always, to overlook the river. Her face was drawn. She fell to reflecting on her life and the changes a couple of years had brought.

As so often still, John Branagh was in the forefront of her mind.

She kicked her shoes off and drew her feet up beneath her in the big, soft armchair. The doorbell rang. Could it be John?

Her face fell when she opened the door and saw Francis Delmara standing there, his arms full of flowers. Hastily she summoned up a welcoming smile.

"You're looking good, beautiful," Francis drawled. "Aren't you going to invite me in?"

"Yes, of course," Sheila said vaguely. "Come on in. I'll make some coffee."

"I'll make the coffee," Francis corrected her. "I know where everything is. And I'll put these things in water."

"They're lovely. Thanks." Sheila bent her head to sniff hopefully at the hothouse freesias and roses, but of course they had no smell.

Francis disappeared into the kitchen and Shelia retired to her seat in the window.

The fleeting sunshine gleamed for a moment on the lightly moving ripples on the river's surface. The bank was edged with grass and a tree stood up bare-branched at the edge of Sheila's view. Suddenly, with a stab of pain, she was back again walking along the higher reaches of the Lagan with John Branagh.

She wondered what John was doing now, where he had gone after the police arrived, whether she would ever see him again.

As it happened, John Branagh was engaged at that moment in a process best described as tearing up the Royal Victoria Hospital by the roots in an attempt to find out what had happened to Sheila Doherty.

Chapter 61

John had begun early that morning by ringing one number after another until he had discovered that Sheila had been taken to hospital to stay overnight. Then he had arrived in person and had raged through the wards like a tornado, severely disrupting hospital staff and routine, until a nurse had told him severely that Sheila had signed herself out that morning. No, they did not have her address and, if they had, they would certainly not feel at liberty to give it out to all and sundry.

John felt weak and devastated.

He had done everything he could and had finally managed to free Sheila from her captors the previous night. He had watched Sheila being carried away, white-faced and unconscious, before his eyes, from the scene of her imprisonment.

At first, slumped down with his head in his hands, he had been unable to move, shaking from sheer relief.

Then he had spent hours giving his statement to the police, waiting, then repeating what he had to say to more and more senior officials before being finally released, told to go home and rest.

Instead, it was then that he began phoning, using all his newspaper contacts, trying to find out where Sheila had been taken.

It was Brian Gallagher, his colleague on the BBC news programme, who first gave him any clear information.

Brian, as a staff reporter, had been one of the first on the scene. When John managed to reach him on the phone, he sounded upset and shaken, very different from his usual calm persona.

In response to John's urgent demands, he told him "They were carrying some people off on stretchers to the Royal. You might be able to find her there."

Brian didn't ask the reason for John's urgent questions. Outside his professional duty, he was not an inquisitive person. He asked so many questions in the course of his work that out of working hours he just wanted a rest from it. He was bone tired. The small hours of the morning were growing into bigger hours and he was still awake.

So then John began on the Royal Victoria Hospital.

In the end, he took the line he should have followed in the first place and rang his sister Mary. Mary didn't know Sheila's new address but she was willing to do what John shrank from doing and ring Sheila's parents. As a friend of Sheila's, Mary had no trouble getting the address of the apartment from Kathy Doherty. She also learned that Sheila had fainted and had spent the night in hospital but was otherwise unhurt.

John's first feeling was of overwhelming relief. Tears of reaction pricked his eyelids.

Sheila was okay.

Then he began to wonder.

Was there any point in going to see her? Would she even want to see him?

He had ended their relationship a long time ago, or so it felt. Was there anything there to take up? Or should he be satisfied that she was all right and continue to keep her safely out of his life?

He walked aimlessly along, trying to decide.

When he looked up and saw that he was outside the block of new apartments where she lived, he found himself laughing.

He could no more resist seeing her for himself than he could fly. His next move, if any, would depend on her response.

He rang the bell of Sheila's apartment just before lunchtime.

Sheila came to answer it almost at once.

She was still barefoot and half asleep from her long daydreaming and reminiscing in the armchair by the window. For a moment it seemed her mind was playing tricks on her, translating the recent vivid memories into hallucinations.

"John," she said, after a thunder-stricken moment. "Come in."

John came in, feeling awkward.

"Hullo, Sheila. About last night. I wanted to see if you were okay."

"Come upstairs," Sheila said faintly. "I'll make a cup of coffee."

She turned and went up the carpeted flight. John followed. His legs felt strange and shaky.

He came into the apartment behind her, blind to everything but the sight of Sheila.

"Sit down," Sheila said. She had forgotten for the time being about her offer of coffee. She felt as if she had been stricken dumb.

John walked over to the window and stood with his back to the room, looking out.

She had not said "Good to see you again" or any of the other commonplaces. Was it because she thought this meeting too important for that sort of thing? Or because she was not glad to see him, and wished he hadn't come?

He stared at the river.

Presently Sheila's voice spoke just behind him.

"John?"

Then Sheila said "Are you - ?" at the same moment that John said "Sheila, I – "

They both said "Oh, sorry!" and then laughed.

"Let's sit down," said Sheila.

They sat side by side on the big comfortable sofa.

"I wanted to be sure you were all right," John said abruptly.

"Yes. I haven't thanked you properly yet for what you did. I'll say it now. Thank you." Sheila sat silently for another few moments. Then she looked up into John's face with determination. "John – why did it matter to you what happened to me?"

John took a deep breath.

He was about to speak when a voice sounded from the kitchen. "Ready at last, beautiful!"

Sheila stood up. She remembered through a haze, and as if from a long time ago, that Francis was in there. Making coffee. The kitchen door swung open and he backed in, still talking, carrying a tray with coffee pot, cups and one of the roses he had brought in a small slim vase.

"I feel like a dutiful husband bringing breakfast in bed to his lovely wife on Mother's Day."

Francis Delmara.

John stiffened. He felt a pain in his chest as if someone had stuck a knife into him.

Francis, on the contrary, seemed fully at ease. He clearly remembered John but nothing in his words showed this.

"Sorry to interrupt," he said easily. "Sheila, beautiful, sit down and enjoy! But those clothes, darling! You really must change before some photographer gets himself the scoop of a lifetime by snapping Sheila Doherty in school uniform!"

"Francis, you know it isn't school uniform," said Sheila, laughing. Francis Delmara always managed to amuse her. "And I'll change when I want to! Thanks for making the coffee."

John swallowed the lump in his throat which was making it impossible to speak. He stood up.

"I'll go on, then, Sheila," he said abruptly. "Glad to see you're okay."

Sheila stared at him. "You don't need to go, John. Please don't worry about Francis. He won't be staying long – will you, Francis?"

"No, I must get on," said John obstinately. "I have to get to work some time to-day, I suppose."

He walked past Sheila to the door and opened it. For a moment he hesitated, looking round at her.

"So that's Francis Delmara," he said. "The one you've been working for all this time. Living with, too, apparently. I wish I'd known. Maybe I wouldn't have bothered –"

He broke off. For a moment he stood staring at her.

"I'm glad you're okay," he said.

Then he was gone.

Sheila stared after him. She could hear his footsteps running down the stairs. She started to run after him, trying to say "But I'm not," finding that the words wouldn't come.

The outside door slammed.

Francis Delmara said something.

"Sorry," Sheila said blankly after a long pause. "I'm sorry – I didn't hear what you said."

"It doesn't matter," said Francis. "Why don't we sit down?"

He took Sheila's arm gently and lowered her onto the big chair.

Sheila sat quietly. Her mind was whirling.

She could not believe that John Branagh had come back into her life and then left again with hardly a word.

She was also finding it next to impossible not to break down into uncontrollable tears.

"I want to get you away from all this as soon as possible, Sheila," Delmara said. "You need time to recover from the shock." He didn't specify which shock, and Sheila was grateful that he didn't. "I want to arrange a holiday for you in the Pacific islands and then some shows in America. Will you come?"

Sheila nodded. She needed time before she could speak without breaking down, but she could nod.

"Good," said Francis briskly. "Some time before the end of the week, then."

Which was why Sheila, on the other side of the world, heard nothing about Phil's arrest until many months later.

Chapter 62

Delmara Fashions arrived in New York to find the press only too happy to give them whatever publicity they wanted.

Harrington Smith's name for Sheila, the Ice Maiden, had caught the public imagination and there was an eager market for stories about her and about her private life.

The capture of Sheila and Rosemary Frazer Knight was a great focus of interest, and although neither Delmara nor Sheila wanted to talk about it, let alone make use of it for publicity purposes, they soon found that they had no choice in the matter. The New York papers carried repeated stories about Sheila's escape and the burning of Mrs Knight until the subject was at last done to death.

Sheila discovered in herself a new desire for excitement and luxury. She had decided that John Branagh was out of her life now for good. His sudden reappearance, and equally sudden exit, seemed to have finally cured her of the lingering hope that he would sometime or other come back to her. He had come, it hadn't worked, and now there was nothing left to hope for.

Meanwhile, the world was full of other men who seemed to find Sheila attractive.

Life became a series of new meetings, dates, parties and evenings out.

Sheila worked hard and played hard. She went with Delmara to show off his best lines to private customers, to display the goods to clothes stores who were considering a cut-price range of the most popular dresses, to carefully set-up lunches with financiers who knew little or nothing about clothes but who might, perhaps, be charmed into investing in Delmara Fashions by the beauty of his leading model.

Delmara began to worry about her health. She had lost half a stone but this seemed only to add to her ethereal attraction.

She was interviewed on television by a chat show host who wanted her to talk about the hostage situation or her own love life, and enjoyed evading his questions and giving him less than nothing for his pains. She met the rich and the famous, and had a much publicised fling with a film star notorious for his good looks and his success with women which the newspapers insisted resulted in the breaking of the film star's heart. She dined, danced, and drove out always with a fresh admirer and could not lose her heart to any of them.

When they had been in New York for three months, Pat Fitzwilliam, his leg healed and his spirits high, came over for a trial race and immediately sought Sheila out.

"It's grand to see you again, me darling!" he said, sounding amazingly Irish and familiar among the American accents. "Looking as lovely as ever. What's this I hear about yourself and Kurt Paston?"

Kurt Paston was the film star whose heart Sheila was said to have broken.

"I don't know. What is it you hear?" Sheila asked teasingly.

She was very pleased to see Pat again, especially as her last sight of him in the hospital bed could now be forgotten, together with all the other memories of that dreadful time. He seemed like an old, close friend, someone with whom she could relax and be herself.

"Well, whatever I hear, it's time you forgot about him and thought about me instead!" said Pat, light heartedly. "I'm going to take you out to the racetrack this afternoon, okay?"

"That sounds good, Pat. And will you take me for a spin in your racing car?"

"Ah, well, now, Sheila −" Pat hesitated. "Anything for you, my darling girl, but these racing cars are a bit fragile. There's no way I'd be allowed to do that. Besides, there's only room for one!"

"I know − I was only teasing. But you can let me drive your own car instead − how about that?"

Pat, who was never without a car for his own private use, and who had lost no time in acquiring a shift stick Ferrari to replace the Lamborghini he had left behind him in Ireland, agreed laughingly.

"But can you drive, Sheila?" he asked, "or do I have to teach you first?"

Sheila, who had bullied Frank Doherty into teaching her to drive as soon as she was seventeen, looked indignant.

"Certainly I can drive," she assured him, omitting to say that Frank's old Audi was a very different proposition from a Ferrari. "And I expect, if you'll give me the benefit of your expertise, that I'll soon be even better."

At the first opportunity, Pat drove her out of town, heading into Connecticut and found a wide stretch of road for the experiment.

Sheila found herself experiencing a touch of nerves as Pat pulled in to the side of the road and made way for her in the driving seat.

"What happens if I smash your beautiful car?" she asked playfully. The long thin lines of the gleaming red bonnet stretched before her as she settled herself at the wheel.

"Just so long as you don't smash your even more beautiful self!" Pat joked, concealing an undercurrent of worry. Like most good drivers, Pat hated to be driven. He would be relieved to find Sheila as capable in this area as in all others.

The smooth, powerful engine purred as Sheila pressed lightly on accelerator and clutch, and slipped into gear. With a speed which sent her heart into her mouth, the car leapt forward. Resisting an instinct to clutch feverishly at the wheel, Sheila deliberately relaxed her grip and felt the steering respond to the light pressure. They raced down the wide carriageway.

"By heavens, you can drive, all right!" Pat said admiringly and Sheila laughed breathlessly. The wind rushed past, lifting her hair and streaming it backwards. She felt an exhilaration which had been missing from her life for months. The spring sun shone down and she felt its heat for the first time since the start of winter. Unconsciously she increased her pressure on the accelerator and the car shot forward.

"Careful, my darling girl!" Pat exclaimed. "You don't want the speed cops after you!"

"I suppose it wouldn't do," Sheila agreed. "What Delmara would call bad publicity."

"It might be a good idea to turn off the main highway," Pat suggested. "Take the next right. There's a very pleasant road after a few more turns, more like the countryside than the city, and quite a decent pub not too far away."

"Fine." Sheila duly turned right. She slackened her speed in deference to the narrower road but continued to move faster than Pat thought safe.

It was as they turned a sharp corner that it happened. A large American car, taking up far more than its share of the road, came careering round the bend and was almost into them.

Sheila instinctively pulled to the left.

A split second later, she realised that this was the States and that she was meant to be on the right hand side of the road.

She tried frantically to correct.

Everything suddenly changed to slow motion.

There was the enormous car on the verge of crashing into them.

There was the squeal of tyres.

Her heart was pounding.

Then Pat's hands on the wheel, wrenching it over and the other car sweeping safely past.

Sheila let her breath out in a sobbing gasp. The Ferrari, which was heading into the verge, was righted almost miraculously by Pat's skilful hands and pulled in well clear of the bend.

Then Pat's arms were round her and she was weeping tears of reaction into his shoulder.

"Oh, Sheila, darling," Pat said thickly.

His lips came down hard on hers and, for a moment, they clung together, kissing frantically.

Then Sheila drew back and laughed shakily.

"Sorry – and thanks."

"Never mind about that," Pat said hoarsely. "Sheila, I love you. I want you. Don't hold me off any more."

All at once a wave of longing went over Sheila, for the safety and security of a man's arms around her and a man's love to protect her. Pat was strong and warm and kind. She was very, very fond of him. She knew that. Why hold back?

She said nothing.

"Let's get away from this public road," Pat said abruptly. "Here, move over." He got out and went round to the driver's side while Sheila obediently slid across to make room for him.

Pat drove with a mastery which increased his attraction for Sheila.

She had thought of him as just a young man who admired her.

Now she saw him again in his own element, exhibiting a natural grace and control which was impressive.

What was she waiting for, Sheila wondered. Where would she find a better man than this one?

John Branagh. The thought forced its way unbidden into her mind and was vigorously pushed out again. John Branagh was nothing to her any more, for she was clearly nothing to him.

They were far away from the main highway now and had come by a series of winding roads to the side of a river.

Pat pulled up beside a clump of trees, parking on a flat piece of rough grassy bank out of sight of passers-by. He turned towards Sheila, leaning over to kiss her.

The over-hanging branches of the tree brushed lightly against her head. Fresh, new green leaves, bright against the red gold of her hair.

Pat caught his breath and gave a groan of desire. His arms went round her again and their lips clung together.

Sheila let herself surrender to the urgency of his passion, feeling her body respond to his warm strength. She put one hand to the back of his head and held him lightly, feeling the soft wiriness of his hair beneath her fingers.

She had gone far beyond thought or conscious desire. At the back of her mind, out of reach of any response, she knew that she was behaving cruelly.

Pat was going to be very hurt if she let him think that she cared and he then found out that she didn't. She didn't really care for him in a serious way. But he was so close, so loving –

A sudden cracking noise from above their heads woke her abruptly from her half trance. There were leaves drifting down from the tree above. Pat started back and looked up. Sheila followed his gaze.

Sticking out among the branches of the tree, they could see a foot.

The foot was wearing dirty white trainers.

The foot was attached to a leg wearing jeans.

Pat jumped out of the car.

"You! Get down here! What the hell are you doing?"

For a few seconds there was no response, then as Pat roared again, a face poked itself out among the leaves.

"It's okay."

"No, it's not okay!" Pat shouted furiously. "Get down here till I murder you!"

"Press," said the face. "Just looking for a good picture of Sheila Doherty here. I followed you in my Chevy this afternoon. Good publicity for her, you know."

"Good publicity!" Pat was so angry that for a moment Sheila thought he would explode.

The journalist was staying well out of reach, up the tree, waiting for Pat's anger to cool down.

"It's all okay," he said again. "I'm Al Riordan, I do the 'Highlights' column for the Gazette. You must have read it? I'm not intending any harm to you or Sheila - honest!"

He had misjudged his man. Far from cooling down at the explanation, Pat's anger boiled over.

"Come down outa that or I'll bloody make you!" he swore and made a leap for the lower branches.

Sheila watched, torn between a desire to giggle helplessly and horror, as Pat pulled himself up into the tree and seized the intrusive journalist by the arms. The two men struggled furiously, Al Riordan intent only on escape, Pat endeavouring to pull him to ground level in order to fight properly.

When you took account of the law of gravity, the struggle could not last long.

Within minutes, both men came crashing through the branches and rolled on the ground in a confused heap. Al Riordan, who if not brave was cunning, twisted himself free from Pat's grip and staggered to his feet. Pat seized him again by one foot, hauling himself upright, his right fist landing in a hard, accurate kidney punch and his left following up in a hook to the jaw which left Riordan dizzy.

The journalist got to his knees and prudently stayed there for a moment while Pat towered over him, uttering threats, waiting for Riordan to get to his feet.

"Get up, ye dirty so and so! Get up till I knock ye down again!"

When he realised that Riordan had no intention of taking advantage of this offer, Pat seized him by his tee shirt, shook him violently, and dragged him to his feet. For a moment which was filled with terror for Riordan, Pat glared at him longingly.

Then, turning him round, Pat sent him on his way with a kick and a push.

He turned to see Sheila watching him from inside the car.

They looked at each other, Pat with the fury dying out of his face, a leaf caught in his hair, his knuckles red and raw, Sheila more dishevelled than he had ever seen her, with an expression from which the alarm had not yet vanished,

Then, slowly, a grin spread over Pat's face and Sheila found herself giggling. A moment later, they were both laughing helplessly.

"Sheila, it's as well that Riordan guy was so yellow! If he'd stood up to me I'd likely have killed him and then where would we be?"

Pat got back into the car.

"Serves us right, doesn't it?" he said. "We should have had more sense. Bound to be one of those guys around most of the time."

"Well, that particular one won't be back in a hurry," Sheila said. "I just hope he didn't get any photos before you got him."

"Photos?" asked Pat, looking blank.

"Yes, didn't you hear him say he wanted to get a good picture of me?"

"So he did," agreed Pat. "I didn't listen to him too carefully, I was too hopping mad."

"He had a camera slung round his neck," Sheila added. "I noticed it bobbing about when you were kicking him on his way."

Pat looked thoughtful. Then he laughed again.

"Chances are the film will be spoilt after the rough treatment the camera got, not to mention himself. Anyway, there's nothing he could have snapped that I'd be ashamed of."

"Yes," agreed Sheila dryly. She did not add that five minutes later it might have been a different story.

The mood had been broken. Sheila and Pat drove back to the highway, found the pub Pat had mentioned, actually a four star restaurant, and ate a pleasant meal in their usual low key harmony.

The heightened emotions of the earlier afternoon were temporarily forgotten and Sheila, for her part, was greatly relieved. She was not ready for any major life choices at the moment and she knew that Pat was not looking for anything less from her.

As for Pat, he was aware that the change of atmosphere had ruled out any hopes he had had for now. He was content to wait. There would surely come another time.

Chapter 63

Al Riordan's camera had not been damaged. The following day's Gazette carried a large and prominent photograph of Sheila and Pat in each other's arms in the convertible. The details were blurred but there was no doubt about who the two people were or what they were doing.

The caption underneath read:

ICE MAIDEN MELTS!

Delmara laughed but Sheila could see that he was not best pleased. He warned her to be careful. The American press were far more enterprising and persistent than anyone in Ireland and they would go to any lengths to get a story.

"The moral is, beautiful, don't do anything you wouldn't want to see splashed over the front page," drawled Francis. "This one is harmless enough but next time it might not be."

Sheila knew that he was right.

She was still on the track of enjoyment, determined to get something out of life since she did not seem able to get what she had originally hoped for. but she decided to be more circumspect in future.

Al Riordan's photograph was syndicated widely and was given due prominence in local Belfast newspapers.

John Branagh saw it, as he saw everything about Sheila, and experienced his usual painful reaction.

He told himself that it was time he stopped feeling like this about someone who had long since gone out of his life. The shock of seeing that the man he had found kissing Sheila beside the Lagan was still so much a part of her life had gone deep. It seemed clear to him that Sheila had no further interest in him. Now there was this other man. She was promiscuous, he told himself. She would never settle down in one permanent relationship. He was well rid of her.

That same night, he invited Rosie to go to the pictures with him, and while there he held hands with her and kissed her.

Afterwards, he drove up above the city and parked in a secluded spot where they could look down on the lights of Belfast reflected in an orange glow unto the night sky.

Rosie was eager for his caresses and John, hurt more deeply than he realised by the photograph of Sheila in the arms of another man, accepted the comfort she offered. He made love to her, entering her body with a fierce satisfaction.

Afterwards he was filled with a deep disgust and self loathing.

"I'm sorry, Rosie," he said harshly. "I'm sorry."

"Don't be sorry, John," Rosie said. "It's what I wanted."

But John could not be consoled.

He had broken his own rules yet again.

He hated himself for what he had done.

Chapter 64

Phil's trial for drug related offences was a headline affair. Gerry was thankful that the new proposal for trial without jury had not gone through. It was difficult enough as it was.

There seemed to be no evidence to support Phil's story that she knew nothing about the gun or the heroin. He was very much afraid that she would be found guilty on the first charge, possession of an unlicensed firearm. That in itself might not be too bad. The thing that really worried him was the second charge, which covered possession of a shipment of heroin not for personal use and, following on from that, a third charge of intent to deal. If Phil was convicted on this charge, the sentence would certainly be jail.

Davy Hagan, like Sheila, knew nothing about Phil's arrest. He was still off the scene. As Phil had suspected, he had been flown over to the Middle East and was trying to iron out by means of bribery some hold-ups which had arisen with the pipeline. He had volunteered for this job. It had always been Davy's way to throw himself wholeheartedly into whatever he believed in. He had decided to work with O'Brien. Once he had made that decision, he was determined to do it to one hundred per cent of his ability.

Phil was on her own.

Through the entire ordeal, she clung to one idea. She would keep Davy out of it.

None of her family, not even Gerry, knew that the flat was his or even that he and Phil were still so close. It seemed that the police had not checked up on the name of the rent payer on the contract. If they had done so, Phil was ready with her story of an unofficial sublet, but it was never needed. Were the PSNI, she wondered, only too pleased to have caught a drug dealer and reluctant to do anything to spoil their case?

The only person who ever raised the question of Davy Hagan's possible involvement was Gerry Maguire. He knew that his sister had gone out with Davy for a while and he was well aware of Davy's views, although he had never shared them. Now he began to wonder if, through knowing Davy, Phil had been introduced to ex-paramilitary, drug pushing circles and had been made use of. He suggested this to

Phil on one of the few occasions when he was allowed to see her but Phil denied it vehemently.

"It has nothing to do with Davy Hagan," she insisted. "I don't know how the gun or the drugs got there. I don't have any friends who could have been responsible. Someone, some stranger, must have had a key to the flat. Someone who rented it ages ago, maybe, and held on to a copy of the key afterwards."

It was a weak story and Gerry knew it. But failing any other explanation, and with no evidence to back it up, he had no alternative. He had to present it in court. He wished very much that some alternative would miraculously appear.

But this wasn't an episode in a TV drama.

One of the worst aspects of the case, Gerry knew, was Phil's own attitude.

She insisted repeatedly that she was innocent of any knowledge of the gun or any involvement in drug dealing.

But even Gerry could see clearly the overall feeling of guilt, some sort of guilt, which undermined the impression her words made.

"Phil," he told her energetically, "you need to convince the jury - the judge too, but mainly the jury. You need to make them say to themselves "I don't believe that young girl knew anything about it." And you're not trying! When you say "I didn't know anything about drug dealing activities," it just sounds as if you were lying, and not even lying well. You've got to do better that that!"

"I'm sorry, Gerry," Phil said, her lip trembling. "I do try."

Something inside her, a gnawing guilt, would not allow her to speak convincingly. As more and more reports of the death and injuries at the Magnifico filtered in, Phil became convinced more surely that some of the responsibility was hers. If only she had found some way to tell. She had wanted to warn Sheila but she had failed to give a general warning with enough detail to make it believable.

She had put Davy first, as she had always done.

The guilt weighed heavily on her and made it impossible for her to declare her innocence in the ringing tones of conviction.

As the day of the trial approached rapidly, Gerry became more and more worried. He had brought in the senior partner in his firm, James Kennedy, for advice and help. Kennedy had recommended an excellent barrister friend, Scott Worthington.

So far, so good.

But even the eloquence of Scott Worthington would need some facts to work on and some support from his client. Gerry was very much afraid that there would be neither.

Chapter 65

Mary Branagh became aware of Phil's arrest and trial only belatedly. She was working hard towards an MA, missing Orla Greaves who had left for Africa at the end of the summer, and ignoring news broadcasts as far as possible. She overlooked the initial headlines on Phil's arrest.

Only when a friend mentioned it casually one day did she realise what was happening.

"This girl, Phil Maguire, is she the one who used to be a friend of yours?" Carmel asked, rustling the leaves of her newspaper as they sat at coffee in the Students' Union. "I seem to remember you mentioning her name."

"Yes, I've known Phil all my life." Mary dragged her thoughts away from the details of her teacher training course. "Why, what about her?"

Carmel told her.

Mary was horrified. "Phil! But Phil would never do anything like that! How can anyone possibly think so?"

"They seem to be sure enough about it," Carmel said dryly. "But they could be wrong."

"They *are* wrong," Mary stated categorically. "How terrible for Phil. I wonder if I can get to see her?"

"I doubt it," Carmel said realistically. "You aren't a relation. But if she's convicted, you'll be allowed to visit her then."

"Oh, don't, Carmel!" For once, Mary, who loved bluntness and honesty, was upset by bluntness from someone else. "She couldn't be convicted."

When the day of the trial arrived, Mary went to the court. There was nothing she could do to help, just by being there, but she felt somehow that Phil might like to see a friendly face among the crowd.

When she arrived at the Laganside court, she was horrified to see the crowds outside the courthouse. There was continual shouting and jeering, all aimed at Phil. At the bar of public opinion, Phil was condemned already.

Mary made her way inside and found her way to the correct courtroom. She was nervous, not knowing what to expect.

Presently the judge appeared, the jury filed in and Phil was brought up into the box. She looked pale and strained.

When she was asked how she pleaded, it seemed to Mary that her "Not guilty," given in a low voice just audible to the listeners, was strangely uncertain.

It was all over very quickly.

The prosecution gave its evidence: the policemen, Sergeant Glover, who had been in charge of the raid on the flat, and one of his colleagues who had actually found the heroin and the gun.

Scott Worthington, looking tall and impressive, questioned both men but without producing anything useful as far as Mary could see. The best he could do was to induce the sergeant to admit that Phil had seemed astonished when the things were discovered.

The most damning piece of evidence was his statement that the raid on the flat had been carried out on the basis of information received that the flat had been used for drug connected activities.

"I prefer not to say more on that point, my lord," said the tall, thin, moustached sergeant turning to the Judge "on the basis that it might endanger my informant." And to Mary's surprise, the Judge accepted this.

An avid reader of detective stories, Mary had a firm belief that hearsay evidence was not permitted in a court of law. Apparently things were different in the Northern Ireland of today.

It was this background, now firmly lodged in the minds of the jury, which, Mary realised, was likely to make them believe in Phil's involvement.

She looked forward hopefully to hearing Phil speak for herself.

Surely, when they heard her, the jury were bound to appreciate Phil's straightforward character.

But it was with a sinking heart that Mary heard Phil give her evidence.

Scott Worthington did his best. He led Phil gently through her story, establishing that she had had the flat for only a few months and that the previous tenants might still have access. It seemed quite plausible to Mary while the barrister was making his point.

But Phil's faltering co-operation, her downcast looks and her almost inaudible answers undermined all his efforts. Mary found it almost impossible to understand why Phil did not deny her guilt more forcefully.

When the prosecution lawyer stood up to question her, Phil's response was even worse. Question after question was answered in the same colourless, unconvincing way. And when the Crown Prosecutor asked "And have you ever noticed any sign of these imaginary 'former tenants' in and out of your flat? Has anyone else ever seen them? Has there ever been anyone else with the sort of access to your flat which you are suggesting?" Phil suddenly lost all trace of colour.

She stood silent, gripping the edge of the box.

For a moment, Mary was certain that Phil was about to faint.

Then she managed to speak.

"No – I suppose not."

It was a bad moment.

Mary knew that the reactions of the jury must be, like her own, of doubt.

Why, if Phil was speaking the truth, did everything she said sound like a lie?

The jury were out for what seemed like a very short while.

While they debated, Phil was taken back down from the box. So far she had not noticed Mary's presence but, as she turned to leave the box, Mary managed to catch her eye. For a moment, Phil looked at her friend. Mary smiled encouragingly. Phil looked at her, then smiled back. It was not her old cheerful smile but it was still a smile, and it made her look, Mary thought, more like her real self. Then she was gone to wait for the verdict.

It was a tense wait but one which was soon over. The jury filed back into the box. Phil was brought back up. The clerk called for silence.

Then the foreman of the jury was asked to give the verdict.

There were three charges.

On the first count, possession of an unlicensed firearm, the judge asked "Do you find the prisoner guilty or not guilty?"

It was no surprise to anyone present when the foreman answered "Guilty, my Lord."

There were two more counts, dealing with the heroin, each much more serious. Mary had hoped that this time the answer would be different. But she knew in her heart of hearts that she was being over-optimistic.

She heard only what she expected when the foreman replied twice more "Guilty, my Lord."

Phil had gone very white.

Mary longed to be able to go to Phil and put her arms around her. Instead she could only wait in suspense as the judge prepared to give his sentence.

"Prisoner at the bar," he began, "you have been found guilty of some very serious charges. The evil of illegal drugs must be rooted out from this country. Leniency will only result in further death and misery for the innocent. I therefore sentence you as follows. On the first charge, possession of an unlicensed firearm, I consider that this offence is in itself a serious one. As a first offence, I am prepared to give a sentence of two months imprisonment. On the second and third charges, of possession of an amount of heroin not just for personal use, and of intent to deal in this illegal substance, I feel obliged to exercise my discretion, and impose a sentence which reflects the gravity of these crimes. Since this is a first offence, I will not impose the full term which the law allows. I sentence you to two years imprisonment for each offence, the sentences to run concurrently."

Two years.

Mary felt her mouth drop open. Surely it was impossible!

But it was not impossible.

Indeed, the commentators on the news that night seemed to feel that, if anything, the sentence was too lenient. The recent spate of drug-related deaths had roused a desire for blood in the local politicians and reporters. There was an almost universal cry for tougher measures.

Poor Phil, thought Mary. No-one seemed to doubt her guilt. This was no Agatha Christie story where Poirot or someone would turn up evidence to prove the heroine's innocence even after the jury had found her guilty.

Phil was to go to prison.

How would she bear it?

Mary shuddered again at the thought.

She longed to be able to change things and see Phil walk free. She was still convinced of Phil's innocence. But it seemed that she was alone in that belief.

Phil had been sentenced and the sentence would be carried out.

Chapter 66

To Phil, her arrest and trial had passed like a dream. A bad dream but one which somehow could not touch her.

She came back to reality when, sentence having been passed, she was taken down to the cell in the Lagan Court and told that she would be transferred shortly to Maghabery.

Suddenly, the knowledge received like a cold shower of water in the face, Phil realised that none of this was a dream. She was really in prison, and would be there for most of the next two years - or perhaps less, with remission.

Annie Maguire came to see her on the next visiting day. She had been in court but apart from that had only seen Phil on one brief visit since her arrest. For Phil, the sight of her mother's pain made everything much worse. She was thankful when the visit was over.

"I didn't do it, mammy," was the first thing Phil said.

"I know you didn't, Philomena," said her mother. "But everyone else thinks you did. That's what I can't understand. How can an innocent girl end up like this?"

Phil's eyes filled with tears. "Oh, mammy, I'm sorry," she whispered.

"You've nothing to be sorry about," said her mother. "I told you, I know you had nothing to do with any drug dealers."

Phil looked away, and could say nothing.

When her father came to see her on the next visiting day, it was just as bad. Phil could only feel relief when she was alone again.

Mary had written to her and asked to be allowed to visit if Phil wanted to see her. To Phil, the prospect was one to look forward to. She need not feel guilty towards Mary. Perhaps it might cheer her up.

She had begun to find herself accepting the prison routine as day followed day. She had been given some work to do in the kitchen and found that she could chat on a superficial level with some of the other women. But there was no-one she felt might become a real friend. It would be good to talk to Mary.

All the same, there was an awkwardness for the first few minutes. They sat across a table in a room where many other couples were seated in the same way, and looked at each other. There was a buzz of conversation all around them. The prison officers stood to one side out of earshot of all but the loudest remarks.

Mary looked at Phil. She was wearing prison uniform which looked rather more like a shapeless overall than anything else, and no make-up.

She was still looking pale and very far from the bright, light-hearted Phil of their schooldays. Even in their recent meetings, when Phil had more often than not looked down-hearted, she had never looked like this.

"Well, Mary," said Phil, after a pause. "It's good to see you. Thanks for coming."

"Any time," said Mary. They both laughed awkwardly.

"I can't understand how this has happened," Mary said suddenly. "You, of all people, Phil – the last person to hurt anyone."

"Oh, don't, Mary, don't!" Phil cried suddenly. One of the warders looked over and Phil, recollecting herself, said nothing more.

Mary leaned forward. "What is it, Phil? Tell me."

Phil looked at her for a long moment. "Mary, I haven't told anyone else, but you're different. And you already know part of it."

Mary nodded encouragingly.

"The thing is – " Phil said, and stopped. "The thing is – I didn't know anything about the gun or the heroin. But – there were other things – things I couldn't help knowing – things I heard about by accident. I couldn't tell anyone without giving away how I knew." She stopped again

Mary smiled at her. "It's all right, Phil. You needn't say any more. I understand."

"I don't want to mention any names," Phil said quickly.

"Of course not," Mary agreed. To herself she said "Davy Hagan. I might have known that if Phil was in trouble, he would be at the back of it." But aloud she said only "I understand."

"So I wasn't guilty of the things I was tried for," Phil went on quietly. "But I was guilty all the same. Guilty of concealing knowledge that could have saved peoples' lives. I can't live with it, Mary. I couldn't fight the accusations in court, even though Gerry and the solicitors kept trying to make me, because I felt that I deserved it all. And now I can't escape from the dreadful feeling of knowing what I've helped to cause. What am I to do?"

Mary reached out and took Phil's hand in her own.

"I do understand, Phil," she said. "I want to help." She was quiet for a moment, then she said "Phil, do you remember going to confession when we were kids?"

"Yes. It's a long time since I've been," Phil answered. "Not since Davy and I - " She left the sentence unfinished.

"I've been thinking," Mary said. "It seems to me that sometimes it's necessary to confess and to hear a human voice say that you're forgiven. It probably doesn't much matter who says the words. Do you think it would help you to do that now?"

Phil thought for a moment.

"I wonder if it would, Mary?" she said slowly. "I think perhaps it would."

"We could try, if you like. No-one would hear us. There's so much noise all around."

The two girls bent their heads in the middle of the busy room. Their hands were clasped across the table. In broken, halting words, Phil poured out all her sorrow, her guilt, her repentance. As she did so, she felt a great weight lifting from her heart. When she had finished, she continued to sit with bowed head for a few moments while Mary, speaking very quietly, tried to adapt for this strange situation the familiar words of forgiveness and absolution.

When she had said everything that seemed appropriate, she looked up. Phil's head remained bowed for another moment, then she too looked up. Her face was calm, her eyes bright with tears.

"Thank you, Mary," was all she said, but Mary felt relief flooding her.

It was the old Phil again, freed from the burden she had struggled with, and ready to go on with her life.

Chapter 67

For Phil, prison was not an easy life. Its main problem was monotony. Phil, used to lively companionship and mental activity, found it difficult to adapt to the daily routine of laundry or cleaning or cutting vegetables. After the first month, she began to realise that she needed to occupy her mind and that she would be allowed to carry on research for her MA if she applied to do so. The opportunity to do something different was a great help.

More than anything else, she missed Davy.

Davy had known nothing of what was happening to her until the trial was over and, by the time he came back and learnt that Phil was in prison, she had been there two months.

On the instructions of the drug network, he stayed away from her.

O'Brien was also in prison with the others who had taken part in the abortive snatch.

There had been so many recent blows, these arrests, and the loss of a full consignment of heroin and of a safe store house with the raid on the flat.

But the remaining traffickers were determined not to lose such a lucrative business. They were operating under the motto of business as usual and didn't want to risk losing another valuable asset in Davy.

To visit a convicted dealer would be to arouse suspicion against himself which, once aroused, would be easily confirmed.

Phil realised all that.

Nevertheless, her heart ached for him.

Mary continued to visit her on a regular basis. Her visits were a source of great comfort. Phil felt a new lightness now and the relief from the crushing weight of her guilt was the one thing which made it possible for her to face each new day, even in Davy's continued absence.

She moved about her tasks in the prison with a quiet, composed mind, taking each day as it came and finding, after the routine had become accustomed, a strange satisfaction in the manual work as well as a lifeline in the mental stimulation of research for her MA.

The months passed and, for Phil, being in prison became, in a way which frightened her when she stopped to think of it, a way of life which it was hard to believe would ever change.

She had made few friends and none of those were close.

Only one girl, a nineteen year old jailed for her part in a robbery, became more to her than a vague face and a name. Arlene Montgomery, a lively good-natured girl who seemed to have wandered into crime as much from a friendly reluctance to turn down the suggestions of her mates as for any desire for gain, made it hard by her repeated overtures for Phil to ignore her. It was as impossible to overlook her as if she was a friendly puppy continually jumping up to be patted.

So Phil talked to Arlene whenever necessary and vaguely missed her when, her year reduced to six months, Arlene finally disappeared from the prison orbit.

When she had been in the prison for almost six months, Phil was approached one day in the TV room by a woman who had not previously spoken to her.

She was tall, thin, and had an indescribable air of toughness.

"I've a message for you," she said to Phil quietly, speaking without apparently moving her lips. "Be in the toilets at four o'clock."

Phil would have preferred to keep away from the woman. She suspected that the message was to do with her supposed drug dealing connections. There was nothing she wanted less than to speak to anyone on that basis. However, she was curious.

When four o'clock came, she went to the toilets.

The woman's name, she remembered now, was Margaret McCleary, 'Big Maggie' to the rest of the prison inmates.

They stood side by side washing their hands and Big Maggie said in her almost motionless style "I have a letter for you from a friend. The initials are DH. It's hidden in a safe place. When can you come for it?"

Phil was glad she had come. She thought for a moment.

"I'll be working in the library today, after tea. Can you get it to me there?"

"I'm never there myself. I don't want to do anything unusual. But we'll see. I know someone who goes there from time to time. I'll get her to bring it."

Phil sat at her accustomed desk in the library, with a book open before her, staring at it sightlessly.

DH

The initials are DH.

It seemed like a lifetime since she had heard from Davy.

It was impossible to read, impossible even to imagine what he would say in his letter.

Impossible to do anything but wait.

A slight, blonde haired woman sat down opposite her. She carried a few books which she set halfway between herself and Phil. She drew one of the books towards her, opened it, and sat quietly reading.

Time passed.

The woman glanced up, saw that the prison officer in charge had her back turned.

With a slow, careful movement – much less noticeable if the warder turned round, than a quick snatch – she took the top book from her pile. She placed it almost by Phil's hand.

She caught Phil's eye and winked at her.

Phil looked down again.

When she was sure that enough time had passed and that she was in control of her actions, she reached casually for the book.

The letter was between the pages, towards the middle.

Phil put a sheet of file paper on the open book, wrote some meaningless notes, then lifted the paper together with the letter and put it on top of her other notes.

Presently, she closed up the book again and pushed it back to the centre of the table.

Later, she read the letter in the privacy of her own bed.

It was not long.

Dear Phil, Davy wrote,

I don't understand what happened. I know that you, of all people, would never have got mixed up in anything. I've just got back to the country. Some friends told me where you were, but not why – no details at all. I'm hoping to get this to you secretly but it may not reach you for quite a while yet.

I can't write openly, or visit you, or I'd be attracting suspicion to myself and it wouldn't take them long to confirm it.

I may have to leave the country again soon, in any case.

I've been told not to go back to the flat because apparently it's a known address, now. I'm devastated at what you're going through. I wish I could help. I love you very much.
I don't want to sign my name in case this goes astray but you don't need to be told it. I love you, I love you, I love you.

There was no signature. The rest of the space was filled up with kisses.

Phil felt a warm surge of emotion as she read.

She kissed the paper and put it inside her bra, next to her heart. It was prickly and a bit uncomfortable, and she wouldn't dare walk round with it, but it was nice to keep it there for a while.

Soon she would have to think of somewhere safe to keep it.

So Davy had only recently come back.

He seemed not to know that it was the discovery of the gun and the drugs in his flat which had led to Phil's imprisonment. His friends must have decided to keep him in the dark. She could see that it would have been hard for him to find out from anyone else without giving away his connection with her.

Phil was glad he didn't know. If he felt that her conviction was his fault, he would probably do something quixotic. Give himself up, most likely.

And what good would that do?

They wouldn't believe that Phil was innocent. Since she was his girlfriend, they would simply think that she and Davy had been working together.

It would just mean that they would both be in prison, and in Davy's case, perhaps for much longer. Phil knew that she had got a lighter sentence because of her age and her sex.

And once they had Davy's name as a drug dealer, they could probably dig up a lot of other things against him.

Phil shivered at the thought.

Chapter 68

There were no more letters from Davy.

Phil didn't know whether to be glad or sorry. It was difficult enough to keep one letter hidden in the exposed, public life of prison where everything was open to regular inspection. She switched hiding places regularly and several times narrowly escaped having the letter discovered. To keep a series of letters hidden would have been impossible.

She considered more than once destroying it, eating it perhaps, but could not bring herself to do this.

The letter had become a talisman, a guarantee that she would someday see Davy again.

She made no attempt to write back. She had nothing to say.

She needed to see him face to face before the right words would come.

And the days went on.

Soon, unbelievably, she had been in prison for almost a year.

She was to get full remission for good behaviour. Taking into account her time on remand, this meant that her sentence was almost up.

She had become so used to the prison routine that she felt panic-stricken at the idea of making decisions for herself again. She had lived for nearly a year in a cocoon where everything was organised for her and there were no responsibilities. Now, suddenly, as the time of her release drew ever closer, that was finished with.

She felt naked and new born.

Life outside the prison was something unreal, a dream she had had long ago and could only vaguely remember. Her family and Mary had faithfully visited her and written but this had not been enough in itself to sustain the reality of that other life.

She spent as much time as possible on the research she was doing into the life and poetry of Byron. This was a third world into which she could sometimes vanish. She would move around in a daze, thinking about the "mad, bad, and dangerous to know," poet, and about his circle. She was only recalled when someone in the daily life of the prison stepped outside routine to ask her something which required thought to answer.

But as the time of her release approached and a date had been set which was almost in sight, Phil began to worry.

Would Davy know that she was getting out?

Would he be able to find her?

Would he still want to?

She decided that she must make some contact with him.

The only way she knew how to do that was through Big Maggie.

The easiest way to find Big Maggie was to keep an eye out for her in the canteen. Phil hoped that she hadn't been released. It was several weeks since she had seen the tall, thin figure about.

It took three days of watching before she spotted the big woman at last. She stood a few places ahead of Phil, with her tray, in the queue for dinner.

It was easy to follow her to a table and slip in casually beside her.

"Haven't seen you around, lately, Maggie," began Phil in a friendly way.

"I've been in the infirmary," Big Maggie told her briefly. "Appendix."

"Oh, dear, sorry to hear it," said Phil, reflecting that this was one of those social lies. Actually, she felt little or no concern about Big Maggie's health. She just wanted to make use of her. "Okay, now?"

"Yeah," the woman grunted, eating fast. "What do you want?"

Phil's heart missed a beat. Was she being so obvious?

Was everyone, prison officers included, wondering why she was talking to this woman who was not even an acquaintance of hers, let alone a friend?

But a moment later, she regained her calm. She had done nothing suspicious. She had no particular seat in the canteen unlike some of the prisoners who always sat together.

There was nothing strange in her happening to sit beside Big Maggie.

"Yes," she admitted. She looked round nervously and kept her voice low. "I want you to get a message to my friend. You remember DH?"

"And supposing I can?" Maggie asked.

"Well, can you?"

Maggie glared at her for a moment, then made up her mind.

"Yes."

"Thanks," said Phil. "Will I pass it to you in the library like last time?"

"No. Janet got out months ago. Observant, aren't you? See me in the toilets after this."

"But I haven't written it yet," Phil protested. "That's no good."

"Okay. Tomorrow, then. After dinner."

"Thanks," Phil said again.

She made no further attempt to speak to Big Maggie who seemed to want to be left alone to eat as quickly as possible without the bother of talking.

While she was working in the library that evening, Phil managed to scribble a brief note.

Dear Davy, she wrote
I will be getting out on 28 Jan. If you want to get in touch, ring me at my parents.
I love you.
Phil.

There was so much else to say but somehow a letter was not the right way to say it.

As the time drew nearer, she became more and more nervous of seeing Davy again.

He was part of the unreal world, the outside world, now.

Would she still feel the same about him when they met?

Would he still feel the same about her?

Did she really love him or was it all just a delusion, a game she played?

So many things had happened since she last saw him.

Those things were real. The drugs, the interrogation, the trial, the year in prison.

By comparison with those things, her feelings for Davy seemed to have faded into an insubstantial, imaginary emotion.

Only when she saw him again would she know how much reality was left.

She met Big Maggie in the toilets, as they had arranged, and gave her the note. The sleazy surroundings seemed to increase the dreamlike, nightmare quality of the whole thing.

What had her love for Davy to do with all this?

There was no means of telling if the note had reached its destination. She had no reason to trust Big Maggie but equally no reason not to trust her. The big woman was acting out of her own strange loyalties. She had taken trouble to deliver Davy's letter to Phil. Phil supposed she had been asked to do this through some criminal communication chain.

She could only hope that for the same motives Big Maggie would deliver the note Phil had written to Davy.

On the 28 January, Kevin and Annie Maguire, with Gerry, came for Phil.

Chapter 69

It was a bright, sunny day, cold but clear.

Phil came out through the gates and paused for a moment to shield her eyes from the glare.

Her parents saw her and waved.

Then they ran towards each other.

Phil found that she was crying as Kevin, Annie and Gerry each hugged her and fussed over her. Gerry seized her suitcase and Kevin took her hand to lead her to the car. Annie, on Phil's other side, kept her arm round her daughter's shoulders.

Suddenly they were real people again.

For the first few days, Phil relapsed thankfully into childhood.

She allowed Annie to look after her, to cook tempting meals, put hot water bottles in her bed, run hot baths for her, and generally behave like a hen with one chick. It was so lovely to sleep in a soft, comfortable bed, to wear clothes of her own choice, to sleep or get up when she chose, to sit around reading or watching television if she felt like it.

But then a restlessness came over Phil and she began to feel the need to become a whole person again. She spoke cautiously to her mother about perhaps going out – taking a bus into town, looking at the shops for an hour or so. Annie encouraged her to go but when it came to the bit, Phil was very frightened. She felt sure that everyone would be looking at her.

It took several attempts before she could bring herself to go out. In the end, Annie came with her and that seemed to make it easier.

Phil was glad that she had made the effort. Each time it was easier. After the first week, she was able to take the bus by herself and felt secure that no-one was interested.

She was still reluctant to leave the house for long. She told her parents nothing about Davy but said that it was possible that some old friends might want to contact her.

"If anyone rings me while I'm out, mammy, be sure to get a number where I can ring back."

She developed a habit of listening with one ear for the phone to ring, no matter what else she was doing. Her mother noticed that she was becoming jumpy, and worried about it, but said nothing.

Annie Maguire was so glad to have her daughter safely back that at first it was enough in itself. Presently she would hope to see Phil getting her life together again but, for the moment, even the family relationships were fragile things to be dealt with carefully. She showed Phil her love in practical ways. But as far as knowing her daughter's thoughts, she was aware that Phil was practically a stranger.

Then one evening the phone rang and it was Davy,

They met one evening in late February, when the first traces of spring were stirring in the light breezes and in the scent of new blooming flowers.

Phil had wondered if he would be the same person, if she would still love him. But from the moment of hearing his voice on the phone, she had had no doubts.

He came towards her across the grass of Botanic Gardens where they had met so often before and, as he came near enough for her to see his face, Phil saw the smile, half rueful, half doubtful of his reception, which had twisted her heart so often before. Then she was running, running and his arms were round her.

It was one of the most perfectly happy moments of Phil's life.

Davy lifted her off her feet, swung her round and set her down again. Her heart felt like bursting as she kissed him back and clung to him.

"Oh, kiddo," he said in a trembling voice. "I love you so much."

He was thinner and pale and, after the first moments, when she was able to look at him properly, Phil could see the changes. He looked older, more definitely an adult – a man, not a boy.

They began to walk hand in hand along the grass lined paths.

"What happened? What happened, Phil?" Davy asked. "I couldn't believe it when I heard it."

"How did you hear, Davy?" Phil asked.

Davy hesitated. "Well. I was out of the country for over four months. Sorting out problems. This is completely top secret, Phil. I was in Lebanon. When I came back, someone had cancelled the lease on the flat and I was told to go on over the Border. I'm based there now. I come and go. I was told, when I got to the Dublin HQ, that you had been arrested and given a two year sentence but nobody down there seemed to know why."

"I think," said Phil slowly, "I think they did know, Davy. I wasn't sure whether I would tell you this or not - I don't want you to feel responsible. But I've decided now that I should tell you. Here's how it was."

She spoke slowly and with difficulty, stumbling and repeating herself in the more traumatic places but eventually the story was clear.

Davy was silent for a moment

When he spoke at last he sounded very angry.

"I didn't know any of this, Phil. I swear it."

"I know that, Davy," Phil said quietly. "I never had any doubt of that. If you had known, you'd have made a fool of yourself by making a statement in the hope of freeing me. And the only result would have been that you'd have been in prison too and for far longer. That's why your friends kept it from you."

"They had no right!" Davy broke out violently. "They should have let me decide for myself. Of course I would have come forward. I could have convinced the court that you were completely innocent. They treated me like a child. And you, Phil – they put you through hell, kiddo, when it could have been prevented!"

Phil was silent. She had said all she could in order to be fair. A hope raised itself unbidden that Davy might be so disillusioned with his drug associates that he might make a break. But his next words quenched the hope stillborn.

"I understand why they did it. A lot of money's involved. They couldn't risk a line from me leading back to the centre of the gang. They have their rules. But, Phil, a few more months and I'll have enough in the bank in Switzerland to finish with them, to leave this country for good and set up a life somewhere else, somewhere safe."

He looked down at Phil and his voice hardened again. "But I'll break someone's neck for this, all the same!"

Phil shivered.

"You're cold," he said in sudden concern. "I shouldn't keep you out here!"

"I'm okay," Phil said. "But let's go for a drink or something."

"No," said Davy. "I'm supposed to keep a low profile. Pubs in this area wouldn't be a good idea. Come on, I'm staying not too far away. We'll go there."

Taking Phil's hand, he led her through the gardens with their scattering of new purple and white crocuses, and out by the far entrance. There was a maze of little streets there.

Phil followed as Davy walked rapidly down one after the other until he came to a terrace of tall houses mostly divided into flats. It was very like the flat he and Phil had shared in Thomas Street and Phil could not prevent another shiver as she looked up at the building where Davy had paused.

"In here, kiddo. We'll soon get you warmed up."

He gave her arm a reassuring squeeze and they went inside.

Upstairs, Davy unlocked the door to a flat which was much smaller than the familiar one in Thomas Street and less shabby. They went into the kitchen where Davy switched on a heater and filled the electric kettle.

"You need something warm to drink," he said. He sounded embarrassed.

Phil looked at him in surprise.

"I'm not specially looking for coffee, pet," she said. "I thought you were going to warm me up yourself?"

Davy found that he had forgotten Phil's forthrightness. He burst out laughing.

"Oh, Phil, Phil, I do love you!"

She came towards him and reached out to put her arms around him. Davy held her tightly but said in a troubled voice, "Kiddo, I didn't intend anything like this to happen. "I'm not – well, I'm not prepared."

"I don't care!" said Phil passionately. "I've been wanting you for so long. I don't want to wait any longer."

Davy bent his head and kissed her.

"Phil, I want to say something important."

She looked up at him, surprise in her eyes.

"Phil, I want us to get married. I want you to come with me when I leave. I want to be able to look after you."

Phil said nothing.

"Oh, I know what you're thinking," Davy burst out. "Look after you! If it hadn't been for me, you would have been fine. But I didn't know that, Phil, and I've been wanting to say this to you as soon as I saw you again, so I'm saying it anyway. I know I'm saying it all wrong. But I need you, Phil. Will you marry me?"

"Oh, Davy – it's what I've always wanted."

Phil knew that she was trembling from head to foot. It was true, it was what she had always wanted. But now that it had come, she was frightened.

"I want you to come away with me, kiddo. I told you that I'm living across the Border now. There'd be room for you where I am and you'd be safe."

Suddenly Phil realised why it had all seemed too easy.

"Davy, I can't"

"What do you mean?" He was thunderstruck.

"I mean I can marry you, yes, but I can't marry what you're involved in. I can't go and be part of all that." She shook her head vehemently and tore her eyes away from him. "Don't ask me to, Davy – you know I can't."

"Phil, you must! I can't manage any longer without you." He put his arms around her and gently turned her head until her eyes met his again. "I love you, Philomena Maguire."

"I love you, David Hagan."

He bent his head and kissed her. They clung together, feeling the familiar warmth of body to body. Davy groaned and held her closer.

"Oh, love. I want you so much."

"I want you, too, dear."

Then there were no more words but only loving.

Chapter 70

Sheila came back to Belfast, a few months after Phil got out of prison, in a strange mood. She had spent the last year moving from place to place with Delmara fashions as Francis set up communications all over America and Europe. She had had a number of holidays but had not returned home for any of them. It was as if she wanted to cut her links with her background. The Sheila who had grown up in Belfast, and who had been in love with John Branagh, was a different person.

Over that year, Sheila had got on with her life. She adopted a policy of work hard, play hard. There were fashion shows, photo sessions, private showings for privileged customers, designing sessions with Delmara and the cutters and sewers. Then a round of parties, drinks, swimming, tennis, sailing.

And always new men, new admirers, but no one who meant more to her than pleasant company and friendship.

It was the news that her father had had a heart attack that finally brought her home.

The letter had followed her from California to Hawaii where she was having a short break after a lengthy photo session for a French magazine. After a strenuous few days of holding one pose after another and always making sure her hair, her face and her clothes were perfect, Sheila was glad to lie in the sun and relax. The silver sand shimmered, the water lapped at regular intervals, the shady umbrella was a refuge from the fiercest heat.

Chloe had been with her for the photo session but Sheila's holiday was a solitary one. She was not lacking in offers of company or invitations to join one or other group of jet-setters, but she had found in herself a desire to get away from the noise and the pleasure seeking, and to be alone. She lay in the sun or the shade, sipped long cool drinks, ate what she chose from the dinner menu, read light fiction and slowly unwound from the stress of the last year.

Walking slowly up to the hotel from the beach one afternoon, she found a letter from home awaiting her. She went up to her room to shower and change before dinner. Then she sat down on her bed to read the letter.

"Now, don't be worrying, dear," Kathy wrote, "because your daddy's getting over it fine. It was a bit of a shock at the time, but the doctor says that it's just that he's been working too hard. If he takes it easy and eats a better diet he'll be all right. I'm making sure that he does, don't worry."

Sheila felt a pang of mixed anxiety and guilt.

How long was it since she had seen her parents? If anything were to happen to her father ....

She must go home straight away.

That was the beginning and end of her thoughts on the subject.

This was a holiday. She wasn't due back at Delmara Fashions for another two weeks. There was nothing to stop her.

She took the first available flight home and touched down at Aldergrove International Airport two nights later. It was a dark, rainy evening, as great a contrast with Hawaii as Sheila could imagine. It was late April and still chilly, especially in the evenings.

She had phoned in advance and her parents were there to meet her in the Arrivals Lounge.

Sheila was surprised at how glad she was to see them, especially her father. He was looking older, she noticed with a touch of anxiety, with his hair sparser and greyer than she remembered. Her mother, on the other hand, looked just the same as ever. Her hair was, if anything, blacker. Sheila grinned privately.

"How are you, Dad?" she asked straight away.

Frank smiled. "I'm fine, Sheila, just fine. A lot of fuss about nothing."

Sheila gave him a hug. "Just the same, you have to take it easy, right?"

Kathy said "I make sure of that, don't I, Frankie?"

"She does, she does," Frank agreed. "A terrible woman, she is. She never lets me do a thing, these days." But he was smiling and Kathy smiled back at him in harmony. To Sheila, who remembered her parents' relationship as stormy, it seemed that they were getting on better now than she had ever known.

"C'mon, lass, let's get your bags and get on home," Frank said, and Sheila felt the warmth and security of his words lapping her round.

It was as they sat round the fire later drinking tea, catching up, as Kathy said comfortably, on the gossip, that Sheila heard for the first time about Phil's arrest and trial, and her year in prison.

Kathy spoke also of Roisin Boyd Cassidy's sudden death. Sheila had heard of it last year from Delmara, and had managed to deal sufficiently with her own grief and guilt at the time.

"Isn't that the woman you met in Dublin, Sheila?" Kathy asked her. "You mentioned her more than once. A famous fashion designer in her day, you said. I thought it must be her when it came on the news."

Kathy knew nothing, Sheila realised, of any drug connection. Nothing had been proved after all. The suspicions must all have been hushed up. Sheila couldn't help feeling glad of that at least.

It was that same evening, as they sat by the fire, that Frank Doherty found the opportunity to speak to Sheila.

Supper was over. Kathy had gone to bed.

Frank lay back in his armchair and Sheila, finding comfort in the situation, crouched at his feet on an old cushion, her head against his knee.

"There's something I've meant to talk to you about, love." Frank said presently.

He seemed to be finding it difficult to go on. Sheila smiled up at him and said simply "Well, dad? Whatever it is, out with it."

Frank grinned. "Right you are, Sheila, girl.

"I remember telling you, years ago, when you were just a little lass, that you were called after my granny, Sheila. Her maiden name was O'Hara."

Sheila stiffened.

"Yes, dad," she said after a moment. "I remember."

"Well, love, that isn't the whole story. And I've always meant to tell you the whole of it. Her name was not just Sheila. It was Brenda Sheila O'Hara. When she married my granda, she gave up calling herself Brenda and she was married as Sheila O'Hara, which made her Sheila Doherty. She died when I was about six or seven and my granda Frank died a few years later when I was eleven. My dad, he was a Frank, too, died later on when I was eighteen. By that time I was set up in a decent job, sales rep for Nicholson's and ready to move on to better things – which I did. When I met your mammy and we got married I never thought to talk much to her about my granny. But I always meant to pass on to you, Sheila, some day, what she told me about her past. Especially I wanted to give you this. You're old enough now to understand, I guess."

Frank paused, and fished in his pocket for a slim book covered in battered brown leather – a diary, Sheila saw.

"She left me this. Her thoughts about her life, I reckon you could call it. I want to give it to you now.

"My granny worked as an undercover agent against the British when she was just a kid in the first troubles. But she came to regret it bitterly, she told me, when she saw the death and the bloodshed that followed. All she ever wanted was to bring freedom to the ordinary people. But I guess it's never as simple as that. She put some of what she felt about it in this diary."

Sheila sat with her head bowed.

Then she looked up at Frank and smiled.

"I'm very glad you've given me this, Dad. When I was in Dublin, people said I was very like someone called Brenda O'Hara. I think this diary - and what you've told me – will explain a lot of what they said."

"Good," said Frank briefly.

Then he spoke again. "One more thing, Sheila. Remember, your grandmother was a good person. Don't be in any doubt of that. She did what she thought was right."

"I don't have any doubt of that, daddy," said Sheila, and found the tears creeping into her eyes.

Later that night, she sat up in bed, cuddled under the bedclothes, and read Brenda O'Hara's diary.

2 May 1923.

They shot my darling Patrick. What am I to do?

14 July 1923

Yesterday my beautiful son was born. I will call him after his father.

28 August 1925

My little Patrick is gone. He was so frail, so helpless. Now I have nothing left. Is it God's judgement on me for betraying my family and my side? For breaking all the rules? No, I don't believe He could be so cruel!

14 February 1927

Today I met a man called Frank Doherty who offers to find me a job in his office up in Belfast, working at typing letters. My struggles over the past year to learn this skill have at last brought a reward!

16 January 1928

Frank has been so kind. He tells me I am worth my weight in gold to him in his business. I don't believe him, but it's nice to be appreciated!

18 January 1929

Frank has invited me to come to dinner and meet his mother. I feel very nervous about it. I think she is a rabid protestant and I am afraid she will hate me if she finds out about my past!

20 January 1929

Dinner passed off well. Frank's mother had no idea about my story.

15 March 1930

I talked to Frank about Patrick, and my family, and the secrets I passed on. I feel very ashamed but Frank seemed to understand it all, and not to mind. He is such a kind man. I can't believe he can forgive me for the past.

10 August 1930

I have told Frank I will marry him. He is so kind and loving. I look forward to the future with amazement. So much that I have done, he is willing to forgive. I never knew someone like my Frank could exist. God must have forgiven me. He has given me such happiness!

8 September 1934

Today my little son was born. We are going to call him Frank, after his dear father. If he grows up to be half the man my Frank is, he'll be the best.

Sheila felt the tears trickling down her cheeks.

She remembered her anger against Brenda O'Hara when she had first heard her story. Poor girl, she had suffered enough and had regretted her part in the violence of those days. Sheila felt glad that she had come to a happy ending after all.

She felt no shame after all in carrying the name of this sad woman into a new generation.

Chapter 71

Phil was living at home.

When Sheila went round to see her the next morning, although Phil seemed glad to see her, there was an atmosphere of constraint. They had not seen each other for so long. So much had happened.

Sheila knew very little about the reasons for Phil's arrest.

They sat on Phil's bed as they had done so many times before.

"I don't know what to say," Sheila said slowly. "I want you to know, Phil, that I've never believed you had anything to do with dealing drugs. It just wouldn't be you, I'm sure of that."

Phil looked at her blankly for a moment, then she smiled. "Sheila, I'm really glad you said that. I hoped the people who knew me well wouldn't believe such things of me but it's good to hear it said. Oh, I suppose I might as well tell you, Sheila." She paused and grew rather pale. "I know I can trust you."

"Yes."

"I was in Davy's flat and when the police raided it they found a gun and some heroin. So I was arrested for possession and I couldn't say it wasn't my flat without involving Davy. And you're never to tell anyone this, Sheila Doherty, or I'll never forgive you!"

"Oh, Phil! Do you mean to say that you went through all that just for Davy Hagan? I could kill that fella!"

"Davy matters to me," Phil said.

"Yes," Sheila agreed. "I've always known that."

"So you see, there wasn't any question about it. I couldn't give him away. He would have been in far more trouble than me if I had done that. They couldn't prove anything much against me, but Davy – well, once they had his name, there might have been a lot of things."

Sheila said nothing.

Phil went on. "I trust you not to tell anyone that, Sheila. But even if you did, he's living safely over the Border now. He gave up the flat in Thomas Street long ago and there's no way he could be traced to it even if they had his name."

"Thomas Street?"

"Yes, 3a Thomas Street. We shared it, more or less, for a few months. At least, I spent a lot of time there. But now, I never want to see it again." Phil shuddered.

Sheila stared at her.

For a long moment she was unable to speak.

"3a Thomas Street."

The words echoed round her mind.

She relived again the moment when she had spoken to Constable Kirk in the ward of the Royal Victoria Hospital.

She had been eager to help in any possible way to catch the drug dealers and gangsters and prevent a repetition of the previous night's horrors. She had found it difficult to betray Mrs. Boyd Cassidy but had felt bound in the end to give the police her small piece of information, which could not, she felt, lead to Mrs. Boyd Cassidy's actual arrest, but might help the PSNI with background. And now, by an extreme irony, her piece of information, leading to the raid on the flat, had put Phil in prison for over a year for nothing. For nothing. Talking to Phil now, Sheila was quite sure of her entire innocence.

She found that she could not believe what she had done. And yet it was true.

For a moment, a craven thought crept into her head, that Phil need never know it.

But what would be left of their friendship then? Phil and Sheila had never lied to each other.

Sheila swallowed something in her throat and spoke.

"Phil, I didn't know until this second that you had anything to do with that address. Oh, Phil, I'm so sorry! It was me. I told a policeman that that was a drug safe house. I found out accidentally. I read a letter down in Dublin that made it clear. Oh, Phil, if I'd had any idea! If there was anything I could do to go back and undo what I did!"

Sheila put her head in her hands and the tears burst out.

Phil came closer and put her arms round Sheila's shoulders.

"Don't cry, Sheila - don't cry. It's all right. How could you know? I shouldn't have been there. I shouldn't have gone on seeing Davy when I knew what he was getting into. But I couldn't seem to stop. It was my own fault it ended up the way it did — I knew that at the time."

Sheila turned her face into Phil's shoulder and the two girls, hugging each other, wept together.

At last Phil, with a shaky laugh, drew back and wiped her eyes with one hand.

"Look at us, a couple of eejits!" she said. "Here, have a fag, Sheila, and don't cry on the match!"

"No, thanks, I don't smoke now," Sheila apologised. She managed a grin. "You're just the same, Phil Maguire, laugh at anything."

"Oh, Sheila, it's good to talk to you!" said Phil impulsively. "I've missed our chats. Mary's been great, coming to see me, but she went off to Iona a while ago and there's been no-one."

"Iona? What's there?"

"It's a Christian community. Mary's going to live in one here. It hasn't been set up yet but it won't be long now, she tells me. I suppose she's gone to Iona to get a bit of practice."

"Mary? In a Christian community? What, like being a nun? You must be joking!" Sheila exclaimed.

"Well, not exactly," said Phil. "It's a mixed set up, for one thing. Protestant and Catholic, male and female. And they don't have to be single. She'll have a job as well during the day, teaching."

"It still doesn't sound like Mary."

"She's changed a lot," said Phil. "And yet – I don't know – she's the same old Mary in lots of ways. But she's got something. Peace, I think. She helped me a lot in prison. I tell you what, Sheila, when she gets back, we should get together, the three of us. It's been ages, hasn't it? I think she'll be home in a week or so."

"Yes, that would be good."

Sheila thought, but kept the thought to herself, that she would be very glad to see Mary. But the most important thing about it, to her, would be to hear Mary speak of her brother and to learn where he was and what he was doing.

A week later, Mary came home from Iona.

Iona is a small Scottish island where some Christians had formed a community in the footsteps of St. Columba, the missionary saint who sailed there from Ireland in the sixth century.

Mary was feeling full of excitement and enthusiasm.

It was the first time she had had the opportunity to live the sort of life she hoped would be hers for the future and she was delighted to find that, far from disappointing her, it had fulfilled all her expectations.

Her first move was to phone Phil.

They had met a number of times immediately after Phil's release but Mary had been away for several months now and she was anxious to see if Phil was in better spirits and beginning to take up life again. When Phil told her that Sheila was at home, and suggested that they should all three meet, Mary agreed with pleasure.

"It'll be like being seventeen again!" she said happily.

"Yes," said Phil in a constrained voice. "Yes. That'll be good."

"Is anything wrong, Phil?" Mary asked. "You sound – well –"

"I can't tell you over the phone, Mary. Wait until we get together."

They met the following day in a bar familiar to them all from their teens. It was as if the years had rolled away and they were back in their last year at school with everything before them.

For a while they chattered and laughed together, falling into familiar turns of speech and jokes which had kept their savour. But at last a silence fell, and Phil gave a sigh.

"So much has happened since the night we met here last when our final A level exams were over, do you remember? We were celebrating a touch of freedom. It's hard to believe. Seven years ago, very nearly."

"Yes," agreed Mary. "I didn't know that night that I was going to get so deep into drugs and waste a year of my life."

"But yet, Mary, things have turned out better for you than for any of us," said Sheila.

"I'm very happy," agreed Mary, smiling. "There's nothing in my own life I would change right now."

"You're lucky!" burst out Sheila. "There aren't many people who can say that."

"Why, Sheila," Mary said in astonishment, "haven't you got one of the best lives anyone could have? Success, money, travel –"

"But the only relationship I ever had that meant anything to me didn't work out," Sheila said. She looked away from Mary and Phil and gazed into her glass.

"John?" Mary asked gently.

"Yes."

"I think he still cares about you, Sheila," Mary said.

"Well, if he does, he's got a funny way of showing it," Sheila said. The note of bitterness in her voice was unmistakable.

"Maybe he will, now you're back," Mary said. "How long will you be here?"

"Not long," replied Sheila. "I told Delmara I wanted an extra few weeks because of my dad, but he needs me back by mid June at the latest."

Mary said nothing more but privately she made a resolve. She would speak to her brother and discover for herself the state of his feelings. Surely, if he really cared for Sheila, he would not be such a fool as to let her go again without a word.

But remembering John's stubbornness from childhood, she was not so sure. Better to say nothing to Sheila until she knew if her words would have any effect.

"And then there's me," said Phil. "Look what happened to me!" She adopted a half joking tone but neither of her listeners were fooled.

"Have you thought about what you'll do now, Phil?" asked Sheila.

"You have your MA now, haven't you?" added Mary. "There are lots of things open to you."

"Perhaps," said Phil. "Yes, if my prison record isn't a handicap!"

"I don't think it will be," said Mary seriously. "You could apply for a post lecturing either at Queen's or at a further education college."

"I suppose so," agreed Phil. Her voice sounded strange.

She sat silently for a moment, looking down.

Then she raised her head and looked first Sheila, then Mary, full in the face. Her expression was unfathomable but her voice held a desperate gaiety.

"There's only one thing may get in the way of my brilliant career, girls. I've been trying all evening to find a way to tell you. I got the results yesterday. I'm pregnant."

Chapter 72

John had never officially moved out of his parents' house although he had often talked of it. But he spent so many nights away from home with one friend or another, or on engagements for the BBC, that he could be hard to get hold of.

Mary realised with some surprise that it had been months since they had met or talked.

He was making a cup of coffee in the kitchen when she caught up with him. Their parents were both out. Taking her opportunity, Mary lifted down a mug for herself from the cupboard.

"Hi, stranger!" she said. "Is there enough water in that kettle for your little sister to have a cup?"

"Should be," John replied. He waited while she spooned in instant coffee and sugar, then poured in the hot water. "Put the milk back in the fridge, then, when you're finished with it."

They sat at the breakfast bar and sipped slowly.

John sighed in satisfaction. "I needed that," he said. "Well, Mary, and how's life treating you?"

"Can't complain!" said Mary lightly.

John was silent for a moment, nursing his mug of coffee in both hands as he leant forward over the breakfast bar. Mary watched him thoughtfully.

"And what about yourself, big brother? Are *you* enjoying life?"

John laughed.

"Mary, I'd be lying to you if I said I was."

Mary sipped her coffee and waited.

"Oh, life's okay, I suppose. I like my work. I'm doing well there. They're giving me my own programme in September, the start of the new season, did you know? That's a mark of strong approval. But, I don't know. I used to think there'd be more to it than this. There never seems to be much point any more."

Mary said nothing for a few moments. Then she remarked casually "There's an old flame of yours back in town. Sheila Doherty. Have you bumped into her yet?"

"Sheila Doherty!" John's voice held a world of bitterness which told Mary more than the longest, most eloquent speech.

"Yeah."

"That's somewhere else where I've messed up," said John at last. He spoke slowly. The words seemed dragged from him. "It was my fault, you know, that we broke up. I've come to see that lately." He stopped, gazing into his cup. Something in Mary's silence, a warmth, a quietness, allowed him to go on. "I was a fool. Very self-righteous. I knew it all. I made judgements, wrote people off. Wrote Sheila off. Labelled her. It was my own insecurity, I see that now. I had a list of rules for myself and for everyone else. If anyone fell down on those rules, I despised them. And yet I knew I hadn't done so well on the rules myself. That's mainly why I gave up the priesthood as an ambition. I could see easily enough that I wouldn't be able to keep to the requirement for celibacy. But I laid it on myself even more strictly, that I would keep to normal rules, chastity outside marriage, and I expected everyone else to do the same or else they were trash. What a mess I've made of my life."

"It's not really about rules, John," said Mary cautiously.

He looked up suddenly and smiled. "Hey, listen to me feeling sorry for myself! It's a bit late now for regrets and for all this self-analysis."

"It might not be," said Mary softly.

"Oh, Mary, of course it is!" he burst out. "What would Sheila Doherty want with the likes of me now? A world famous model, going with racing drivers and film stars and the like? She's probably forgotten my name and, if she hasn't, it's only because she remembers what a clown I was! The last time we met, it was very clear that she had no more interest in me!"

"I think you're wrong there, John. I wouldn't be surprised if she still remembers you very well."

John looked up at her and grinned, raising one eyebrow sceptically. "Only as someone to avoid, I guess."

"I had a drink with her and Phil Maguire yesterday," Mary told him. "She hasn't really changed. I don't think she's very happy."

John's expression changed suspiciously. "Oh?" was all he said.

Mary wondered if she should go on.

Then she decided to risk it.

"I think the ball's in your court, John. Do you want to play? Sheila won't try to contact you. She thinks you despise her. But I don't see the point of throwing away something you both seem to want, something that could be good, just because you're afraid to make the effort to find out for yourself if it might still work. Why don't you give her a ring?"

"Because," said John angrily, "I don't even know her number. She has an apartment by the river but her phone is ex-directory."

"But *I* know it. Here."

She took a slip of paper from her pocket with the number written on it and placed it on the table in front of him.

John's face was inscrutable,

Mary felt that she had said enough.

It was up to him, now. If he wanted to take any action, he knew how to do it.

She changed the subject and began to talk of other things.

Chapter 73

Phil had no way of getting in touch with Davy, or none that she wanted to make use of.

He had gone straight back down south after their brief time together, and although he had tentatively suggested that he should give her a name to contact if she wanted to get a message to him, she had rejected the idea. She wanted no more guilty knowledge to weigh her down.

By the end of the summer, she longed to see him.

Her pregnancy was becoming noticeable and she had eventually, with difficulty, told first Gerry and then their parents.

It seemed to Phil that she had brought them problem after problem.

She was moved by their cheerful acceptance of her announcement.

All her life it had loomed over her as the ultimate disaster - her upbringing had underlined it constantly - to be fool enough to become pregnant outside marriage - to have to break it to her parents that she was pregnant! Suddenly it was not so bad after all.

Annie fussed over her and Kevin expressed, awkwardly, his intention of helping in any way possible.

Phil told them as little as she could about the father but they guessed, and she reluctantly confirmed to them that it was Davy.

She explained to them that he was out of the country and unreachable. What they read into that she had no way of telling.

She had no-one but her family to turn to at this time. Mary had moved into her community and Sheila had gone back to Delmara Fashions in mid June.

Phil sank back into the warm cocoon of her family and focussed more and more on the new life growing in her womb.

Davy had returned to his hideout near Dublin.

He lived a strange life there which he still found it hard to accept as normal. He thought of himself as a businessman, not as a crook, but although he tried hard to believe it, he knew, when he allowed himself to think about it, that it wasn't the truth.

He had been allocated a room to himself in a house which held five other men, all gang members. Most of his time was spent chatting or playing cards with these men, eating, or sleeping.

Then there would be brisk, active intervals, when he would be driven off, sometimes to an area he could not easily identify, to take charge of consignments of drugs and see that they were safely shifted to a safe place and in due course delivered to the next link in the chain who would split the stuff up into smaller lots and pass it to the street traders.

He grew used to crawling, face down, through fields in the Border area, avoiding the Customs and Excise men, waiting for the lorry to arrive with the goods and be unloaded, then slipping silently across by unofficial, unapproved roads. As the weather grew colder again with the approach of winter, this became a less and less pleasant experience. On one particular night, a barking dog alerted the customs men to the existence of himself and his companion before they had reached their position. They spent a long, cold half hour almost submerged in a nearby stream before it was safe to escape.

On another occasion, Davy managed to stumble over someone lying in ambush.

The man's yells at once gave the alarm so that Davy and the other men with him were forced to fly for their lives amid a shower of bullets, leaping over hedges and ditches and racing across fields until they were safely out of range.

It wasn't the customs men or the police.

There was no way they would have been firing like that at random, without warning given.

Davy knew quite well who it was.

Big Jim Murphy. The gangster whose men had beaten Davy up years ago now, before he threw his lot in with O'Brien. These were his men.

There had been gang warfare between Murphy and O'Brien and their men in the early days of the peace process. Things had been more settled for a while, as each realised the other was too strong to be pushed out altogether, but with O'Brien in jail and likely to be there for a long time, Murphy clearly felt it was a good opportunity for another push.

Often, too often, now, drugs were going astray. The lorry would turn up empty or not at all. It wasn't that the Customs and Excise men were seizing them on entrance to the country. If that was happening, they would be eagerly publicising their success.

There was something else behind it. Murphy had an informer, someone who was telling him dates and places so that he could intercept the loads.

There had been shootings, too, mainly in the North, but not only there.

One day late in October, Davy was summoned with a number of others to a high level meeting.

The atmosphere was charged.

"There've been too many mistakes recently," Sean Joyce said grimly. Since O'Brien's arrest and imprisonment, it was mainly Sean who had taken on the leading role. "It's Murphy and his gang, I know it is. They think now O'Brien's out of the way, they can take over, hijack our stuff. It's got to come to a show down. Davy, you have experience of these guys. You know who most of them are. We'd like you to set up a meeting with them. We'll get together and see what can be arranged by way of drawing up boundaries, identifying each other's territory."

Davy was in full agreement. He was certain that the present situation, where nothing was being achieved, needed to change. If nothing was done soon, it would be better to forget the whole business and get out with what he had. He had sacrificed a lot for this last effort to make enough to give him and Phil what he thought of as a good future. But it had gone on now for too long. It was time to win or lose.

In a remarkably short time everything was organised.

Davy sent out feelers to the people he knew best on Murphy's side. Would they be up for a high level meeting? Would Murphy himself be willing to come to an agreed place with some of his henchmen to meet Sean Joyce and a picked few supporters, or would they prefer something a bit more low key? Davy and a couple of others could have a preliminary meeting with some of Murphy's men if that would be better.

Word came back by devious routes. Murphy himself wasn't prepared to come into the open just yet. Maybe at a second meeting.

Meanwhile, some of them would meet Davy and others at an address in Belfast which, they claimed, was neutral ground.

Davy wondered. It didn't sound like neutral territory to him.

But Sean was happy enough to go ahead on Murphy's terms.

Davy, a youngster called Paddy McCormick, and a stout, balding man known as Shorty McFee, were picked to go. Late on the chosen night, they piled into a black BMW and drove off, heading north out of Dublin.

When they came within reach of the Border, they moved off to one side, turning into a narrow, minor road. There were no soldiers, no police even, at the main Border crossing points these days, nevertheless Davy felt it was wise to keep as much out of sight as possible. They crossed by one of those small cross-border roads which some few years ago had been constantly dug up by the Army to prevent just this sort of ingress by terrorists, and as constantly mended again by the local inhabitants.

It was a pitch black night. There was no one about apart from their own car. They travelled slowly and cautiously, driving only on sidelights, until they were well away from the border area.

It seemed to take an eternity before they reached the outskirts of Belfast, and stopped.

Davy got out.

The meeting place was a small farm house on the east side of the city.

Davy knew that they weren't far from it by now. His instructions had been detailed and explicit. They should be driving down the next small lane on the right, he reckoned.

Standing beside the car, he addressed the others.

"All right, boys. Take it slowly now. We'll park here and go forward on foot. It's not so much that I don't trust Murphy as that I don't trust Murphy."

This raised a weak grin from Paddy and Shorty.

"What I want to do here is go in by the back way across the fields so they don't know we're coming until we're there, see?"

The other two men nodded. To them it made sense. Never throw away an advantage. Take the other side by surprise when you could.

They went ahead, moving like shadows ready to retreat if necessary, across the damp fields beside the narrow country lane.

Davy came at the rear. He was watching carefully for any sound of movement, any ambush, any betrayal, from that direction.

After twenty minute's slow, careful advance, they were within sight of a small farmhouse set on a slight rise in the ground, almost a hill.

305

There was a light in one of the downstairs windows. This would be the place.

Davy called a halt.

"Okay, boys. This is it. We go in slowly, keeping a look out all round, okay? I'll knock and give the password. You two keep back until I signal you forward. Guns out and ready, but for any sake don't be firing unless there's good reason. This is meant to be a friendly meeting, right? Any questions? No? Okay, then."

They moved forward again. Below them, the dark was chilling. The lights of the city gleamed. In the small hours of the morning, they were fewer and more scattered. Davy had a strange, momentary feeling as if he was one of the ancient army of Brian Boru advancing on the enemies of Ireland.

Then the feeling faded and he was sharply aware of the buildings below him. In the sleeping city, few but police and criminals would be awake, he thought.

He went to the back door of the building and rapped sharply.

"Who's there?" came a quiet voice, sounding, to his satisfaction, surprised.

Good, thought Davy. They didn't hear us coming, then.

"Captain Kirk and his two Klingons," he said, just loudly enough to be heard.

Whoever had suggested the passwords had been a Star Trek junkie, he thought with an inward grin.

The door swung open.

Davy saw that he was facing a gun pointed straight at his face.

"And we're the Daleks," said a rather louder voice giving the counter sign.

"So now you can put the gun away," Davy said. He raised his own. "None of us need them."

"Okay," said the man, who Davy now recognised as Johnny McCann, the one of Murphy's henchmen he had mainly dealt with in setting up the meeting. "Call in your mates."

Davy turned round to signal to Paddy and Shorty.

As he did so, he heard a noise behind him, a click from McCann's gun. He recognised it without a shadow of doubt for what it was. The sound of the safety catch on McCann's gun being released.

Almost before he had recognised it, a warning bell went off in his head.

In the split second while he was still identifying the sound, he dived sideways out of the light streaming from the farmhouse door and began to run, heading back towards the others, leaping wildly over the nearest wall at the edge of the farmyard and crouching down for cover.

Suddenly the place was full of noise.

Shots, voices shouting.

There was no need to warn the other two men to keep back.

The noise was enough.

The place was in an uproar. Men armed with guns were pouring out of the building, far more of them than the agreed three. Shrieks and groans pierced his ears. Someone had been hit but not one of his own men, he thought. The noise came from just outside the house. One of Murphy's men. Shorty or Paddy or maybe both must have opened fire when they realised they had walked into an ambush. He heard the sharp noise of many shots.

Davy fired, aiming as best he could at the muffled figures to be seen against the light from the doorway.

His instinct to distrust Murphy had been right, he realised. They should never have come here, never have risked setting up this meeting.

In the darkness it was hard to see who was doing what. The sounds of fire from nearby him told Davy that Paddy and Shorty were still there. Time they stopped firing and got safely away. Davy moved cautiously forward, trying to see over the rough wall to find someone to fire at.

He automatically fired and reloaded, fired and reloaded. A dream took possession of him. He was fighting, protecting his own men, destroying the enemy.

Davy thought of the many men who had been in the same position as him throughout the history of the world. Soldiers fighting for something. Some of them fighting for a cause they believed in. Some of them fighting for a reason they could not fully understand.

He thought of his grandfather and his uncle fighting for the freedom of Ireland. He thought of all those people who had fought on both sides in the recent Troubles.

What cause was he fighting for?

He thought "How did I get myself into this position?"

Had he made the right choice?

Was anything good going to come of it?

Had he wasted his time?

The thoughts ran through his head.

Davy banished them.

Concentration was the important thing at this moment. He could not afford to be side-tracked.

Perhaps, when tonight was safely over, he might rethink what he was doing?

He fired again and became aware that Paddy and Shorty must be safely away. He could no longer hear the crack of their bullets close to him. There was only the enemy fire.

It was time to retreat. He had unwittingly moved into a more exposed position than he had realised. The dream had carried him forward, firing, loading, moving forward, firing.

It was time to go.

He needed to be careful to find cover.

He glanced round.

He was still crouched behind a low wall within range of the farmhouse. There were a number of outbuildings quite near.

He needed to make his way to the next building to his rear and then from there on.

Bending low, keeping his head down, he ran quickly across a short piece of open ground to the nearest building.

There was a bang and the sound of a bullet cracking, and a sharp pain in his shoulder.

Davy ran on, half bent over, and rounded a corner to safety.

For a moment he paused there, aware that he had been shot, as yet feeling only the beginning of pain.

It would be worse presently, he knew.

He raised his gun, hurting his arm in doing so, and fired again.

It was important to get away now, before it became more difficult to move.

He fired again, then ran quickly to the next cover.

As he crossed a wide piece of open ground between buildings, he realised that there were more bullets than before whistling past his ears.

He had made it. There was another wall between him and the bullets

But there was still a long way to go before he would be safe.

Should he wait or try to move on more quickly?

If he waited, McCann and his men out there in the dark might come closer, might catch him up.

Davy decided not to wait.

Bent low, he dashed out from behind the wall where he had stopped to shelter and made for the next building.

He was half way there when a bullet struck him in the back and then another. He fell forward, his gun flying from his grasp.

For a moment he tried to crawl onwards. His eyes seemed to be growing puzzlingly dim.

"Phil," he heard a voice muttering. Was it his?

"Phil."

As he crawled on, he could see her clearly just ahead of him, laughing at some silly joke he had made, throwing her head back and pushing back her dark hair with one hand.

"Phil," he muttered again. "Oh, kiddo. Oh, Phil."

Then the picture began to blur and a silver lake crept up and over his eyes, blotting out everything else in a liquid pool, drowning his thoughts.

And then there was only darkness.

And a bright light.

Chapter 74

Phil heard on the six o'clock news that a man had been killed in the course of an inter-gang gun fight.

The identity of the man in question would be announced on the following day when his family had been informed.

To Phil, expecting her baby in the next few weeks, the blow when it came was cushioned by its unreality.

Only later, when she held her little boy in her arms and traced his father's features in his face, did she find herself weeping helplessly.

Mary heard the news in the communal living room where she was sitting with the other members of her community after supper. Unlike Phil, when she first heard the name, Mary wept.

Later, she went quietly into the room which had been set aside for prayer and knelt at the small altar.

"Lord," she said, when at last she could say anything, "forgive us and help us."

Then she bent her head into her hands and remained there motionless, unable to find further words while the tears fell unheeded.

"What's to become of this country?" she thought, and struggled against the despair.

It was some time before she found words for her prayer again.

At last she became calm.

Then, taking herself to task for her weakness, she set herself to pray for Phil and for the child who was to be born.

After this she prayed for Sheila and for her brother John as she had done so many times.

Finally dredging up the words, she prayed again for this poor country which she loved.

For an end to death and violence.

* * *

Sheila had gone back to work again.

She was feeling increasingly unsatisfied with life.

But when Delmara rang up to check if she would be available in mid June as they had agreed, she could think of no reason to refuse.

Her father had recovered from his heart attack. She couldn't hang around at home forever.

Francis had set up a number of shows in Dublin.

Sheila felt that she would enjoy meeting some of her southern friends again. She wondered about Sebastian O'Rourke. What did he feel about her now?

But apart from this, a fleeting thought only, she could raise little enthusiasm for the programme before her.

She had been badly shaken by the news of Phil's imprisonment. Phil had told her not to be silly when she had spoken of her own feeling of guilt and responsibility, but although they had moved back into their old friendship without another word, Sheila had not managed to rid herself of the guilty feelings.

On top of that had come the meeting with Mary and the revived memories of the past. Sheila realised, with a sickening pain, that she had not succeeded either in getting rid of another feeling, her feeling for Mary's brother. John Branagh still mattered.

Sheila felt helpless, trapped in her own emotions.

Everything she had been doing for the past three years, the career she had built for herself - had it all been meaningless, a game to distract her from reality?

She did not intend to contact John herself. He had made it very clear, she thought, that he never wanted to see her again. If he had changed his mind, why did he make no move?

She had broken all his rules, why should he feel anything for her but anger?

So by mid June, she was gone and did not know that, only days later, John phoned her apartment. When the message on the answer machine told him that she had left the country, he rang off without a further word.

Chapter 75

John heard the news about Davy Hagan's death with a horror which surprised him.

He and Davy had never been close friends. Their ways had long since separated.

But Davy, like others who had been shot over the past few years, had been at school with him, and now had gone.

How many of his school mates were left, he wondered?

Where had all their bright hopes for life vanished to?

And his own life? Where had it gone?

A new determination grew up in him, hardening into a resolve not to allow his life to vanish, like Davy's, without at least attempting to make it different.

He thought again of the conversation he had had with Mary when he had admitted to her some of the mistakes he had made. He knew now that the breakdown of his relationship with Sheila had been his own fault. He had condemned Sheila, when in fact it was his own insecurity which was to blame.

Mary seemed to think Sheila still cared about him. Was she right? He found himself hoping desperately that she was.

He needed to find Sheila and to tell her that he knew now how badly he'd treated her. Would she be prepared to listen? Was it still possible to get his life, both their lives, back on track?

There was only one way to find out.

* * *

Late in December, just before Christmas, Francis Delmara set up another show in Belfast.

Sheila felt that she would enjoy going home, seeing her parents, seeing Phil's new baby. But apart from this, she could raise little enthusiasm for the programme before her.

Her thoughts went constantly to John Branagh the last time she had seen him.

He had been so angry, so jealous when he had realised that her employer, Francis Delmara the fashion designer, was the man who had kissed her by the banks of the River Lagan. Until he saw Francis at Sheila's apartment, he hadn't known.

He must have believed that there was some still sort of sexual or romantic relationship between them.

He had, as always, Sheila thought, given her no chance to explain. Francis Delmara had long ceased to be more to her than an employer and friend. She smiled wryly to herself when she remembered that it was jealousy of Francis which had first caused John to break off their relationship. There had never been anything but a slight attraction on her side and whatever there had been on Francis' side had by now disappeared with the need to maintain their business relations on a secure footing.

John saw the posters advertising that Sheila Doherty was back in town for a fashion show at the Hilton Hotel as he drove through town on his way to the BBC building one morning in the run-up to Christmas.

All thoughts of arriving at work on time flew out of his head. He turned the car abruptly, earning a series of shouted curses from the drivers nearby, and sped in the opposite direction towards the Hilton.

He parked at random and burst into the hotel, making straight for the reception desk.

"Sheila Doherty?" he demanded. "Is she staying here? I know she has a show here in a few days. Is she in the building now?"

But Sheila wasn't staying in the Hilton, nor was she there practising, and no-one at the Hilton admitted to knowing where she was to be found before the date of the show. The pretty, dark haired receptionist, who thought John looked cute and sexy, would have been very happy to earn his gratitude, but had to tell him, regretfully, that she had no idea where Delmara was holding his trial runs.

John stood in the car park with the light sleety rain falling on his hair and face and phoned Sheila's flat, but there was no reply. He realised she would have to be out practising somewhere, since she wasn't at the Hilton itself. But where?

John moved heaven and earth to find out, calling in all his contacts, built up by now to considerable numbers during his time with the BBC. Reporters, people in the fashion business, celebrities he had interviewed. None of them knew anything helpful.

John stood in the now heavy sleet, feeling near to despair.

Suddenly his mobile sounded. It was his mate Brian from the BBC calling him back.

"I just thought, have you tried Kevin Kernaghan?" Brian said. "He's a guy who plays five-a-side with me, so I can give you his number, and his girl friend Chrissie works part time for Delmara Fashions. She a hairdresser, I think, or some such. Anyway, maybe worth a ring?"

John rang.

* * *

The rehearsals for the new show were taking place in a hall normally used for plays and concerts. Instead of the usual catwalk curving down into the audience, there was a platform of uniform height.

Sheila found it hard to relate her movement across this stage with the more intimate descending walk into the heart of the audience.

However, she was a professional by now. It was up to her to do her best.

"When will we get a chance to practice in the real setting, Francis?" she asked.

"The Hilton's function rooms are booked up until the day before the show, Sheila," Delmara explained briefly. "You'll have plenty of time then." He turned back to his immediate preoccupation, adjusting the length of the gown Chloe was wearing to suit the height of her shoes.

The door at the far end of the hall burst open.

Sheila felt her heart jump out of her body.

It was John. John Branagh.

Banging the door shut behind him, he strode down the hall, ignoring the stares of the assembled models, dressmakers, hairdressers and the designer himself.

He came to a halt in front of the platform and stood there, legs planted firmly apart, one arm shielding his eyes to let him see through the murky gloom.

"Sheila Doherty!"

"Yes, John?" Sheila gulped. She felt oddly breathless, unable to speak in more than a croak.

"Well, Sheila Doherty, are you going to marry me or not?"

Sheila gave a funny little yip. She could feel her heart bounding in her breast.

"Don't you think we've wasted enough time already?"

Kicking off her shoes, Sheila flew to the edge of the platform.

"Oh yes, John! Yes, John!" she shouted, as the breath flooded back into her lungs.

Then she gave one final blissful squeak of happiness and hurled herself down into his arms.

John, his feet still firmly planted, was able to catch her with only a slight rocking motion.

His arms went round her, hard and strong, his lips found hers and he held her against him as her knees began to quiver and give way.

The kiss went on for a long time.

Then John raised his head, looked round him at the gaping audience and said, speaking firmly to Sheila alone, "Then come on! I've got a licence here and I've booked a slot at the registry office. No time to waste. The taxi's outside."

He took Sheila by one arm and began to lead her along the hall.

"But, John -" Sheila began weakly, looking down at the model dress she was still wearing.

"What? Do you want to change your mind? You don't think we've messed around long enough? I've been a complete self righteous fool, okay, but I don't mean to be any more. Maybe I've grown-up a bit, or something. Once and for all, Sheila Doherty, do you mean to marry me?"

The dress could wait. She could give it back to Delmara later, when she talked to him about breaking her contract.

"Yes, John," Sheila said meekly and allowed herself to be led, shoeless, along the hall to where the taxi was waiting outside.

Made in the USA
Charleston, SC
30 April 2011